MEN·ON·MEN
6
·BEST·NEW·GAY·FICTION·

EDITED AND WITH AN INTRODUCTION BY
DAVID BERGMAN

A PLUME BOOK

PLUME
Published by the Penguin Group
Penguin Books USA Inc., 375 Hudson Street,
New York, New York 10014, U.S.A.
Penguin Books Ltd, 27 Wrights Lane,
London W8 5TZ, England
Penguin Books Australia Ltd, Ringwood,
Victoria, Australia
Penguin Books Canada Ltd, 10 Alcorn Avenue,
Toronto, Ontario, Canada M4V 3B2
Penguin Books (N.Z.) Ltd, 182–190 Wairau Road,
Auckland 10, New Zealand

Penguin Books Ltd, Registered Offices:
Harmondsworth, Middlesex, England

First published by Plume, an imprint of Dutton Signet,
a division of Penguin Books USA Inc.

First Printing, September, 1996
10 9 8 7 6 5 4 3 2 1

Page 363 constitutes an extension of the copyright page.

 REGISTERED TRADEMARK—MARCA REGISTRADA

ISBN 0-452-27708-6

CIP data available upon request.

Printed in the United States of America
Set in Janson
Designed by Leonard Telesca

PUBLISHER'S NOTE
This is a work of fiction. Names, characters, places, and incidents either are the product of the author's imagination or are used fictitiously, and any resemblance to actual persons, living or dead, events, or locales is entirely coincidental.

For John

For lóve's more impórtant and pówerful thán
Éven a príest or a pólitícián.
—W. H. Auden

CONTENTS

don't want to give the impression that I have anything against a certain sweetness and kindliness in writing, as long as this sweetness does not become cloying. Paul Gervais' "Love in the Eyes of God," Karl Woelz's "Cartography," and Philip Gambone's *"Gioia e Dolor"* all add enough piquancy (enough *dolor*) to make the sweetness (the *gioia*) tasty.

There is perhaps another source for what one critic saw as the roughness of these stories, and that is that I seem to be attracted to stories whose themes if treated honestly don't open themselves to neat conclusions. One of the directions that gay culture has gone as it has been increasingly challenged by queer theory and queer activists is to test the boundaries of sexual identity, class identity, and the intersection of race and ethnicity with sexuality. These are issues that do not lend themselves to neat presentations or clear closure if treated honestly and seriously. Over and over again I found the stories that most interested me, excited me, and stayed with me were those stories that showed how men negotiated differences of race, ethnicity, class. Achim Nowak's "Graham Greene Is Dead" is an excellent case in point. A German-American, he finds himself involved with a Trinidadian of Indian extraction during a revolution instigated by Islamic Africans against the black Christian government. Sandip Roy addresses the issue of race and ethnicity from the point of view of an Indian student who finds himself drawn to a blue-eyed African American. Even when the sexual attraction is *not* interracial or interethnic, the couple is made aware of race and ethnicity. In Jason K. Friedman's "Massage," the fact that the two protagonists are Jewish adds to the tension. But ethnicity isn't always a source of tension. In Philip Gambone's and David Vernon's stories the ethnic difference between the lovers is less a problem than their attitudes toward family and intimacy.

If contemporary gay thinking questions the boundaries of gay identity, it has also reinforced gay distrust of realism and fiction as categories. Gay fiction has for some time been driven by what looks on the surface to be two opposing passions: a desire to write both realism *and* fanatasy. Thomas Glave's remarkable tale "Their Story" is one of several he has written about the Trinidadians who reside in the North Bronx, where Glave grew up.

want the book to reflect in some measure the diversity of gay experience and gay literary styles while maintaining what I believe are the highest literary standards.

But what are those standards? Are they anything I could formulate in a precise way? Over the years I've tried to articulate them, if for no other reason than to understand my own limitations and thereby stretch them, but I must admit I haven't made much headway.

In a review of *Men on Men 5*, one critic described the style of some of the stories as "rough." I was a bit surprised by the term since I think that one of my faults is being a bit too elegant and prissy. I'm not certain what the critic meant by "rough," but I think he might have meant that the stories aren't necessarily neatly laid out, that the prose is willing to allow itself to reveal the emotional pressure under which it was produced, and that the conclusions are far from finished and closed off. Robert Browning, a poet I much admire, has one of his artist characters say "a man's reach should exceed his grasp/Or what's a heaven for." And I suppose I prefer stories that struggle toward a largeness of vision and a complexity of experience they don't quite have under control. If this is what the critic meant by "rough," I suspect most of the stories in the collection have a certain roughness about them. I find that stories that don't have this rawness tend to be overcooked, mushy, bland, or to mix metaphors, have the kind of sanitized, odorless neatness of television.

The rawness that I'm looking for comes mostly in two varieties. There's the rawness of subject matter, the rawness you can find in Bruce Benderson's "Blades," or in Kevin Martin's "Crack," two stories that deal with people living at the extremes of American life. There are stories like Philip Gefter's "Elizabeth New Jersey" and Norman Wong's "Andrew and I" in which something grotesque emerges in unlikely places. Interestingly enough, when the subject matter is a bit raw, I find that the most successful prose is often restrained, simple, chaste. But there is a kind of stylistic rawness that I also admire—a style of Faulknerian excess and abandon. J. E. Robinson's "Waiting on Eurydice" and Thomas Glave's "Their Story" both seem to come out of a whirlwind of language. I admire this style all the more because I have never been able to write this way. But I

this collection represents is the twenty best gay stories I have
read in the last two years.

Perhaps one way of dispelling the illusion that *Men on Men* is
some kind of well-established institution is to give you the low-
down on its editorial process. Here is the elaborate system by
which stories get chosen: I place announcements in journals
across the country, appear at writers' conferences and other sym-
posia, and tell everyone I know to spread the word of mouth
that I am looking for stories for *Men on Men*. As a result the
news has gotten pretty widely disseminated. The stories then
come in. My letter carrier complains that I get more mail than
anyone on his route, and to be sure, I've gotten about 900 stories in the last two years, almost twice as many as for *Men on
Men 5*. Usually after I come home from teaching, I lie down on
a blue velveteen sofa bought the year I graduated college and
read the stories that have arrived. There is no screening com-
mittee except that I sometimes ask my lover to read over a story.
He's not a literary person, but he loves to read, so he gives me
a fairly good window on the reactions of the kind of intelligent,
general readership *Men on Men* has built up over the years. I
write back to authors (usually within the month) either to tell
them why I can't take the story or to ask if I can hold on to a
story for later consideration. A month before my deadline, I sit
down with all the manuscripts I have pulled aside, about 5 per-
cent of the ones I've received or about forty-five stories. It's then
that I whittle down the semifinalists to the eighteen to twenty
that will appear in the volume.

I find this last stage in the selection process the most difficult
and painful because all of the stories I have set aside are worthy
of publication. I know there will be a number of very good
writers—better writers than I am—who will be hurt and disappointed by my decision. Worse still, it is almost impossible to
justify these final decisions which are admittedly very personal
and highly intuitive, as well as highly practical. For it is at this
final stage that I must consider *Men on Men* as a whole. I don't
want all the stories to be about coming out, or AIDS, or family
problems, or finding a lover, or breaking up with a lover. I don't
want all the authors to be established writers or complete unknowns, or from a particular region, ethnic, or racial group. I

MEN ON MEN 6: INTRODUCTION

• DAVID BERGMAN •

When I took over *Men on Men* after the death of George Stambolian, I was excited about editing a series that had become the preeminent venue for new gay fiction. What I didn't realize was that in the eyes of many people, I was taking over the helm of an institution. They saw publication in *Men on Men* as bestowing on the writer and his work some seal of queer literary approval. As a result, authors have begged me by letter and agents have beseeched me by phone, believing that the acceptance of a story in *Men on Men* will mean a book contract. Moreover, readers tell me that they look toward the publication of *Men on Men* every other year to find out who the new "canonized" gay authors will be.

Although this attention and confidence is flattering, it is misplaced at best. I hardly want to feel like a one-man College of Cardinals, although I have always liked that particular shade of red. Nor does publication in *Men on Men* swing so much weight with increasingly bottom-line conscious editorial boards. More important perhaps, nothing will so jeopardize the quality of *Men on Men* than believing in its own power to wield institutional authority since institutions by their very nature avoid risks and shun pleasure, and one of the things that has made *Men on Men* so valuable is that it has been both daring and fun. Thus, the first thing I want to do in this introduction is dispel any illusions readers, critics, authors, agents, or editors might have. All that

This ghost tale is at once fantastic and a faithful portrait of a community. When the narrator of the story tells us that he was there and saw it all, we inhabit that queer space of the realistically fantastic or the fantastically realistic. The teenage boy in Wayne Scott's "A House of Difference" lives in *Lesbian Rage*— at least that is what everyone calls the apartment house where he makes his home—another queer space that mixes the realistic and the fantastic. Perhaps the most subtle example is J. E. Robinson's "Waiting on Eurydice," which Robinson imagines as occurring sometime in the near future, since the casual relationship between whites and blacks of both sexes is not quite a reality, yet not quite impossible either. But the clearest example is James Purdy's "The White Blackbird." Purdy is one of America's most important writers, whose first books appeared in the mid-fifties. His work has always frustrated critics by defying the usual categories. Although "The White Blackbird" has the feel of a fable or fairy tale, Purdy insists that the basic premise of birds stealing a woman's jewels is based on an incident from his childhood. And although there is nothing explicitly homosexual about the story, it is a very queer tale indeed.

After a reading in San Francisco, a handsome man came up to me to complain that *Men on Men* never had any stories about married men who were gay. "Do you mean gay men who tried to hide the fact by getting married?" I asked. "No," he said, "gay men who also want to be in a marriage with a woman." I'm not sure that this collection will satisfy that particular reader's needs, but I began to be more alert to stories in which the gay/straight dichotomy is challenged, as it is in Bruce Benderson's, Thomas Glave's, Kevin Martin's, Wayne Scott's, and Karl Woelz's stories. Gender roles are challenged in yet another way in this collection. There seem to me more drag queens in this volume than in the last. I'm not certain how to explain this phenomenon. I certainly didn't set out to find such stories. Perhaps our attitudes have changed enough about drag to excite renewed interest in it. Drag is no longer a humiliating compulsion but a liberating masquerade in Bruce Benderson's, Philip Geftner's, and Wayne Scott's work.

AIDS continues to be a subject for gay writing, but not as it used to be. It forms the background for how we live now rather than the foreground it once occupied. William J. Mann's "Tricks of the Trade" deals more explicitly with AIDS than any of the other stories, yet in that story it is part of the intricate interweaving of lives and generations—a fact of gay life that forms an element in the way we live now. In Richard C. Zimler's story it is a fact that stares the protagonist in the face although it takes him a long time to see it. But in most of the stories it is one of the facts of gay life which is dealt with (or not). Gay writers have taken on the strategy of the "Old Masters" in W. H. Auden's "*Musée des Beaux Arts*," who, while never ignoring "suffering," realize it can never be the entire picture of our lives.

Other themes continue to be important to gay literature, but these, too, continue to change over time. Family matters were always a vexed subject in earlier gay writing. Now we see stories that explore a much wider range of approaches to families. Jim Grimsley, one of the more exciting new novelists, provides a story in which the family by putting pressure on the protagonist to marry actually forces him to come out. In Karl Woelz's "Cartography," the son of a gay man urges his father's lover to solemnize his relationship to the father. It is the very absence of the usual tension that makes Woelz's story such a delightful surprise. In David Vernon's "9.2," it's the family's wholehearted acceptance of their son's relationship with his partner that seems to be driving the two lovers apart.

I have some very personal reasons for loving many of the tales. Paul Gervais ends his story by having one young man walk on the back of his college roommate who suffers from chronic back problems. I have a bad back, and I have frequently asked boyfriends to walk on me, and I have gotten the same strange response that Gervais' protagonist gets. Yet my decision to include "In the Eyes of God" is not a personal whim. Since reading this story I've learned by talking to friends that back-walking is not uncommon, and yet I have never before read about it. Gervais' story has the kind of freshness I very much admire—finding something that can speak to our common experience but which no one has thought of writing about. But, of course, throwing up a mirror to our lives is only one of the more powerful things literature can do; just as exciting is its ability to open up doors to experiences that are far from our own lives and give us the tools not only to understand them but participate imaginatively in them. In good literature the end result of either opening a door or holding up a mirror is the same: As in Richard C. Zimler's masterful short tale, "The Most Obvious Place," we can be shocked by the familiarity of otherness and the otherness of the familiar, shocked and a bit relieved.

The ability to effect the shock of recognition and a realization of shock is one reason that gay writing is for me—as it is for many readers—the most exciting area of American literature today. Consequently, these stories aren't just great stories for gay readers; they are powerful stories for anyone interested in fine writing and serious fiction. As gay fiction continues to push against the stereotypical boundaries not only of race, class, and gender but also of content, genre, and style, I find that it reexamines and reimagines not just what life is for me as a gay man, but what this society is for everybody. As a result this work increasingly transcends the ghetto from which gay literature was born while staying faithful to the lives of men-loving men.

Baltimore, January 1996

BLADES

• BRUCE BENDERSON •

It's a classic cowhide purse for a middle-class lady, brown and unremarkable, with a simple gold-plated clasp. It took a leather-worker's thick, curved needle and some fishing tackle to sew the razor blades along the inside, like a circle of jagged teeth above the open straight razor at the bottom.

Flip the purse open. The upscale odor of sour tanning is all that you'll notice, before the icy slice of razor's edge makes you howl. You yank out a bloody hand—learn to keep your hands to yourself.

Her own dark hand is nimble. Its bones can collapse past the defense zone of razor-blade teeth to the big roll of bills perched next to the straight razor. They thread twenties from the purse like magic tricks, smoothing them into a limp curve over the knuckle of a big forefinger, letting them float onto the bar counter to the tinkle of her silver bracelets.

In this dim light, she seems to be a big-boned lady over six feet tall, with a provincial hairdo tapering at the earlobes, in a tidy silk shift appropriate for the office, and a single strand of real pearls. It's only the span of many silver bracelets on the big wrist that seem slightly odd, and the fact that she's sitting in this dank, dark hole.

The hole is of the disappearing center-city sort, where mostly male prostitutes or transgenders sell sex to older men to get the drugs they want. Homosexual behavior pays the bills, even though the atmosphere seems hyper-hetero. Queens snap at sulky homeboys wearing gold jewelry or the bead necklaces of gangs, while lustful, mostly drunken businessmen still carrying attaché cases ogle one or the other from the shadows. But she is imperiously beyond the darkness, supposedly immune to all the excitement over strong contrasts of gender, miles above the seedy envy of money, in her very perfect world of idealistic romantic interests.

He is slouched by her side in a concave curve, his wiry legs dangling from the bar stool; his full, curvaceous mouth welded to the bone structure of a lean face. Dead almond eyes under gleaming licorice strips of hair yanked back wolfman style. His sixteen-year-old chin sports just enough hair for a scraggly goatee. For those with unarmed purses, this is the archetypal WANTED bulletin. The nerves that control the face muscles are already dead to scrutiny, the eyes apathetic to the camera flash at Central Booking. From the dark drapery of the oversized clothing poke big, adolescent bones. In this dim light, within the black walls, from certain angles, the clothes make the body look puffed for challenge, like a threatened cat raising its fur like porcupine quills to look bigger and fiercer. The clothes could also be hiding a weapon, lost to potential friskers in the folds, or a second set of clothes, worn underneath by someone with no fixed place to live.

The teeth are jagged. The upper row, anyway. The upper row of teeth are rotting, chipped by accidents or brawls. But then the lower row . . . They're all gold. Sleeves of gold molded perfectly over the contours of his real teeth. All nine in front. So that his real teeth are probably rotting underneath.

The gold teeth flash their predatory grins at the big, pleasant-looking black lady with the new purse from which money keeps appearing to pay for alcohol. They are drinking Amaretto. There is feminist bravado in her warm brown eyes under the copper eye shadow. Her voice is sibilant but a little schoolmarm-ish. With soft, curt remarks and dismissive gestures she makes known what kind of woman she is. In charge of her own life. Undaunted by the fact that he is half her age and three-quarters her height. Never paying for sex, by the way. But maybe she'll

cook a feast for him later, when they get hungry. He'll be hungry
real soon, he mentions, scanning the bar with blank eyes and
poking a thumb into a pocket of his oversized jeans, while the
fingers splay impudently across the top of his thigh toward the
crotch.

Two days ago she recovered from that fever. A fever she
would never mention here. She only comes to this hole to avoid
the censure of a world that faults her for being too tall. That's
all there is to it. So why give wind of the elaborate procedures
that were carried out two days ago?

Two days ago, she turned her kitchen into a sterile laboratory.
With the help of her girlfriends she rinsed the sink and fixtures
with boiling water and scrubbed the countertops with bleach. A
friend who works as a plastic surgeon's assistant was visiting. She
and the friend laid out the sterilized instruments, the plastic
bladders of silicone and the syringes of estrogen, on gauze-
padded sheets, set out alcohol and cotton for prepping. A long
line of customers snaked out of her kitchen into the hallway of
her building. Some had self-anesthetized with medications rang-
ing from crack to Percodan. The first of many wanted loose
silicone added to her breasts, which had already been created
two years ago using silicone bags. But this procedure was
cheaper. Others wanted prominent cheeks or chin extensions to
make the outline of their faces more heart-shaped. Then there
were those who wanted enormous buttocks or hips to appear
even more curvaceous. She herself only wanted more shapely
thighs as her legs tend to look too gangly and male.

The injection of the silicone causes enormous bruises. In some
places layers of plasma surface and smart like a bee sting. She
had to sleep with a pillow under her knees because even the
slightest pressure in the swollen area of the injections was
excruciating.

But the worst was the fever. It spiked up and down hourly for
two whole days. It burned her eyes in their sockets as if they
had been replaced by acetylene torches. Her tongue felt heavy
and sandy against her dried-up palate. Slowly the fever melted
the fear into a hot trickling. The trickle became a sun-warmed
brook. She began to float on this lightly rippling brook. Her

body was weightless. The rivulets became cool, flowing through her limbs and swirling around her splayed fingers. The tiny waves were like the satiny skin of an adolescent against which one slides one's hand. There'd be no harsh sex to contact at the end of the long stretch of rippled skin, only this endless sliding. This was the clean love for which she was in search, and now she had found it, but as she had expected she could not in the face of it move her body. No one but no one need know about this fever. How could they ever understand?

The flat, oval face of the romantic interest is watching the new-smelling purse with veiled curiosity. The long, dark hand with tinkling bracelets slides inside the purse again and comes out with another bill earned from the silicone sessions. The boy's eyes gleam with interest. She asks him to go to the store and get both of them packs of cigarettes and mints. He slides off the bar stool to attention. His hand curves over the fresh bill. Her prideful eyes sparkle with Amaretto as she watches him shuffle toward the door. She loves the stiff, thrusting walk, the ill-intentioned slouch, the pants hanging from his skinny hips. She imagines, mistakenly, that all eyes are fixed on the line of sight linking him to her proprietary gaze.

What she doesn't know is hidden under the drapery, criss-crossing the lean, nearly hairless chest and severing his nipple, fanning out from his rib cage almost all the way to his navel: a vast constellation of welted scars, still tender to the touch after almost a year. And inside his brain is the muffled memory of a searing incident: black sky in a dark park. An overheated crack pipe quickly stashed in his pocket, so hot that it burns its way to the flesh of his lean thigh. He's trying to hide the smoking crack pipe from the olive eyes of a rageful dealer to whom he owes money, as a quick, dull stampede of feet approach from behind. In the park with the broken streetlamps he feels the pressure of metal against his muscles as he is backed against a wire fence. It bulges behind him like a hammock while his feet scud uselessly forward.

Then there are the endless jabs and slicings—like children poking curiously with sticks at a big dead animal—the points sinking in and popping out; edges of blades making ribbons of the T-shirt and crosshatching the skin of the chest; and a close-up of crusted knuckles around a knife handle, while another big calloused hand encircles his neck and presses the back of it against the fence.

He tries to drop his jaw low enough to bite one of the fingers. But the grip tightens, the slicing keeps happening until he feels himself slump down slow-motion: liquid is seeping out in a pissing feeling; a warm weakness, like a brook trickling in the sun. His limbs flow deliciously away like a hand sliding down the satiny skin of the most beautiful girl's body. And there'll be no recriminations at the end of the long stretch of rippled skin, only this endless slide.

He stops at the entrance to the store, feeling the bill against the pads of his palm. A magnetic pull is coming from the corner where little magic vials are sold. But the black bitch's purse constantly giving birth to those twenties has a stronger shimmer.

He pokes the bill through the scratched slot of the plastic antitheft shield, and two packs of Newport and a roll of mints spill back, followed by clattering coins and some folded, grimy bills.

Back where the purse is, the hole has swollen full of people. Boisterous and impatient. They push by him without so much as a "sorry." They really should watch themselves as somebody could end up in the toilets with a skull split open. The tall black bitch who claims to be a real woman doesn't bother telling him to keep the change when he holds out the coins and crumpled bills with the mints and Newports. And she seems to want to sit here all night. If she is a woman, there'll be a slippery pussy into which to plunge, but at the very least tits to suck and the padding of an ass against his thighs. There'll be an apartment somewhere, a bed and a shower, and maybe a full refrigerator.

Then there's that purse.

Much later, it is nestled between their hips on the back seat of a taxi, upon which her long-boned body is folded into thirds, her pressed-together knees improbably high. The not very serious fantasy of reaching across her lap to open the door and shoving her out of the taxi as the light changes flashes through his mind. Then all of it is erased by the murky row after row of faceless buildings, his body moving through night . . .

Entering her apartment like they now are, you might remark that her sober middle-class image was being compromised. It's not just the many feminine icons replacing genuine accoutrements of a woman's life, as in the bathroom. It's the shabby compromises of the city outskirts poking through the brave attempts at upper-class ascendancy: that laminated breakfront imitating a European antique or the knock-off country flower print on cheap curtains and couch covers; the sound system with its many luminous readouts showing itself off in a corner.

He is wild about that sound system. There are CDs piled everywhere. The latest ones. He rifles through them, letting out gasps when he discovers some of his favorites of the moment. Her mascaraed eyes glue themselves with sullen suspicion to his hand movements. He feels the look but pretends not to, rakishly poking the first CD into the system and then striding toward her. As he grinds against her to the music, her eyes peer vigilantly from above, on the lookout for the hand that might reach for a weapon. She is caressing him through the baggy clothes with the covert agenda of frisking. But the hard curves of his body and the flat stomach remind her of those delicious, dizzy slidings. His calloused hands clasp her flesh, and the lush padding of his lips suffocates her. Her tongue begins to swirl against the gold teeth, and the musty smell of his body makes her feel weak with intimacy.

He, for his part, is quickly surveying her body, spanning different parts of the skeleton with his caresses to make a diagnosis. Is it a real woman? The buttocks feel too sculpted, but the arms snaking over his back have the creamy, yielding texture of femininity. The tops of the thighs feel pliant and meaty.

He decides not to worry about it. When he pushes her backward she obeys, collapsing onto the big matching-print bedspread. Looking down, you'd see her long, twisting figure cradling his smaller clenched body, which is lunging. Then her panty-hosed legs rise, opening along either side of his narrow hips, as the skirt hem inches up her thighs. The legs hover in the air, then snake around the narrow waist, expertly edging the pants and undershorts down to reveal smooth, hard buttocks dimpled at the teardrop tops.

What a fool she is. Not to have had him remove all his clothes before her body got trapped underneath his. Not to have had him put the clothes away from the bed. Out of the pants he still wears the weapon will pop. Or from his socks. He'll hold the point of the blade to her neck while she is pinned beneath him and leave her bleeding like a pig.

Just let him try it. At the least sign she'll lunge upward with superhuman strength. He'll go flying off her and hit the wall. She'll pounce on him and hold him by the hair while her fist smashes cartilage and gold-sleeved teeth pop from the blood-gushing mouth. And what will she do with all that gold? Should she have it melted down? Make that plain heart-shaped locket she'd been thinking of getting?

The pants are already off and kicked to the foot of the bed. The room is a cavern of thickened breath. Hands are reaching behind her to unzip her dress.

He won't find out. *Ever.*

Her passion will overrule all his explorings. As he lies naked on his back, his body will be claimed by her hungry mouth. She's already flipped him. He's stretched his arms over his head. His legs dangle submissively from the edge of the bed. It's safer this way, she tells him. You won't get the rest of me until I know you better. The teasing tongue and slippery mouth glide in cool pleasure over his thighs and crotch, tracing their way through the thicket of his groin to—

No! He grasps both of her ears to keep her head from moving. Not up there.

A feeling of insult gushes through her. Molten offense. *He knows.* Isn't she good enough? Why's she got to keep her mouth below the waist?

He just . . . doesn't want to take his shirt off.

Teasingly, she pinches the hem of the T-shirt and begins to lift it. His hand locks over hers. His mouth compresses.

She swings her feet to the floor, and cups her chin in her hands. The unzipped dress slips from one shoulder.

Take your shirt off, she orders sulkily.

No!

Her hand snakes to his thigh and slides onto his crotch, begins its rhythmic stroking. Harder and harder his penis gets, deeper and more rhythmic his breathing . . .

Take your shirt off.

No. Never.

But this time something tells her not to withdraw. Her hand lingers at his thigh, caressing it reassuringly. The story of the scars unfolds. The scars were an unzipping. His skin shredded like ripped clothes letting life out through the seams. An enormous loss. And even when the blood had been replaced and the wounds had closed, he never got everything back. All of it went down a size.

In fact, he doesn't take his shirt off. He wears it even when he's alone, quickly shedding it to wash and then putting one on again. The sight and the memory of vulnerability are too much for him. . . .

A barely audible hum deep in her throat. Her warm, brown eyes flooded with a look of compassion. How unconcerned with scars she is, how eager to lightly caress his whole body with her hands and mouth. How she dreams about and prays for that moment of trust. How this chance for him to get used to his new body couldn't be better. With the help of someone who really likes it . . .

The shirt slowly peeling upward . . . Past the flat nub of the navel and the bloom of almost invisible hairs leading toward the sculpted chest, under the wide net of crosshatched scars.

They hurt a little, he says.

Breath held. Her hand barely grazing the skin, contacting the net of welts.

Both of them breathing. Stooping, she runs her moist lips over the pattern, stops to tease the intact nipple, the soothing hum still vibrating in her throat. Over and over she lathes the chest with an adoring tongue, the sides of the rib cage, the burn scar at the hip.

The moistened chest feels healed, he thinks. She's reforming it for him with her mouth. Slowly but surely his breath comes easier and the muscles relax. The suction on his body sends waves of soft pleasure coursing; his hands encircle her neck and pull her toward his crotch.

Afterward her head is cradled on his chest. Their guards drop. She drifts into sleep with the feeling of being in the natural world. A small sigh of ease from his gently parted lips. I bet I'm going to be here for a while, he's thinking as he loses consciousness, his chest naked for the first time since . . .

The middle of the night. A scarred angel in her arms. Against her cheek in the darkness the edges of the welts. Waves of tenderness are enveloping her. She is thinking, tomorrow . . . after she has cooked breakfast for him . . . he will discover that she has given him some money. Not for sex. But because she knows he has no cash . . .

The best idea would be to get a fifty from the roll of bills now and slip it into the pocket of his pants lying at the foot of the bed. . . .

No embarrassment. She can put the purse somewhere safe and not have to think about it.

She slips out of bed and feels her way to the corner of the couch where the purse is lying, pausing a moment to think of what has been lulled into sleep on the bed. Her eyes are full of astonished tears of gratitude, reverence for her rescued child. She feels woozy with tenderness as she sticks her hand into her purse too carelessly.

It nicks her finger.

She puts the purse in the bottom dresser drawer and tiptoes to the bathroom for a bandage. Then she sinks beside the unveiled beloved, who has shifted his back to her so she can't see his open eyes, which are staring at the bottom dresser drawer.

Until his lids fall closed.

And the orbs begin to twitch.

And he dreams yet again of shrieks slashing the black air.

TRESPASS

• DAVID EBERSHOFF •

Through the hydrangea leaves, Boyd and I were focusing on the hot asphalt of San Raphel Road. Camouflaged in the bush, our eyes at tailpipe level, we were waiting for the right car to drive by. We'd been balancing on the balls of our feet for nearly an hour, hopeful in the last weeks of summer that we could get in at least one good round of Hubcap before heading home for dinner.

Just as we were becoming bored and sweaty, Boyd's ears perked up and turned like a cat's. A chugging noise was coming from down the road, and he picked up his polished Mercedes hubcap as if it were a Frisbee. "Sounds like a Chevy," he said. "It's a pickup, Mitch. A four-by-four. You'll see." Sure enough, a few seconds later a boxy silver Chevrolet with a lawn mower strapped into its bed careened down the road. "Yup," Boyd said, tugging at his shorts. I'd been asking my mom to lend me a hubcap off her Chevy, but she kept saying she didn't think it was a good idea.

My own hubcap, shiny and spoked, had originally rolled on the back wheel of a Buick parked in an empty and poorly lit section of the Pasadena Plaza's parking garage. "Even though it came off a Skylark," I told Boyd, "it'll do for any souped-up special-edition car. Fat cats love spokes. It'll work on a Lincoln or even a Cadillac."

The hydrangea bush was on one of the fancier streets in Pasadena where the houses were hidden behind ficus-covered walls and oleander bushes. It was a perfect street for Hubcap, much better than our own neighborhood where the lawns were yellow and brittle and the shrubbery solitary and shaped like lightbulbs.

"The right car will come along," I said.

Next to me Boyd was rubbing the black ball of a pill bug up and down his thigh, from the hump of his kneecap to the frayed hem of his cut-offs. His face was fixed with a quiet concentration, but then suddenly he snapped his thighs closed as if he'd noticed me peeking up his shorts. From the way his face coiled up, I knew he was about to take off. Checking his watch, he said, "That's it for me. I need to go over to Mr. Bowman's."

"Who's that?"

"One of Jessica's neighbors. He's on vacation, and I'm taking in his mail and watering his plants. Gotta do it by five because I'm going over to Jessica's after that."

"I'll go with you," I offered.

Boyd thought for a moment and then said, "Fine, but you're not coming to Jessica's."

We hid our hubcaps beneath a pile of wilting leaves, and I followed him out of the bush. We walked by Old Man Norman's brick mansion and turned onto the dead-end street where Jessica Frank lived. When we passed her Spanish house with red roof tiles, Boyd's elbow nudged my ribs and he said, "Did I tell you her parents are out of town?"

I nodded, not wanting to say anything because I might have let on that I thought Jessica Frank was sleazy.

A small, tidy lawn sloped up a hill to Mr. Bowman's house, a one-story gray bungalow with a porch and large, bloomless camellias shading the windows from the California sun. Boyd and I walked up the oil-stained driveway, Boyd shaking in his cupped palm the kitchen door's brass key.

With the blinds drawn, Mr. Bowman's kitchen was veiled in a cool, gray light. I liked the feeling of the air on my skin, which was still warm and sticky from running around. "Who lives here again?"

"Some dude my mom met at a Christmas party. I think that's

where she said she met him. But you never know with her. She'll talk to anyone."

I followed Boyd down a long hall with wood floors. On the walls were framed photographs of white-water rafters, mountain climbers, and wind surfers. "My mom's the same way," I said. "We were at the Price Club this morning and she just had to ask everyone what they thought of the Medfly sprayings, if they thought malathion was really as safe as the government says it is." I laughed, hoping Boyd thought it was funny, too. "She just can't keep to herself."

Boyd unbolted the front door and went out to the porch to fetch the mail. I could hear a squeaky metal lid lift as I looked around Mr. Bowman's front hall. On a side table was a blue pottery lamp glazed in something that looked like milk. Next to that was a glass bowl filled with keys, a yellow diving watch, and a bent photograph of two handsome men, nearly identical, with red parkas and skis, their arms across each other's shoulders. They were on a snowy mountain next to a sign that read: *Attention! Vous vous trouvez sur une piste hasardeuse!* I didn't know why (did that mean hazardous?), but the picture began to kindle a heat in my stomach.

"This guy gets so much mail," Boyd said, coming inside. "This all came today. Every day there's just as much."

"What does he do?"

"My mom says he's a big lawyer downtown."

"He is?" I weighed the risks of asking more questions, not wanting to appear overly interested. "Where'd he go on vacation?"

"Hiking in Switzerland." Boyd went into Mr. Bowman's book-lined living room and knelt in front of a wood-trunk coffee table where the previous days' mail was neatly sorted. "My mom said I should keep his mail in piles for him." He efficiently separated the mail into stacks of magazines, junk, bills, and envelopes that looked personal and private. Coming across a post card, he held it up and read it, and then flicked it over to me. On one side was an oil portrait of a young man with a green ascot and a brown mop of hair. The painting looked old. The other side said it came from the Picasso Museum in Barcelona, Spain. Then I read the sloppy note.

A genius has worked on every corner of this town, and here's another example. You were right, three days is not enough, and I've adjusted my schedule. (Who needed that duty-free shopping trip to Andorra anyway.) Met a terrific guy named Persio who took me to a tennis club forty minutes outside the city and we played three sets on the finest clay I've ever seen. (Who cares that I lost.) Can't wait to hear *your* tales. Love, Jason.

My eyes bulged. Certainly I'd misunderstood everything I'd just read. The words must mean something else to Mr. Bowman and Jason, I thought. They couldn't be about what I thought they were about.

"The guy's a fag," Boyd said.

A bubble popped in my head. "How do you know?"

"Look at the card, blind man."

I read it again and then looked back to Boyd.

"Love, Jason," he cried, his voice pitching high. "Screwed a dude on a tennis court."

"It didn't say *that*!"

"It might as well have. Here, give it back to me." He plucked the card out of my fingers and went back to the mail pile. "Look at this," he said, holding up a tissuey white envelope. "Looks like a letter from his mom."

I picked it up. It was from Mrs. Eugene Bowman of Oshkosh, Wisconsin. "Do you think his mother *knows*?" I asked.

"Fags tell everybody these days," he said. "Okay, I'm done. Now let's get out of here."

"Tell everybody what?"

"That they're fags. Come on, let's blow this place."

"That's it? Don't you do anything else for him?" I kept looking at the envelope from his mother.

"I told you it was easy. I get five bucks for five minutes of work."

"What about watering his plants?"

"Only every other day."

"Even in this heat? It's 100 degrees out there."

"Maybe you're right," Boyd said. "I mean the guy is paying me five bucks. I might as well do him a favor."

I followed Boyd around the house as he nosed a green plastic watering can into pots of spider plants and ivy. "You really think he's a fag?" I asked as Boyd trickled water into a yellowish fern hanging in the bathroom.

"Hey, my mom told me first. If you don't believe me, look around."

I *was* looking around, but there was no proof. The bathroom was just like the one my brother and I shared: Square-inch white tiles paved the floors and larger ones covered the walls. Two towels, one brown the other white, hung askew on the towel rack. There was a stack of magazines next to the toilet, *Time* and *National Geographic*, the same magazines that rested on my parents' toilet tank. A sliding door to the mirrored cabinet above the sink was partly open; on the glass shelves inside were the expected items: the stem of a red toothbrush, a razor-blade cartridge, a scum-rimmed glass, a blue bottle of cough syrup. Boyd saw me staring into the cabinet and opened it further with an outstretched finger. "Look at those."

"What?"

"The rubbers!"

"Where?"

"Those round, gold things."

"They look like chocolate coins."

"Well, they're not."

"Just because he has rubbers doesn't mean he's a homo."

"Trust me, the guy's a fag. Now let's get a move on. Jessica's waiting for me." He plucked a condom from the shelf and slipped it in his pocket.

Suddenly I felt slow and behind, incapable of catching up. Boyd had said he'd done it with Jessica, but had he really?

He switched off the light and headed toward the kitchen. As I began my first step to follow, my eyes made one last sweep across the bathroom. In the shower-tub was a double-hung sash window with panes of bubble glass. A hair-thin shred of sunlight pushed its way under the bottom of the window, and instantly I knew it was open and unlocked, that there was a way back into the house, and with that burning in my head, I took my position behind Boyd, tracing his steps across the kitchen's white linoleum floor and out the door into the brown heat of Pasadena in August.

"Mitch, do you want another wing?" my mother asked, floating a platter of barbecue chicken under my nose. Unable to eat, I politely turned it down. The line of sunlight shoving its way under Mr. Bowman's bathroom window was all I could think about. With my eyes open I could still see it floating in my vision, blazing on the sight of my short mother and her orange chicken. It took the center stage in my brain the way I guessed a burglar might imagine a golden key swimming in his mind or a safecracker might hear tumblers clicking in his skull. All evening, since Boyd locked Mr. Bowman's kitchen door behind us, I'd been feeling the preguilt of a klepto—helplessly aware I was about to do something wrong.

"Boys, your father and I are thinking of going to the movies tonight. It's too hot to stay home. Any takers?" In her yellow checked sundress, my mother looked like a little girl, her chest flat and her straight gold hair pulled back in a tight braid.

"Nah," my older brother, Charlie, said. "I'm going to Michele's. They've got A.C." He was seventeen, had sideburns growing halfway down his cheeks, and, though a football player, got better grades in school than I did. For the most part he'd been ignoring me for the past year ever since he'd found under the mattress of my bed—who knows how?—my stash of jockstraps stolen from the gym. The only thing he said was, "Can't figure out what size you are?" and, because he had something to lose in revealing his little brother as a jock thief, he'd never mentioned it to anyone as far as I knew.

"I may go to Boyd's to go swimming."

"Sounds like the troops have plans," my balding father said to my mother. He was tall and pear-shaped, with wide dark eyes next to his fleshy nose, and I often tried to ignore how similar our faces were. "But I want everyone home by ten. The paper says they're starting the spraying then. Says they found another Medfly on a lime in San Gabriel."

"I just don't understand how they find the little things one at a time," my mother said.

"Mitch, you're responsible for making sure Jane is inside." The owner of a pet store, my father was particularly worried about the effects of the malathion on Jane, our Great Dane.

"You know, Mitch and I took an unscientific poll at the Price Club this morning," my mother said. "And we found that four out of five people don't believe the government on this malathion business. One out of two think they're overdoing it with the nightly spraying. And one third of all our respondents don't even believe the Medfly exists. What do you think of that?"

"Proves the people know," my father said.

My room's walls were covered with corkboard, and after dinner I started throwing feather-tailed darts at the red and white targets I'd tacked up. You'd be breaking in, I warned myself as I shot darts into the corners of my room. A neighbor might call the police. *Jessica Frank* might call the police! You could wind up in jail, I whispered, aiming for a bull's-eye above my bed, both disturbed and pleased that that wasn't enough to keep me away. The cool air in his house had touched my skin in a way I'd never known before. It was like crawling into bed on a winter's night and discovering only after taking in the warmth of the heavy bedclothes just how deep the chill had set into your bones. Once you're warm you never want to go back out into the cold.

Hot, I lay on my back on my narrow bed, and I threw a purple dart into the ceiling. The strip of sunlight burned up there, too, like a neon tube. My heart continued to pound in my throat, where it'd been lodged since Boyd spewed the remarkable phrase: The guy's a fag. I wanted to go back to his house and find out exactly what that meant.

Once my parents and Charlie left, I put Jane in the back and headed off into the night, making it to Mr. Bowman's in five minutes on my bike. Unlatching the high blue gate to his backyard, I wheeled in my bike, its chain clicking like a mother's *tisk! tisk! tisk!*

An avocado tree, its branches spread over the yard, had bombed the grass with its overripe fruit, and I felt one squish softly beneath my tennis shoe. The peeling frame of the bathroom window peeked from behind the tree's knotty trunk. Kicking through a tangle of ivy, I wedged myself between the tree and the house. It felt like I was watching a movie starring myself, and there was nothing I could do to stop the main character from going ahead with the stupid thing he was about to do.

The window's screen covered my fingers with black dust as I tried to shove it up. Just get inside, I thought. Just get in there by yourself. I started sawing at the screen's lower corners with my house key. My fingers moved inside the slits, searching for the sliding latches. They were stiff, not easy to release, but I worked to pry them free. Go, go, go! The voice in my head was like a coach. Hustle on inside. *It's never too late to go home*, the frantic voice of hyper Mitch Hatch chimed in, seeming already to belong to another, dimly remembered fifteen year old. But nothing was going to stop me from entering the house. The boy I once was who would have stayed home and taken novels under the sheets with him—the boy I was before the first corn-silk hair sprouted on my ankles and between my legs—was gone now, his last traces eliminated, and as I raised the screen and then the window's lower sash, I whispered into the dark space of Mr. Bowman's bathroom, "That wasn't really me anyway."

A glow of light from a lamp in the front hall came into the bathroom, which appeared bigger from this angle. I stood in Mr. Bowman's tub and touched his green bottle of dandruff shampoo, the same kind my brother used. I closed the window and switched on the light. Gray scum glazed the bath's white porcelain, and a pad of dry silvery hair lidded the tub's drain. Swiftly I went to the medicine cabinet, and the condoms. I took one out of its wrapper and rolled the dusty latex in my hand and over my fingers and then put it in my pocket. The cabinet's other half, which Boyd hadn't opened, held more of the same: yellow mouthwash, a pack of Q-tips bound by a rubber band, a cake of face soap, and a clear plastic bottle labeled "SLICK—*The Personal Lubricant*." Carefully I rolled the bottle in my palms, turning it like an artifact. Maybe this could tell me something about a fag's life, I thought. I squeezed a drop of the clear fluid onto a fingertip and rubbed it into the scratched-up skin on the back of my hand. It felt like the perfumed oil Boyd's mom once brought back from a tennis ranch in Arizona. One night last spring, when we began lifting dumbbells after school, Boyd invited me over and asked me to give him a massage with the contents of the little blue vial. "All great athletes get their muscles rubbed," he said as he lay on a towel on the maroon carpet in his bedroom. He was wearing baggy red swim trunks, and as

I gingerly worked the rose-scented oil into the skin of his arms and chest, I watched a small lump rise in the nylon of his bathing suit. I told him I'd do his legs too, but instead he sat right up. "No way, only my arms are sore," he said, the corners of his mouth hanging down in distaste.

I put the bottle away. I'd been rubbing the shiny liquid into my skin—my thighs and shins and stomach and neck—for nearly a quarter of an hour, transfixed by the shellac it left on my body. With a wet washcloth I cleaned myself up. It was getting late, and thinking of Boyd had made me anxious. He was probably down the street fingering Jessica at that very moment. He'd probably told her he was taking in the mail for her homo neighbor, and they would share a disgusted laugh as Boyd's mouth nuzzled her long, tan neck.

But there was still the mail to look at. In the living room I reread Jason's card. It actually was about one guy meeting another. Shit. It really can happen. Then I held the letter from Mrs. Bowman up to a light. Was it possible that she knew? Through the envelope I could only make out the words "Your father's fishing magazine." I flipped it over. Against the lamp I could read something about "your news." And so without thought, without reservation, with my head dizzy and my prick hard, my fingers crawled out of my pocket and slit the envelope's seam.

Dear Matthew,

I know it has been over two months since you wrote us with your news, but it still feels to me like it is the same afternoon that I opened your letter and that I am still standing in that awful hot sun we had in that heat wave in June. I started reading your letter in the driveway and the sun and your news just stopped me right there. (Dad and I have repaved since the last time you were here so you don't know how black and hot and *tarry* that asphalt is.)

Even though you thought it would not surprise us, well it did. It really did surprise *me* is what I should say. It had never occurred to me, never crossed my mind. I know, as you pointed out, that you never talked about dating girls in college or law school or since you moved to California, but I always thought you just decided not to tell your father and me about them. Plus, you've always worked so hard I thought you were paying attention to your career just right now. No, I never once thought of anything else, that you might be anybody else. Not just once. How could I?

So, I was standing there at the end of the driveway reading your letter, just all worked up by the news in the first paragraph, when Mrs. Broak, you know what a Mrs.-butt-my-way-into-everything she's always been, sneaked up behind me. She literally tiptoed right up behind me until she could look over my shoulder. Then, pretending to be casual, she asked, "What're you reading?" Well, she startled me so, and that sun and the wavy heat coming up from the asphalt and your news, everything just turned me around. Before I knew what I was doing I said, "Can you believe it? Everything in today's mail was junk, all garbage, nothing but missing children notices and book club offerings," and I lifted the lid to one of the cans at the end of the drive (it was trash day) and threw the whole day's mail into the garbage, bills, your father's fishing magazine, your letter, *everything!* She just startled me so.

When I finally got rid of Mrs. Broak, I went inside and sat myself down in the front window. Two houses down across the street I could see Mrs. Broak do the same thing in her living room window, and we both just perched, our eyes on the garbage can, me waiting for her to get up and go to the bathroom, she waiting for me to give in and go and dig the mail out of the trash. Now I couldn't do that, not with the talk that would follow. So about two hours later I just watched the Garbage Men empty the trash cans into their truck and drive away the day's mail.

Not to worry, the bills of course came again the next month, and I went out and bought your father a new copy of *The One That Got Away*. But your letter was gone and I never even finished reading it and of course I never got to show it to your father. Since then I have often thought that maybe I misread that first paragraph, and that it did not say what I thought it said. In fact I was nearly convinced of that until the other night when I was standing in the kitchen making a lasagna and all of a sudden I was struck that we hadn't heard from you in over two months. I said to myself, Joanie, things in life don't turn out as you planned for a reason, and maybe Matthew didn't marry Allie Shenk the way you were so certain he would when he was in the eighth grade, but you've only got one son on this planet, and that's one more than Emily Broak, so don't screw this up, Joanie, you hear me?

Your father of course doesn't know anything about your letter but I think at some point we should tell him. So, what's the next step? Where do we go from here? Just like the time when you were in college when you took us on the foot tour of Boston (what was that called, the Freedom Trail?), that's a perfect example of how you've always been so good at showing us the way. We need you to do it again.

Love,

Mom

Panicked, I looked around Mr. Bowman's living room, expecting to see my reflection in the glaring eyes of witnesses and the police, jury, and judge. For the first time in my life I felt the despair of committing a crime. The envelope was slashed beyond reasonable repair, and unless I confessed there'd be no way to return the letter to Mr. Bowman. I folded the letter back into its envelope and then put it in my pocket.

Poor Mrs. Bowman. I imagined her waiting daily in her front-window chair for the mail to bring her son's response so they could reconcile. I pictured Mr. Bowman coming home nightly throughout the summer in a poplin suit and sorting his mail looking for a reply from his mom. Each night, in a quiet moment, they both would say to themselves, "Nothing," their voices trailing off in soreness. Mr. Bowman probably was clambering around the mountains of Switzerland wondering if there'd be word from his mom when he arrived home.

I stepped back into the shower to climb out of the house. Resting on the tub's deck was a wood-handled back scrubber. I thought of the day when Mr. Bowman would come home from his trip, riffle his mail, and then climb in the shower, disappointed that his mother still hadn't written. His back would be quilted with muscles and brown from hiking shirtless along Alpine cow paths, and under his showerhead he'd run the brush's horsehair bristles up and down the furrow of flesh that traced his spine.

At the redwood picnic table in our burned-out backyard, my mother passed around a stainless-steel platter piled with blackened meat patties the size of silver dollars. "I just love miniburgers," she said, dropping one into Jane's begging jaws. My mother was talking about the people she knew whose lungs had become itchy or who'd broken out with bumpy rashes, all the result of the malathion, she presumed. "It's no coincidence," she said. "It's Agent Orange all over." I could barely follow her sentences. The only thing I could think about was the letter in my pocket. I could almost feel it there against my thigh, throbbing like a fresh cut. I was too afraid to leave it anywhere, fearful that someone might find it or, even worse, that I might carelessly forget I had a problem to fix. I'd been trying to think of what I'd want done if I were the one who'd just confessed everything secret and important about himself to his parents.

I couldn't eat anything, so I quietly handed off my four miniburgers to Jane.

"Don't think I didn't see that, Mitchell," my mother clucked, her chin in her hand. "Don't think your mother doesn't see everything."

Earlier in the afternoon Boyd and I were hanging around the hydrangea bush for about an hour, but no cars with hubcaps that matched ours drove by. "We need another hubcap or two," Boyd said. Our bare thighs were brushing up against each other in the bush's shade. Wiry black hairs poked out mine, but Boyd's thigh was as smooth as the inside of an arm. My leg was thicker than his, too, and as we crouched our upper legs pressed together like two uneven butt cheeks. "We need something in the low end. Something for a plain old Toyota. Or a Honda hubcap would get us lots of business."

"If you want a Honda one, I'll get it, Boyd."

"Only if you *find* it. You can't rip 'em off of cars anymore."

"Why not?"

"Because that's stealing."

"What about playing Hubcap?" I asked. "Isn't that lying and

deceiving and being mean?" A black Volkswagen putted by. "So what's the difference?"

"There's a big difference, man. Hubcap is for kids playing around. Ripping things off is for another crowd. Crooks. Cat burglars. Felons." Boyd then broke into the details of last night at Jessica's. When he started telling me how she'd worn her wet bikini beneath her tank top, I wondered why life had set things up so that Jessica Frank would fascinate Boyd yet leave me numb and bored. What was it about her and every other girl I knew that turned me into a fifteen year old unlike everyone else? It used to be that in the hydrangea bush I often felt that, after all, Boyd and I were pretty much the same, and my vague longing for him and a few other guys at school really wasn't as serious of an isolator as I feared. But ever since Jessica's parents went out of town leaving her and her older sister, Joyce, alone, Boyd had made even our Hubcap command center another setting to point out that his life was proceeding nicely while mine was on the brink of careening out of control. He made me feel like a drunk driver cheerfully skidding across a lawn in the instant before he plows through a living-room window.

My mother was convinced the malathion was the reason I wasn't eating. "It's not that," I tried to tell her the next night at dinner.

"But how would you even know?" She threw a pop-up bun at Jane, who was busy gnawing at the flies on her tail. "I'm worried about where you'll get your nutrients if you don't eat your dinner. Won't you have a hot dog?" Her small fist gripped a long barbecue fork, and its two gouging prongs sparkled in the late evening sun, winking like my mother's eye. She and I had always shared a wink as our secret gesture of love. I had never seen her wink at my brother or my father or even Jane the Great Dane. When I was little and she called me Monster, I would walk around, skinny and awkward, thinking I would grow up to be just like her, and sometimes, as I perched on her tiny lap, my bony limbs locked around her neck and waist, I would tell her I wanted to be her exact twin. "You can be whatever you want to be," she'd always say, and my child's fist of a heart would swell with relief. As I grew taller and skinnier, my mother's lap had a harder time holding me, but I would wiggle my way onto her. Finally one day when I was eleven, long before I knew anything about myself and my looming adolescence, she said to me, "You don't really want to *be* my exact twin, Mitchell. You want to *marry* her." With that, she neatly scooted me out of her lap for the last time and then called over Jane, who, though slobbering and huger than me, took my warmed place. Stunned, I looked in my mother's pie-shaped face for an explanation, for our wink, but she was already focused on brushing the oil out of Jane's coat and did not notice me slink away.

Charlie was at his girlfriend's tonight, and, looking at my mom and dad's tight faces reminded me of the square of folded paper in my pocket.

"Mitchell?" my mom said. "I'm just going to come out and say it. Are you having trouble with girls? Is that why you're not eating?"

"I know you don't think of me as a smooth operator, Mitch," my father said, chewing his bun. "But I do know a few things about girls and their ways."

"So do I!" my mom chimed in.

Right then, in the faint honey light of dusk, I considered asking them for help. As I watched my parents butter their ears of corn and glare at me with their dull brown eyes, I thought maybe I could split myself open and tell them what had happened. I could explain how Boyd was taking in Mr. Bowman's mail and how something about his house had forced me to do things that I knew were wrong even as I was doing them, how it was hard being different from Boyd and Charlie and all the other guys and all the other girls and even different from all the grown-ups I knew in the world, being the most unwanted thing that each of them could imagine, that I could imagine, and everything in my life would have been okay if it weren't for this one thing, which seemed to be consuming my attention more and more every day, and what would they do if they were me, what would they do?

"If it's about a girl, talk to us," my dad said grinning. "Or maybe it's about a couple of girls!" Then, something in his square face—its similarity to my own, maybe—told me they couldn't help me on this one, that I would have to go at it alone, and that it would be much, much better if I didn't bring this up with them or anyone because this was the one thing they, all of them, everyone I knew, could not, would not, understand.

A few days later I was waiting for Boyd in the hydrangea bush when, hot-faced and puffing, he pushed his way through the leaves.

"Why were you running?"

"Jessica's mom nearly caught me and her going at it behind their garage." The Franks had been back from their vacation for two days. "We were back there and Jessica had her blouse open and my zipper was down and all of a sudden we heard footsteps rustling through the leaves and somebody was coming back there and then Mrs. Frank called out, 'Jessica?' " Boyd was lying on his back and his raised T-shirt exposed the shallow cove of his navel. Speaking towards the sky, he continued, "So, I just grabbed Jessica's arm and made her climb over their back fence with me, but she got scraped up pretty bad. I told her to go home and tell her mom she fell off her bike and then I jammed over here. The whole thing sucks."

"Maybe you guys should take it easy now that her parents are back."

Boyd's head turned toward me. He snorted, his lips twisting, and said, "Easy for you to say."

I wanted to ask him what he meant, but his likely answer scared me. He could confront me here and now, I thought, but what would I do, what would I do as he called me a fag, a fucking homo? I could take my first step toward coming clean about Mrs. Bowman's letter if I looked at him right now and sternly said, What do you mean by that? Tell me what you mean. I dare you . . . But I knew I would deny it, every bit of it, and swear on my life that he was more wrong than he'd ever been.

Then suddenly the clicking sound of a powerful engine came drifting from down the road. Boyd's eyes bugged. "Mitch, what's that?"

"Sounds like a diesel," I said.

"That's not just a plain old diesel." He sat up. "That's no lawn mower, Mitch. That's a Mercedes. It's a Merk, man!"

"You sure?"

"Sure, I'm sure. You watch. We've got this one. Meet me back in front of my house 'cause this one's going to fly."

"I'll be there, Boyd. Good luck, man!"

Next to me, Boyd stood up, bending so his head wouldn't stick out with the pompom blossoms. He gripped his hubcap between his thumb and his index finger, readying it. The coughing diesel was making its way down San Raphel and as it curved the bend, we saw, sure enough, it was an early eighties night-blue Mercedes sedan. Driven by a lady who looked older than our moms, the car sloped by our hydrangea bush. As soon as we could see its rear license plate (it was one of those vanity plates that said BLUBLUD), Boyd whipped the hubcap out of the leaves and sent it whizzing through the air. It landed on the center yellow line just behind the car's bumper and skidded harshly across the asphalt, scraping loudly, one or two sparks shooting out. The Mercedes' brake lights burned red. Boyd hopped out of the bush waving his hands and shouting, "Hey, lady, your hubcap! Your hubcap!" He ran to the spot where the hubcap was twirling on its rim like a quarter. He scooped it up with both hands and held it over his head. "Your hubcap! Look!"

The Mercedes' door opened and the driver stepped out, visoring her flat hand above her eyes. The woman was wearing a purple and silver jogging suit and a large sparkling cocktail ring. She seemed confused, her face stuck and her mouth ajar. "What?" she said.

Boyd was jumping up and down. "Your hubcap came off!" he yelled. "Look, it just flew off! Here it is!"

"Oh, my goodness," the driver said, her hands patting at her blond helmet of hair.

"It just popped off," Boyd said, still bouncing on his feet.

"Why, thank you. I heard that terrible scraping noise and I thought what on earth? Aren't you nice to stop me like this because I would have just kept on driving, you know these days I don't stop for anything."

Then Boyd took off with the hubcap under his arm.

"Hey, where are you going?" the woman cried. "Where are you going with my hubcap? You come back here!"

The woman started chasing Boyd down the street, her fist raised and her breasts bouncing back and forth like tether balls.

Eventually she stopped and watched Boyd sprint to the end of the block and then disappear. I knew he'd used our planned escape route up a lemon tree and then along the brick wall of Old Man Norman's property to the opposite side of the block.

The woman was in the middle of the street, chugging for breath. Behind her, the Mercedes' door was open, its engine still on. She set her hands on her hips and then walked back to her car muttering. Bending over at each wheel, she began examining her car's condition. When she arrived at the fourth intact tire she angrily cried out, "What the hell's going on here?"

I couldn't wait to report to Boyd his Hubcap success. I was desperate to share something with him, something laced with emotion, and this seemed about the best chance I'd get for a while. A Hubcap victory like this—it'd been so long!—could help him forget, I believed, his feeling that a rift was subtly spreading between us.

I met him in the driveway of his parents' house. He was sitting cross-legged on the cement, hidden behind his mom's yellow minivan. A two-liter bottle of Coke poked out between his legs, and a drop of sweat was moving down each of his temples. Looking up he said, "I got her, man."

"She was pissed, too."

"How pissed?"

"She was talking to herself and I heard her say she was going to call the police. Then she got on her car phone, so I think she actually did it."

"Did she see you?"

"I don't think so."

"What'd she do when I took off?"

I told him about the lady's confused reaction, emphasizing the corny details like her wide butt sticking out when she bent over to investigate. I started to make up a part about her farting, but just then Jessica appeared at my side.

"Hi," she said.

"Jessica!" Boyd jumped up. "Did your mom figure anything out?"

"I don't think so." She had big beige bandages on her knees, and her blond hair was pulled back into a bushy ponytail, making her look even taller than she was, which was taller than both of us.

"Jessica," I said. "We just nailed a blue Mercedes in Hubcap. Totally got her!"

"Look, Boyd," she said, glancing around. "Can we go inside?"

"Yeah, sure," he said. "Catch you later, Mitch."

"Bye, Mitch," Jessica said.

I headed back to the hydrangea to deposit the Mercedes hubcap. For some reason, I knew it was over. I had a feeling that was our last round, and Boyd's hubcap next to my spoked one would now rest in the underbrush of the hydrangea for a long time to come. Through the seasons they would stay there, rusting and sinking into the dirt, undiscovered for a year or two, until somebody's gardener took on the special project of cutting back the shrubbery on the street.

As I shuffled along the sidewalk, I saw a cop car turn onto the street. Not even knowing what block I was on, I started running. It wasn't the hubcap in my hand that I was so worried about. Instead, all I could think about was getting caught and having my pockets emptied. They'd find Mrs. Bowman's letter. That would be it. Everything would crash, and maybe I'd get out of the hubcap charge but I'd be booked on burglary and mail theft. Oh my god, and I kept running, my lungs banging for air. Boyd would never understand how this had all happened, no one would. They'd never listen to my side of the story. I didn't even risk looking back to see if I was being followed.

I finally made it back to the fancier part of the neighborhood where there were walls and gates and overgrown bougainvillea and hibiscus. At last I saw a tall box hedge I knew how to cut through. At its base there was a spot where the branches thinned, and I tunneled through it and then sneaked along the bamboo-lined border of a deep yard that belonged to a widow. Once I hit the back wire fence covered with passion plant vines, I jumped over it and crawled my way across three more backyards until I found a slouching woodpile to hide behind.

Until twilight I crouched there, guilty from Boyd's sin, and with his hubcap locked between my knees. And as I waited for the safety of night, my heart knocking with terror, I read over and over Mrs. Bowman's letter.

The night before Mr. Bowman's scheduled return, I rode back to his bathroom window. Once inside I went to his bedroom door and peered inside. After the chase, I almost ripped up the letter and buried it next to the woodpile. I almost convinced myself to forget trying to fix anything. How much longer would my luck hold?

A green down comforter was lying sloppily on his double bed, his pillow dented with a sleeper's ghost impression. On the other side of the room was a black dresser. On top of it were a neat stack of Mr. Bowman's stiff attorney-at-law business cards, a column of pennies in an ashtray from a hotel in Tokyo, and an unframed photograph of a man with gold ringlets of hair propped on a sofa reading a book. With his wire glasses and the concentration on his face, I could recognize Mr. Bowman. Of course it's him, I thought, feeling as though I'd met him long ago and something important, like affection, had already passed between us.

A dresser drawer was open and inside were rolls of black socks and squares of white handkerchiefs. I fingered them and cautiously creaked open the drawer below it. It held Mr. Bowman's boxer shorts, each with a different design. Green tennis rackets, orange Japanese fans, one pair had a map of Missouri on the seat. Feeling as though I had a right to do it, I dropped my tan corduroy shorts to the ground. In the dressing mirror on the back of Mr. Bowman's closet I saw myself with my pants down. The thick hair on my legs looked like matted fur, my briefs were too tight, and the stubble on my chin was oily. What was I? I knew, but nobody else, except Mr. Bowman, would if they were to come across me now. I was just trying to make things as right as I could get them for Mr. Bowman and his mother, and for me. In spite of this, it seemed entirely possible that the next thing that would occur on the face of the earth would be the flashing of the judging world's camera bulb, capturing me in an inaccurately guilt-loaded shot: the hubcap-stealing, trespassing child, shorts around his ankles, lifted letter in the pocket, sex swollen and leaking, his hand caught in the underwear drawer.

I yanked down my briefs and replaced them with a pair of Mr. Bowman's boxers that had golden roasted chickens, steam rising off the crispy skin, printed on the cotton. Big in the waist and thighs, the shorts' roominess pleased me; I liked the feeling of air crossing the skin of my groin and rear. I was excited, but I hadn't slipped on Mr. Bowman's underwear for the same reasons Boyd went to Jessica. What would Mr. Bowman want me to do about the letter? In his boxer shorts, in his dim bedroom, with the dust of his floors collecting between my toes, with my pulse echoing in my ears like a steady knock on the door, I might be able to figure it out.

I came to realize that Mr. Bowman and I would become friends out of all of this, that we would look at each other and think, Me too, me too. And as I lay down on the floorboards in the long shadow of his bed, my eyes staring at the blank ceiling, I could see the potential of my life more clearly than ever before. It was like the time when I was eight and I begged my soccer coach to let me play goalie even though I'm not much of a catcher. From my whole team to our opponents to my parents, everybody knew I was the worst goalie in the league, but I still thought I was pretty good until I let eleven shots fly into the orange netting, four with my fumbling assistance. Sometimes the person in the center is the last to figure things out about himself.

Eventually I stood up with a plan. Sitting at his desk, I turned on his computer. Here he must have written the letter to his mother and here I would write him a letter, print it out, and paper-clip it to his mother's and leave them both in his underwear drawer.

On a blank screen the letters I punched appeared, explaining who I was and how I ended up in his house reading his mail. Unfolding the story, I wanted to tell him how I'd planned none of it and I apologized for invading his privacy.

After days of 100-degree weather, Mr. Bowman's dark house was no longer cool, and as I typed, hunched on his cane-bottom chair, sweat spread across the small of my back and between my legs. My cramped fingers continued to type as the night slid on and my palms grew damp. The first page of my tale, then the second, then the fifth burned on Mr. Bowman's computer screen. A dull pain crept into my curved spine, but I didn't slow to straighten myself. It was getting late, and I still hadn't gotten to the part how I'd considered showing Mrs. Bowman's letter to my own mother, hoping we could use it as a model of how a mother and her gay son could work things out. How I might have really done it, too, if Michele hadn't pulled up in the driveway and dumped dumb, drunk Charlie at our door.

I continued to type nervously, the pressure of time and heat closing in on my opportunity to report all that had happened. In the summer sky I heard the thudding whir—at first distant and soft, then approaching and menacing, just like in the movies—of the Medfly helicopter brigade aerosoling the neighborhoods with fog banks of malathion. The whipping blades told me I was late getting home and Jane was now whimpering in our backyard. But I couldn't stop, not just yet. My head peered over the keyboard, the cords in my neck stretched taut. The tendons in my wrists stiffened with ache. My fingers typed even faster, misspelling almost every other word, but I still needed to tell Mr. Bowman how he could contact me so we could meet, and just at this moment I heard a noise from the kitchen door, and my fingers stopped, skipped a beat, and then began pounding again. I was so close to done, and the letter could explain it all better than I could. Footsteps moved down the hall, and I hunkered closer to the computer screen. I imagined Mr. Bowman's blocky face would first screw up in confusion, but soon it would expand and relax with sympathy. "What's going on here," he would gently say, rubbing my neck, somehow knowing exactly how I'd ended up in his house, at his desk, in his underwear. I craned my neck to line my vision with the door frame, my fingers still working, and just as Boyd and Jessica tiptoed forward and squinted into the gray computer glow of their borrowed love nest, their dewy faces stuck in the silent instant between rosy excitement and ashen disgust, just at this moment, when before I would have only felt the tent of my soul collapse, just then I realized that I was no more evil than Boyd, that if he could seek pleasure so would I, and that passion for us all would remain a troublesome thing.

MASSAGE

• JASON K. FRIEDMAN •

You pace the block above and then the block below. You don't want to appear overeager. You don't want it to seem you're expecting more than your hour's worth. At ten to eight, all paced out, you're on his block, and there's the house, just as he described it over the phone: mustard-colored, barnlike, surrounded by a chain-link fence. A single tree in the front yard. You have lived in this city a year and still don't know the names of the trees. As you lift the latch on the gate you notice, under the tree, a gray cat taking a shit. Its eyes meet yours and you turn away.

You wonder how many windows give onto this spot, how many eyes can see, through the branches of all the nameless trees, all the men who must lift this latch. It stays light quite late this time of year in this place. You head around back, to his apartment.

You knock on the screen door and your name sails through the big lighted kitchen, cluttered with chairs and on every surface magazines and broad- and spike-leaved plants and glasses of cuttings. Then he appears, shirtless, in longish green underwear. You are both the same type—swarthy desert people—but unlike you he is compact and muscular and tan, with long, curly hair like Samson. He looks like you perfected. He smiles easily and takes your hand in both of his, as if you were old friends or ex-lovers, as if you had not just met at the gym.

That was last week. After showering, both of you had hard-ons. With practiced modesty you held a towel in front of your crotch and went to the bathroom. He took a chair by the row of lockers, pretending not to notice you. His penis jutted out like a club. He put on his socks first. You kept trying to make eye contact. It was important to make eye contact before sweating it out in the sauna. Finally his penis drooped and he put on his underpants. You came out and started getting dressed. He smiled at you, told you you had a great dick. You returned the compliment. On his way out he handed you a business card.

He leads you to a little room off a bathroom. There's a light fixture with two empty sockets and one dim bulb. A beige carpet. A window with a spider plant in it and the blind dropped. And in the center of the room, the table. He tells you to take your time undressing, then lie on your stomach, facing the wall. He tells you to call his name when you're ready.

You call his name and instantly hear his tread. He directs your head to a towel-cushioned headrest, so that you are looking down at the carpet. Then you feel his hands floating insistently up your legs like an air-hockey puck, hovering over your ass fuzz, one on each cheek, then coming together, clasping, at the top of your head.

"Breathe deeply," he says. "In and out. In and out." He tells you that this hour is about you. He says it's not often in the busy workday that you can spend time just taking care of yourself. His voice is deep and even, his touch is at once firm and gentle.

You close your eyes and drift and almost forget why you came here—to be humiliated. Oh it became clear soon enough, that afternoon in the gym, that he was never going to have sex with you. When he handed you his card—a line-drawing muscleman's naked back chopped along one edge, a row of interlocking triangles in a band under his name—he told you not to worry, he was licensed and legit. You almost said you'd prefer him unlicensed and illegit; instead you simply smiled.

Of course, you resolved not to call. But every day you examined his card and rehearsed his words, wondering what message he was trying to convey. When you called he had no idea who you were. Then when you explained, he said he gives a sensual massage but won't jack you off at the end. Which is what some people expect from a massage. Which he has nothing against morally but that just isn't what we're trying to accomplish here. You said almost nothing except to make arrangements.

Music is playing, a blues singer with a velvet voice. You can't make out the words. Better to concentrate on your humiliation. You were not a fool at the gym; you became one only when you picked up the phone. A sucker, a chump. You'd never seen him before last week. You imagine him making a single appearance at every gym in the city, collecting clients at every stop, the way he has collected you.

"Breathe," he says, rubbing hot oil into your back. "Breathe."

You lift your head, facing the wall. "I imagine bodies are just bodies to you."

He thinks for a second, then says, "No. Not really."

But you persist. "It must just be a different way of perceiving the body. Different than the rest of us, who take a healthy sexual interest in naked men."

He's pushing against your lower back. You expect him to pound harder to match your hostility but his touch remains even.

"No," he says. "These girls I used to work with were like that. They would have, like, five clients in a row, so people really were just pieces of flesh to them. The day that happens to me I stop doing massage."

He's doing this thing with the flats of his hands, skimming between your shoulderblades and sailing up into your hair.

"Plus," he says, "I'm selective about who I work on. I only pick guys I'll enjoy being with. And I only have one client a night. It's just a supplemental-income thing for me."

So you have been chosen. Two members of the Chosen People in a dim room in an ugly house in a strange city, but only one of you is the truly chosen. This is supposed to make you feel better?

"At least you're being honest," you tell him. "To admit you're getting off on this. And why should you have anything to do with anyone else if you're not being paid for it, right?"

He's doing something to your neck. His furry navel is staring you in the eye. He is not wearing underwear under his underwear. Your gaze drops to his socks.

He kneads between your shoulderblades, harder and harder, suggesting a movement toward something, but the bright pain you feel at the base of your neck comes out of the blue.

"Tell me if I'm doing this too hard."

You laugh, and his thumbs press into either side of your neck. Your head jerks and the pain comes up behind your eyes. You bite your tongue so you won't cry out.

His fingers slide down the side of your neck, reaching for your throat. The balls of his hands meet at your nape. His grip tightens and you can only hope—

Then he lifts your head and holds your face in his greasy palms. Your eyes meet his, which are deep and liquid and filled with concern.

"I'm going to stop hurting you now," he says. "So you can stop calling me a whore."

You close your eyes. "I never said that."

"It doesn't bother me." He sets your head back down. "It's easy enough to own negativity."

"You're a licensed professional," you say. "I'm the sorry one here."

"You're just human."

You lie there with pain's echo ringing in your ear. The pain itself allowed for nothing else, no other feeling or thought, but this fresh memory of hurt connects with the memory of hurt you came with today and sends you deep into yourself.

M's absence has hurt more than you could have imagined. A different, deeper hurt than the one you had felt so often, especially toward the end, when every word out of his mouth gave you a queasy, hunted feeling. He was older, more experienced, smarter, so you trusted his every word. And he encouraged you to trust. After you moved in together, his advice multiplied. *Don't eat so much, don't eat so quickly. My last lover had an eating disorder and I can spot the signs.* Then: *Think carefully before you open your mouth. Nobody has any idea what you're talking about half the time.* Finally: *I want you to try to calm down a bit. I didn't want to say this, but I can see that mental illness runs in your family.*

It was all for a purpose, he assured you. In bed he whispered mysterious lines that sounded vaguely encouraging: *It's just a matter of actualizing yourself. If and when that happens, none of us will be able to stop you.*

He moves around the table and begins lifting your right flank. You start turning over.

"No, don't turn over. Don't do anything at all."

In his voice are no traces of aggression or defensiveness, only kindness. He continues this lifting business, on one side and then the other. You relax and let him do whatever he wants. "Good," he says. "Just put yourself in my hands."

You have never had a professional massage before, but now the moment has come that surely splits them all down the middle. He tells you he's going to pee and that when he comes out of the bathroom, we'll start on your front.

You have a hard-on. True, you're a hornier man than most, but who wouldn't be excited in this situation? Still, you don't want to appear overeager. You don't want to appear eager at all. As soon as the bathroom door closes, it sounds like a fucking gusher in there. It is hard not to overinterpret this. He did not get excited working on you. He wants you to know this. But at least he's giving you time to shed the signs of your own arousal. You think of being chased by thugs in some unknown part of this city. Grotesque sex scenes melt into one another.

When he comes out you stare up at him apologetically. "I'm afraid I'm incorrigible," you say.

"I'm that way, too. Don't worry about it. Just go with what your body tells you."

Then he tells you to lie back and breathe. He starts on your legs.

"Some of these guys," he says, "are lying there, and you can tell they're praying, 'Please don't let me get a hard-on, please don't let me get a hard-on.' What kind of way is that to relax?"

You close your eyes and try not to imagine M's hands on your legs. He was, naturally, expert at giving massages and would give you one when he was particularly pleased with you. After dinner parties where you had been charming and well-spoken. Like some kind of goddamn trained porpoise—or were they dolphins?—the ones they had at Six Flags in that place so far away and so long ago, the ones that sang "Happy Birthday" to you when you were a kid.

"But you can understand where they're coming from, can't you?" you ask.

"Excuse me?"

"Why guys are embarrassed to get a hard-on. You tell them this isn't a sexual experience and then you come out in your underwear and start rubbing your hands all over them."

"It's sensual. There's a big divide in the massage community between sensual and so-called legitimate massage."

"Whatever you want to call it, you can't tell me that getting a massage isn't an erotic experience."

"I work with it," he says, then picks up your left arm. "No, just let it hang limp. You don't have to do anything. Good. That's it."

"And take a look at yourself! You're driving me crazy just looking at you. How is this supposed to help me relax?"

"Breathe," he says. "Breathe. You know, you really do have a great dick."

You don't want his fifty-bucks-an-hour flattery. You close your eyes, cursing under your breath, willing him to hit you, to leave you with something real, something you can see and touch.

But he keeps on, rubbing your chest in circles, passing the warmth of his hands into you. It's clear that your easiest question will not be answered, your slightest wish will not be granted, but what did you expect? Try to work with it. Try not to think about it. Try not to think about anything, try to lose yourself in the blues singer's voice. You still can't make out words, only open endless vowels, endless and deep. Your arms are limp. Your dick is limp.

The next thing you know you feel bristles against your lips. You look up and there's his chest sailing across your mouth as he stands behind your head and reaches down for your belly, thighs, everything but what's between your legs. He rubs you wherever his hands land.

You open your mouth and breathe, breathe, taking it all in, then letting it out. He draws back and then lunges down your body again, and for a moment you can smell his breath, a meaty smell that you inhale and hold in. Then his bristly chest against your lips and you are practically kissing his pumping heart and suddenly your eyes tear up behind their lids.

You cannot remember ever being this close to another person besides M. And for the last year you did not even sleep together. And when it was over, when it was clearly over, you started up with the guys at the gym, that gym with the sign in the sauna saying KEEP YOUR HANDS TO YOURSELF/YOU'RE BEING WATCHED under the video camera that everyone knew was a prop yet still held you in its gaze, so that you might have started off with a hand on each other's dick but in your haste to finish were soon on your own, eyeing the fogged door or the blind camera or sometimes even each other, but truly, finally on your own.

As you dress, coffee begins grinding in the kitchen. You hope he won't offer you any. You want this to be a sign, the first, that he has a life outside of you.

In the kitchen he's standing there at the sink with his arms folded across his chest. The sky has turned that cyanic color that will ease into black. "How are you doing?" he asks.

"I'm not quite sure," you reply. Your neck aches, your shoulders are sore, your legs are stiff. Look at him, how comfortable he must feel in his body. You are not exactly comfortable in your body. But in your secret heart something has lightened. You feel soft at the core, ready to burst into laughter or tears at the slightest provocation.

But if this session was about you, it was also about him. So you say, "And how are you doing?"

But he only laughs. "Now wait a couple of hours before you jack off. Let that energy spread to your whole body, not just your dick."

And then, after you've handed over the cash, he has the grace to hug you, to participate in the experience—the emotions—he has just disavowed. You press against him. Your arms meet around his hot back and you hold on for dear life.

GIOIA E DOLOR

• PHILIP GAMBONE •

The Pellucca house—Charlie had only recently stopped thinking of it as *his* house, too—was on a shady side street in the still largely Italian neighborhood off Main. In the twenty years since he'd moved out, Charlie had witnessed its transformation from the inconspicuous working-class house, circa 1910, where he had grown up, into a place with two extra rooms (a den and a glassed-in porch), a new kitchen, a new bath, a finished basement, a flagstone patio and built-in grill, new shingles over the clapboards, and triple-glazed replacement windows everywhere. Every two years, his father repainted several rooms. Charlie's mother often said that if she hadn't been a bookkeeper, she would have been a decorator. "Adeline's Interiors" she would have called it.

Charlie unlocked the door with his own key. It was the key Pop had given him at the airport three years ago, just before he and Adeline left on their retirement trip to Italy.

"Just in case," Pop had told his son, pressing it, like a St. Christopher medal, into the palm of Charlie's hand.

Now, for one brief moment as he fit the key into the lock, the key he had since kept, religiously, on his key chain, Charlie felt a tremor of dread. What if he found a calamity inside: his father dead of a heart attack, his mother collapsed on a wet bathroom floor, her hip broken, her skull fractured? He pushed open the door and called out.

"Eh, the absent-minded professor returns!" Adeline exclaimed.

She came, almost rushing, into the hallway, looking overjoyed to see him, and dressed, too, for an overjoyous occasion. She was wearing a sharply tailored pair of white pants and a knit sweater in a color Charlie knew she would call "oatmeal." The sweater was embellished with seed pearls and bold, geometrical shapes of fabric in shades of pink, silver, and sandy brown. On her left wrist was a heavy gold bracelet. And her hair—the thin Gennaio hair that Charlie had inherited (though not the color, which for the last twenty years his mother had tinted blond)—was done up in her favorite set: a light tease and curl with lots of hair spray.

"The absent-minded professor returns again and again, you mean," Charlie corrected, giving her a quick kiss on the lips.

In the last few years, he'd noticed that his mother's hands had begun to wrinkle and that the skin under her neck was loosening up, but by and large Adeline Pelucca could still pass for a much younger woman, a sixty year old, maybe even fifty-five.

Charlie moved into the hall, letting his mother greet Dennett. He watched how she kissed him—affectionately, but with a tinge of formal politeness—as if she were saying, as she always said, that her home was open to anyone Charlie brought home, although after eleven years Dennett was hardly just "someone Charlie was bringing home." Still, he and Dennett, despite those eleven years, six of them owning a house together, were not officially out to his parents.

"Oh, how beautiful!" she exclaimed, taking the pot of tulips that Dennett had brought. "Boys, these are lovely."

"We thought you'd like the color," Charlie said. He shot Dennett a quick glance, as if to apologize for the "we." It was Dennett who had remembered to buy flowers.

"Oh, I *do*. I love them." She kissed them both again.

What story, Charlie often wondered, did his mother tell herself to explain Dennett's presence in the family? Whatever the picture she'd put together—"Charlie's good pal," "Charlie's house partner," "Charlie's bachelor buddy"—whatever innocuous category she'd found for Dennett, Charlie knew Denny had been deemed acceptable, which was the most important category of all. Dennett was polite and well-mannered, *gentile*, as Nonna Gennaio had once said, lending her language as well as her approval. Good-looking, too, and, though in a different way from Pop, a "sharp dresser." Dennett had other qualities that Adeline probably also appreciated, qualities that *their* language, the language of gay men, had terms for: Dennett was "straight-acting, straight-appearing." He'd been an easy one to take into the family.

Adeline led them into the kitchen, which was, like the rest of the house, immaculate. She set down the pot of tulips and immediately began peeling off the purple florist's foil wrapped around the pot.

"*Cafone*, huh, Adeline?" Dennett asked. Over the years, he had picked up a little bit of dialect.

Adeline laughed. "See?" she said, looking at Charlie. "Denny knows. Oo, my little adopted Italian." She took off the rest of the purple foil and stuck it in the kitchen waste basket. "There! Doesn't that look better?" she asked, handing the flowerpot to Charlie. He set it down on the kitchen table, next to two platters of hors d'oeuvres.

"Oh, I've been so *sperut'* to have you home for dinner!" she said.

"Ma, we were here three weeks ago."

"Eh, I'd be thrilled if you boys would come every week." She turned the flowerpot a quarter turn to expose another tulip blossom. "Guess what I'm making for dinner tonight."

There was such a tickled look on her face that Charlie would have known, even without smelling the aroma in the air.

"Spaghetti with lobster," he said.

"*Yes!*" Her voice bubbled with excitement, like ladlefuls of red sauce with lobster poured on top of everything. "With fresh lobster, not the frozen." She lifted the lid from one of the pots on the stove. "Smell." Charlie took a whiff. "You, too, Denny," she coaxed.

"Wonderful," Dennett agreed. "Adeline, I'd love to spend a Saturday at your side learning some of your recipes."

"Anytime, anytime!" she said. "You hear that, Charlie?" She turned back to Dennett. "You know, Denny, when Charles' grandmother moved in here with us, she hardly allowed me into the kitchen. My own kitchen! Can you imagine? At ninety-two, she still wanted to be the queen of the roost!"

"Nonna was quite a gal," Charlie offered.

Adeline went over to the cabinet where she kept the liquor and brought out a bottle of scotch and some cocktail glasses.

" 'Quite a gal' doesn't cover half of it, Charles." She set the scotch and the glasses on the table and shook her head. "No, she was a wonderful lady, but she could also be—God forgive me—a bitch sometimes."

Charlie turned to Dennett and translated: "Nonna liked having things done her way."

Adeline opened the freezer and pulled out a container of ice cubes.

"*Her way!*" She set the container down. "Charles, you were always Nonna's favorite. You don't know the half of what your father and I went through those years after Nonno died. Ask your sister sometime. She knows."

Charlie began to pour the scotch.

"So why'd you and Pop ever invite her to live here?" he asked. "I mean, couldn't Nonna have gone to live with Zi'Carolina?"

"Charlie, she was my mother." She made it sound as if he had just asked the dumbest question in the world. Then she smiled. "And when I get to be Nonna's age, you boys are going to take me in, too, right?"

Charlie looked down at the the platters of hors d'oeuvres. "Sure, Ma."

"Eh, that doesn't sound very convincing," she said. "I guess your father and I will have to move all the way across the country to live with your sister."

One platter contained olives, pickled hot peppers, and slices of pepperoni; the other held cubes of mozzarella, provalone, and cantaloupe. Charlie picked up a single piece of cantaloupe.

"Here, Charles, do it right." She handed each of them an hors d'oeuvre plate. "Make up a little plate for yourself. Take some of everything." Charlie put the cube of cantaloupe on his plate. "Have some pepperoni," she told him. Dennett was filling his plate: melon, cheese, hot peppers. "See," she said, "Dennett knows how to do it." She looked at their plates. "Ah, now isn't that nice? *Salute!*" She raised her glass of scotch. They clinked glasses.

"Where's Pop?" Charlie asked.

"Down the cellar. He's painting." Adeline went to the basement door and yelled down, "Vincent! The boys are here." When she got excited, her voice turned loud and husky like Nonna's.

"So, Adeline, what's new in the house?" Dennett was the one who always remembered to ask.

Adeline turned and smiled. "Look around, Denny." Her eyes went over to one of the counters. When Charlie looked, he saw a new set of ceramic canisters. They were peasant Italian: grapes, leaves and vines painted in bold, bright colors.

"I was admiring those canisters," Dennett told her.

"Aren't they *gorgeous*?" she asked. "They were on sale. Marked down from a hundred twenty dollars. I thought they were just so festive and gay."

The door to the cellar opened and Vincent Pellucca came into the kitchen.

"Hey, hunger draws the wolves from the forest!" He shook Dennett's hand warmly, then gave Charlie a kiss on the cheek. "Did you boys forget where we live?"

He was wearing his bulky Italian sweater with the heavy collar and looped belt. They'd bought it on the retirement trip in Rome, at a shop near the Spanish Steps. Charlie knew that his father thought the sweater made him look sexy.

"So, what are you drinking?" Vincent asked.

"Scotch," Dennett said. "How about one, Vincent?"

"Ah, now you're talking!" He clasped his hands together and rubbed them vigorously.

Dennett began to get up from the table.

"Sit, Denny, sit," Vincent said. "I'll get it."

He went over to the liquor cabinet. Charlie noticed a slight limp in his walk.

"What's the matter with your leg, Pop?"

"Eh, what do you think: *'a vecchiaia*." He stretched out the final syllable in a long, agonized wail. "You know *'a vecchiaia*?" he asked Dennett. "Old age."

"Oh, Vincent, stop it," Adeline scolded. "You're not old. Your father looks great, doesn't he, Charles?"

With his plump, rosy cheeks, thick head of silvery Pellucca hair, and his wardrobe of sharp clothes (bought "at the better discount stores," Adeline always emphasized), Vincent Pellucca often looked—again, Adeline's expression—"like a million dollars." This evening, though, Charlie thought his father seemed a little rundown.

"Did you fall, Pop?"

"No, I didn't fall."

"So what's with the limp?"

"Eh, who knows." He sounded irritated. "I told you, *'a vecchiaia.*"

"I've been trying for three weeks to get your father to see a doctor," Adeline said.

"And what's a doctor gonna say, huh?" Pop snapped back. "What? That I need a new leg?" He turned to his son. "It's sore, that's all. I think I pushed myself a little too hard on the golf course a few weeks ago. But your mother, she has to make it into a case where I'm dying or something." He poured a generous amount of scotch into his glass.

"Oh, I am not!" Adeline said.

"Ma, if Pop says he's okay . . ."

"Eh," she said, dismissively. "Your father wouldn't go see a doctor even if his leg started turning green. He always puts off decisions for later." Suddenly, she began to chuckle. "You know, if important decisions were up to your father, I'd still be single." She reached over and pinched her husband's cheek. "When we were courting, he was so shy. So *pauroso.*"

Charlie knew all the inflections of that word, *pauroso*—timid, fearful, shy—and he guessed it probably did describe something of his father when Pop was young. He guessed it still applied. Pop had never been as eager to forge into new territory as his wife. He'd been a dry cleaner for over forty years. He liked his golf and his TV programs and his basement painting studio. Without a lot of fuss, he went along with Adeline's dreams, with her plans and ideas of what had to be done. The decision to send Charlie to prep school that summer, and Jacqueline the following summer; the clothes, the music lessons, the vacations the family took, the remodeling and redecorating of the house; moving Nonna in when Nonno died; the retirement trip to Italy—all these steps along the way of their forty-year marriage were ones that she had taken and that Pop had obligingly followed. The family joke was that Adeline had proposed to Vincent, but Charlie had always figured that the joke told something of the truth. Pop went along with things. His friends called him a good guy. Charlie wondered if his mother hadn't spent her entire life trying to make sure that her son wouldn't be quite the same kind of good guy her husband had been.

Pop sat down at the kitchen table and tasted his drink. "Ah, that's better," he said.

"Vincent, try the mozzarella," Adeline said. She turned to Charlie and Dennett. "It's fresh." Charlie took another piece of mozzarella from the platter. "Angel, is that all you want?" she asked.

"Ma, when I'm hungry I'll take more."

He glanced at the kitchen clock. It was his opinion that a three-hour visit was acceptable. Three hours and he did not have to feel guilty. He had two and three-quarters hours to go.

They ate in the dining room, using Adeline's new china. When Nonna died, she had sold off most of the old stuff: both Nonna's furniture and hers, even the vanity with the three mirrors on hinges that Charlie had liked to play with as a kid whenever they went to Nonna's for a visit. All of it was gone and in its place Adeline had assembled a new environment that Charlie hardly recognized.

"Boys, take more," she said, motioning toward the platter of lobster and spaghetti.

Charlie helped himself to a small second portion, then passed the platter to Dennett.

"Ma, whatever happened to that big red lobster platter you used to use?"

"Oh, I got rid of that." She passed him the sauceboat. "What was I going to do with that thing anyway? It was too big for your father and me, too heavy."

There was something almost magnificent about the way his mother had so easily cast off the past. It was as if she had discovered that in all this making over there was some power to stave off bad things, especially those biggest of all bad things, old age and death.

"That platter used to come in handy when you and Jacqueline were little," she went on. "Remember the Christmas Eve fish dinners? When Nonno and Nonna and all the aunts and uncles used to come over before midnight Mass? That's when I needed a platter like that. But now, who has that kind of company anymore? Of course, if my kids would give me some grandchildren . . ."

"Ma," Charlie pleaded.

After the spaghetti, there were chicken cutlets, fried cauliflower, mushrooms and peas. For dessert, his mother had made another of Charlie's favorites, a barley pie with bits of chocolate and citron.

"Eh, I have to wait for my son to come home to eat like this," Pop said, as Adeline placed the pie in front of Charlie.

"What do you mean?" she said. "Oh, Charles, don't listen to him. I treat your father very well."

Charlie shook his head. "You two."

Adeline touched Dennett on the shoulder.

"Forty-one years, Denny. Vincent and I will be married forty-one years in October. What do you think of that?"

"It's wonderful," Dennett said.

She laughed. "It better be. We're too old to get divorced now, right?"

"I can't imagine you and Vincent not being a couple," Dennett told her.

Adeline bent down and pressed her cheek into Dennett's.

"Oo, I love this one!"

She went around the table with the electric percolator, a new one, Charlie noticed, while he served slices of the barley pie. Suddenly, she stopped short.

"Oh, Vincent, look at you! Paint all over your good sweater." She grabbed the hem of her husband's sweater and brought it up to his face. "Look." Charlie could see a large, shocking pink smear.

"Damn it," Vincent muttered, rubbing at the spot. It was dry. "Damn it." He rubbed again, then looked up at Charlie and

Dennett. "Eh, so now it'll be my painting sweater." He opened his eyes wide and shrugged his shoulders.

"Your good sweater!" Adeline went on.

"Adeline, pour the coffee, will you?"

"He paid tens of thousands of lira for that sweater," Adeline announced. "What a ruination."

"Christ, Adeline!" Vincent slammed the palm of his hand down on the table. "It's gone, okay? How much of a tragedy do you want to make of it? It's *gone!*"

Charlie caught Dennett's eye.

"What, Vincent!" Adeline's voice was raspy now. "You couldn't have changed your sweater before you went downstairs?"

"Ah, go on," Vincent mumbled.

"Go on yourself," Adeline shot back.

Vincent got up from the table and made for the cellar door.

"And where are you going?" she called out. "Honestly, Vincent, sometimes I just don't understand you."

"And sometimes I don't understand *you!*" He slammed the door behind him.

Adeline looked at Charlie and Dennett. "Tell me," she said. "Tell me."

Charlie made a take-it-easy gesture with his hand. "*Pace, pace.*"

"But what is it with your father sometimes?" She put down the percolator and looked at Dennett. "I bet your parents don't fight in front of company, do they, Denny?"

"Oh," Dennett said, "they have their moments."

"Yes, but not like this, right?" She laughed. "Only the Italians. We're a fiery race, Denny. Not like you calm, quiet Norwegians."

"Ma," Charlie begged, "sit down and enjoy your pie."

He took a bite. The familiar tastes returned, a complex mixture of flavors and textures: the sweet of the barley filling mixed with the bitter of the dark chocolate and the chewy, tangy surprises of the candied citron. Ma had learned the recipe from Nonna.

"It came good, Ma." Sometimes the expressions of the older generation of the family just spilled from his mouth spontaneously.

"Thank you, angel. I'd make one for you every week if you'd come that often for dinner. Tell him, Denny."

Dennett laughed, a laugh that Charlie guessed was itself a complex mixture of things.

"Ma, you went through a lot of trouble for us," he said. "Denny and I really appreciate it."

"No trouble at all, angel."

"You know, Ma," he said, laying down this next idea as gently as a china tea cup, "maybe Pop gets jealous when you focus all this attention on us."

She looked at Dennett, shaking her head incredulously, then back at Charlie.

"Eh, come on, Charlie," she said in her voice of long experience. It was—this exasperated *eh*—as far as she would ever go toward explaining the mysteries of her marriage to him, her angel.

Downstairs, Charlie found his father working at an easel. He was wearing a pair of half glasses and a loose-fitting cotton smock. When he retired, Pop had signed up for oil painting lessons with the adult education department in town. They'd started him off on still lifes, then landscapes. Now he was working on portraits, copies of old masters.

Charlie stood back, watching him work. Pop was putting finishing touches on a new portrait, a blond, blue-eyed woman in a low-cut dress that showed off her decolletage. Her hair cascaded in voluptuous curls down her neck and bare shoulders. He was working on her lips, which were fleshy and slightly parted in an alluring smile. At last, he spoke.

"The one time I don't wear my smock, and I get paint on that sweater."

"I bet there's an Italian saying for that, too. Right, Pop?"

Vincent turned around and looked at Charlie above his half glasses.

"No, but there's an American one: 'Shit happens.' "

Charlie laughed. His father moved away from the easel to get a better view. His limp was noticeable again.

"Speaking of which," Charlie said, "Denny and I discovered squirrels in the house this week, behind the walls in my bedroom." Now that he and Dennett had stopped sleeping together, saying "my bedroom" wasn't even a lie anymore.

Vincent walked back to the easel and added a daub of color to the canvas.

"That's shit all right. What're you gonna do?"

"I don't know. Any ideas, Pop?"

Vincent offered a few suggestions. Each was something that Charlie and Dennett had already considered.

"Well, you'll think of something, I'm sure," he said. "You two have solved every other problem you've ever had with that house."

Charlie pretended to be paying attention to the tubes of paint on his father's table. "We haven't solved *every* problem, Pop."

"Yeah?" Vincent asked, still concentrating on the painting. "Well, everything takes time." There was the slightest bit of weariness in his voice. "*Tèmp e paciènza*," he said. "You know that one? Time and patience."

For a few moments, neither of them spoke. Charlie kept watching his father work on the portrait.

"So, who is that?" he asked.

"It's my imagination," Pop said. "I'm painting this one from my head. *È 'na bellezza*, no?"

It was another of Pop's expressions. When Charlie was a boy, whenever Pop saw an attractive woman, he'd ball up his left hand and bite it real hard. "*Managgia! Che bellezza!*" he'd say. "Damn, what a beauty."

Charlie studied the painting more closely. "You did this from your imagination? Pop, that's great."

"I'm going to call her Sonya," Vincent said. "Sonya the Swede."

"Has Ma seen this one?"

"It's a surprise." He dipped his brush in and out of a little cup of turpentine and then started to wipe the bristles on a piece of old facecloth. "I'm making it for her birthday."

In his mother's aesthetic, Charlie figured that Pop's paintings were kind of *cafone*. But she had found a place for each of them: Pop's copy of a portrait of Jesus in the bedroom, a Dutch landscape in the bathroom, the Mona Lisa down here in the basement. Others she'd convinced him to give away.

"It's really impressive, Pop," Charlie said.

"I dunno. Do you think your mother'll like it?"

"Of course."

Vincent dipped another brush into the turpentine. "Maybe I should make her another landscape instead."

"Hey, Pop, do what you want." Charlie had intended this remark to be full of permission, but it sounded more like the kind of thing his mother would have said: full of other, unspoken messages.

Vincent continued to clean his brushes. Charlie watched the steady, competent way his father went about even this kind of task. There was so much patience in everything his father did.

His father turned to him. "*You* want it?"

"Gee, Pop, this one was supposed to be for Ma, no?"

"I can make her another one." He wiped off the last brush, keeping his eyes focused on the canvas in front of him. "You think it's any good? Tell me straight."

Now that he was approaching forty, Charlie was finally beginning to see that it had always been possible to be straight—that old kind of straight—with his father. Vincent Pellucca had grown up in Akron, commanded a tank in the Second World War, come home, set up a dry-cleaning business, gotten married, had two kids. When, after college, Charlie told his parents that he wanted to become a Trappist, his father's only comment had been, "If it makes you happy, son, God bless you."

Charlie pursed his lips. "I mean, I don't think it's my favorite one of yours, Pop, but you're the one giving it to Ma. The question is, do *you* think it's good?"

Pop shook his head amusedly. "Charlie the Diplomat." He laid his brushes on the lip of the easel. "Come on, let's go have another cup of coffee and see what your mother is up to." As he pulled his shoulder back to remove his smock, he winced.

"You okay, Pop?"

"Eh, Charlie: *Gioia e dolor*. I got joy and I got sorrow." He stretched out the vowels in long, mournful pitches, as if he were singing.

A memory came to Charlie of the summer his father bit his hand so severely that he developed an infection. It took most of that August for the inflammation to subside, and a couple of times they had to take him back to the doctor's to clean the wound. Charlie could still remember his father's hand gloved in gauze; could still picture how he kept gnawing at his fist anyway, right through the bandages, whenever he saw a pretty woman.

"*Gioia e dolor.*"

"Yeah, I know, Pop," Charlie said.

Vincent looked up, his eyes roaming studiously over his son's face. Charlie touched him on the shoulder, digging his fingers into the bulky softness of the Italian sweater.

"Sometimes, Ma drives me crazy, too." He sighed. "Like the way she keeps calling me 'angel.' "

"Angel, huh?" Vincent moved away from Charlie and hung the smock on a peg. "Do you remember the summer we sent you to that fancy prep school and you started calling your ma 'Mother'?"

"I did?"

"Mother," his father repeated, exaggerating the sound, emphasizing the foreignness of it. "*Mother.*"

"How long did I do that?"

"For a few months. Mother this, and Mother that."

"Really?" Charlie had no recollection of it. "Did Ma ever say anything?"

"Just once. She asked me what I thought it meant."

"And what did you say?"

"I told her that you probably thought it was a nicer name for her. That made her feel better."

"She was hurt that I called her Mother?"

"Sure. It wasn't her name."

They were climbing the basement steps now, Vincent first. His limp was obvious.

"You know, Pop, that was really a very important summer for me." It was the summer, his seventeenth, that he'd first fallen in love with another boy. He wondered if he could ever tell his father all that.

"Good," Vincent said. "I'm glad it was, son. We always wanted the best for you kids."

"What did you and my mother talk about?" Charlie asked Dennett.

They were driving home, Dennett at the wheel. The heavy dinner had made Charlie sleepy.

"Oh, the usual," Dennett said. "Decorating, flowers, your father, you."

"Me?"

"Your mother always talks about you, Bubellucca." He glanced in Charlie's direction. "She asked me if I thought you were happy."

"What!"

"That's what she said."

"How the heck did that come up?"

"I don't know. We were talking about your uncles' old greenhouses, and all of a sudden she brought up that guy who was killed this week at the drug company protest. Did you hear about that?"

"Yeah, I heard about it."

"She said she thought it was so sad, not just that guy's death but all the people dying of AIDS."

"She said that?"

"Yes. And then, out of the blue, she just asked me if I thought you were happy."

Charlie shot Dennett a look. "Why? Does she think I'm going to chain myself in front of a drug-company delivery truck or something?"

"Who knows," Dennett said.

Charlie shook his head.

"She doesn't get it, does she? I mean, she assumes that you have to be unhappy or depressed or something in order to show some moral courage."

"Charlie, she's concerned, that's all."

"About *what*?"

"Probably about AIDS. She's probably worried about whether you're infected or not."

Charlie snickered. "Technically, she doesn't even know I'm gay."

"Technically," Dennett agreed.

"Why doesn't she just ask if she wants to know?" he said.

"Bubellucca, she's your mother. She doesn't know how to ask."

"Well, damn it, I'm her son, and I don't know how to tell her," Charlie snapped. Silently, he watched the traffic. After a minute, he said, "So, what did you tell her?"

"About what?"

"When she asked you if I was happy."

Dennett looked over at him. "I told her you were."

Charlie closed his eyes.

The next thing he knew, his head fell forward and he jerked awake. He turned to Dennett.

"You doing okay? You want me to drive?"

Dennett laughed. "I'm fine, Bubellucca. Why don't you just keep your eyes closed and let yourself go to sleep?"

There was nothing Charlie wanted more, but he felt he should keep Dennett company while they drove back home. He tried watching the road, but the steady rhythm of Dennett's speed and the stuffiness of the car made his eyes heavy . . .

The car jounced over a pothole.

"You okay?" he asked again.

"Go back to sleep," Dennett said.

Charlie sat up and rolled down his window. A chilly rush of air hit his face. He rolled the window up again. This time, when his eyelids drooped, he gave himself over to it. After all, Dennett would be careful; he wouldn't drive them off the road or into oncoming traffic. It was one of the things he most liked about Dennett, how safe he was.

ELIZABETH NEW JERSEY

• PHILIP GEFTER •

The affair had begun with the intoxicating glamour of a love story: *Boy meets boy. Next thing they know, they're on a Swiss Air flight to Paris.* Roman was still working for *The Downtown Weekly*. He had arranged the trip to Paris not a month after he met Keith, proposing a story for the paper as a legitimate pretext for a romantic adventure with a new boyfriend. It wasn't the first time he had felt like Don *Quixote* in the guise of Don *Juan*. Infatuation seemed to be his windmill, despite his awareness that it is nothing more than a hallucination of the libido.

Keith had been just his type—the kind of handsome young man with classic features and dark hair who always caught his eye on the street or at a party or in a restaurant. From their first intimate dinners in his apartment and their lingering Sunday afternoons in bed, Keith had presented himself with worldly aspirations. Roman thought he had finally met someone who shared his sensibility, his curiosity, his love of language, his regard for visual form and music. He thought that Keith shared his imperative to forge new ways of being in the world.

On their second day in Paris, Keith cut a classically handsome figure on the Rue Napoleon: button-down shirt; navy-blue blazer; jeans; Weejuns. He looked like he had been dressed by his mother, and Roman dressed him again in his mind: He imagined him with longer hair, wearing a white T-shirt under a loose-fitting black linen jacket, black jeans, maybe a pair of brown suede boots. They sat down on the terrace of the Cafe Flores.

How are you feeling? Roman asked.
Keith sighed. *Overwhelmed.*
Why?
With a breathless awe in his voice, Keith said, *I just can't believe I'm in Paris, France.*
Roman shook his head. *You don't say Paris, France, Keith. That's an address on an envelope.*
But it's so amazing.
It's like saying you live in New York, New York.

Roman had wanted not a protégé, but an equal, someone he could grow with and learn from; someone who was good for him, who could foster his talents, challenge his thinking, take him forward. Keith had begun to fail him and Roman felt disgusted.

Soon, his made-to-order Adonis began to disintegrate around anyone who was well-known or attractive or smart. The less self-possessed Keith became, the more Roman's patience and consideration descended into an exasperated antipathy. Keith tagged along, unable to assert himself, unwilling to make a decision, incapable of holding up his part of the bargain, his end of the table. Roman felt responsible for him in a way he hadn't anticipated, and claustrophobic in a way he couldn't endure. Yet, the more dismissive Roman was of his behavior, the more dependent Keith became.

Roman had looked forward to the idea of staying at the illustrious *L'Hotel*, where, on his deathbed, Oscar Wilde was quoted as saying, *I'm dying beyond my means.* One morning, sitting at the small rosewood table in their room, Roman sipped his coffee. The gauzy white curtains swelled in the soft morning breeze. Sunlight shimmered across the pale yellow sheets. He gazed at the fresh peonies on the dresser, struck by the pink dewy petals against the green velvet walls. The colors elicited in him a sweet, heightened calm, the membrane delicacy of the blossoms a poignant contrast to the quicksilver pace of his cosmopolitan life. He pulled apart a croissant, dipped it into his coffee, and looked up.

Keith was walking toward the table with two beauty-parlor clips on either side of his forehead to dry his hair in place.

Do you ever think about being a woman? Roman asked Keith as he sat down.

Keith's face turned red, and he stared into his coffee for a long time. Then, as if to mock Roman, he said, *I get sexually excited when I imagine myself as your wife.*

Roman looked at him, perplexed. *Do you remember our first night together? The way you rejected my advances?*

Keith poured steamed milk into his coffee, his hairclip catching the sun. His strange, vacant smile indicated some private, treasured reminiscence. *I thought someone like you would never even talk to me. You walked up to me and asked me what I was thinking about. No one ever approached me with that line before.*

You said you couldn't remember.

I was overwhelmed. And, then, when I found out who you were . . .

Roman raised his eyebrows.

I mean, well, knowing your name from the paper, Keith said. *Your column. I was meeting someone famous.*

I'm not famous. Roman said, exasperated. *Christ.*

You were so handsome.

You told me I had bad breath, Roman said, shaking his head.

I was nervous, Keith said. *I didn't know what else to say.*

Oh, so I became a victim of my own attributes? That's not very nice.

Keith dropped his eyes, and fingered the table. *You haven't been very nice to me ever since we got here. I'm not even sure why you wanted me to come.*

It was true, and Roman sighed. He didn't know what to say. He seemed forever to be looking for a perfect romance where *desire* plus *glamour* created *magic*. But every time he reached for this fairy tale in his life, he seemed to depart from the course of reality. He dipped the rest of his croissant into his coffee. *I thought it would be fun, that's all. I just didn't expect you to rely on me so much. It's awkward. It makes me uncomfortable.*

I don't want to make you uncomfortable.

Well, then, don't try to please me so much. Don't seek my approval. I can't stand it. Try to please yourself. Take some initiative. I'll respect you more.

Later that morning, Roman had become more playful. He suggested going shopping. They *were* in Paris, after all.

In fact, Roman said offhandedly, flipping through a magazine, his eyes falling to an ad for Azzadine Alaia, and holding it up for Keith to see. *If you really imagine yourself as my wife, maybe you'd like to go shopping for that little black dress.*

Keith laughed, and sat down on the bed. *A dress? I don't know.*

A little dress. A wig. Some make-up? Roman flicked his eyebrows, prodding him.

I've never done that before, he said, half-smiling. *Maybe it would be fun.*

Roman had worn a blue seersucker shirt that afternoon, a gray linen jacket, jeans, and white canvas bucks. Keith wore his Brooks Brothers blazer. They strolled into Chanel, and a *vendeuse* approached them.

Bonjour, messieurs, she said in her most ingratiating singsong French.

Bonjour, Roman said, matching her good humor. *Parlez vous Anglais?*

She responded with a tight little smile. *Oui, yes, of course.*

We're looking for a suit. For my friend, here. For a party. A costume party. Would you have one in his size?

But, monsieur, you want a Chanel suit? she asked, masking indignation behind clenched teeth. *I do not know if we will have one this size.*

She walked to the back of the store, and returned with a navy-blue cotton-gabardine suit, white stripes on the pockets of the jacket, and gold buttons. She held it up to Keith's chest, but the shoulders were too narrow. *This is the most large we have*, she said with obvious satisfaction, pleased that such sacrilege could not be perpetrated on so serious an article of clothing.

They walked toward the Place de la Concorde, and, in Keith's first act of will during the trip, he insisted on going to Yves St. Laurent. Roman was happy to comply, if only to encourage his initiative. Keith liked one particular dress with a high collar that fanned into a narrow decolletage. A thick cinch belt, a long flowing skirt, smoky blue with gold embroidery, festive and feminine, frilly and flamboyant. The kind of dress a rich suburban matron might wear to a fancy luncheon at the Pierre.

I think a low neckline would give you away, Roman pointed out.

Yeah, Keith said, disappointed. *I guess you're right.*

At lunch, they both ordered *steak frites* and a bottle of Bordeaux, and considered the kind of woman Keith should be aspiring to.

What's your mother like? Roman asked Keith. *How would you characterize her type?*

He thought about the question. *She's tall like Rosalind Russell. She has short, dark hair. She likes bright colors. I don't know. Rosalind Russell and, maybe, Shelley Winters.*

That doesn't make any sense.

Well, she's neurotic like Shelley Winters.

But they're so totally different, Roman said, sipping his wine.

What about your mother? Keith asked.

Roman laughed. *A cross between Maude and Medea*, he said. His mother was a driven, productive woman who never cared about clothes. She had larger concerns: Justice for the poor. Civil rights. Court cases and class-action suits. Labor disputes. Marches. Rallies. He always liked her the most when she was focused on a mission. *She was more Elizabeth Taylor-like*, he said. *Not beautiful the way Liz was beautiful, or stylish, but she was sexy in that dark, voluptuous way Liz was sexy. Martha in* Who's Afraid of Virginia Woolf. *That's what my mother's like. Ballsy. Mercurial. Nuts.*

How did she dress?

Roman tried to picture her when he was in high school. *In*

the snapshots I have of her, she was a lot more stylish than I actually remember. When she had to, she wore simple black dresses. A thin string of pearls. I always wanted her to look like Liz Taylor in Butterfield Eight.

She was beautiful in that movie.

Did you ever dress up in your mother's clothes? Roman asked, biting into his raw steak.

When I was really young. But then I stopped when my brother called me a fairy.

Roman laughed out loud. *Once when I was four or five, I put on my mother's shoes, and one of her sweaters, and a pair of shorts on my head as pretend hair. I walked outside and stood on the front porch waiting for someone to walk by to see if they thought I was a girl. But nobody was around. That was as a child my only foray into crossdressing.*

Do you think all gay men dress up in women's clothes when they're children?

No, but I bet a lot of drag queens end up looking just like their mothers.

It was several hours later that they walked down the Rue Danton when Roman spotted a perfect 1950s dress on a mannequin in the window of a curio shop. It was black, which he was partial to, and it had a collarless neck and short sleeves. Roman imagined Keith wearing it with white stiletto heels.

The proprietress sat on her small throne in the back of the store, draped and layered in necklaces and bracelets like a weathered old Madame who had truly seen it all. They asked her if Keith could try on the dress. She opened her fan and pointed at a velvet curtain. Roman perused the rhinestones and pearls and sapphires and rubies in the glass cases while Keith was changing. He had been drawn to a pair of dangling earrings in the shape of heavy crystal teardrops when he spotted a choker of fake pearls. He looked up as Keith emerged from behind the curtain. Keith threw out his arms, stamped his foot in a flamenco gesture, and laughed out loud.

Roman couldn't believe the transformation. A dress designed for the contours of a man's body. A dress to make a woman out of anyone.

Divine, Roman proclaimed. *Brilliant.*

Do I look like Elizabeth Taylor? Keith asked, giggling, swept into the possibility.

More like Elizabeth New Jersey, Roman said, leaning back against the counter, his laughter becoming almost uncontrollable. *Here, the perfect necklace for Miss New Jersey. Try this on.*

Keith, with his high cheekbones and beautiful lips and wavy black hair in a little French cocktail dress from the late 1950s. . . . The pearl choker was simply too eloquent for words. Something moved inside of Roman. A weight tingled at the tip of his penis. He paid for the items, smiling at the old woman as he collected his change.

At the Galerie Lafayette, they bought lingerie, makeup, shoes, and a wig. Roman concluded that underneath Keith's tentative reserve, there was a floozy at the core. *No wife of mine is going to wear purple lipstick*, Roman said at one point, unequivocally. *It isn't sexy. Neither is that bouffant.*

Put in that way, Keith acquiesced to Roman's taste. Straight black hair parted to the side and falling to the shoulders. A soft red lipstick. Black heels. Sheer stockings. A little smoldering restraint. A modicum of style. At the perfume counter, Roman sprayed a sampler of Chloe on Keith's neck.

Back in their room, Roman poured himself some gin, arranged their purchases around the blue-dusted armchair by the window, and sat down.

Okay, my darling, he said softly. *Strip.*

Keith obeyed. He took off his loafers and slipped off his socks. As always, Roman was struck by his beautiful feet with their vaulted arches and sculpted toes. Keith unbuttoned his shirt, and unzipped his pants, stepping out of them one leg at a time, hopping as he tried to keep his balance, leaning against the wall. He stood there naked, his swimmer's body at the very top of its form, a delectable servant awaiting the next command.

Put these on, Roman said, dangling a pair of black lace panties from the tip of his finger.

Keith slithered into the panties, and pulled them up around his thighs.

Hide your dick.

Keith strapped his erection under the tight black lace, and Roman's erection swelled. He handed Keith the bra, and watched as his muscles rippled under spaghetti-string straps. Keith picked up the wig with both hands and sat down in front of the mirror. He tucked his hair underneath, lining it with his finger, separating the bangs, shifting it into position, sucking in his cheeks. He began to paint his lips with lipstick, and Roman had to unzip his pants from the mounting excitement.

Elizabeth, he said. *Try on your new dress for me. Audition for the role of my wife.*

Keith stood up and wriggled into the dress, arranging it around his waist until it fell in place. He slipped into the heels, then turned around with his hands clapped together at his chin. He smiled seductively.

Oh, my God, Roman breathed. *I've created a goddess.*

Keith's eyes twinkled. He waltzed over to the armchair, and knelt at Roman's feet. Long black hair fell on Roman's white boxers. Keith took Roman's dick in his hands, and, as he slid his lipstick-red lips around it, Roman dropped his head against the chair, moaning with pleasure.

Roman pulled Keith toward him, and he sat down on Roman's lap. Roman felt the slinky fabric of the dress against his own hard-on. He took Keith's face in both hands, and kissed him. He locked his lips around Keith's mouth, and sucked on his tongue, tasting lipstick. He smelled the sweet, heady fragrance of Chloe as he rubbed the palm of his hand against the stubble on Keith's face. He touched Keith's erection inside the lace panties. . . .

Roman lowered him onto the carpet. He licked Keith's neck and unzipped the back of his dress. He pulled the panties down to his ankles, flipping them off and tossing them away. He grabbed Keith's hip, then his legs, sliding his finger between the cheeks of Keith's ass, tapping the tight membrane donut. He

spit into his own hand and wiped it in Keith's ass. Gazing into
Keith's eyes, he lodged his hard dick in between his cheeks.
Do you want me to fuck you? Roman whispered in his ear.
Ohh, Keith sighed.
Can you take me?
Darling.
Roman dropped a condom into Keith's hand. *Put this on me.*

As Roman slid inside, Keith moaned. His lips parted. His hair
fell across the carpet. Roman thrust all the way inside and inched
out slowly, feeling Keith relax, finding the rhythm, and losing
himself in a dense, hot animal stupor. Soon, he felt the con-
tractions deep inside Keith, the pulsations of Keith's erection,
the warm liquid spurts against his stomach, until a string of
nerve endings tingled at the tip of his own penis and an explosion erupted from the base of his spine.

LOVE IN THE EYES OF GOD

• PAUL GERVAIS •

I was a freshman at St. William's, a Catholic college for men.
It was in northern Vermont, near Sharples, an old mill town.
These days, I get news of the place through out-of-date issues
of the alumni magazine passed on to me by Craig Marcuccio.
Once, I was listed among the missing. Now, I'm just forgotten.

Less than two weeks into the term I was on my second roommate. The first, John Wylie, wore a broad smile on his face as
he slept, but scowled by day. He was proud of his Celtic roots.
We're a warm and generous people we are, he said, liltingly.
Evenings, he'd rattle through his box of fine chocolates like a
wren among fallen leaves; not even when the box was full did
he think to offer me a buttercream. To teach him a lesson, I
went downstairs to the candy machine and bought two Mars
Bars. Want one? I asked. No thank you, he said. I have some
candy here. His preferred drink was Jack Daniel's. I didn't know
if that was vodka or gin until the night I tied one on with him
and his rowdy, fast friend, Leo Doyle. The next morning I woke
to find a mound of thrown-up spaghetti simmering on my electric blanket, looking no worse than it had the night before on
my cafeteria tray. I took a lot of ribbing for that bad form from
two Irishmen who prided themselves on their genetically acquired ability to hold liquor.

Later that morning John said:

If it's all the same to you, Steve, Leo and I would like to room together. You wouldn't mind living with Andy, would you?

Andy Dover was Leo's roommate. I'd never exchanged a word with him until he stopped me, moments later, in the corridor.

So what do you say, he said; wanna room together?

Leo, in the distance, chanted HUNja, HUNja, making the hand-job gesture with his pumping fist, his voice echoing up and down the cavelike hall. Andy and I stood there, breath suspended—two marked victims in *Night of the Living Dead*. I accepted Andy's tepid proposal. That afternoon, a four-way trade was effected.

Prior to our double divorce Leo Doyle had made cruel sport of the fact that Andy Dover's mother had taken great pains to decorate the room he and Andy were assigned. Over the summer, she'd sent for the dimensions of windows and beds, making curtains and matching spreads. I could live, by modest compromise, with the dark-green checkered fabric she'd selected, with the braided rug, with the colonial rocker and turned-maple floor lamp, but I wondered how long I'd last with Mrs. Dover's good son whose apparent sound mind and morals went all too well with the homely decor. Apart from a certain gentleness, uncommon in these halls, Andy and I seemed to have only one thing in common: electric blankets.

On his side of the single, wide, built-in desk we two boys were meant to unnaturally share stood his gallery of family photographs. Our first evening together he introduced me, by way of these pictures, to his mother, father, and little brother. His mother was of Swedish descent, he explained, and this accounted for his big bones.

Kids used to call me Hands, he said.

Hans? Hans the Swede?

No, Hands, he said, pinching the air like a lobster with his own two.

Oh, yes, I remarked. They *are* large.

This is my dad, he said, bringing me to a summer day of their recent past in what was clearly a northern clime.

His father was Italian by background—his name had been Doveri before he changed it. The same thick lips that made him appear eager, influential, made his son look provided for, influenced.

Andy, smiling like a parent, said, And this is my little brother. Joey was just twelve years old. He'd come as a surprise. Joey's the greatest kid, Andy said. He's a gift. He's got an amazing IQ.

Where were these pictures taken? I asked.

At Skytop, he said, with airs.

Where's that?

New York. Upstate. Don't know of it?

No.

You're kidding. Never even heard of it?

No.

He thumbed through the standing rack of folders he kept on the shelf above the one that displayed his family photos. Here it is, he said. This is their brochure.

He handed it to me. His fingers were lean and gangling. I looked at the cover. An old northeastern grand hotel with begonias out front in paisley-shaped beds.

It's just the greatest place, Andy said.

I flipped through the expensively produced booklet. Horses. Tennis. Boating. Golf. Lunch.

Fun for the whole family, I said, jealously—I had no family life anymore.

It was getting late and I was ready for bed. Life in this institution exhausted me. Billymen, as St. William's boys were called, roared in their doorways at all hours like lions at the mouths of their dens. Evenings they were especially restless. The walls, floors, and ceilings resounded with their fiendish cries. They had a language all their own; I couldn't speak it, but unfortunately, I understood. Fucking was their staple expletive. Holy fucking shit. Jesus fucking Christ. Horror fucking show.

Our beds were against opposite walls, the wide expanse of cold floor between them broken only by the oval braided rug, the rocker, the floor lamp. I went to my bed and undressed, sitting down. I slept in just my underpants as John Wylie did. I turned on my electric blanket and set the dial to seven. I pulled back Mrs. Dover's green checkered bedspread and got in under the covers, turning off my bedside lamp. The bright overhead light still blazed in the pocked, fibrous ceiling.

Andy removed his sweater and lay it folded on the chair beside his bed. He took off his shirt—it wasn't a shirt I'd ever have bought or worn. He was down to his undershirt, an article of clothing I'd never been taught to need. It was a bit shrunken, not at all new. It gripped him in tight wrinkles at the armpits. Its short sleeves were beaked. He drew the T-shirt over his head, narrowing himself to shed it. You don't wear pajamas? he inquired.

I looked him in the face. But soon my eyes fell to his bare chest. Nah, I said, as if I'd renounced pajamas long ago and not just last week.

He took off his pants, and quickly, his briefs—everything he owned was from Alexander's, he'd boasted, earlier. He was comfortable naked in company. In an odd series of movements, he joined his hands behind his back, reaching one arm over his shoulder while sending the other around from below. He flexed a complete group of muscles and something went CRACK, loudly.

My back, he explained, half apologetically.

Oh, I said.

I have trouble with it.

I see.

I looked him up and down, hoping he wouldn't notice. Perhaps it was true what people said about hands and penises. He resembled those medical illustrations of the human body, every particularized muscle clearly discernible under his taut, hairless skin. He'd been a diver, he said earlier, the star of his high-school team. I thought, How odd that he's come to a college that has no swimming pool.

His pajamas were pressed under his pillow. He put on the bottoms first. They hung loose at the waist, falling so low that the high curves of his rear end remained uncovered by all that gathered flannel. He put on his pajama shirt, switched off the overhead light, and got in bed, saying:

Night night, sleep tight, don't let the beddy bugs bite bite bite.

Night, I said.

Just as I'd drifted off to sleep, Pete Foley, the hall monitor, opened our door with his skeleton key—this to prevent our panty raiding nearby Mount St. Mary's. He flipped on the light for a look, waking me. I turned my back to him and faced the cinderblock wall whose sharp edges were dulled by layers of rubbery green paint. I splayed my hand against it. It was cold and sticky to the touch. They couldn't have built these accommodations to better resemble prison cells. Misplaced in this bed, in this room, on this campus, I felt sick in the heart, if one could be sick in the heart. Soon, the walls rumbled again: a final play-off, resistance against discipline. I covered my ears, turning down the flaps, but the roar got louder still, like the sound a train makes emerging from a tunnel, huge, unstoppable.

I took my hands away from my ears. I thought I was going to cry.

I wanted to go home.

I had no home, not really.

I don't belong here, I said, softly, but aloud.

Did you say something? Andy said.

No. Nothing.

It was Sunday. Andy's alarm sounded at what seemed like dawn. I hadn't set mine. When he went down the hall to the bathroom I dozed off.

In a while, I opened my eyes. Andy was back, dressed in a jacket and tie. The jacket was a contemporary plaid which brought to mind the window plan of a tall, dark office building. With his tie falling to a reasonable length in front, he was left with a scant five inches in back.

Get up, get up, it's morn-ing. Get up, get up, it's morn-ing.

It might be morning, I answered, but it's Sunday.

We've got twenty minutes to get to mass.

I don't go to mass.

He looked confused. Why not? he said.

I'm an atheist.

Yeah, right.

Andy found, with ease, among his things on the shelf, his prayer book. I wondered, Whatever happened to mine? My father gave me one for my tenth birthday. It had a black, soft leather cover, and its edges were trimmed with gold. There were ribbon markers sewn into its binding, in every color of the rainbow. It made me feel accomplished in faith to follow the liturgy on my own. I would turn the onionskin pages with care, posed with my prayer book in hand like a revered member of the celestial hierarchy, forcing myself, the whole time, to be surprised by what I seemed to already know. It ended up puppy-chewed and broken, that prayer book of mine, but in what forgotten drawer who knew?

An hour had passed. I got up and went to the window. I pulled the cord on the blinds; a cold northern light seeped in through the louvers. It was early September, but in this polar microclimate the ground was white with frost.

I looked off toward the chapel. It was the campus centerpiece, we were told, its spiritual and architectural hub. As I contemplated, uninspired, its contorted buttresses and folded wings, its doors burst open and groups of Billymen rushed out. Most of them headed straight to breakfast at the Student Union cafeteria. But one, only one, came walking toward the Quad, toward Curtis Hall where I lived. His hair was brown with auburn highlights and it stood firm in natural waves. His shoulders were wide, his clothes were plain, but his bright face was all contrast: dark eyebrows, dark lips.

He opened our door with his key.

I came to get you for breakfast, Andy said. I didn't want you to miss it.

Thanks.

Get a move on then; what are you, anyway?

The smoky cafeteria echoed the din of an activity I'd never known to be so noisy. Andy and I fell into place at the end of the line. Looking up at him gave me a cramp in the neck and so I discouraged conversation with one-word responses to everything he said.

Though I'd not been at all anxious to view the contents of the steam tables, it seemed to take forever to get there. Cold toast awaited us, a quaking mountain of it. Eggs, gummy side down in deep stainless-steel trays. Some things I accepted, some I declined. Discretion seemed to make no difference in how I felt once I'd eaten; everything from this kitchen made me a little bit sick.

The tables were built to accommodate eight. We sat at an empty one, across from each other.

Andy said:

So how's life, Peter?

Peter?

Peter Prep. That's your nickname, didn't you know?

No.

That's what they call you on the floor. Cracked me up.

I blushed.

So what prep school did you go to, anyhow?

Thomas, I said.

Oh yeah, Thomas. I think I've heard of that.

I thought, I'm sure you haven't.

Where is it?

Boston. Back Bay. It's not like a country prep school, playin' fields and all. It's a city school. The city's its campus.

I went to Fordham Prep, Andy said. It's not really a prep school, though. Jesuits. How could it be?

I think I've heard of it, I said. In fact, I hadn't.

I worked at my eggs. I ate only the yolks, soaking them up with toast as my grandmother used to do. She called the yolk the *sausette*.

Andy said:

When I first saw you, I thought, Dressing like that, he's got to be from Park Avenue.

Oh? I said. I had no idea how Park Avenue boys dressed.

Yeah, Andy said. Like, I could picture you getting in and out of your father's Cadillac limo in front of the Colony. That hair of yours is great.

I don't know what the Colony is, I said, but my father isn't rich.

Could have fooled me.

I dress like this 'cause I like the look, that's all. I'm not puttin' on the dog or anythin'. It's just a style thing. My father's a druggist. I'm from Massachusetts, not Park Avenue.

I know where you're from, Andy said. You told me. What was that town called?

North Tewksbury.

Oh yeah. What is it, one of those perfect little New England

villages, a whitewashed church, everybody walking around in
tweeds?

Nah, bunch of farmers down there. Baptists.

Baptists? Isn't that more like in the south?

Yankee Baptists around us. Dairy farmers. They're pretty nice
though. They don't bother you or anythin'.

Andy had a pack of Winstons. He eased out a cigarette with
his stiff, long fingers and set it between his lips. He offered me
one.

Don't smoke, I said. Remember?

Sorry, he said, refolding, precisely, the cigarette pack's tiny
foil wrapper. Just being polite, he added.

On our way out we stopped at the bulletin board. Andy
pointed to a notice. I read it to myself. The first meeting of the
Choral Society was to be held that afternoon at three. Andy said:

I want to get into at least a couple of activities. I think they're
very important. I'm a good singer and I like it. I had the lead
in *Bye Bye Birdie* at Fordham. I was Birdie. Ever see it? The
musical comedy?

No.

It's great. Had a lot of fun. Birdie's modeled after Elvis, you
know? Turning toward me he bandied his legs Elvis style, jit-
tering. Gotta gotta gotta, he sang, in a throaty voice like the
King's. A couple of Billymen passed, raised their eyebrows and
smirked. I threw my gaze to the bulletin board, pretending I
didn't know him. A notice caught my eye:

Ski Team
First Meeting of the Season
Sunday, September 28
Football Field
2:30 P.M.

I showed Andy the sign.

Going out for it? he asked.

Ya, I said, I'm goin' out for it.

Andy said:

I hate it when people drop their g's at the end of gerunds.
Did I do that?

Yeah. You do it all the time.
Hunh, I said.

Skiing was the one sport I was good at. I was fast and I was tricky. I could do the latest wildcat jumps, spread eagles, and tucks; I always landed on my feet. Wedeling was my specialty; I could do a dozen quick turns in a ten-foot vertical drop. I could herringbone uphill as fast as most people skied down. Skiing was my passion; I hated summer—I was a boy of winter. All my skiing life I'd wanted to race, but living so far from the mountains, I never had the chance. I looked forward to proving myself in competition. I knew I'd do well.

I put on a pair of corduroy jeans; they seemed right for a ski-team meeting. I wore a cotton turtleneck shirt and moccasins I'd made myself from a kit. They were meant to be true moccasins, like those the Indians wore, but the only authentic thing about them was that they had no soles.

I had never in my life walked out onto a football field. Football was a sport I didn't know how to play, having grown up in the country far away from ballfields and boys who frequented them. I opened the stadium's chain-link gate. I entered the silent, unfamiliar forum with the caution of a Christian looking out for hungry lions.

There was a boy in sweatpants doing stretch exercises. He was sitting on the grass beside a powdery white sideline. What does all this have to do with skiing? I wondered. These boundaries, these goalposts and bleachers.

The boy grunted and worked his hamstring.

Ski team? I asked.

He had two hands on the tip of one foot and was pulling at it, grimacing. That's what I'm here for, he said.

The open space around us was desolate and cold. I lifted my eyes, searching for a humanizing reference in the landscape. Those were the Adirondacks I saw, gray, unbeckoning, beyond the lake I couldn't see. I turned around completely and looked the other way. Mt. Mansfield rose in the near haze. I remembered a childhood visit to Stowe, the first ski trip of my life. It was back when we were still a family, vacationing together, my parents, my brother, Renee, and me. Renee and I slept in a

dorm. But it wasn't like the dorms here at St. William's. Everything was made of wood, warm and resonant, the walls, the beds,
the lamps on the walls. A thick blanket of snow covered the
streets, rooftops, pine trees. It was as if you were tucked into an
enormous feather bed whose cushions under and over you were
as soft as they were sheltering.

The wind blew. I turned up the collar of my jacket. My grandmother used to say:

The wind she blow on Lake Champlain, by 'n' by she blow a
hurricane.

Three guys approached. My eyes were tearing up in the wind
but I could see by the cut of their clothes that they were Billymen. One of them slipped a knit ski hat over his head, but he
still didn't look like a skier. Real skiers possessed a natural dig-
nity. Billymen did not.

A few others straggled in through the gate. They were all tall
and amply built. They seemed to know each other from previous
seasons.

Fucking cold, one said.

Fucking right.

Fucking wind.

Freezing my fucking balls off.

They jumped in place to warm themselves like football players
on the line.

The one with the hat had a clipboard. By his superior air and
the deference he was given I could tell he was captain of the
team. He said to me:

You, what's your name?

Steve Lamont.

I looked at his face as he wrote it down. Perhaps he was handsome, in his Irish, Robert Redford sort of way. He asked:

How long you been skiing?

Since I was ten.

Good skier?

I shrugged, modestly.

Ski the expert trails?

Oh sure.

Ski parallel?

Course.

Ever race?

No.

Fucking never raced, he said, drawing a laugh out of his teammates. Terrific.

Pointing his pencil at the redhead on the ground, he said:

You, you a good skier?

No, said the boy, standing up. I was heartened to see that he
was shorter than I.

Medium good?

I never skied before.

Some fucking season coming up with *this* bunch of fruity
recruits.

Billymen snorted, laughing.

See the fucking ribbons and cups fucking piling up like fucking shit in a hole.

I'm a runner, said the redhead. My coach said I have the mak-
ings of a champion. I'm here to learn. I'm not afraid to admit
it. I'll ski circles around you guys in a month. Watch me.

The captain handed him his clipboard and pencil. Well fucking be my guest, he said.

The redhead smiled, a good sport.

Another guy appeared, walking with a pair of ski poles.

Who's this, the captain said, fucking Rick Moriarty?

The guy fell into an egg position, letting out a hoot and a
laugh, instantly gaining everyone's respect. How I wished I too
could have proved myself. If only there had been snow on the
ground. If only this had been a slope and not a flat field.

The captain said:

O.K. guys, now listen to me. My name's Kevin Jenny. I'm the
captain of this team. O.K.? Any problems, you come to me,
O.K.?

O.K. cap'n, somebody said.

It's a fucking early season up here, Jenny said. Fucking snow's
already falling on Madonna. The first meet's scheduled exactly
one month from today. That'll be with Putney. Now let me
make one thing clear right off. We're a club team, O.K.? What
does that mean? It means we're not on the A circuit. It means
we're not up there battling Middlebury who's got their own

fucking slope right in the backyard. We do slalom and giant slalom only. No downhill. He paused for a minute and looked us over. His eyes met mine before he said:

Oh, I've had dreams of turning this club into a first-string team. But I'll tell you something right here and now. With this fucking lot of pussies I'm looking at, them dreams of mine are going up in vapor like this shit that's coming out of my mouth. See it. Fucking smoke.

Laughter all around. These guys loved their captain.

Lot of work to do, Jenny said, so we'd fucking better get started. He stepped back and turned to the open field. We've got some running to do here, O.K.? The course starts under your feet. We'll make a run of the complete circumference of this fucking field here. We're doing three laps. This isn't a fucking race. I'm not interested in who wins. This is training. Let's work on these fucking legs so that when we finally get up there on the course you fucking fruits won't come swishing to me with, Thay man, you didn't tell me it wath gonna be like thith!

Oh, you're cute, somebody said.

Jenny pounded his clipboard once. O.K., team, he said, that's enough sewing-circle bullshit. Let's get to running. Take off. We're fucking outta here.

I looked down at my feet. I'd worn the wrong shoes. I looked at everyone else's feet. They hadn't. How had they known enough to wear running shoes? The posted notice in the Student Union had said First Meeting, not First Training Session. What should I do? I wondered. I couldn't have gone back to the dorm to change into sneakers. Because there was no physical education at Thomas School for Boys, I didn't own a pair.

I was the last to start. Running, I measured the distance between the rest of the team and myself by the freshly powdered lines we passed. How quickly the gap between us grew. I wasn't used to running, but these moccasins made it impossible. Had I had the right shoes on my feet I might have been no slower than the straggler in the bunch, the guy who'd carefully shed his ski poles to find himself trailing everyone but me.

I ran as best I could, trying not to whip my shoes off to the wind. The others, even the straggler, were coming up the other side. The redhead was out in front. He ran to be the winner. It was as if he hadn't heard the captain say, This isn't a fucking race.

I thought, I'll have to run faster. At any cost. My inferior performance was looking more and more ridiculous. I picked up speed. One shoe flew off, falling yards behind. I stopped to retrieve it. In pivoting, I lost the other one. I collected them both and slipped back into them.

I ran.

Even the straggler had completed one lap. The rest were well into their second. I'd barely made my first turn around the end zone. I was out of breath.

I'd taken off my shoes by now. Carrying them as I ran, I must have looked like a girl on a beach, in the grip of a romantic impulse brought on by the drama of sand and surf.

The team had completed three laps and had gathered at the starting point. I chose to abandon my run and join them. In the center of the field I put my shoes back on and walked.

When I reached the group all eyes were on me.

Wrong shoes, I said, hoping they'd understand.

My explanation was met with an array of puzzled looks, self-conscious laughs.

Jenny said:

That's all for now. We'll meet again on Wednesday. Same time. Eventually it'll be Monday, Wednesday, and Friday. Any questions?

Heads turned. No questions.

We're outta here, the captain said.

I looked down at my moccasins. I remembered when the kit arrived. I'd sent away for it to the Seven Sisters Indian Trading Post, in Brayton, South Dakota. How disappointed I was when I opened the box and examined its contents. The leather was blackened with a dye that didn't look at all like something the Indians might have known. Funny, I'd never for a moment liked these shoes.

Hey Lamont, I heard the captain say.

I looked up. He was walking my way. I had a pain in my side from running and the ache must have shown on my face. I felt a little nauseous, too. But so what. Perhaps I'd do better next time—that is, if they'd have me a second time. I thought, I'll go into town on Monday and pick up a pair of sneakers. Perhaps I'd run on Tuesday, on my own, building up my stamina.

My teammates were filing out the gate. The captain stood before me. I looked him in the eye. He was so serious he was fearsome. The wind picked up. I shivered and said, with a little laugh:

The wind she blow on Lake Champlain . . .

Jenny said:

For your information, Lamont, this is a training session, not a fucking fashion show.

He vaulted off, a peculiar swing to his walk. The chain-link gate banged shut behind him.

By 'n' by she blow a hurricane, I said.

Someone had slipped a couple of pamphlets under the door. I picked them up. *The Unmentionable Sin*, the booklet was called. It was written by a certain Father Louis Wendell, SSW. I'd never heard of him, but perhaps he was on the faculty.

I was sitting in the rocking chair reading it when Andy came in.

Look at this, I said. They've supplied us with some reading material. Your copy's over there. I held up mine.

What's the unmentionable sin? Andy asked.

Guess.

Whacking off?

Listen. I read:

Masturbation is a complex and sensitive problem that can't be solved in one fell stroke. . . .

Andy laughed.

Don't laugh, I said. Our parents are paying for this. I read on:

If you're in the habit of abusing yourself, it's time to take the matter in hand. . . .

You've got to be kidding, Andy said, laughing hard.

That's what it says, right here. Take the matter in hand.

Andy said:

According to Leo Doyle they put saltpeter in the food.

What's that? Saltpeter.

It's supposed to keep our peckers down.

The food tastes like it's full of it.

Think so? Andy said. I still wake up in the morning with a hard-on. Don't you?

Well . . . ya, I said, embarrassed.

Later, we locked our door against roving intruders and listened to Mozart's *Requiem*—Andy's record. Andy sang along. He was a base baritone.

> *Laut wird die Posaune klingen,*
> *Durch der Erde Gräber dringen,*
> *Alle hin zum Throne zwingen.*

He isn't a very good singer, I thought. But he loves the music.

He was sitting in his rocking chair, holding the libretto in his lap. I lay on my bed. He'd enjoyed, he'd said, his first meeting with the choral society. For Christmas they'd do Benjamin Britten's *A Ceremony of Carols*, transcribed for adult voices. Andy'd been assigned a solo and was pleased.

And so the evening passed in this fashion, the two of us in our room listening to Mozart as all around the Beachboys battled the Rascals who were battling, in turn, whatever Billymen horror show ensued—tonight it was all over *The Unmentionable Sin:* JERKaw, they chanted.

My skis stood in the corner next to Andy's pair of Harts. As the music played I gazed at them. They were the best skis in the world, Head Competitions; I'd worked the whole summer in a Greek restaurant to buy them. Strange, I used to find such beauty in that pair of skis of mine. Tonight, they couldn't have interested me less.

The music ended in a noisy chorus, deferring to a harsh chaos that like serpents ate its way through our masonry walls.

JERKaw.

Andy rose and put away his record as if he were a priest handling the consecrated host.

I was tired. I sat up on the edge of my bed and undressed. I got under the covers leaving my clothes in a heap on the floor.

My roommate had better manners. The metal chair beside his bed had become an ingenious valet stand, the run in the middle of its back a convenient pants hanger. I watched him take his clothes off. I watched him crack his back, his hands joined contortedly behind him, one elbow raised. I noticed with interest that there was very little hair under his wide, muscular arms where the skin was still whiter than the rest of him. His waist was as small as mine, yet his shoulders expanded above it to a wide stately breadth. CRACK. He put on his pajama bottoms and got in bed without the tops. He reached over and turned out the light. Night night sleep tight, he said.

Night, I said.

But I didn't fall asleep. I planned my escape instead. I would take the bus to Laconia where, for the past two years, my mother had lived with my Aunt Caroline. Since my mother left us I hadn't seen her, not even once. In all her frequent letters she begged me to visit, and yet I never did. She'd be thrilled to find me at her doorstep, this I knew. How sympathetic she'd be when I'd tell her about my big mistake, that I'd made my way to a hostile land where my feet were frozen in place on the cold, forbidding ground, that I'd come to a school where I didn't belong, where out of a thousand young men I was the only one like me, the only one.

Pete Foley opened the door, startling me. I'd already made myself comfortable in my mother's and Aunt Caroline's home, but now I felt sick to my stomach to see where I actually was.

The room went dark again. Pete pushed the lock button on the doorknob, then pulled the door closed. The night was eerie in its cocked silence which with dawn would suddenly spring.

Andy said:

You awake?

Ya, I said.

Would you do me a favor?

Pause. What?

Would you walk on my back?

I was confused. What do you mean, walk on your back?

It's home chiropractic. You wouldn't believe how it helps. My little brother Joey does it all the time. He's the perfect weight. But you can't weigh much either. How much do you weigh, anyhow?

One twenty-five.

Yeah, you'll do. Would you mind trying?

Sure, I said.

Andy got up. The room was all blue shadows and yet I could see him. He went to the braided rug and lay facedown on the floor. O.K., he said.

I got out of bed. I walked barefoot across the cold linoleum floor then stood at the edge of the rug beside him. What do I do? I asked.

Just step up onto my back. One foot at first.

His pajama bottoms fell low on his rear end. He sent a huge hand to pluck the cotton fold from the peach cleft.

I stepped up onto him. His body was warm underfoot. His clear skin shone the way a glow-in-the-dark Madonna does when you'd just turned out the lights.

Am I doin' O.K.?

Ooh, he said, softly moaning; it was like the sound you make when you take the matter in hand.

I put all my weight on one foot, centered at the small of his back, then placed the other one beside it.

Oh, he said. Ooh.

I stood there, my arms extended for balance.

Walk, he said.

I raised one foot and placed it in front of the other.

Ooh.

I adjusted myself in my underpants. There was no saltpeter in the food.

How'm I doin'? I asked.

F-ine.

Oh good.

I walked as far up on his back as I could, then halted and turned around. It was a vantage point I'd come to. Great beauty burned before me with the white glow of a snow-covered valley. From this crest I'd gained I saw the path that led me here, its heaving, twisted way to the horizon, yet I cared only about now, this moment in which, having traveled so far from a troubled past, I doubted the reality of what my memory told.

Take a step, Andy said, and I walked, buoyant with wonder, like an astronaut on the surface of the moon.

THEIR STORY

• THOMAS GLAVE •

And then in those afternoons that yet were to come after so many other events of that time and our days too had passed over into our dreams, even after all details and memory had merged into those rivers of our nights, you would see the two of them there walking together, past our windows, past our front porches and our doors, through Sound Hill: Mr. Winston and Uncle McKenzie. In summer, the trees fluttering down their eyes and watching so quietly the heat-drowsed life along those streets; the smell of the Sound (the water only yards away behind the farthest of our houses) hanging heavy through the air as first one pair of dark hands from behind a fence, then another and then still another, waved at them in greeting, and large heavy dark eyes all along that street—through the heat, through our dreams—looked out from every other memory with easy smiles of recognition.

You will not see them walking quite that way now, and our summers too have grown more silent. But even then, as starlings chattered overhead and our backs strained over hedges and coaxed geraniums to turn their hands to the sky, you knew that it hadn't always been that way: that the faces of those two, and later our own, had not always borne that sadness; that once, you remembered, there had been more of a lift to those old shoulders lately so rounded, and a spryness to the step that no winter of the heart nor mind could remove. Some of the older folks, like my grandpa, remembered that time so many years ago when Mrs. Winston also had walked through our streets: the iron-gray hair framing the heart-shaped face, the heavy body that had known many years of difficult labor, the pair of long brown legs ending in bright sneakers beneath a flowered dress; remembered (and carried into the dream) that voice singing away the long hot days in her garden down by the water, where, among those hydrangeas and the peonies that had done Sound Hill proud, she had worked tirelessly in a relentless quest for color. And memory of her could not be summoned without bringing to mind Uncle McKenzie's wife Icilda, and the smells of curried goat and ackee and codfish that had always breezed out of her kitchen. In that time, when the world still allowed those of us who were young to be children, scraped knees and pop eyes turned up without fail at Mrs. McKenzie's front porch for Jamaican bun-and-cheese not even the best of the Jamaican bakeries in Baychester and up on Boston Road, even years later, would equal. There, between taste-swallows of an island of whose mountains we knew nothing, we always greeted Uncle McKenzie, who inevitably found time to put himself all up under Mrs. McKenzie in that cluttered kitchen—"a goddamned kitchen jack!" her voice shouted as her always-crisp housedress rustled in ferocious blue; as, softer, came, "Here, pickney, take it, nuh?"—and we felt the caress of rough brown hands we also carried later to our dreams.

Uncle McKenzie was play uncle to all of us: What you Americans call play uncle this or that, we in Jamaica call pet name, he said, and that is mine. And so, without fear of what was to come later, reaching up to those hands and running back out into that time of protected ignorance, we called him Uncle, for the rest of his life, in fact, as we ate bun and hard dough bread and gizzarders conjured out of that distant unknown place called *Trelawny*, from where they both had come, and where, they always told us, lived creatures called *duppies*—ghosts.

Ghosts in and of themselves wouldn't have been enough to scare us in Sound Hill. In our isolation in that forgotten and far-off North Bronx part of the world, so far removed from the churnings of a city whose streets permitted their prisoners no real vision of the sky or light, we had already known them. We had learned long ago that even the vaguest rustle of a bedroom curtain on nights of the most abject loneliness only betokened —in most cases—a visitor of the gentlest and most yearning benignancy, longing from so far off (within that other darkness, emblazoned by that light we couldn't yet see) to share and comfort our solitude and theirs. We knew they came and went as surely as the summers came and went until our fire-shadowed days of autumn; there were beneficent ones and those troubled and—depending on how one had treated their personages in life—those who could bring terrible dreams and vengeance. All of them, if permitted by us the living, possessed the power to access and decipher our thoughts, appetites, memories, devotions, regrets, and even our most secret and thwarted obsessions; mostly when we walked those night rivers of painful remembrance, which was often. So that even many years later, when so many of us had moved out of our parents' homes in Sound Hill and into (smaller, lonelier, meaner) apartments in the city, leaving behind the lilac fragrances of those ghostly night walks, we would summon again to the rushings of our own shame just what had happened with Mr. Winston and Uncle McKenzie, as we learned the truth.

When Mrs. Winston died—Miss Ardelia, we called her—all of Sound Hill turned out for the funeral. Because we had no church of our own, it was held at a church way up in the Valley. Midway through the service, all the ladies, my mama included, bent low over their knees and raised their palms high up in the air—supplicating that light which had never been kind but which they so devoutly believed would someday fall from the unyielding sky and maybe even now, especially now, Jesus, descend into their reaching hands; as their men, like my daddy and grandpa, sat like stalwart sphinxes beside them—afraid more then and always of the quiet storms building within themselves than they were of the future explosions a lifetime of such storms could cause at any moment to rip open the tender flesh of their hearts. Mr. Winston was the worst. His daughter and son-in-law came all the way from San Francisco to see Miss Ardelia put to rest; they had to help him into the church because his own knees would not. That last week of spring he had turned sixty-six, and last June he and Miss Ardelia had made forty years together. "A man can't take but so much," my mama said. "Taxes, killing, young people dying, Social Security that don't feed nobody. That's all one thing you could put into a box and just say God help you try to sleep at night. You'll lay off worryin and go on to sleep when you get tired enough. But a wife sick so long and then to go off like that and leave him, sweet Jesus. A man can't take but so much. Especially a man like him."

Mama was right. That day when we were all in the church up in the Valley feeling the spirit and Miss Ardelia's spirit too with Mr. Winston bawling and then being real quiet and then the light that wasn't ever kind falling over us and us listening to the preacher's words about how Miss Ardelia was now with the Lord our shepherd in the sight of all His goodness and His grace, I watched Daddy holding on real tight to Mama's hand as he looked straight ahead and held me too and I knew she was right. Everybody's mama knew and everybody's daddy—those who were there—knew too. Mr. Winston was a soft kind of man, good soft—the kind you had always seen on those later spring and summer and even winter evenings walking down past the fences and the lawns with Miss Ardelia almost-tall at his side— walking, you remembered, a little stiff; joking with Noah Harris and Hyacinth-who-danced about how that lawn sure enough looked like the ragged-torn side of some trifling nigger's head, hadn't they never heard of Bill and Acie's Lawnmower-U-Rent on Gun Hill Road?; greeting the Walker twins, Timothy and Terence, telling them apart only because of the fiercely protective look and arm-about-the-shoulder Timothy always had for his born-twenty-six-minutes-later brother; making Yvonne Constant, the quietest little girl in Sound Hill, look up for more than a second and even smile; with Miss Ardelia not humming quietly then to herself as she often did but just smiling and laughing softly once in a while; admiring O.K. Griffith's irises or Johnnyboy's front-yard eggplants; putting a hand now and then again to that white straw hat she always wore on warmer days; then the two of them walking down to the Sound, when you would hear the man's soft voice telling her how someday when they had not three but four grandkids he would build them all a sailboat and take them up off over the water, past Westchester and Connecticut on one side and Long Island on the

other, and wave to all the rich whitefolks who'd be watching
with the same wide-open eyes they'd always imagined us to have,
and say Hey, y'all, looka here!—I got my family out with me
for the day.—So whyn't y'all let them maids and chauffeurs free
for a day so they can come on with us for a swim?—Hush up,
Win, would come the woman's voice then: very like a flute, more
light than sound; as you imagined her resting a thin hand on his
thin shoulder still moving with the laughter he had learned to
embrace as joy—a small, pithy sort of joy, but the form and
shape of joy enough. The hand would remain there, moving over
the joy, as the curve beneath it leaned slowly into the arm and
hand, feeling it long after eyes and flesh and desire had joined
and gone home to watch the nightly news, watch the outer darkness descend, watch the inevitable. There, where eyes mattered
less than touch, the feeling continued, you knew, as we felt the
hint of it or the breath or the moment amongst ourselves, even
long after everything had happened.

How, then, did those future events come to occur? Some
would say later, after they were over, that they had begun with
a sort of blindness. Uncle McKenzie's blindness, after Icilda
McKenzie's death a few years before from a cancer that in her
earlier years had begun gnawing away at the smooth flesh of her
breasts like a tenacious but unasked-for lover, been arrested by
several pairs of surgical hands, savage machines, and scalpels, and
skulked in her body for twenty years until, the tenacious lover
finally turned vengeful, it had silently exploded into her brain
on that gray morning none of us would ever forget. After the
explosion and the memory, Uncle McKenzie did become blind.
From that morning on, he had been able to see nothing except
that long dim pathway leading yet further down into a valley of
utter silence, where all trees and even the most humble ground-
dwelling creatures had long ago learned not to weep, stricken
with the knowledge that all about them grew the most unima-
ginable sadness which no tears could redress. So that, as our
restless spirits showed us, it wasn't quite a literal blindness. And
then some of us thought that actual no-sight might have been
almost a blessing on those nights we dreamt Icilda McKenzie's
ghost came back in her aching grief to wander past our sleeping
houses, past the house of her dead friend Ardelia Winston and

so many other passed-on or sleeping friends who wept and reached out to her from the endless sorrowing rivers of their dreams, until she found that particular green house down by the water she was looking for: where the kitchen still smelled of bun and curried goat and calves'-feet jelly, and pictures of Discovery Bay and Port Maria hung on those weary walls; yes, that house, whose structure was of slight wooden frame like all the rest; where the walking shadow paused for a moment to embrace those summer-night delights of ripe apricots still hanging on the front-yard tree her own living hands had planted so many years ago, the dark man with that bit of the sea in his voice laboring not far from her. Then, like that which she had become and which the object of her eternal searching desire was fearsomely becoming, she entered the house—patting the claypotted geraniums on the front porch to make sure they were still properly dry in that season of frequent thundershowers; as she drifted upward into the room whose walls had watched her die from the tenacious lover's grasp; where the mirrors had watched her watching herself making love throughout the years to him whose sleeping, trembling cheek she then, in the dark, began to stroke; caressed the grieving forehead; kissed, with the fleeting touch of ghost-love, those lips so lately useless throughout the new appalling silence of so many sightless days; as he, mired in the mud of that dream-riverbank that continued to hold him fast in the wretchedness of his own despair, called out to her from a place she could not reach him, to save me, Icilda, help me, Icilda, I'm ready to go now, Icilda, I'm ready. I'm ready. She would calm him then. For while she could do little or nothing to lighten the blindness of his days, which she anyway spent on the banks of a distant shore he wouldn't know for some time, she was able at least to quiet the fury of his nights. When, in that dark solitude, he awoke sweating and fever-pitched, grasping the air wildly and crying out for her, feeling the pounding of his heart and thinking, praying, that this might be the heart attack at last, Heavenly Father, O Jesus, that would finally bring him closer to her and allow him that sweetness of resting his fevered head in her cool lap once again, forever, she was there—just behind him, out of his sight but close enough to lay her hands on his neck and rub him there, pulling him with that gentle, ghostly insistence back down into the twilit country of sleep and the river where, at least for the space of that time within earthly boundary, he could rest his fatigue on the shore and listen in peace to those rushing waters.

In those hours of silent, immeasurable time between two worlds—one raging, the other in the most unknowable and confident serenity—what secrets, we wondered, what wisdoms did she share with him? Our own dreams never told it all, being currents allied with the nocturnal unspoken mysteries of death. But we learned then, as everyone gradually discovered, that only those ghosts we knew among us were capable of telling the complete truth, unencumbered by twitching lips or the diurnal cutting of an eye. They alone possessed the fortitude and the power, buttressed by the breadth of eternity, to stare down the remorseless intelligence that outlined and directed our destiny. Fearing death—perhaps because we did fear it—we knew that their knowledge was infinitely greater than our own not only because they had already faced what we feared—loss of life and the awful pain-resonances of human grief—but also because they had long gone on to whatever it was our surviving hopes, wisely or in pathetic human foolishness, insisted we continue to believe in. Our spirits, like Icilda McKenzie's, had only to face the circular time of what to us for our time on earth would remain unknown, as we yet walked through our days and nights in constant fear and avoidance of the certainty and ostensible closure of death. So that when the living, fretting Uncle McKenzie stuttered out the pain that had so tightly coiled about his heart and spirit, protesting the entry of yet another presence into his dreams, wanting only her in the flesh, in his arms again, or himself with her on that farther shore, she the wiser spirit would shush him who was still her husband and lover; whispering to him that he must allow to occur what was beyond his power to alter; that, soon, some night, they would again be joined in always-time, and that, for now, he would do best to listen to the sounds of all those other wandering spirits, who—for all he knew—might be bringing him news of her sojourns on those quiet shores along which she had so lately walked. Oh, she was strong, our night rivers told us; she would never allow him to descend of his own miserable willingness into the deeper parts of that current from which, for him, at this moment in his destiny, there could be no return. In her patience, and from within that firm and infinite resolve deepened by the requisites of death, she soothed the bitter maledictions of his raging heart until the restorative river-melody sighed once again in the more steady sound of his breathing. It was then—only then—she knew that she could (as she must) remove her hand from the relaxed grip of his and, just that way, a vision diminishing, a force once again released, make her way once more out of that bedroom and down the stairs, out into the sleeping world so uneasy from its own day-terrors, to walk again in her own aloneness until the unrevealed hour when the longing of their separate courses would again meet for all time in that other world of light.

Thus, in that way, until the end, some of us thought, Uncle McKenzie's nights gradually came to be illuminated by those private moments of transcendent vision, even as his days began to descend into that most terrible form of blindness which preys on the living bereaved. It wasn't long afterward that we saw how he began to stumble, not walk, through our streets he knew so well. When, one evening, he fell down on the sidewalk in front of O.K. Griffith's irises, O.K.'s boy Walter R. later told his daddy that, as he'd reached out to help the old man to his feet, Uncle McKenzie had looked dead straight up at him, right through and past him, as if seeing a sunset world behind and beyond Walter R.'s nappy head, and in the most terrible earth-filled voice had whispered, "Icy. *Icy.* Got to get home to help Icy wit the curry goat. She waitin pon me, you no see, pickney?"—so that later Walter R. would tell his daddy too that the look in Uncle's eyes—that vacancy which saw nothing in this world except those sunsets laying waste desolate fields beyond a river which in daytime did not exist—had terrified him as much as the hopeless weight of those old, fragile bones held up in his arms. Later that summer, when the police brought Uncle McKenzie to Noah Harris' doorstep with the news that he had been frightening women at the Pelham Bay bus stop by asking them through his tears if they had by any chance, please, seen his wife Icilda walking through the river, several of us wept into the most private spheres of our own hearts, feeling the dreadful certainty that, from all appearances and more, Uncle McKenzie wouldn't be with us much longer. It was as if, seeing what was to come even very much later in the ashes of tragedy and reborn gods whose acts would forever terrorize our survivors, and not having the good sense to run even then from what would be that later horror, we sought in both Uncle McKenzie and Mr. Winston a glance of the forever-survivor, who might lead us into a possible future and more fearless resketchings of ourselves. In our sorrow for him, we were obviously feeling also a more prescient sorrow and fear for ourselves, sharing the knowledge that even more unnerving than the final rivers of our dreams were those inescapable deserts of our surrender to the ashes of the future.

But then—thank God and the spirits—through the workings of unseen guiding hands, it came to seem an almost natural occurrence that, neither too soon nor late, the stronger of the two personalities between the two old survivors began gradually, cautiously at first, to guide that one who had fallen to his knees with the scent of a dead woman's curried goat still in his nostrils up to his feet and to a place where, far above that night river, two old wrinkled men could begin to weave out the intricate patterns of their common distress; as the trees in that place gazed down upon them with wise and silent knowledge of the miracles humans might yet achieve after so much time of blinding loss.

And so it happened. As the hazed languor of those late-summer days crept into the cooler fires of the coming nights, we began to see them—bent-backed, shuffling, wary of step—more together: in the steady company of shared grief, perhaps, but also in the occasional slow surprises of that elusive light that children, and all others who find they still have much to discover in the world, know. Thank Jesus, our mamas murmured, because a man at that age needs someone he can slap thighs with and trade jokes with about the good old days that were already past most of our recalling, and about which practically no one wanted to listen anyway beyond the necessary polite smile of one minute or less. So that, even years later, well into the time of our own separate and lonely autumns, we would think back on our pleasure at the sound of their mingled voices, low music frosted by age, as Mr. Winston guided Uncle McKenzie down to the Sound they both loved; relating to him over their slow steps the joke about rescuing the maids and chauffeurs from the whitefolks. It began there—the slow unraveling of a tale of his grandchildren in San Francisco, who knew only what the evening winds and their parents' whispers told them of their grandfather's distress, were sent by their mother and father to "quality" schools where they were taught nothing about themselves, and —most unforgivable—had been raised by the lawyer his daughter had become and the architect his son-in-law had always been not to believe in spirits. That was why, he told Uncle McKenzie, those two children had learned all about the lives of so many important people and all the gleaming cities they had built in the snowy wastes, the anchors they had tossed on the coral reefs, the radioactivity they had brought to sun-scorched deserts high above the secret lairs of scorpions, and even the luxury housing developments they were planning to erect on all the bright planets still reflecting the moon's ageless light on the earth, yet to this day could not have midnight conversations with their departed grandmother, who, like Icilda McKenzie, also walked steadily between this world and that one. None of his living people knew how to listen to the older spirits, Mr. Winston said, nor to those tall trees in the South he remembered that still brought the tortured last words of so many skeletons that only some years ago, and even yesterday, had swung in white silence from those long branches, a length of charred bleached bones and shame drying in the sun. So what kind of way to raise children was that?, he asked; and Uncle McKenzie only shook his head and said that it was no kind of way at all, Massa God, for pickney must raise up to know the spirit and true. Amen, intoned that other, thinking again of Miss Ardelia; and they would stand there for a while, looking out at the glistening waters of another vision, another dream, as the hushed waters of the Sound lapped up at their feet on shore.

The days grew chilly; the light thinner; late flowers offered up to us their resolute and noble last, falling fast before the proud marchings-in of our stately chrysanthemums. We returned to the dreaded boredom of school, weekend leaf-raking, honors projects; our grandmamas again turned to preserves, worryings about the world and scoldings; our parents once again every day rode the Sound Hill bus to the Pelham Bay station to their jobs in the city and back again. Between these dull, regulated spaces in our lives and nights of TV telling us how not to think and feel and what winter would bring, we heard: Mr. Winston, with Uncle McKenzie at his side, leaning on O.K. Griffith's fence; regaling his companions, O.K. and Walter R. with that long-ago truth he had never forgotten, about how the most persistently disapproving eye to his marriage had not been Miss Ardelia's mama and daddy but her grandmama, who had died six years before the marriage yet had insisted from that calmer world on making an appearance at the wedding of her beloved third granddaughter, and who indeed on that hot South Carolina June day had appeared in her cream linen suit—spanking new as forty years before—that had matched her cream high-heel shoes and the yellow-cream flowers on her hat. Settin up there big as day, Mr. Winston said, and didn't leave off bugging 'Delia bout what her duty as a wife was till two weeks *after* the honeymoon. Even then they'd still been aware that she had been lingering, a presence, carrying her aroma of mint jelly and beeswax through the big new house young Mr. Winston had moved into with his young bride; a presence gently ruffling lemon fragrance through the bedsheets before the newlyweds turned in for private hours of love; plaiting Ardelia's hair with gardenias throughout the night as the bride slept in her husband's protecting arms; dusting off the kitchen table, always leaving behind her beeswax scent, scolding Ardelia for walking around like a lovestruck rabbit instead of with a broom in her hand; until, on a gray humid afternoon which promised a cooling absolution of rain, the old lady felt the ponderous weight of an earlier rain in her soul, and, her face wet with sudden tears, cried out, "Your grandfather's calling me! It's time to go home for good! He's calling me!"—and, bestowing one final kiss on her granddaughter's stricken face, disappeared into that seamless memory of rain, drawn back into her lonely husband's embraces awaiting her at the edge of the world. In that moment the young bride put a hand to her own cheek and felt her grandmother's tears, which would remain there and bring to her face a glow of supreme life touched with an implacable sadness her husband would not be able to caress or kiss away until eleven days and twelve nights later, when Ardelia would sit up abruptly in bed to cry out "Nana's home! She's with him!"—and sink with a sigh of deepest relief and contentment, yet edged by a lingering melancholy which would never completely leave her, back into her husband's waiting arms. The earliest dreams began then. Late one night, the elderly couple returned to the newlyweds from an uncharted place on the other, broader side of the world, where, nightly, it had been said, the sea crawled with a maroon skin beneath a ceaseless moon, and in every tide carried back to shore the intoxicating unmistakable scents of beeswax and mating crabs. "Me and 'Delia never was much for writin letters," Mr. Winston said then, "but can't nobody write letters to folks passed on no way. But with the dreams at least we could *see* em." It had remained that way always, he said, as O.K. Griffith snorted and said he didn't believe in no ghosts comin back like that and leavin tears and whatnot on people, especially on people that young; Mr. Winston just came right on in with Hush up, boy, letting O.K. know he hadn't hardly lived his life yet and probably still didn't know the difference between a real live ghost and a baby 'coon's fart.

A shining then. Uncle McKenzie's face. Almost wet with the memories that until his last hour on earth would call to him from the framed photograph of Icilda as a young girl, kept on his night table, close to his heart. With those elbows easy on fences, at the side of his indomitable-spirited and trusted friend, what occasionally came close to the surface in him was clear. And, watching, as we did, you would feel that gladness for him in the something—a flicker of that other, deeper knowledge he hadn't yet either named or uncovered—that, anticipating the gift it would shortly bestow upon him, had for the immediate present transported him, too, back to those days of his youth.

So, then, should any of us really have been surprised, to discover that—quite suddenly, almost forever—all memory of the present was swept up into that slow breeze's beginning and the signaling thereafter of evening's arrival off the Sound, as that other aged voice we knew so well began recounting once again the events of that time of the relucent miracle of the dolphins, who, in a sadness so grievous it couldn't be shared even by the spirits of countless other creatures long ago hounded to extinction, and bearing in their eyes the foreknowledge of an impossible destiny even the most self-aggrandizing marine biologist couldn't explain, had begun to wash up and suffer out the last days of their stricken dreams on that long, thin palm-lined strip of land Uncle McKenzie's countrypeople at that time called the Palisadoes, which years later would be renamed for one of the nation's most illustrious and forthright heroes, whose name, even in times of willful collective amnesia, would never be forgotten by the wisest. No explanation ever emerged for the dolphins' appearance on those shores, nor for that deep lingering sadness in the eyes of so many once-sleek sea acrobats which, particularly in that part of the world, had been known to chase sharks to the farthest ends of archipelagic exile, rescue children from foreign ships in distress, scratch their own backs on the spines of silent sea eggs in that tropical midday heat, and—most astonishing—balance in perfect stillness on their fins in the undulating open sea, bottlenoses stiffly pointed toward shore in upward-facing attention, when, at events of great historical moment, the anthem of national pride and independence was sung by uniformed schoolchildren at the Prime Minister's residence. They had faithfully guided fishermen at dusk past hordes of camera-wielding tourists out to the deepest, bluest waters where green-dreadlocked mermaids and their seaweed-bearded lovers (the older, oceanic true brethren of the Maroons) forever sang the wistful political songs they would later bequeath to the beloved dreadlocked singer who, until his untimely death some years later (attributed to cancer of the brain because of his love of that special weed, but strongly suspected by the informed to have been engineered by predatory northern intelligence agents) would, with the peerless talent bestowed upon him by the sea and the sky, sing those sunset chants of hunger, suffering, and triumph before endless mockeries of justice, with a style which would catapult both him and that green island of blue mountains into fame throughout the world, which, nonetheless, would continue to insist that what the poor everywhere really needed was charity, only charity, don't you know.

The dolphins continued to suffer. The wails of their dying

young could be heard all over the tin roofs of those shacks in neighborhoods on the other side of the harbor, in the western part of the city, and even up in the hills, in the larger homes of those who blocked their ears with mango leaves to keep out the suffering creatures' cries, and who daily told their maids not to speak amongst themselves in those spotless kitchens of such things as dying sea mammals on the causeway and those terrible visions of hunger and prostration before death. Three hundred dolphins arrived on Monday, by Wednesday there were close to seven hundred, and by the week's end over a thousand; in the midst of their agony they continued to horrify curious witnesses with their grotesque dying smiles, as, shrinking further into the suffocating indignity of their last hours, they dreamt still of leaping away days on the open seas where, so it had always been known, only one man had ever walked. Why the rass were they so desperately unhappy, everyone wanted to know, and why the backside had they struggled to the land's end of these particular shores? Those questions were never completely answered, Uncle McKenzie told us, but still in horrendous numbers they continued to wash up, continued to die, continued to decompose beneath that trenchant sun with those gruesome grimace-smiles beneath their bottlenoses. Even if they had been edible no one dared eat them, for to do so in that region would be supreme and utter blasphemy on the spirits of those deities who, even after so many years of modern building on their sacred lands, continued to appear nightly in the surrounding waters and in the hills, and who centuries ago had taught the first inhabitants of the region exactly what the sea offered and what it withheld. So that it was finally clear to all, even to the wealthy who stuffed their ears with mango leaves and studied North American TV programs in order to expand the vacancies of their own minds and lose the precious music of their accents, that without doubt the condition of the dolphins was inextricably linked to the nation's condition, which at that time (and, it seemed, forever before and since) was gripped in the stern throes of not-enough, the wretched condition the singer crooned about. A mean little thing, not-enough. But big. Nasty. That had crept through every tin-roofed shack, pissed its salty waste beneath ragged clothes-lines, pecked at the scabby feet of bangbellied children, cutlassed off a woman's arm for her bracelet on a city bus, buried a woman at age nineteen with deep scars on her wrists and an undetected form in her belly, planted want in sixty hearts in a town of one hundred, burned to death in a rumshop a young man who had in his short life cartwheeled seven times over the taste of Irish moss, raped sixteen virgins in a neighborhood known for fierce allegiances, enticed down the narrow throat of a bewhiskered man the bitter taste of a certain drug (and thereafter his own death), rallied even the soaring black john crows to fight over those slim dungheap pickings, and frightened away those who, from behind the gilded window bars of their inherited hopes, at the end of those long curving driveways of their aspirations, fled in terror to the warm, palm-filled city of exiles on the northern continent, where not even those palms, though more decorous, were indigenous, and where the only dolphins to be found were those which performed in glass tanks for tourists. It was a terrible time, Uncle McKenzie told us; although the man they called the Prime Minister was a noble spirit and stout-hearted, of a long line of men who had arrived in the world at birth with white hair and blue eyes which, while revealing little of their origins in Africa, yet even at that tender age gleamed with a fierce national pride and love of the people. During the sixth week of the dolphins' visitation, his blue eyes gazing out calmly enough yet sternly at millions of television viewers one evening, he announced that enough was enough, the dolphins were obviously a sign to everyone that it was time for wide-reaching reforms, *all* of our people have to be fed, we will *not* wind up like our neighboring nations to the north and east, we'll all have to tighten our belts and share the little we've got, I don't want to hear any complaints from those of you with mango leaves stuffed in your ears, if you don't like it we've got five flights a day to that northerly city of exiles, that noxious sinkhole of traitorous Swiss-bank quislings and dictators' descendants, make your choice. Not even twelve hours were allowed to pass until dawn of the following day, when, in frenzied riotousness, those who stuffed mango leaves in their ears, along with those who someday hoped to, launched a national campaign of outrage against the dolphins and the poor who had befriended them. That, Uncle McKenzie told us, was how he first met Icilda. She was out there on the causeway on the evening of the first anti-reform protests, a young girl kneeling by the side of the road in a yellow dress, a pink bandanna on her head, scorning the clamorous reactionaries who endeavored to convince her of the wrongful actions of the Prime Minister, as she nuzzled against her face a dolphin dying yet struggling to give birth on that narrow shore. It was the same creature that, the week before, had with that irrepressible smile shared with her forty-plus tones of the secret dolphinic language, confirmed in those same secret tones that she and the nation's wisest should never *ever* put even the smallest amount of their trust in bakra men, confided the as yet unrevealed truth that one distant day in the future the Rastas would finally be regarded nationally with the proper reverence they deserved, and, with that disarming prescience known to southern sea mammals, assured her that the moon's reflection on night waters was of course, as always, a matchless ally in the pursuits of youthful romantic love. Enraptured by that vision of a young woman in a yellow dress kneeling with the head of that sickly dolphin in her lap by the side of the road thick with riot-noise and human greed and anger, Uncle McKenzie made his way through the protesters to she who would shortly become, and remain long after her death decades later, the woman of all his dreams. He begged for her hand which up until then had known no other man's touch, and, oh, how he'd had to convince her, he told us, and console her too in her youthful grief after the dolphin's passing and the appearance of those five stillborn young; yet he managed to assure her that, yes, he too was pro-reform, progressive, anti-imperialist, and, no, he didn't stuff his ears with mango leaves, he had no dreams of a large house at the end of a winding driveway while people suffered in silent hunger on land and dolphins died on shore, he too despised the transnationals and the inhuman global straddlers, and no, Icilda, I've never loved anyone up until now, my love, my heart, the spirits of the blue mountains were saving me and all my youth for someone like you, Icilda, Icy. To hold. To hold this way. Come. They were married one year later with the white-headed Prime Minister's blessings and the voice of the singer behind them. Four years later, guided by the spirits of those dolphins that appeared in their dreams in gratitude and remembered solidarity, they journeyed north to a city of steel, bridges, tunnels, black water, concrete-colored skies, and unsmiling people who raced through their days in order to die sooner, all of which, however unsettling, would grant the two some promise, an agreeable sort of happiness, and years of passage in each other's arms; during their waking hours far only in literal distance from that green island that never left them—"Home," Uncle Mc-Kenzie would say then before the grave watchful eyes of O.K. Griffith and Mr. Winston, "That still my home, you see. And I going home someday to die"—standing very still then, seeing nothing, we thought; seeing again Icilda on that distant shore, the dying sea spirit in her lap; as all of us, moved by that tale of events and places we hadn't yet known and still hoped for, sank back into our selves, holding within, and in the truest part of our hands, those singular visions which still took the immediate shape of flesh in an old man's eyes. Mr. Winston would touch him on the arm then, lightly, drawing him and all of us back to the present and Sound Hill as the light began to fail with the merest murmur about our shoulders. Then they would depart in silence. Even then it was apparent to us how united in soul and reach they had become, stepping out from within those twilight afterthoughts to descend further, arise ever higher and higher and *higher* into the time-fields, the caresses, the—*!!here we are, my love!!*—of ghosts.

One. Become one at last. So the words and the news came down to us, over us, quickly and silently taking shape, a whispered intelligence out of that most unending of currents that first slowly and now more quickly was rushing us all on to those final events. The first of which came with a shock: that, all at once, and for some time after, we couldn't tell either of them apart from the other. It was as if, overnight, as we slept, they had traded each completely for the other: it was Mr. Winston, not Uncle McKenzie, whom we watched winter-wrapping Icilda's nine backyard fig trees, muttering all the while about the duppies them that did live pon the hill just so and the damnblasted obeah woman who did live in May Pen, thief from the people them in Mandeville, vex up a whole heap of boogayaggahs in Half Way Tree and then when you hear from the shout did die in Spanish

Town with nothing but a blasted rass-goat f' come sniff up her footbottom. It was Uncle McKenzie, speaking with all the life-knowledge so sonorously contained in Mr. Winston's voice—or so we thought, their voices and faces also having somehow become each other's—who laughed out of Miss Ardelia's side porch step about how he hadn't never in his life trusted no peckerwood and how these folks up north didn't know diddly squat of what they was missin compared to what we had back home—then all at once, in self-conscious laughter, became confused between NAACP, PNP, and JLP. And then it was quite clear to us from the way that laughter soughed up between them that they had at last discovered between themselves the completely possible yet still unnamed actuality of love; which, while perhaps not yet manifestly real to them except in the current-realm of dreams, had, further back in time than any of us could guess, been predetermined by that same constant pair of unseen guiding hands—both through their shared dreams of each other and by way of those spirit-linkages of the past. So that we knew the presence of their wives nightly hovered above them in munificent protection as the two of them, furtively at first, and with a hesitation formed by decades of adherence to the most championed and unquestioned conventions, began to reach out and across those dreams to hold first the divined presence of the other, then the actual other; holding each other's dream-spectres and then flesh as once they had held their wives; becoming in those still hours wife and husband and lover to each other. The current of that love swiftly filled out every lonely space of the two old men's reawakened hearts, filling them with that presence—mainly their newly discovered love and desire for each other—they had before sensed only on the edge of a further darkness, beyond the edge of the sea, and had never questioned. The current allowed them nothing of fear or shame. For by the time their lips brushed in dreams, then across those luminous and shifting night-fields when their shared tongues and skins and even the blood beneath were the same, we knew that they had walked enough with each other along the shores of death and grief so that at last, without any great effort, they were able to read each other's desires in every shade except green, had acquired the difficult skill of summoning one another out of har-

rowing dreams to the calming kisses and entry of the other, and
ultimately possessed no fear whatsoever of wading through each
other's night rivers in search of all the untold secrets lying at
rest there. It really was as if, aloft in the pursuits of those new
vision-gifts, they were finally free—not of care, but of the
weighted vain nuisance of hope; for by that time they knew with
certainty, rather than hoped with fear, that someday they would
be united in complete silence and light with their wives and each
other; in that certitude knowing that they could love each other
without the abstractions of hope because the gift was already
theirs: there remained nothing more to hope for except the gift's
expansion into their unity in death.

So watching them, dreaming them, we too learned. Learned
that the hunger for those whom we love, knowingly or not,
doesn't die. Doesn't die even when the spirit stoking the needing
fails, or when the watching eye glimpses the ghost-warning of
its own impending death. We knew that a hunger so keen as
Uncle McKenzie's and Mr. Winston's could not at their time of
life either die or be destroyed. In our part of that hunger and
yearning, as we slept and dreamt of them and moved ourselves
back and forth rhythmically across the sheets pressing with our
own unappeased desires so urgent and wet against the flesh, we
watched them straining along the steep banks of those rivers,
burying their faces without rest in all that grew there; their
mouths open, then filled, heavy with each other's pulsing flesh;
their wrinkled hands moist from those rivers shared, as, amidst
odors and essences of what only the most private innermost eye
reveals, they thought still of resting the head they rested on the
other in the bosoms of those other two watching ghosts who
met one ancient eye with still another, descending—the lover
of one, the comrade of another, and friends as they had always
been and would be always. There.

—So it was and would be we remembered as our days whitened further into deep winter and the sweep of that new silence
all around brought forth the events which began with the memory of the smell of curried goat in a dead woman's kitchen and
would finally unite the four of them forever.

*That was how it began, we remembered   Yes, right there, slowly,
inevitably, the windcurrents of that time and the season carrying the*

predictions of the long endless winterdark to come and then the attractions of love and recollection beginning in a dead woman's curried goat across the wide and far blue sea and the echoings too of years from that place of blue mountains and trees where so many years ago a young girl in a yellow dress had knelt by the side of a road with the face of a dying sea creature in her lap: the smells of embraces and memory lifted without end over every horizon of our dreams: then the dreams of the sleeping revolving earth as the singer crooned on about the poor whose bellies could never be full especially with the sad meat of their hearts fed upon by those who lounged at the end of long driveways and stuffed mango leaves in their ears: they at first paying no heed, do you remember, to the miraculous arrival of dolphins upon those shores and later to the memory-scents contained in the smell of curried goat from a dead woman's kitchen carried through that spiritforce to the sleeping nostrils of Uncle McKenzie who beneath spiritual vigilance slept in Mr. Winston's enfolding arms: until he our Uncle awakened on that morning which would signal the beginning and end to all things, the first of which was in that moment a walk through the unfolding winter dream that led him down those icy pathways and winterquiet streets and through the frostcolored late morning out of Sound Hill and up through Baychester and the Valley and then still up and over westward to White Plains Road where the music shops and the food shops and the stores with red black and green in their windows and too with green black and gold lined that avenue so noisy with traffic and the grumblings of that elevated subway above: and now mark that, yes, even in that coldness young men were out feeling their bones and early morning rage with each other in the streets: mark too how then he Uncle McKenzie with a light step walked past them to that grocery store owned by his countryman who would sell him those two pounds of goatmeat he our Uncle planned to prepare at home for them alone, the two of them who were Mr. Winston and himself, because this was and remains for all time and ever after their story, remember, their story, yet to be a tale of our remembrance of the past:

—To walk out of there, Uncle McKenzie, white of hair, tall of stance, so lately light of step and always given to that deep music of ageless mountains beating within the blood: walking, yes, still smiling within the welcome hoarfrost of that private dream, except that that day Icilda was not walking with him, she could not come in those

*looming moments to steer him from danger as had always been her
province and willful destiny both before and after her own death, for
that day the dolphins of the past were calling her back to them across
the channels of memory, beckoning, urging, so that thus called, you
understand, so summoned back to that grievous suffering of the past
and to that one in particular who with its dead young had returned
to her walkways after so much infinite time, she could not refuse: and
forthwith journeyed back across the seas and mountains and scorpion-
filled deserts to that place and hour of the protestors and again to her
own youth in a yellow dress and a pink bandanna, holding once again
in her lap on that narrow causeway beneath the palms of her youth
that desolate bottlenose as she soothed the feverish sorrow plaguing the
air so that she couldn't be there, you see, which would be* here *in this
time and place when that man she had always loved now walking in
a winter dream of another waiting man held always close in their love
and shared waiting for death, he the aged morning walker of that day
suddenly awakened out of the cycle of snowflakes kissing his face on
White Plains Road to see with horror and shock:—*

They're killing him, Icilda

*—he thought: awakening then yes to see the young men who were
his countrymen two of them or no three no* FOUR *raining blows down
upon that young boy outside the music shop blaring a song of the singer,
raining blows upon the boy's head, the boy there no more than fifteen
years old holding up his useless hands, screaming, and now how true
it came to be then that yes, revelation, a hungry mob is an angry mob:
Icilda, he thought as they reddened the snow with their fury and rage
and called him Battyman and* You goddamned fucking battyman *and*
kill him the fucking battyman *because:*

*—: oh but they must have heard something about him, you see, or
perhaps they thought he was looking at them in a certain way, whatever way he was looking at them, if he was looking at all: which to
them would have been* that *way, the way men do not, musn't look at
men,* that *way, they'll kill you for it;—or maybe, who can tell, at one
time in the past he might have been clad in shorts, tight shorts showing
too much, too little, the wrong shirt, the walk too fast, arms too slow,
eyes too wide, lips or mouth or nose or who can tell?—but in any event
it was notright notright*

*so now kill the bastard little battyboy son of a bitch they said
killing him Icilda*

:—he thought amidst the screams, shouts: and in that one instant he our Uncle McKenzie as we watched in our dreams and screamed for him to leave them alone, not to go near them, we screamed to him but him not hearing:—he our Uncle McKenzie went forward with cries/shouts/trembling rage of

Leave him alone
Why you beating him
Leave him alone

—his greatest mistake we knew as we watched and shouted and tried to reach him through the dream, pull him back: but couldn't awaken from it ourselves as we watched dawn on Uncle McKenzie the horror that his longtime comfort with the world of ghosts who loved him had scarce prepared him for the world of the living who did not: nor for the rageworld of the young who loved the old less than they loved themselves (which they did not), having been taught by everyone one thing only which was destruction, an outcome for which they too (also having known not-enough, the hot piss of it down their throats, the shame of their bones whitening in the sun and eternally the unsatisfying blood beyond their hands) were destined; his greatest mistake, knowing nothing of this rage until

then the noise began filling up the whitening air whoops shrieks frenzy finding another source for that fear the driving forward of it seeing only this latest enemy seeing in that hysteria not really him hearing only the voice forbidding feeling the ancient shame of their bones whitening in the sun one pushing along the other for O violence we have done/shall do again they thought in that screaming as their bones whitened in the sun the howl deep within their skins For yet might we live they thought yes through the blood they thought live precious precious and the sacrifice blood and the bones the skin the knife for sacrifice there

then raining blows down upon him upon the thin whiteness of his head beneath the whitening sky

so there began the red beneath the blows and the sacrifice darkening the skin

darkening the snow and the field of the dream suddenly so dark: seeing now there in the red Uncle McKenzie on his knees: the goat meat fallen beneath him: the red over his eyes: the knife glittering in the red: we couldn't reach you Uncle couldn't hold you through the dream could only see you there

falling
falling
   the red over your eyes now over all our eyes too for we too were
responsible: had been dreaming of safety far too long: believing our-
selves safe for a time not only from death but from the self-stalking,
the fear: which wasn't to be feared so much in the night rivers of our
dreams but here: right here always here in our days our violent
waking days
   So that it was
   had always been
Red.
Then darkness.
Leaving him there.

   The police were able to identify him because he always carried
his Social Security card. From Sound Hill, they ascertained from
his address; had living kin who did not reside in either the city
or the state. Who would have to be contacted. Which O.K.
Griffith did. And the victim: would have to be taken to a city
hospital, the police said, since no one was able to say anything
about the condition of his insurance or even if he had any. That
city hospital, not far from the Pelham Bay train station, which
was where Mr. Winston and the rest of us found him: not in a
room but on a dirty stained stretcher in the emergency room
because there were no rooms, you see, so many people were
dying, they said, this one and that one: Don't you people know,
we've got a fucking huge-ass disease out there that's killing everyone, and then so many of these sluts coming in with their
faces bashed in, goddamn dope addicts and crackheads and all
these young punks too with their guts or the few brains they
have left shot out, we're living in violent times, it's a violent city,
we're inundated, you'll have to be patient, we'll get an intern to
tend to him as soon as we can, what do you expect, a miracle?
—rushing through the cold white glaringness of so much human
misery, holding their breath as we held ours so as not to inhale
those odors, piss, shit, antiseptics, blood: so as not to believe,
please, that Uncle McKenzie so suddenly was going to die that
way in that place he had avoided for so long as men forty and
fifty years younger than he turned up there without fail and

nameless in the redred on nights of the full moon, bullets deep
in their brains, knives plunged up to the handle in their throats:
no, not die there, we said, not on that low flat white hard stained
mean metal stretcher jammed between every other and every
other going on and on down the hallway and all holding a dying
hand reaching out, a shot-up stomach, a bleeding head and Lord
Lord Jesus we thought what kind of world was this what kind
and what was happening what had been happening to us
always?—The entire world screaming, except for him: laying
there only; eyes closed; not speaking; not even dreaming for
once; merely waiting as Mr. Winston clutched his hands there;
then bent over him calling *Now you Mac;* putting his own face
next to that face; begging between those dry pleadings, kisses,
unheard assurances, please Mac. Now Mac. Come on now, Mac,
now can you raise up, Mac, please, or can you hear Mac. It's
Win, Mac. Mac.—Then we looked not at Mr. Winston but into
the eyes of those passing who had looked into his eyes looking
into the closed face of his friend and lover and saw in their eyes
beginning the low dark storms of that incredulous and loathing
disgust. The bitterness of knowing yet knowing nothing, un-
derstanding nothing beyond the storm. Then feeling our own
rage. Waiting with Mr. Winston. Seeing nothing more. Waiting.

(*Wondering later was it all part of some other dream or real. Know-
ing that it was real.* Seeing him open his eyes. One time only.
Filled with that same redness that never left him. Looking out
right then almost steady at the one touching him. Both looking.
Deep. Longslow. The fearpain in the redness for a moment leaving him. Then closing his eyes again. Saying something. Quiet-
quiet. Low, from deep down in the red and the night river rising.
Saying, Icilda. Icilda girl, I finish. Finish in this country, Massa
God. I finish. . . . Winston. Jesus—:
—Don't bother go on with that—the other touching him saying. Uncle McKenzie's voice coming out of him. Standing over
him next to him still touching. Not caring not mattering either
who looked or how. But then all at once couldn't find what he
was looking for behind those closed eyes. Not anymore. Not

anywhere. But wait. Maybe. Maybe . . . —but no. Couldn't find it. It was gone. All gone. What he was looking for. What had been there. Inside those eyes. Between the hands. Deep in the chest. The light.)

Six hours later Uncle McKenzie stopped breathing. There, amidst the noise, in the clutter of all that stench and suffering, he just stopped. There was no time for any of us to say or do. It happened so very fast, was suddenly so quiet. And then, as one of us who had maintained watch throughout the entire time there would later report, it was in that precise moment that a very old woman who yet somehow bore the incandescently transfigured face of a young girl, with dirt on her knees as if she had recently been kneeling by the side of a road, and with a pattern of wetness on the lap of her yellow dress as if an apparition from the sea had only just lain its head there in a struggle between birth and death, walked unseen by all the nurses into that emergency room and over to that particular stretcher, lowering her wet, gleaming face over the face of the man who lay there; saying something to him in that moment which caused him immediately to sit up, lower the stretcher's protective side rods, step to his feet with the renewed vigor and erect stance of a man fifty years younger, beckon with his face also newly transfigured to Mr. Winston watching in disbelief as the woman too beckoned to him, grasp his hand firmly, warmly, and walk the three of them hand in hand down the dirty passageway under the dim fluorescent lights past the stink and noise and cries, unseen by the nurses and out the door to where, sheathed in light beneath a new white straw hat, waited another woman, who with that same odd yet joyous and almost otherworldly youthful lightness in her step, joined them—taking hold of Mr. Winston's free hand as he continued to hold Uncle McKenzie who held also the hand of the woman in the yellow dress as she smiled back at him and, so walking, led them all on. Farther on. And on. Walking.

The nurse was examining the body of the man on the stretcher. Then said, quietly, The patient has expired. I'm so sorry. So very very sorry. Please accept—said something else we couldn't hear. And made the sign of the cross.

Mr. Winston was found dead in his house in Sound Hill at three o'clock that afternoon. His eyes were open, gazing out intently at something which in that wider, more silent distance might have figured as a distinct and even familiar form taking shape. The gaze remained intact beneath our ministering hands. It was then that we noticed his left hand was clenched tight shut, as if holding something both withheld and held. The balled, curled-up fist staunchly resisted our attempts to open it. It was as if, quite by a last willful effort of the heart and thereupon inevitable, what remained held so tightly within had in lasting partnership with the holder sworn that it would not ever, and could never, be removed—as if the silence out of which the grasp had been formed exceeded both within and without, on every side and for all time, the imagined silence of death.

The funerals for Uncle McKenzie and Mr. Winston were held two days later at our church up in the Valley. After the services they were laid next to their wives and each other.

Yes. We were there.

COMFORT AND JOY

• JIM GRIMSLEY •

The sound of a voice stopped Ford in the hallway outside the lobby of the hospital, an eerie minor-key vibrato, pure and clean, singing without accompaniment, tingling the skin at the back of his neck. Ford, then a fourth-year medical student, was only dimly aware that the hospital sponsored a Christmas concert, but here it was, spilling over from the lobby to surround the Information Desk and congest the elevator court. Curt Robbins, the resident who was in charge of Ford for that month, cursed the traffic and the delay for the elevator, but Ford moved away from him into the fringes of the crowd, feeling the silence of those around him as the song hovered in the room. The voice rang on the tile walls and terrazzo floor.

The man who was singing stood on a raised dais, nearly blocked from sight by a structural column. He was an odd, tall man, angular, with a childlike face, a high, clear brow, dark hair and a full, soft mouth. His face was cleanly planed, his jaw all sere lines. His lips caressed each syllable of sound from the tip of his tongue. At first Ford thought him homely, maybe because his face was unsymmetrical, slightly skewed on one side, as if the head had been squeezed slightly at birth; but after listening for a while he could no longer be sure.

The song kept him there. In the midst of the decorated lobby, trimmed in potted poinsettias, the familiar carol belied the joyous season and mocked, gently, the attempt at gaiety through evergreen and velvet decorations. This man's song was about the sadness of Christmas, and the singer, as far as Ford could tell, was aware of it, was in fact filling the spacious room and all its occupants with the certainty of it. Tidings of comfort and joy. Ford was mesmerized.

The song ended and the singer received his applause. It seemed to Ford that those who had listened to the true nature of the altered melody applauded, as he did, with vigor surpassing the usual polite appreciation. He watched the man, the slim figure and odd face, descend and vanish quietly into a knot of congratulatory friends. For a few more moments he watched, before shaking his head clear of the echo of the voice and song. Finding Curt Robbins, who had stayed to listen, rapt as Ford, they resumed their duties. But as the elevator opened to carry him to the ninth floor, Ford spied a stray concert program skewed beneath the edge of a sand urn. He lifted the bright green and red xerox, reading the names of the singers, the Bell Ringers from Coral Baptist Church; Amanda Zed, operatically trained, business office; and Dan Crell, who worked in clinic administration as an administrative assistant. Ford folded the paper and tucked it into his pocket.

Later that same evening, in the apartment he shared with his dog Hammond and a friend, Allen Greenfield, he found the program again. He unfolded the paper and read the name again.

He hummed a few notes of the carol idly and thinly, with only white noise from the refrigerator for accompaniment. He tossed the program into the trash along with the rest of the paper to be purged from his pockets. The song would not leave his mind, by now almost maddening, for it had stuck in his head and replayed itself all day. He picked up the program again and carefully smoothed the paper on the counter.

When he finally threw the thing away, he had the feeling he would remember the name. Dan Crell.

Months later, Ford moved into a house on Clifton Heights, a pretty brick bungalow with a deep yard stretching back to a patch of woods and a mostly dry creek bed. Here he lived alone with his dog. He had bought the house using income from a trust established for him by his grandfather. He had reached his late twenties, and his parents reminded him regularly that he ought to be thinking about marriage. His parents were certain to continue their lectures on the subject.

Ford was aware that he would never marry and, in fact, often wished he had the courage to tell them so. But the thought was amusing in some way. Honesty. With the white house, the cool rooms, the yard filled with oleander, the dark gardener moving among the blossoms. Honesty alongside the cool china, the polished silver, the framed pictures of parents, grandparents, great-grandparents, collateral couples, the great paired beings of his past.

By early fall, his parents' concern over his matrimonial future became acute. At dinner with his father one evening, the two of them supping in his father's club (which remained a men's club even though women occasionally won membership), Dr. McKinney, Senior brought up Ford's last girlfriend in Savannah, Haviland Barrows, who had recently married Red Fisher, one of Ford's high-school acquaintances. "Settled right down in the historic district in a little stoop cottage. Renovated beautifully, right out of a textbook. I don't think that's such a bad way to start out." Father dabbed his lips nicely with the napkin, preparing to engage his almond torte. "Of course, he'll get the Jones Street house when his grandfather dies. Your uncle Hubert drew up that will. God knows what she gets. From what I hear, some of the Barrows don't have a cent."

"I hope she's happy," Ford said, signaling the dark waiter to bring more coffee. "She deserves it."

"I never did understand how you let her get away, son," Father said.

"I wonder if I'm likely to get married at all," Ford answered.

"What are you talking about? A fine, good-looking boy like you, a doctor, even if you're the wrong kind of doctor. You should have been a surgeon, I've told you that before. The fact that you're a pediatrician will always disappoint me. But we're talking about marriage. Of course you'll marry. Your mother and I wonder why it's taken you this long."

"If it's taken this long," Ford said, "that has to be because I've wanted it that way."

"Nonsense. First you had to get through medical school,

that's what we've always expected." Dr. McKinney adjusted his collar. Ford spooned his own torte. "But now you're out of medical school and it's time to think about your future. You're going to be a busy man and you need someone to take care of you at home."

"You got married when you were in medical school."

"That was different. When your mother and I were coming up, people got married when they were younger. These days it's better to wait, the way you have. But you do have to stop waiting sometime." His father laughed, self-consciously, underlining the jovial atmosphere he attempted to create for serious discussions.

Later they discussed his trust funds and other financial matters. Ford asked after his mother. Father answered that she was well. The conversation cooled even further, and the two men parted company in the porte cochere as the liveried driver handed Father his car keys. At the last moment, the elder doctor said to the younger, "Don't forget we talked, Ford. You need to think about what you're doing. You need a wife."

The two shook hands, and in his father's eyes glimmered ghost lights of real affection, sodden and restrained.

One morning, Ford became aware of someone watching him from the back of a nearly empty hospital elevator.

Headed for the operating room, Ford wore surgical scrubs; but the only top he could find was too small. The sleeves rode indecently high on his shoulders, revealing round deltoids and post-summer bronze. Ford's radar alerted him that the young man at the back of the elevator found the sight of Ford's shoulders appealing. Ford allowed himself to return the young man's gaze coolly.

But the face surprised him. Ford searched for the young man's identification badge, hanging from the pocket of the requisite oxford shirt. Mr. Crell noted the motion, and this discomfited Ford somewhat. He felt suddenly naked, but met the young man's gaze again.

This time Mr. Crell averted his eyes, as if shy. The moment gave Ford an interval in which to study the face.

He noted smooth white skin, a strong shape to the face, cheeks slightly concave, and a shape of mouth along which Ford could see himself running the tip of his thumb. Thumb tracing those rounded lips, the strong line of jaw. The face broadcast innocence, as if a child were entombed in the bones; then the memory of what a voice might sound like, emerging from that face, caused Ford to ache a little. He remembered the man's voice with a shiver, and longed to hear it again.

"This is our floor," said Crell's companion, a nurse whom Ford had failed to notice.

"I guess I'm falling asleep," Crell said, "it's all those late nights," easing away from the elevator door. Even in those few words Ford could hear the singer in Dan's voice, the rich soothing undertone that, for a moment, filled the elevator car. That was it, or so Ford thought. But as the elevator doors began to close, the young man looked back at Ford.

A few days later, after twelve hours of a twenty-four-hour shift, he went to the hospital cafeteria for breakfast. Seated with Curt Robbins were Russell Cohen, Allison Roe, and a couple of other residents. Ford rubbed his night's growth of beard in the midst of a discussion of a juvenile who had been admitted to the ninth floor with acute diabetic ketoacidosis. Robbins described the fruity smell that accompanies the onset of this state, and Ford settled back to listen.

But across the cafeteria, framed by louvered windows and yellow blinds, Dan Crell carried a breakfast tray to a seat. He set his tray onto the table and arranged himself behind it, unlidding hot coffee and releasing steam from the styrofoam cup. When Dan finally looked up, he found Ford watching him and immediately returned his attention to his tray.

Ford found himself staring too, and averted his attention to Allison Roe's onyx ring with the diamond at the center of the setting. He lost all contact with Curt's explanation of disease process and felt his breath come short. What attracted him, nearly more than any physical part of Dan, was what he could feel from Dan across the room. He told himself this was not the time to approach Dan since meals at Grady were as much a part of teaching as grand rounds, but when he glanced at Dan again, he felt a hand tighten on his chest.

When he stood, Dan watched him.

He studied all the changes in Dan's face as he crossed the room—frozen unbelief, recognition, the whiteness of terror. At the table he loomed over Dan, whose cereal spoon was suspended in midair. "Good morning," he said, "can I join you for a minute?"

"Please." Dan looked down at his cereal.

They sat together through a brief silence. Not for a long time had Ford read so much in another presence. He felt himself opening and relaxing, drawn to the body across the table as if they were falling toward each other. Ford cleared his throat. "Well. I've been seeing you around the hospital. And I was wondering if maybe you would like to have dinner with me."

Dan laughed. Shock registered in his expression. "Have you been planning this for a while?"

"I saw you in the elevator. I liked you." Ford blushed himself, as if he had never admitted to liking anybody before. He glanced at the table of physicians still engrossed in their medical discussion. He said, "I need to get back to my ongoing learning experience before my senior resident comes after me. When can we get together?"

They negotiated the date, shy of watching each other but drawing out the process in spite of Ford's need to return to his duties across the cafeteria. Ford was on call for several nights running, and Dan was busy with rehearsals for a play at a local theater. They settled on Friday evening in a week, and Ford noted the engagement in his pocket calendar. This business finished, they parted.

The short walk across the cafeteria divided his life by apprehension, beginning with Allison Roe's quizzical glance. They had all been watching. What would Allison say if she knew Ford had asked the man to dinner?

In his pleasant kitchen on a morning when he was free of hospital duties, he understood his courage to be failing. He sensed that he himself would have some large decision to make if he were actually to go through with this appointment, and something about that thought made him afraid. Nor was he interested in pursuing the fear to its roots and giving it a name. The notion that he could hide from the fear appealed to him instead. He sat in the early quiet on his side porch, wrapped in a thick sweater against the December chill. Holly in the sideyard gleamed deeply green. Loneliness poured into him with the stirring of winter breezes, but even in the cold he sat on the porch for a long time in his pajamas and sweater, bare ankles in bedroom slippers, whitened fingers on the warm mug.

He tried to remember the feeling that had led him to cross space, to sit down at the table of a stranger and ask the stranger to take a meal with him. A different feeling from approaching another man in a bar: a few nights of sex, then the occasional embarrassed glances exchanged afterward when, cruising once again, they crossed paths. He tried to think of the last time he had slept with a man after taking a meal with him, and he could not remember anybody since college. He pictured the stranger's face, but the image formed only as a blur in his consciousness.

By the time he left the porch he had resolved to break the date. He wrote a note to Dan, mailing it to his hospital address. Ford simply wrote that the dinner they had planned was proving impossible for him to schedule. He signed himself "F. McKinney" and attempted to make the scrawl as little like his usual signature as possible, in case Dan Crell attempted to make some sinister use of the note.

When he sealed the envelope he felt a brief, precious moment of relief.

On the Friday of the impossible dinner, with Christmas looming the next week, Ford headed through first-floor corridors toward the Pediatric Appointment Clinic where he was scheduled to see patients under Dr. Milliken's supervision. Though the clinic occupied a large area on the second floor of the hospital, Ford went to the trouble of descending one floor and crossing to the clinic on that level. Out of fear. Dan Crell's office lay on the second floor in a suite of offices between the two clinics.

But Ford found Dr. Milliken at the juncture of corridors near the first-floor lobby, standing in a large crowd, and as Ford approached, Milliken signaled him. Ford smiled the crisp smile of the proper young medical resident, heading toward his Chief of Service. "I want you to hear this," Dr. Milliken said, and a piano struck soft notes as across the crowded lobby Dan Crell mounted a dais and prepared to sing.

"Let's see if we can't get closer," Dr. Milliken whispered. "He has a wonderful voice."

Ford muffled his panic and followed, trapped. Dan began to

sing a lullaby to the Christ child, a song Ford had heard in his childhood but not since. At the first full notes, a ripple of recognition passed through the gathering; then rapt silence fell as the voice swelled to fill the lobby, to permeate every corner. "Loo lay thou little tiny child," the young man sang, and the mournful tones sent a chill through Ford. He lost himself in listening. His eyes followed every movement, tracing the slim figure of the singer as the song poured from him, the radiance of the sound matched by the luminescence of his face, his flesh, his wholeness. While Dan sang he remained oblivious to everything around him, motionless but for the throbbing of his tender, touchable throat. Again his singing told those who listened that the joy of the saved is the sorrow of the saviour, that the tiny child might wish another fate. Again in minor keys and throbbing tones he undercut the merry decorations of the lobby, and from within Ford responded, once again, with the same deep sadness.

The song ended, the last pulse vanished, and the room exploded into applause, far greater than Ford's memory of the year before. Dan received this quietly, with a look of deliberate containment. The stillness of his features burned an image into Ford. Before descending from the dais, with an air of perfect peace as the applause continued, Dan surveyed the crowd.

He could hardly help but find Ford, who stood inches above every other occupant of the room. Their eyes locked, and suddenly Dan's moment of perfect beauty fled. He froze on the dais, broke off the eye contact by act of will, took a breath and gathered himself together, each phase of the change visible to Ford. Dan's flesh went ashen, his eyes dimmed. When he could move again, he let the crowd take him.

Ford's shift ended and he drove to Clifton Heights, where he wandered from room to room.

When the telephone rang he rushed to answer. But this voice was without resonance. His mother had called to ask about his plans for arrival in Savannah, would he drive or would he fly? Her cool questions returned him to the kitchen, facing wooden shelves, studying his grandmother's collanders and the telephone directory. He reached for the directory, saying to Mother, "I only have about thirty-six hours, if I drive I'll do nothing at home except sleep."

"I agree that flying is sensible, Ford, but if you haven't booked a flight by now you'll never get a seat."

"That's not what I told you, Mother. I said I hadn't decided which flight to take because I wasn't sure of my schedule. I have seats on two different flights and I'll know tomorrow which one I'll be on. My travel agent has everything under control."

"I don't mean to be a bore about it, dear, but you know what Christmas means to all of us." She laughed electronically across the scores of miles. "We want to make sure you get here in time for your grandmother's party."

"I get there Christmas Eve," Ford said, "and I'll probably make it to the party but I won't make dinner most likely."

Shortly afterward they said good-bye to one another and hung up, and Ford looked up Dan Crell in the telephone book. There was only one listing under that name, on Blue Ridge Avenue near North Highland. Standing in the dark, taking deep breaths, Ford lifted the phone receiver again.

After a dozen rings he gave up. Maybe Dan had begun his family visit early, or had decided to do something else for the evening, or perhaps he refused to answer the phone. Leaning against the countertop, Ford watched moon-cast tree shadows moving against the windows.

Christmas in Savannah followed the course of every Christmas he could remember. But his family noticed a change in him at once. His sister Courtenay picked him up at the airport, full of news about Smith College and warnings about Dad and Mom. "Sounds to me like they want to start matchmaking for you as soon as you get in the door. They've invited the oldest Stillwell girl to Grandmother Strachn's for eggnog."

"Christ," Ford said, "that's all I need."

"Chin up, Fordie, she's so shy she won't say a word. And she's only tall enough to come up to your rib cage, you can always pretend you don't see her."

"Why can't they mind their own business?"

Courtenay, nearly six feet tall herself, but blessed with the sort of striking beauty that can carry off such height, reached across the car to pat his forearm tenderly. "As far as they're concerned, Ford, your marriage is their business. Family business. Just like mine will be, whenever I get around to it."

"Are you seeing anybody?"

"Oh yes. The same guy I told you about, the carpenter. Mom will love it when I finally tell her about that one."

Ford laughed. Courtenay turned down Abercorn Street and finally onto East Gordon, where Grandmother Strachn's well-kept mansion occupied the corner off Calhoun Square. Ford convinced Courtenay to park on the other side of the square, and they walked slowly through the moss-hung trees, arms around each other's waists.

"Cheer up big brother," Courtenay said, sensing trouble in his silence. "You've always got me. Frankly, it suits me if you wait a long time to get married. As long as the prince of the house is single, the pressure is off the princess."

"I doubt I ever will."

"Do what?"

"Find a wife. Raise a family."

She let the statements stand for a moment. "Are you trying to tell me something?"

He shrugged, affecting nonchalance, but feeling the flutter of tension in his stomach. "I'm not seeing anybody at all right now. I haven't dated since Haviland."

"Is something wrong, Ford? Is there something you need to talk about?"

They looked each other in the eye. Ford smiled wryly. "Are you asking for direct communication, in the McKinney family?" They remained beneath the draping of Spanish moss. Ford reached for another joke but stopped himself. Without a plan for this conversation, he had managed to begin it anyway. "There is somebody I want to start seeing. A man at the hospital."

Courtenay accepted this in silence, gently drawing him against her side. From Grandmother Strachn's parlor drifted the sound of recorded Christmas carols. "Have you talked to Mom or Dad about any of this?"

"Sort of. To Dad. He deflected the whole thing, and I wasn't very direct."

"How long have you known?"

"About this guy? Not long. About me? I don't know. I'm just now getting around to ,facing facts." Remembering the Christmas concert, the empty Friday evening, now a week past but fresh and aching nonetheless. "I haven't been very good at it, so far."

He told her the story of the last few months, including his therapy sessions and his pattern of anonymous sex. Her lack of surprise gave him to understand that the essence of this news neither surprised nor shocked her particularly, and she listened as if there were all the time in the world. Finally she said, "Thanks for telling me. I guess I'm not really surprised; I knew something was going on. You're too good-looking to be having trouble finding a woman."

"How do I deal with Mom and Dad?"

She blew out misty breath, turning to the imposing house that overshadowed them both. "I don't know. Let's think about it." She ran a hand through his hair and pulled him against her side. "But I wouldn't rush into anything."

"If they're planning to parade half of Savannah's finest in front of me, I don't know if I can stand it."

"You're not here that long; hold your breath and drink a lot of eggnog." She kissed his forehead and they wandered toward the parlor lights. "Wait till you get yourself straightened out with this man. Or till you get somebody else you care about. You need a little support before you take on the whole twenty-nine generations of McKinneys and Strachns."

Christmas Eve at Grandmother Strachn's followed a script written before either Ford or Courtenay were born, beginning with the formal dinner Ford had missed, and ending with gift exchanges and halfhearted caroling around the venerable Steinway in the middle parlor. As at most Savannah social occasions, everyone drank throughout the evening, and when Ford entered, still arm in arm with his sister, the room glowed with flushed faces and bulbous noses etched with broken capillaries. Ford greeted Grandmother Strachn at once, seated in her high-backed chair at the center of her family. He kissed the delicate old skin of her cheeks. Aunt Rose had just seated herself at the piano stool and, after Ford had kissed his mother and the other aunts and had shaken hands with his father and the men, Aunt Rose struck up the first chords of "Hark the Herald Angels Sing." Glass in hand, Ford joined the circle of voices. His mother contrived to have Lisa Stillwell stand next to him. They had rounded their way through "Joy to the World" and into "While Shepherds Watched Their Flocks by Night." Flushed with his success (and with what he considered to be his rather good baritone), Ford managed to speak politely to Lisa as Aunt Rose flipped the pages of her yellowed music book. He caught his mother watching with a look of private satisfaction as he complimented Lisa's singing. Aunt Rose reached her destination and struck up the opening chords of "God Rest Ye Merry Gentlemen."

The song catapulted him back to Atlanta. He tried to control himself, but after the conversation with Courtenay, his tenderness refused control and he knew he could not stand where he was. Not with this sinking in his gut. He excused himself quickly. He shut himself in the downstairs bathroom and locked the door, leaning against the wall out of sight of the mirror.

He could still hear the song, but not as sung by his family's ragged choir. The voice in his head, rich and full, filled him with loneliness. But he played the memory through, beginning to end, the sadness and beauty of the voice, and at its end he looked himself in the eye in the mirror. Taking a deep breath, he let go of the ache. "I will take care of this," he said, "I promise," though he himself did not know for whom he had made the promise.

The party ended, as always, with Aunt Rose leading Grandmother to the stairway, where the departing guests lined up to bid her good night. Grandmother's two maids brought coats and hats to the gathered family, and soon everyone bundled up. Ford helped Lisa Stillwell into her white wool jacket with the sprig of mistletoe at the lapel, and as he did, Mother called out, "Oh, and Ford. Borrow Courtenay's car and drive Lisa home, will you? Courtenay can ride home with your Father and me."

Lisa looked at him hopefully and Ford tried to smile. Courtenay gathered herself into her own coat. "Mother, for heaven's sake, I'll drive Lisa home, and Ford can ride along with me if he wants. But I'm not about to turn him loose in my car when he's falling over asleep."

Ford adjusted the white collar of Lisa's coat from behind. "I'd probably drive across the square, tired as I am."

"Whatever you do, don't be out all night," said Father, pulling on his driving gloves.

To appease his mother, Ford carefully held the door for Lisa and walked with her down the stone steps. "It was lovely of Mrs. McKinney to invite me," Lisa said, "my parents are abroad this year and I had no idea what to do with myself on Christmas Eve."

"Mother's so crazy about the holidays, she can't stand the thought of anyone being alone." Ford casually looked over his shoulder to find Courtenay.

She appeared, heels click-clacking on the tabby sidewalk behind them. She deftly allowed momentum to insert her between Ford and Lisa, taking both their arms. "Don't you just love holidays," she said brightly, turning from one to the other. "I used to think December was cold here, too, before I went to Smith."

She and Lisa chatted about Smith as they crossed the square. Ford let himself be pulled along in their wake, playing the familiar, acceptable part of the silent male in female company. Courtenay handed the car keys to Ford, assuring him that she wouldn't let him drift at the wheel, and he and Lisa arranged themselves in the front seat for the short drive to the house on East Gaston. Courtenay maintained a wall of chatter during the drive. At the large, well-lit house, Ford parked in the porte cochere and rounded the car, walking her to the steps and shaking her hand. From the car, Courtenay called, "Call us sometime, Lisa, it was truly wonderful to talk with you!"

Into the house she vanished, casting one lingering glance in Ford's direction.

Courtenay took over the front seat and Ford drove home. "Mother's very pissed that I didn't let you do this little duty yourself."

"Whereas I've never been so grateful to anybody in my life," Ford said.

At home, their father and mother awaited them in the family room. Father knelt in front of the fireplace, stoking the new flames of the fire he had lit. Ford took the small brandy his mother offered, settling himself into the easy chair that faced the Christmas tree. Mother always insisted on two Christmas trees, the large one at the front of the house, for the neighbors, as she said, and the small one in the family room. As Ford sat down, his Father said, "Well, I think Grandmother Strachn and Millie outdid themselves this year. Did you have any of the caviar, Ford?"

"Yes, wonderful," Ford yawned.

"I'm sure Mother had it flown in," Mother said, "she takes care of this whole occasion herself, you know. Rose likes to take credit for it, but Mother's the one who makes the arrangements. I liked those little cheese straws too. Millie makes those so well."

"I'd like to hire Millie away from her," Father said.

Mother laughed, patting her hair with studied irony. "When Mother dies, God forbid, the biggest fight we'll have will be over who gets Millie."

"Rose will keep Millie," Father said. "Don't you think Millie will want to stay with the house?"

"Rose isn't getting that house," Mother said. "What would she do with it? A maiden lady with a house that size? It's ridiculous."

"Please, dears, let's not start this." Courtenay rounded the sofa, barefoot, to nest on the floor beside Ford. "It's Christmas, and Grandma isn't anywhere near dead yet."

"She certainly isn't," said Father. "She's as sharp as she ever was. Don't you agree, Ford?" Father unknotted his tie and unbuttoned the top button of his shirt. Grey chest hair curled over the fabric. Soft firelight rendered him younger, though every bit as stately as usual. "What's wrong, son? You're awfully quiet tonight."

"I'm a little tired from the flight, I guess. I got a good night's sleep, the hospital is pretty slow this time of year."

"I hear good things about you from Carter Thompson. He says your faculty is pretty impressed. He's not very impressed with your faculty, but he says your faculty is impressed with you. I'm glad to hear it. If you have to be a pediatrician, you might as well be a good one." He stared stonily into his drink.

"I don't see much of Dr. Thompson. He spends most of his time at Emory."

"Well, that's easy to understand. He gets at least ten thousand dollars every time he walks into the operating room over there."

"I figured he was doing pretty well."

"How long are you home for, Courtenay?" Ford asked.

"New Year's Eve. Classes don't start for another week, but I'm moving to a new apartment."

"I don't particularly like the idea of your living alone," Mother said.

"Please, Mother, let's talk about this after Christmas, all right? Ford's home and I don't want to argue."

"As long as you remember that we do have to talk about it." Mother's polite voice concealed a well-known blade.

Father eyed him from above the glass. "I thought Lisa Stillwell looked just lovely tonight."

"She has the sweetest little figure," Mother agreed.

"She certainly thinks the world of you, Ford," Father added, weighting each word. "She was quite excited when she found out you would be at the party."

Suddenly Ford remembered the careful telephone interrogations conducted by his mother, each pointedly reminding him of the vital need to arrive in time. A small knot of anger rose in his throat.

Courtenay said, "Lisa certainly does have big front teeth."

"Courtenay!"

"I didn't notice anything about her teeth," Father said.

"You didn't? They're as big as a beaver's."

"Courtenay, that certainly isn't a very kind way to talk about the poor girl. Do you remember how terrible you used to feel when the boys made fun of you for being tall?"

"Yes, Mother, I certainly do. But now I'm six feet tall and drop-dead gorgeous and Lisa Stillwell's teeth are still too big."

Father laughed in spite of himself, setting down the glass on the sideboard. Mother said, "Keith, don't encourage her."

"I'll be perfectly happy to be quiet, Mother," Courtenay said, drumming fingertips on Ford's knee, "if we can just stop talking about that little dwarf."

Ford said, "She's a perfectly nice girl. I just don't want to marry her."

The fire hissed. The top of the brandy decanter chimed. Otherwise the whole house fell silent. Father sipped, swirled the glass, looked at it. "What brought that on?"

"I was trying to be funny."

Mother said mildly, "I don't see the humor."

Father crossed his arms and faced Ford with his legs spread slightly. "Tell me, son, whom do you want to marry?"

"Nobody," Ford said. "Right at this moment."

"Well," Mother said brightly, "I'd like a Christmas cookie. Would anyone else care for one?" She glided from the room before anyone could answer, calling, "Courtenay, come help me, please."

When Courtenay refused to move, Father said sternly, "Courtenay, go and help your mother with the cookies."

"Go ahead," Ford said, patting her head. "I'm fine."

In the uncertain world of gesture, one never knew what would anger Father most. Tonight, that touch on Courtenay's head was it. "That's right, Courtenay," he snapped, "you have your brother's permission to leave."

She stalked out silently. Father faced the curling flames, took a deep breath and waited till his flush had faded. "Now Ford, your mother and I had the best intentions in the world when we invited Lisa to the party. I don't want to hear any more unkindness about that. But let me say this. If she won't do, look for somebody who will. You're too old to be single. When I was your age I had two children, I had settled down, I was living my life. Even in the middle of a residency, I was living my life. That's all I want for you. That's all your mother and I are trying to achieve."

"Maybe what I need to do is stop coming home." Ford set down the snifter beside the chair.

"Don't make childish threats."

When he stood, he towered over his father, and the realization came to him that Father had more to fear, right now, than he did. He spoke as calmly as he could. "This is no threat, Dad,

and I'm not a child. I don't need this. No, listen for a minute."
Ford took a deep breath. "Now, you and mother need to face
facts. I might not ever get married. I might marry somebody
you don't like. One way or the other, it's going to be me who
picks and me who decides." He lifted his overcoat from the
couch. "I'm going to bed. I'll see you in the morning. Tell
Mother I said good night."

Retrieving his overnight bag from Courtenay's car, he lingered in the small garden behind the house, standing beneath
the broad mimosa. At this hour of Christmas Eve the city lay in
silence, occasionally interrupted by the whisper of a ghost of
traffic. He walked to the wooden fence that separated the yard
from the service lane. Wishing for his own bed, his own house,
he studied the few stars bright enough to pierce the haze of
streetlight. Wind had begun to shift, and he smelled the first
dingy scent of the paper plant blowing into the city.

He could find no place for himself here and now, in the backyard of this house in which he had spent most of his childhood,
or in the lives of his parents, or in the smells drifting over his
hometown.

He passed a nearly sleepless night in the room of his boyhood,
long since transformed by his mother into another showplace
for antiques. His speech to his father replayed itself in his head.
Toward morning he dreamed he had brought Dan home with
him for Christmas, a long formless dream that he failed to remember on waking. But the renewed image of the young man
left him aching and full of dread.

Christmas Day passed peacefully despite the tension that remained from the night before. Before breakfast, Mother approached him in the sun room and told him that both she
and his father had agreed to let the subject drop for this trip,
for the sake of the holidays. "But Ford," she said, "it's really
time we had a long talk about this whole subject. This is twice
you've told your Father you don't want to get married. And
while you may be an adult now and this may be your decision,
it's certainly something that involves your family. We all know
how busy you are and how difficult it is for you to travel, so
your Father and I would like to come to Atlanta to talk to you
about this."

"I think that's a better idea than trying to deal with it on Christmas." Ford felt suddenly exhausted.

"Good. Now you think about when you want us to come and let us know. But I'm perfectly serious about this."

"I'm taking you seriously, Mother. I want to talk about this too."

"I thought this was what you and that therapist were supposed to be working on," with a slight lift of her upper lip.

Ford contained a flash of anger, turning away from his mother. "I thought we were going to save the whole subject for another time. All right?"

Through the long day at home, Ford counted the minutes till he could excuse himself and retire. Having prepared himself to discourage any attempt at conversation, he was relieved when none took place. He rose, finally. "Tomorrow morning I'm taking a taxi, so you folks can sleep it off." He rubbed the back of his head idly. "In fact, if I'm going to be awake when I get to the hospital tomorrow, I'd better go to bed now."

Saying good night to all, kissing Mother, shaking Father's hand, he thanked them for a fine Christmas and headed to the bedroom in which he slept as a guest of the house. Knowing now, and vowing to remember forever, that home lay in front of him, in the crass young city nestled at the foot of the Georgia mountains, and not behind him in the aging Savannah by the sea.

Crimson clouds blazed over the eastern horizon for the whole of the short jet flight to Atlanta, and Ford sat suspended in the bleeding light. He tried to remember Dan's face and recalled only a vague blur. Any feeling concealed itself. But later, in his bedroom, memory of Dan's face returned to him, vivid in detail, and Ford remembered the eerie voice, singing not the lullaby of this year's concert but the well-known carol of the year before, *to save us all from Satan's power when we were gone astray.*

Gathering his gym bag, Ford headed to the hospital.

Atop the C wing of the huge edifice the medical school had installed a gymnasium for the use of residents, who were often trapped in the building for long shifts. Ford headed there, parking in the sparsely populated deck and striding through the quiet corridors. Hardly anyone had returned from the holidays. He found the gym empty but for one third-year student, a woman named Dorothy Ballard whom he had met here before. "I stayed in town this Christmas," she said. "I learned a long time ago that going home is useless. My lover made Christmas dinner and we had the best holiday I can remember in years."

"I wish I'd had the good sense to stay here," Ford said, pretending for the moment that this were actually an option.

"Do yourself a favor and get listed for Christmas duty next year."

"I think I'll do that." He headed for the bench press.

My lover made Christmas dinner. He flushed his muscles with blood and oxygen, moving the resistance machine through its courses, building his body like armor. He scrutinized each body part between sets, confirming its thickness of flesh and firmness of tone, eyeing the shape of the parts and the whole. Watching himself. Aware of his need, today, for certainty.

He peeled off the T-shirt. Tensing and relaxing his torso, eyeing the planes and ridges, the gleam of perspiration. Gathering evidence.

He showered in the on-call suite one floor below, stashing his gym bag in the locker and dressing in scrubs. Taking a deep breath, running a hand through his hair to get the look of it just right, he spoke to the face in the mirror. "Whatever happens, I'm fine," he said.

The wait for the elevator seemed endless, but when he entered the car a wave of dread engulfed him. At the outer door to the office suite in which he would either find or not find Dan, he took a deep breath. Let him be here, he thought, let this be over. The other voice attempted to intercede as well, to say, no, not yet, you haven't planned what you're going to say, wait a little while, but Ford placed his hand flat on the door and pushed.

LAWNBOY

• PAUL LISICKY •

There were things nobody knew about me. They didn't know about my old train set in my bedroom, complete with Cape Cods, hotels, signal crossings, and papier-mâché palms, a set that I tinkered with until the ninth grade, then smashed—to my uttermost sorrow—after a fight with my father. They didn't know I could recite a handful of Psalms—the 13th, the 23rd, the 42nd, and the 53rd—completely by heart. They didn't know about my love for the paintings of Hieronymus Bosch, my deep interest in Greek myth, my faith in the shifting weather, or my fascination with Saturn and the outer planets. They didn't know about the day, in my thirteenth year, when out of sheer boredom, I stitched my fingertips together with needle and thread, making an intricate basket of my hand and giving myself a tremendous infection. They all thought I was a good-natured kid, upright and responsible, generous, affectionate, and kind, and of course I could be those things, but there was much more to me than that, a side that unnerved even myself, and this side included William.

William. William the pigeon-toed, William the conqueror. His name, though banal, even after five years, still conjures up an otherworldly thing, not a being of flesh and blood, who sweated and stank, who slept, ate, shat, and died, though I should have known better. I never even told my best friend Jane about him, though she thought she knew me. Well, she didn't.

I was mowing my parents' yard. He was standing between the joewood and the carambola, mopping his tanned forehead with a blue rag. He was watching me, hard, and I made an effort not to notice. He'd been around forever; he had to be almost as old as my parents: forty, forty-two. I'd never even given him a thought. I only knew that he worked the camera for Channel 7 News, had a gentle greeting for my folks whenever he walked his Dobermans, and had the most profound and beautiful traveler's tree I'd ever seen (like me, he loved plants). That was it. He meant absolutely nothing to me, until he stepped forward, then I started noticing: jaw, eyes, hair, smell, hands, feet, mouth. There was a kind of buzz about him, a field of hissing electricity that jerked with my ions and electrons. I felt myself getting hard. I thought: Now you've really gotten yourself into trouble.

"Lawnboy," he said, mocking me. "Lawnboy, Lawnboy."

I pulled back on the lever. The motor silenced. "Is there a problem?" I said, with some irritation.

The hush overwhelmed. Above, dry palm fronds clattered in the heat.

"Can I help you?"

He nodded, shyly. He tucked in his shirt, a striped Haitian thing patterned with yellow parrots. "My lawnmower's broken. My place is a mess. Would you be interested in cutting my lawn?"

My expression dulled. I reacted as if he'd been asking to tap my spine.

"I'll give you twenty bucks. Twenty bucks, an hour a week. No weeding or mulching."

I frowned. I felt simple, my tongue swelling fatly in my mouth. Befuddled. I glanced up at the shocked treetops and saw a sun shivering in a glazed sky. When I looked back at him, his eyes, blue with sprinklings of gold, were watching mine. I thought I detected some fear in them.

"I have to ask my parents," I announced.

I loped through the side door. I crouched, pressed my nose right down into the quarry tile so I could almost breathe in the dust. I was seventeen years old then. Of course my parents didn't need to know. If anything, they'd be thrilled that I'd finally stop moping around the house, dreading the resumption of school. I stood, watching the second hand of the clock make three complete rotations. I peered through the slats of the Bermuda shutter. He was still standing, shifting his weight from foot to foot. I reached into my pants, gave myself a firm and brutal yank. When I looked down, I noticed the trembling of my hands.

"What did they say?"

I bounded down the walk. I tried to seem matter-of-fact, reckless. "They said fine. Fine. When do you want me to start?"

"Tomorrow." He grinned, his shoulders drawing imperceptibly backward. "So we have a deal then."

"Deal." I extended my hand to him.

But he didn't take the hand. Instead, he placed his palm flat over my face, then pushed up, and as I started the mower, I decided he was probably the creepiest, most disgusting individual I'd ever met in my life.

That night I lay in bed, listening to the house. Ice maker, pool motor, air conditioner, computer, oven cleaner. Everything but voices. It was the fourth day in a row that my parents, Ursula and Sid, hadn't spoken. I should have been used to it by now, but their silence only seemed to have gotten noisier, so shrill I pictured it puncturing a hole, the size of a meteorite, through the ceiling. I couldn't be safe from it, not outside, not in my room. I suspected it would follow me everywhere, even after their deaths, till my own death. I glanced at the digits of my clock radio. 10:04. Boy, am I seeing the world.

They shouldn't have gotten married. They hated each other. Anyone could see it in their eyes and their clipped, joyless mouths. It had always been this way. Once, seeing intimations of these same expressions in their wedding photos, I thought, with relief—*ah*—so it isn't my doing. Still, it maddened me that they kept holding on like this. They never dealt with anything. The same way they couldn't deal with me. I mean, I didn't mince or prance. I didn't weave, I didn't dot my "i's" with circles or curlicues, but my eminent faggotry should have been obvious to them. Hello, Ursula. Hello, Sid. Knock, knock. Anybody home?

I fooled with my armpit hair. I was thinking about the beach trip I'd planned the next day with Jane and then I remembered

my lawn-cutting assignment. I ground my teeth. I thought of
his face: the mussed-up brows, the deeply cut eyes. He carried
a smoky smell about him, as if he were burning deep from inside.

"So where are you going?" Ursula said the following morning. Her voice sounded upbeat, despite the goings-on with my
father. At least she'd gotten herself dressed today.

I stuffed a banana muffin in my mouth. "Beach. I'm going
with Jane. I'll be back before dinner."

She pressed the small of her back into the countertop. She
held her thin, pasty arms tightly over her chest. "You're not
going to the beach," she said with a knowing grin.

Crumbs caught in my throat. Did she know? She couldn't
know. "Why do you always have to accuse me? You never believe what I say. You always think I'm plotting, Mom. I think
you despise me."

"Are you going to start with me again? I made a simple psychic assertion. I know you. You're a lousy liar. You can't hide a
damn thing from me."

"Oh yeah?" I laughed, and slammed out the door.

I stood outside William's at 8:54 A.M. I was early, but wanted
to get it over with. The door opened, and he stood there in a
robe patterned with marine flags, a mud mask on his face.

"Lawnmower's in the garage," he said with a husky rasp.

I pulled up on the door handle. The mower hunkered beside
the pool chemicals—a nice one actually, with pretty green
paint and detachable grass catcher. Unlike our lawn mower, a
piece of shit which was constantly leaking gas, this one started
first try.

I bent over, stretched. The grass, a high-quality Floratam, was
pleasantly spongy. I worked up and down, sidestepping sprinkler
heads, guarding the tender young trunks of the palms. I started
making up a song. I frequently made up songs and sang them
aloud, almost yelling them up to the trees.

> Lenny, the lusty Lawnboy,
> Cuts the yards and makes them sizzle.
> Everyone who sees him needs
> His moisture-seeking love-hard missile.

I studied the sliding windows of the house and realized I wasn't going to have sex with him. I didn't know where the warped idea had popped into my head anyway. Once again, I'd allowed myself to get all worked up about someone who was unavailable to me. How hard it is to know people. I used to think that I knew what hurt and bolstered them, but I realized that I could be wrong. Once, I thought I knew my folks. But now they were strangers, as foreign to me as the workings of a nuclear power plant. I looked up at the window again. He was just a regular fellow. Lonely. Dumb. A little fun.

I finished up in record time, forty-three minutes. The yard was smaller than I'd expected. I stepped through the gate, sat, and took in the reeking trees: flame vine, sapodilla, poinciana, satin-leaf, gumbo-limbo, soursop, wild cinnamon. My fingers smelled of gasoline, fertilizer. The lawn, green as mouthwash, glittered in the morning heat. Above me, the sky bubbled and fried.

"Nice tune," William said, stepping outside.

"What?"

"I said I liked your song."

My stomach folded in on itself. "I wasn't singing."

He cuffed the top of my head and laughed. "Sure you weren't. Do you want to come inside for breakfast?"

My words came out sludgy, like juice squeezed from a freeze-damaged orange. I told him that I had to leave, that I needed my payment, please, but he kept scrutinizing me, as if certain he possessed me. I tasted a fresh filling deep in the corner of my mouth. Finally, he reached into his rear pocket and pulled out three ten-dollar bills.

"But this is ten dollars too much."

"Take it."

"It's too much."

"Just take it. Buy yourself some candy."

"I don't need any candy."

"Whatever."

I shrugged. For some reason I felt myself welcoming, letting down the defenses, when I noticed the fractures of light in his eye. I went off. I imagined him capable of all sorts of things. Hangings, slayings, snuff films. Whole freezers filled with kidnapped boys in body bags stacked according to height, weight, race, creed.

"So would you like to come in?" he asked again.

"Sure," I said and followed.

Something disturbing and immature in my nature wanted to startle people. Perhaps it was because I was essentially unstartling in appearance. I slumped through the corridors of my school, Coral Gables High, a quiet, mealy kid with Dumbo-like ears, in flannel shirts, racking up B after B, even though I was most likely a genius. My second-grade teacher, Mrs. Edge, had extracted me from the class and said, "You're too good for us. I'm going to recommend to the principal that you be promoted to the third grade." And she did it, easy as the snap of a finger. These effortless achievements continued until my thirteenth year. I'm not sure what happened after that.

We sat at the kitchen counter. He told me about his ex-wife Lorna, his daughter Poppy at Rollins College, his years in the Episcopal seminary, and of his preparations for the priesthood. I was bored out of my skull. The same image kept drifting across my tired eyelids: a hole in the clouds, torn like a bullet wound, with the sky on fire behind it.

Then I thought about Jane. We were supposed to have gone to the beach. She had to be pissed by now. Or worried. She was always worried about me. Sometimes she told me that if I wasn't careful, I'd be one of those people you read about in papers, carved up like a Christmas turkey, decapitated, lying armless or legless in a ditch. She could think what she wanted. But I knew I was protected. Something, somewhere was watching, keeping me. God. An angel. I could walk through fire, I could thrive through sickness, I could pass through the harshest danger and come out alive, because I was graced, blessed.

I looked up. William was smiling. "You haven't listened to a word I said."

"What?" I put the jar down. The tabletop was littered with the scraps of the peeled label.

"Tell me about yourself. How's school?"

I shrugged. I wasn't going to give in to him. He thought he had something. He thought I was innocent, powerless, that I was going to lie down and take it. He was wrong. I pictured him lying on his stomach in a warm, dark cave. A bowl full of liquid beside his head. How easy it would be to lift the bowl in his moment of peace and kill him.

We were in his room. He sat on the bed while I swayed above him. He unzipped my pants and felt for my dick—a hard, red, glistening muscle. He gripped it, cranked it around. "Beautiful," he rasped, gazing up into my face.

He started sucking me off. It wasn't like I'd expected. I mean, I'd fooled around before, but it wasn't serious sex—not in a bed or anything—and this, I supposed, was serious sex. I wasn't particularly excited. Maybe I was bored, even disgusted. I concentrated on the motions, trying to pinpoint the smells in the room. I thought: bleach, weeds, sweat, funk, hair.

"Good?" he asked, taking a breather.

"Yeah."

We continued. We rolled around on the bed, when a thought, a full sentence, occurred to me: *He is getting younger, while I am getting older.* I didn't know what it meant. I thrust out my leg, kicked over the lamp, then rolled him over on his back, even though he was the stronger. I hiked his legs onto my shoulders, and to my astonishment started fucking him.

"That's it," he muttered. "Fuck your old man, boy. Go boy. That's it. Keep fucking your daddy."

"Shut up," I whispered. "Just please shut the hell up."

A thin cord of electricity quavered up my spine. I realized: this is what I'd always wanted. All at once I departed from myself, turning above the bed like a huge ticking wheel, watching us pushing against each other. My breath was sticking in my throat. I leaned over and kissed the harsh sandpaper of his face. I returned to myself, felt him clenching and relaxing around me, then pulled out, coming across his heaving stomach.

I stood before the bathroom mirror. I stuck a coated finger in my mouth, pushing it around my gums, feeding myself. My body felt new: the blood enriching my face, the muscles sharper as if dug by fine tools. I had something. I had a power all along and hadn't even known it.

But when I walked into his bedroom, I was only the mealy high-school boy again. I eased under the covers, punching him softly on his broad freckled back, waiting for encouragement, or something returned, when he only swung away and rolled on some basketball socks with holes in them. His head appeared to be swimming with thoughts. His Dobermans jumped up on the bed, panting, licking at my bare skin.

"Get dressed, kiddo," he said. "Your parents are going to be worried."

"But can't we do it again?"

"No, that's enough for me." He laughed softly. "Get dressed. It's time for you to go."

"You sure?"

He nodded.

So that's it, I thought. That's what you do. I picked up my clothes from the sweaty heap on the floor. He kissed me dryly on the mouth. I left. On the way home I kept repeating: *I went to the beach. I went to the big beach with my friend Jane and saw palms and sand and girls carrying buckets full of tulip shells. I took a swim and ate a snow cone.*

And that was how it started. Once a week, I went to William's house, mowed the lawn, weeded the garden, and had sex. I gradually began to understand him, his silences and quirks, how he couldn't stand when I nicked the flesh of the century plant or splashed gas near the bird feeders. I learned when to talk, I learned when to be quiet. I also learned not to be resentful whenever he ignored me afterward. We had a pattern. We knew exactly what to expect from one another. No hurts, no disappointments. Not much talking. Sometimes, if we finished up early, he'd take me to the Speedboat Restaurant in Fort Lauderdale and I'd order exactly what I wanted: hamburger, salad, fries, dessert, soft drink. We might have been any other father and son. No one suspected a thing.

One afternoon I saw both of my parents sitting across from each other in the living room, silent. It was unlike them to be together in the same room. I couldn't tell whether I was grateful or frightened. Then it occurred to me that one of them, most likely my father, had cancer.

"Sit down," my father said grimly.

"I already have."

My eyes drifted to the baseboard heaters. It was a murky af-ternoon, threatening rain, and Ursula flipped on the lamp, which depressed me. Lamps are for night, I wanted to say. Their si-lence somehow amplified things: the clicking of a palmetto beetle, the pressure of the palms against the window glass. A stray nerve kept pulsing in the small of my back. I knew what was coming. I wanted to pick up and run down the street.

My mother finally sat forward on the sofa. "You've been spending a lot of time away from us."

Silence from Sid. He slouched low in his seat, curled the edge of his hand over his brow.

I nodded solemnly. "You want me to help out more?"

My mom nodded, then wagged her head. "I'm surprised."

I smiled, because I couldn't contain it any longer, but neither of them smiled back. "I don't understand."

"People are talking."

"Huh?"

She whispered, "Why are you spending so much time with that man?"

I raised my chin. Always what the neighbors thought. Who cared what the neighbors thought? "So what?"

My father sprang to attention. "Don't talk to her like that. That's your mother."

My eyes smarted. Did I know them? All my life I'd come and gone as I pleased. All my life I'd taken care of myself. Even when I was younger they'd never asked for report cards, never taken an interest in my hobbies or projects. I was the kind of five year old you saw circling the shopping-center parking lot on his bi-cycle, dodging cars, bewildering the parents, years before the other kids. And I wasn't complaining, okay? But there seemed to be a tacit agreement that they completely stay out of my business.

"What's this have to do with Mr. Parsons?" I stood up now.

"You sit down," my father demanded.

I didn't sit. They'd never talked to me this way before, and it wasn't going to start now.

"Do you see how he listens?" my father said to my mother.

She ignored the remark. Her lips hovered over the rim of her cup. It seemed that I'd frightened her. "What have you been

doing with that man, dear?" she asked shyly. My mother reached
into her sundress pocket and showed me a piece of wadded-up
paper. The printing was mine. I'd covered the entire page with
the same phrase, in columns, using the tiniest of letters. *I love
to fuck I love to fuck I love to fuck I love to fuck*

"I found this in your notebook. I know I shouldn't have gone
through your things. I know it was wrong, but when you started
withdrawing from us, I didn't know what else to do."

I wasn't withdrawing from anyone. "You had no right, Mom."

"Have you been sleeping with that man?"

"What makes you keep asking these stupid things?"

She nibbled at the corner of her mouth. She recognized the
truth in my eyes. "We're having that bastard arrested."

"Don't talk about him that way."

That did it. My father went for my arm. He didn't punch me;
he didn't do what any regular father would do. Instead, he drew
me to him, somehow rolled me over his knee like a puppet,
and—get this—started spanking my clothed butt for a good
half-minute or so. I was seventeen years old. It was such a comic
thing that I let him do it until we both filled up with shame.

"Happy, buddy boy?" I said.

I laughed all the way up to my room. When I lay facedown
on my bed, minutes later, I was still laughing. Fools. I took
breaths, many deep breaths, breathing, breathing, calming myself down, then reached for a pen, a red ballpoint, and started
punching it in and out of my right palm, deft and precise as a
sewing-machine needle, until I was looking down at a smear, a
little red star on my hand. It was beautiful to see. The house
stilled, and I fell fast asleep holding my beating hand to my face.

I wished I had had more courage. I wished I had held onto
my anger, letting it fuel me, giving me beauty and strength, but
in the weeks that passed something happened. I learned that I
was nothing more than a coward. I no longer could deal with
their scrutiny and assumptions, their empty and implacable
faces. They kept looking at me as if I'd crossed a bridge over a
steaming fjord and had become a stranger to them. What they
did was rob me of my history. I became flat, an outline, weightless. One afternoon, coming home from school, I overheard my

father instructing his lawyer to remove my name from his will. I didn't care about his money. But this erasure from their lives startled me, like an unexpected punch in the neck. I'd thought they'd get over it after a while, that we'd go on and be the family we'd always been, fixed in our silences and resentments. Instead of going back to the way things had been, they grew worse. I hated myself for the poverty of my spirit, for hungering after their love. Once again, I'd misjudged people and myself.

What I did was convince myself to play their game for a while. I had only one more year of school, then I'd get out, hungry and loosed upon the world. What followed was the worst period of my life. I hope I will never do something as stupid and irrational for as long as I live. I nearly killed myself in the process and hurt many others, but I didn't seem to have a choice at the time. I had no idea how lulling and easy it is to hate oneself. I watched my soul shrink then shimmer to a tiny point.

I stopped picking up the phone and answering the door. I even shirked my gardening duties. I didn't even pass William's house, and imagined his lawn grown mangy and foul without me. On my way somewhere, I'd take the long route, around the park, through the college gates, just so I wouldn't bump into him. I lived in great fear of bumping into him, at the drugstore, at the motor-vehicle registry, of seeing the wornout expression on his face: *Why have you done this?*

I devoted myself to becoming a better child. I helped with the garbage, manicured the hedges. I even scrubbed the mold from the side of the house, something that should have been done years ago. I made it quite clear, without saying it, that I no longer had anything to do with William, or with people, for that matter. My parents started treating me better. They actually talked with me, asked my opinions, discussed current events. They'd finally gotten a son, whoever that was, and he was gradually becoming an exemplary young man.

But they didn't recognize the signs of bitterness. For some reason, I wanted all people to know how much I hated them. I wanted to tell them I can play your games, I can live your lies, and it's easy. I did it by making them like me. I began studying all night long. I began achieving perfect grades, throwing off the curve for the entire class. My teachers were amazed by me.

Princeton, Stanford, Cornell, Swarthmore, Yale, Michigan—all of them wanted me by the end of the year. I kept on going. I was giving myself up to the powers. I swam, I ran, I beat off constantly, sometimes so much that it stung to pee. I was burning, a saint, purifying myself in these blaring fires. A dream would often come to me, and I'd force the dream, force myself to watch it, though it made me sick. I'd be standing over my young self, the sweet, boyish, optimistic self, punching his face until his mouth fell open.

We were eating dinner one Saturday night. My mother stepped out, then back into the kitchen, holding a cake rimmed with candles. My father handed a wrapped present to me. Then I realized it must be my birthday. I'd completely forgotten all about my birthday.

"We're so proud of you, Evan," my mother said blankly. "You're doing everything right."

My father added: "I'm so glad you've changed."

I nodded, smiled. I unwrapped my present and stared at the watch in the box. It meant nothing to me. I should have broken it right in front of their needy eyes.

"Thank you," I said humbly, and kissed them. Their foreheads were dry. I might have been kissing the brows of the dead.

Months passed. My friend Jane and I were walking along the bay front. A new high-rise was being thrown up in record time, and we watched the construction workers in their orange hard hats stepping across the open girders. I'd just been offered a full scholarship to Princeton and I supposed we were celebrating that meager fact. I hadn't even talked to Jane in over seven, eight weeks. Somehow I'd learned to live without her in my life.

"Are you sure you're okay?" she said out of nowhere.

"Well, that's a non sequitur."

"I'm serious. Are you sure you're okay?"

"Of course I'm okay. I've never been better in my life."

A green-eyed man with black hair jogged by us. He looked me up and down, grinned, then trotted ahead.

"Did you see that?" Jane said warmly. "Did you see the way he looked at you?"

"Faggot," I muttered, and walked ahead of her.

"*Hey!*" Something wet bounced and spread across my back.

"That doesn't sound like you. He was exactly your type. Have you been doing acid again?"

"I'm not taking drugs, Jane."

She annoyed me terribly. First her judgment, then her rancor. I watched the people walking by us. I watched their stupid, simpering, self-satisfied faces and threw a mental message to each one. *Fuck you . . . Fuck you . . . Fuck you . . .*

"You're changing," she said quietly.

She sat down on a slatted bench. "You used to be so much fun. You used to have such an amazing sense of humor."

"What sense of humor. I was never funny."

"Yes you were. And we always talked when things got bad. We buoyed each other." She folded her arms over her chest, frowned. She didn't talk for a while. "Fucker," she mumbled.

"Fucker?"

"You heard what I said."

"Keep talking like that and I'm going to leave you right here."

"So leave."

It came as unexpectedly as a fish in a flooded street gutter. I glanced to my right and saw William sitting in his parked car, with newspaper and coffee cup. I didn't think he was looking at me. He was simply another office worker spending his break in his car. The intensity of my argument with Jane diminished. I wasn't scared or sick or excited. I'd known this moment would come, but I never thought it would be so dull. My vision went runny; my words sounded stupid in my mouth. I might have been sitting on the mucky bottom of the bay. I glanced again, the car was gone, and I was afraid.

Why the hell hadn't I said hello?

"Are you sure you're okay?" Jane said finally, rubbing the back of my head.

"I guess," I said, and then we went home.

I couldn't sleep. I felt something simmering in my body, a slow cooking, spreading up through the stem of my torso, then prickling, exploding in my throat like salad oil. I wanted to molt, I wanted to cut away the baggage of my skin. I kicked the wet covers off the bed, threw on some clothes, and left the house. I was going to walk it off. I was walking through developments, through people's backyards in the dark, over culverts, canals, swamps, berms, retention basins. Hours had passed. I passed airport runways with their raucous blue lights, sanitation plants gleaming and vast as cities, signs fizzing and sparking, arrows pointing in all directions. Two towns over, the boat factory was working overtime, and the junky hot smell of plastic lingered in the atmosphere. A storm threatened from the Everglades, then receded, pushing the humidity even higher. I took off my shirt and roped it around my waist. I decided to walk and walk, possibly to the Keys, possibly to the Card Sound Bridge, until I finally got rid of this feeling.

Hours later I was standing in William's front yard. I expected the lawn to be overgrown, ruined, bits of scale and dollarweed eating at the turf, but no. It looked even better than before. Moist, lush. I knew it: William had found another Lawnboy. I had lost him for good. I fumbled for some broken shells and started tossing them, one after another, at the glass of the window: *ping ping ping ping*

Was there anyone else at that moment who knew the pressure and potential of changing everything? I raised my hand and linked myself up with him, the longing, imaginary one, then pressed forward, my fingertip upon the doorbell, standing on William's front porch, waiting.

TRICKS OF THE TRADE

• WILLIAM J. MANN •

"Going tricking?" Javitz had asked me, earlier tonight, in that voice that knew the answers to its own questions. I just laughed.

Tricking. Such an odd little twist of a word. As if I would take one of these boys home with me, and rather than sex, I'd pull a rabbit out of a hat. As if we'd get to my door and I'd refuse to let him inside, instead turning to him with a maniacal grin to say, "Tricked ya!"

As if tricks were the antithesis of treats—odious, displeasing, toxic to the system—instead of what they are: the caramel on the apple, the cinnamon in the bun, the cotton candy on the stick. Tricks are how we treat ourselves. Not that all tricks are always so delectable: some of mine have been the proverbial rocks in Charlie Brown's paper bag. But most of them are sweet: Hershey's Kisses. Milky Ways. Almond Boys.

Tonight, it's his nipples that bewitch me from across the room, little pink cones in relief against sweat-dappled copper skin. He moves in a rhythm that repudiates the beat on the dance floor. He wears a vest but no shirt, a grin but no smile.

It has been a summer of random magic, of surprising spirits conjured up between the sheets of my bed in my room overlooking Provincetown Bay. Strangers' kisses have exposed souls to me. The uneven scar on one boy's abdomen and the crinkles at the corners of another's eyes have revealed more truths than I could ever have discovered in a more consistent lover.

It is the last summer in which I am to be young.

"Hi," he says to me.

He strokes his stomach idly. Little beads of sweat leave shimmering trails down the smooth brown flat plain. He can't be more than twenty-three.

"I've seen you around," he says. "You work up here?"

"No," I say, which is a lie. Mystery helps in this town—especially when you're no longer twenty-three. "But you do," I say. "A houseboy or a waiter?" I ask, knowing the options for a boy his age.

"A houseboy," he says.

And so, the script stays on course, except for the brief flutter of my eyelids at that precise moment, when I catch the eye of a man across the dance floor. My breath catches, and I worry that the houseboy notices. But he doesn't—of course not: he's deep into character. Acknowledging my distraction would be akin to an actor on stage responding to the laughter of the audience in the middle of a scene. He carries on, as is proper. But I stumble, drawn by a man across the room, a man I don't know, a man I thought was someone else.

I know no one here.

When I was just a boy, my mother told me a riddle that terrified me. It went something like this: "A girl is put in a room with no windows and only one door. That door is locked from the outside. There is nothing in the room with the girl but a radiator. Later, when they open the door, the girl is gone. What happened to the girl?"

The answer: "The radiator." The *radi ate her*.

That riddle has come back to me now as I sit here on the edge of Javitz's hospital bed. The snow outside batters the windows like a flock of suicidal gulls. It's one of Boston's infamous blizzards, the kind that slicks roads within instants, that drops five feet of snow in an hour. Javitz is my ex-lover. This is his second time in the hospital this winter. He's forty-seven—a terribly old age for me to contemplate ever being.

I'm sitting here now, remembering that riddle, and Javitz asks me about Richard Nixon.

"They're making quite a fuss, aren't they?" he says, watching the TV that's hooked up on the wall. It's Nixon's funeral, and some soldiers are handing Tricia and Julie an American flag.

"It's all very tragic," I say.

"What is? He was eighty-one."

"No, I mean, his life. The disgrace and all."

Javitz makes a sour face. "He was a crook. You don't remember. You're too young."

"I remember watching him resign," I protest. I was twelve, on summer vacation between seventh and eighth grade. My mother remained a die-hard supporter right to the bitter end; we both cried watching the resignation on the little black-and-white TV in the kitchen while she peeled potatoes for supper.

"You don't remember all the terrible things he did. Nobody seems to anymore. He would've been as bad as Reagan on gays and AIDS and all that stuff. Maybe worse."

"How could anybody be worse than Reagan?" I ask.

Javitz closes his eyes. "Luise Rainer was," he says. Talking about politics wearies him fast these days. "Especially in *The Good Earth*."

"I'll say," I laugh. "And they gave her *two* Oscars."

"Count 'em," he says.

"*Two*," we say in unison.

He takes a deep breath, eyes still closed. "We should do a Luise Rainer video festival this summer in Provincetown. What do you think?"

I consider it. Every summer for the last five years, Javitz, Lloyd, and I have rented a place in Provincetown, that little spit of sand at the end of Cape Cod farther away from the rest of the world than anywhere else. How we've managed to do this, I don't know—Javitz on his adjunct faculty pay, Lloyd still in grad school, me barely making enough income to pay taxes. But every year, each of us writes down on a slip of paper the top limit of what we can afford, and then we toss the slips together and add them up. Somehow this quirky little experiment in socialism has worked for us every time.

Once there, we rent old movies—our shared passion—and invite the neighbors. A Dietrich night, a Cukor festival, a Liz Taylor cavalcade.

"All right," I tell Javitz now. "But I can't imagine who'd come to see Luise Rainer."

"Round up your little boys," he says, and his smirk looks even more devious with his eyes closed. "We can tell them she was a great actress. They'll believe anything."

"What's your name?" the boy is asking.

"Jeff," I tell him. "Yours?"

"Eduardo."

We shake hands. Our eyes hold.

And so, another one.

Loving strangers is a heady mix of romance and reality, the sordid and the sublime. I have returned this summer for that mist of sweat across a boy's bronzed back, for the magic that happens when the two of us marry eyes across a dance floor and become forever young.

"Can I still get away with it?" I asked Javitz before I left tonight.

He laughed. "Maybe for another year."

Once, Javitz and I were lovers, when my skin was soft and unmarked like the boy Eduardo's. My face then was not the one that stares back at me now from my mirror, the little pinched lines around my eyes like the marks my mother used to make in the crust of her apple pies. My current lover Lloyd tells me I'm being absurd, that at thirty-two I still have many years left. But I see his own surreptitious look in the mirror, notice the tweezers he's left behind on the sink surrounded by a scattering of bristly gray hairs. Once, we were the boys of the moment, angry young men marching through the streets in black leather jackets covered with crack-and-peel slogans: "Act Up! Fight Back! Get Used to It!" Javitz and his generation had smiled indulgently at us. "Ah, youth," they had sighed. But how quickly our energy dissipated, how quickly boys are replaced. The hair on my head thins out, while in my ears it sprouts cocky as crab-grass. My body might be pumped from an afternoon in the gym, but one hundred crunches a day can no longer dispel gravity's influence on my waist.

"And then what?" I asked Javitz, replying to his comment, trying to mask the honesty of the question.

"I'll see you at Spiritus," was all he said.

That he will still join me there takes courage. Spiritus Pizza is the late-night joint where men gather after the bars have closed, hoping for one last chance to evade the damnation of an empty guesthouse bed. It is not a place for the weak at heart.

Javitz is not weak. He is a tall, striking man, with long black hair and intense dark eyes. Once, when we were lovers, I thought he was the handsomest man in the world, but now we're not lovers anymore, and I no longer think that. We talk little about why I broke up with him; but it's there, every time Lloyd peels off his shirt in front of us to lie in the sun, his skin still tight, his stomach flat. It's there every time I get dressed to go out tricking, and the boys I bring home become younger and younger. Javitz is well known in Provincetown, and back home in Boston, too. "A leading activist," one newspaper account called him, "an icon of the gay community." But it's his loss of muscle tone that makes him stand out from the crowd at Spiritus now, the predictable result of years of antivirals: shapeless calves, spindly arms. And not long ago he witnessed what happened to one man—near fifty, near bald—who dared to assume he could still come out and play.

"Did you smile at me?" this man had asked me, standing on the steps of the pizza joint.

"Sure," I offered.

"Are you trying to pick me up?" he asked.

I was taken aback. "No," I told him.

"No," he echoed, darkening. "Of course not." He visibly slumped, shoulders sagging, like a tire slashed.

A boy beside me began to giggle. "They're going to find him washed up on shore in the morning," he whispered to me.

And they might as well have.

Growing old is not for sissies, Bette Davis once said. But sissies *do* get older. All of us sissies here tonight, with the hot juice of youth pulsing through our veins. Some of us are already well on our way. But what does it matter, Javitz says. Get old or get AIDS: the result is the same. Especially here, in this place: this place of sculpted pectorals and shaven torsos, heads thick with hair and bodies jumping with T cells. But the first wrinkle, or the first purple blotch on your leg, and you are exiled. We rarely question the banishment, dismissing any who try.

"How old are you?" Eduardo asks, as if it were the next logical question in our conversation.

"How old do you think?"

"Twenty-eight?" Last year, it probably would've been twenty-six, but it's good enough; it's what I want to hear.

"Around there," I lie. "And you?"

"Twenty-two," Eduardo responds.

Who has ever been twenty-two? I ask myself. Not me. Not ever. If I ever was, I don't remember. Yet every summer, a new crop is twenty-two, standing at the cusp of the dance floor as if they were the first ones ever here.

"Do you want to dance?" Eduardo asks suddenly, as if it were an original idea that had just struck him.

My line: "Sure."

And so we dance, the prelude to the sex I know will come, predicting the choreography in my bedroom just a short time from now: back and forth, round and round, up and down. We're all one big writhing mass of human flesh out here under the lights: male flesh, young flesh, raw bodies and sweat, humping together, wet luminescent backs sliding against each other, nudging shoulders, hands massaging chests where hard stubble sprouts like rough grass, all of us pushing, shoving, grinding, grunting. I'm reminded of the time the bar threw an underwear party. I came on the dance floor: hands in my Calvin Kleins, hands fighting each other for a turn, hands, hands, hands without faces, and I came onto the floor to prove I still could.

"So what is it that you do?" Eduardo shouts over the music. The inevitable question. My answer will distance us. I'm no houseboy, no clerk at the scrimshaw shop.

"I'm a writer," I say.

Whenever I tell boys that I am a writer, they always respond in the same way. They appear to believe that this is significant, that they should somehow be impressed. "What do you write about?" they always ask in response, as Eduardo does now, a ridiculous question, one for which there is no answer. So I always say, as I do now: "Whatever I can."

Eduardo smiles. He knows he can go no further. He's in over his head.

Was from the start.

The snow blasts the windows again. "Jeff," Javitz says.

"What?"

"Do you remember when we were at Hands Around the Capitol?"

"Yes," I say.

"I tricked with that guy. What was his name?"

"James."

"Oh, yeah. Is he dead?"

"How would I know?"

"I was just wondering." He closes his eyes. "Ask Lloyd. Maybe he knows. He tricked with him, too."

This is Javitz's newest trick: thinking of someone for no apparent reason, someone we met briefly years ago or some friend of his I've never known, and wondering out loud if they're dead. Sometimes I know; sometimes I don't.

But Javitz isn't going to die. Not yet. I sit here, thinking about little girls trapped in rooms with malevolent radiators waiting to gorge themselves on their flesh, and I know that yet again, Javitz will come home, and this time, he'll be able to do a little less for himself than before. And then he'll get sick again, and back here we'll come, and then home again—just as it has been for the last eight years. The curse of the long-term survivor, Javitz calls it.

And of the long-term friend.

Immediately, I feel guilty. What—I'd rather he just die now, and get it over with? I look at him. He's closed his eyes again but I don't think he's asleep. No, I don't want him to die. But what does it matter, he himself would ask, since we already know he's going to—not soon, perhaps, but not many decades from now either, the way it's supposed to happen, when we're both old and gray (he older and grayer than I).

How senseless all of this is. Which is why, I think, my mother's riddle has come back to me now. And why it has terrified me all these years. It didn't make any *sense*, and mothers were *supposed* to make sense. I mean, if what happened to the girl was that the "radi" ate her—what is a *radi*? If that syllable had had some double meaning—slang for rhinoceros or something—it would have carried some logic that would have made the riddle clever. But "radi" means nothing, so how could a "radi" eat her?

Thus I had an image of this heinous radiator coming to life like some mad creature out of Stephen King, and devouring the poor girl. I saw it straining at its bolts and its hot, burning iron elongated into claws, looming over the girl before consuming her into its steaming mouth.

But now, as I sit here and watch Javitz drift in and out of sleep, I think the reason the riddle so frightens me is not so much the monstrous radiator, but the image of the poor girl shut up in a room with no windows, with no way to get out—abandoned, left to die, forgotten. They put her in there and left her all alone, defenseless. And my mother had the nerve to ask: "What happened to the girl?"

Hah. As if she didn't know.

"Aw, yeah, man."

His nipples taste salty, and I test them with my teeth. Eduardo moans softly in appreciation. Rare that a boy's nipples should be so sensitive. Usually takes years.

He's stretched across my bed, still in his vest and shorts. I lick the hollow space between his taut pectorals: smooth warm skin, tasting bitterly of sunblock. He has a fit of passion: grabbing me from behind my head he pulls me down to his mouth, and we kiss hard, clinking teeth, an accidental toast. He rolls over on top of me and kneads my chest, playing top for as long as I let him.

Now his vest is on the floor and my shirt is gone, and we're kicking off our shoes. That's always the most awkward part: the shoes. Unlacing trendy boots—black Doc Martens on him, clunky workboots on me—takes time, and pulling them off of sweaty feet, with moist, unyielding socks, is work. But we manage. He helps me with mine, even going so far as to pretend to lick the scuffed brown leather of my right boot. Oh, how boys like to pretend they're into things that will in reality take them *years* to appreciate. We're soon just in our cut-off denim shorts, legs entangled.

His energy excites me, urges me on. I decide it's time to claim my place on top, wrestling Eduardo underneath me. I grab hold of his nipples and clamp down, little fleshy knobs between my forefingers and thumbs. He groans. I sidle up over his chest and shove my crotch in his face. He bites the faded denim. "Suck it," I tell him, and he moans again.

I wonder how many cocks this twenty-two year old has sucked in his life. Even as he's unbuttoning my fly, I'm doing arithmetic. Even in a moment of such passion, I'm still up on the ceiling looking down. He's twenty-two. Born when I was twelve. When Nixon resigned. He was *five* when I sucked my first cock. *Five*.

But he knows what to do. How *do* boys learn these things? How did I learn?

(His name was Gordon. One of my two best friends in high school. "You've done this before?" Gordon asked. *He* had, of course: with our other buddy, Stick. "Sure," I lied. "Mmm, that's good," he told me, vindicating my make-believe.)

I ease Eduardo up and kiss him. I taste my own cock in his mouth. "You're so nice," he murmurs into my ear, and I bite his neck.

Now he's straddling me, playing with my nipples while I stroke my dick and reach up now and again to lick the head of his. He groans, "Aw, yeah," as I shoot—long stringy ejaculations of white that torpedo across the bed and make me proud. *See that, kid?* Go ahead and *try* to shoot that far. Just try.

He does. And almost succeeds. But I still win.

Then I'm exhausted. "Man," I say, falling back into the pillows.

He lies down next to me, on his side, his nose to my ear. This is the point where they always want to cuddle. Did I say the shoes were the most awkward part? *No*: this is.

"Are you one of those types who kicks a guy out after having sex?" Eduardo says, half-teasingly.

I look at the digital clock next to the bed glowing green in the dust-colored darkness. It's 3:25 A.M. "If you want to stay, you can."

I'm distant. I'm a jerk. He picks up on it. "Do *you* want me to?" he asks in a little voice.

"You should know something," I say.

"Don't tell me. You have a boyfriend."

"Yes," I tell him.

"I knew it."

He sits up in bed.

This, too, is part of the script.

Lloyd—that's my boyfriend—was supposed to come with me to Beth Israel tonight to see Javitz but he got beeped at the last minute. He's a psychologist over at Mass General. Mom always wanted my sister to grow up and marry a doctor; I beat her to it. "Tell Javitz for me," Lloyd said, "he better not die or anything when I'm not there."

Lloyd loves Javitz in a way I can't: free of guilt, free of a history that lingers between us. I envy that love. What must it be like, I wonder, when there's nothing that hangs around in the back of your mind, like dirty socks in a closet, their existence unseen but their presence always known?

Right now the blizzard is whooping and hollering outside like a gang of boys on the street late at night, flushed with booze and hormones.

"How are you feeling?" I whisper to Javitz, who's opened his eyes.

"Tired."

"Yeah, me too," I say. We've watched Nixon's funeral three times on CNN.

"I wonder if I'll see Richard Nixon when I die," Javitz is saying.

Wouldn't make much sense if you do, I'm thinking. The young and the old going to the same place. Big-time crooks and a guy who always counted his change and returned extra pennies. Republicans and angry AIDS activists living together for eternity in a place called "after."

But Javitz doesn't believe in a heaven or a hell. Maybe it's because he's Jewish, and the Jews are pretty ambiguous on this point. But Javitz isn't religious. He just believes in an "after." "Sure," he'd say, when questioned about an afterlife. "This is before. That will be after."

But none of this makes sense. Bad guys don't go to heaven.

Radiators don't eat girls. Generations don't disappear. And people don't break up with lovers they really love.

I love Lloyd. What has been lost in the fires of early passion has been replaced by an enduring respect, affection, friendship. I love Javitz in a different way—always have and always will. I met Javitz when I was just twenty-two, the same age as Eduardo, the boy I fell in love with last summer in Provincetown. Javitz was thirty-six when I met him, just a little older than I am today. He seemed so old to me then: but old in a good way—a way these boys I trick with must see me. An older brother who's still young enough to fuck, but old enough to explain what's going on. Before Javitz all I had been looking for was a place to put my dick. Wide-eyed, eager, and horny, I was new to Boston, having arrived for my grad program at Emerson with all the zest any boy feels upon his first move to a real city. I met Javitz at a poetry reading by Allen Ginsberg, the very first poetry besides Dr. Seuss I'd ever heard read out loud. But what excited me more was the prospect of the boys who would undoubtedly show up. I wasn't disappointed. There were plenty of boys, but it was Javitz who caught my notice, Javitz with his long black hair and smoke-chewed laugh, and the magnificent way he saw right into my terror.

"You there," he said, across the cheese and crackers. I raised my eyebrows questioningly. "Yes, you." He grinned. "You look as if you need someone to show you around."

I did, of course. We made a date for the next night. He took me to dinner at an Italian restaurant in North Boston, with red and white checked tablecloths and carafes of red wine. He promised to show me gay Boston, and if I wanted, gay New York, too, sometime. "Sure," I agreed, awestruck, sitting across the table from him. He knew so much, had been to so many places. I remember how my hair kept falling in front of my eyes as we talked. It was so thick then.

"How old are you?" he asked, sitting back in his chair.

"Twenty-two," I told him.

"Twenty-two? Who has ever been twenty-two?" he sighed grandly.

"You, I imagine," I said, trying to be cute. "Once."

It worked. He winked at me, and both of us were hooked. "So," he asked, next question: "Are you out?"

I lied, of course, and told him yes. Isn't it funny? No one's ever closeted when you ask them. But Javitz, as I was to discover, was a big-time activist.

He has pictures of the very first New York Gay Pride parade in an old photo album. They're pasted down with those little black corner holders, and they show Javitz—back when he was still David Mark Javitz from the Bronx—in his big fuzzy Afro with peace signs dangling from around his neck. A decade later, when he moved here to Boston, he was the first to be arrested for civil disobedience in an AIDS action in front of the State House. I went with him to the planning meeting where he volunteered to do it. Talking about getting arrested made me nervous, but Javitz assured us he'd gone to jail before: he'd been in the civil rights protests during the sixties.

"I was in *third grade* during the sixties," an ACT UP boy with seven piercings through his nose had teased.

"The *entire decade*?" Javitz responded, unruffled. He was fond of saying: "Youth is nothing but an instant in time when we don't know what the fuck we're doing but we believe ever so earnestly in the importance of doing it."

Right now, I can't remember why I broke up with Javitz. I was twenty-six. He'd just turned forty. Maybe that had something to do with it. We lasted not quite four years. I was twenty-six. He was forty. Maybe that was it. But it's hardly enough of an answer: we don't talk much about it, so maybe we'll never know. I do know that I felt a little like a captain deserting his ship, although no one could ever imagine Javitz away from the wheel. Besides, the ship wasn't sinking: Javitz had yet to get very sick, and when he did, I was there. With Lloyd.

"When I get out," Javitz says now, drawing my attention back to him, "we need to get up to Provincetown, start hunting for a summer place."

I nod.

"And then it starts, all over again," he says, looking at me. He gestures with his hand for mine. I take it. "Are you ready?"

"As best as I can be."

"Good," he says, smiling. "That's all they can ask for."

Eduardo is huffing. I hear the caterwauling of boys out on the street, whooping about something. For a moment, I wonder if they're cute, cuter than Eduardo. Off in the distance, the soulful sound of the fog horn, warning ships not to come too close to this place.

"I can't believe you have a boyfriend," he says. "Why didn't you tell me this before?"

"It wasn't relevant," I say. I know my lines.

"What do you mean it wasn't relevant?"

"I mean it's okay," I say. "Lloyd does it, too. It's okay."

Eduardo is shaking his head. "Well, not for me."

"So when *you're* in a relationship, be monogamous."

"You don't get it. I don't sleep with married men."

"Well," I laugh, "you just did." I reach over, putting my arm around him and sitting real close. "Listen, just because I have a boyfriend doesn't mean I can't get to know other people. That's the beauty of being gay. Not being fenced in by definitions, restrictions. I really enjoyed myself tonight. And I'd like to see you again."

"Why?"

Good question. Because you have the most beautiful nipples? Because you give good head? "Because I like you," I say.

"I'm not just looking for sex," he says, in that righteous voice boys use when they are attempting to stand firm for some principle in which they think they believe.

"So you were hoping we'd get *married*?" I ask, with emphasis on the incredulity.

It works. He sounds suitably embarrassed. "No, no," he says, looking away. "But I always hope that every new guy—"

"Every new guy?" I repeat, as if to say: "*Hah!* See?"

"You know what I mean," he says, and of course, I do. Twenty-two year olds need to believe they're no different from what their parents expected them to be. They might be gay, but they're still in search of their parents' lives. Sex is something to be rationalized, even though they're all fucking like little queer bunnies. Sex is the first thing we think of when we come out,

Javitz once told me, and the last. It's hormones that first kick open the closet, but it's our eventual embrace of that primal drive that allows us to finally slam the door behind us, the definitive awareness that we're different from our parents, indeed, from the rest of the world. But it'll take these boys at least until they're thirty to figure this out. It did for me.

So why do I bother? "Do you know how old I am?" I ask, breaking my own rule.

"Twenty-eight," he says, puzzled.

"I'm *thirty-three*." I don't add that come August, I'll be thirty-four.

"No way," he says, and I imagine he's as shocked to learn he's just tricked with a thirty-three year old as he is a married man.

"Yes way," I reply, somewhat regretful of my impulsive confession.

Eduardo smiles. "You look great for thirty-three," he says.

"Thanks. And you look great for twenty-two." I kiss him, hard and deep, on the mouth, to prove that I'm really not such a bad guy. In seconds, he's ready to go again, boyfriend or not. I could kick myself for reigniting his dick: once a night is usually as much as I can handle these days. *Why do I try? Why do I persist?* I'm asking myself as he starts nibbling on my sensitive nipples again. I can almost hear Javitz laughing in the other room.

The snow is letting up. I wonder for a moment if it might actually be over, the storm.

"I hate the winter," I tell Javitz.

He shifts under the thin white sheets. His butt is sore from too much bed time. "That's because you're a summer baby," he says. "Like me."

Javitz's birthday is the day before mine: August 6 and August 7. He jokes that he'll admit to being older than I am: by a day. But the decade between Javitz and me is nearly equal to the decade between me and the boys with whom I most frequently trick. They—bright-eyed little things that they are—look at him across the breakfast table the next morning with a sense of wonder: *who is this man?*

Many have wondered the exact same thing. "What *do* the three of them do together in that house?" the Provincetown gadflies whisper. "Are the two younger ones his slaves? Or is he just their sugar daddy?"

They see us walking together down Commercial Street, shoulder to shoulder to shoulder, Javitz in the middle, the tallest of the three. "Didn't one of the younger ones date the older one for a while? Which one is which? Do you *know*?"

"The older one," a neighbor once told a friend, "is merely trying to relive his own lost youth."

"The younger ones," said another, "are just waiting for the will to be read."

"How to disentangle the myths of age?" Javitz sighed dramatically, sitting on our deck two summers ago, waving his cigarette.

I responded in kind: "How to explain to a world fixated on the paradigm of two the power of three?"

These are the discussions we have, late into the night. I laugh at our pomposity. We like the sound of our voices in the stillness of the night as we solve the problems of the world. I turn these conversations into essays for the queer and alternative press. That's how I make my living, as a freelance journalist. I roll the ideas around in my head, like dough in sugar and cinnamon, thinking them through in odd snatches of the day, at the grocery store, at the gym, between tricks or loads of laundry. Then I bring them up again with Javitz and Lloyd: "I was thinking—" I say, and we pontificate some more.

This is who we are. This is my family—audacious maybe, but constant and unconditional. This is what nourishes me. When my mother turned her back on me, I lost the family into which I was born. But it's what came after that matters—Javitz, Lloyd, and I, a new family, ill-served by definition, constantly changing and accommodating itself. Three working-class boys—Javitz from the Bronx, Lloyd from a farm in Iowa, me from a dried-up little factory town in Connecticut—living beyond our means in a succession of summer houses in the rarefied resort of Provincetown, trusting always in the sustaining power of three.

The images are always there, at the flick of a switch in my mind. Javitz on the back of a motorcycle, riding sidesaddle, being dropped off at 7:00 A.M. by a trick on his way to work. "Who d'you think you are, worrying us all night?" Lloyd asks, only half-teasing. Javitz shakes his long black hair, the curly ringlets still wet from a shower at the biker's house. He adores the attention: "I've never ridden on the back of a motorcycle before," he gushes. "I felt like Nancy Sinatra in *The Wild Angels.*"

Javitz with a tray of raspberry croissants as we get up in the morning: Lloyd and me, Lloyd with a trick, me with Eduardo or Raphael or the kid from the tea dance whose name I failed to get. "Good morning," Javitz says, and the tricks stare in wonder. Would they like a cup of coffee? "Or do you *drink* coffee?" he wonders. Only *I* get the dig.

"Who *is* that man?" they ask again later, as I kiss them goodbye and send them on their way. I just smile—for how can I tell them?

I feel caught in a sticky web that connects two separate worlds: the Boom and the X generations, pre- and post-Stonewall, positive and negative, old and young. But what am I then, if not either? Javitz once said it was my role to bridge the gap, to connect with the children and tell them about what came before. This strange link that I provide, this tenuous grip on history: What good will it do when we too—the ill-defined inbetweeners—are dead? Once I thought only Javitz's generation would disappear, but I was wrong. The boys I knew when I was a boy, the ones who first invited me onto the dance floor, back in 1982 and 1983, in those heady quixotic days when nobody believed it would last this long—they're disappearing too. Sometimes I think I see them, standing there among the children. I'll spot someone on the other side of the dance floor, and I'll think it's Gordon, or Stick, my high-school buddies, the ones I came out with, the kids with feathered-back hair and wide ties whose faces, even now, stare eternally in black and white from the glossy pages of our yearbooks. But I'm wrong: it's never them. I wonder if they're waiting for me, if that's why I've seen them.

But that's not what I fear anymore, not really. I don't know if I have the virus. Last time I was tested I didn't—but that was seven years ago. Still, I haven't been fucked without a condom since 1984, Lloyd even longer. Neither one of us plans on being retested unless it's absolutely unavoidable. What would be the point? To die from an antiviral? If Lloyd were to get sick, I imagine, that would be that, the end of the line for me. What was it that the Wicked Witch of the West said? "The last to go will see the others go before her."

"I'm feeling stronger tonight," Javitz says, shattering my reverie.

I thought he had fallen asleep. I'm still holding his hand, I realize. His words send a weariness all through my body. I look over at Javitz and realize the nurse must think we're lovers. And we are, of course—even though I broke up with him. Yet here he is, holding my hand, never letting go, when I would have thrown it away from me as fast as I possibly could, bitter and resentful at being cast aside for a younger man. But not Javitz: a sign of strength or of weakness, I don't know. Yet it hardly matters: it took courage, either way.

And now he's asleep, his breathing so much easier than it's been for the last few nights, the infection in his lungs apparently beaten. Maybe tomorrow Lloyd and I will come to pick him up, and maybe next week we all will pile into the car and head up the Cape, searching for another house and another year, grateful but also fatigued by yet another chance, another summer, always wondering how many more. But this summer, none of us will be young.

Me least of all.

Eduardo sleeps, finally, like an angel, a child actor in a Nativity play. Adorable. My heart is breaking, as I knew it would. Tomorrow he'll be gone, and I'll miss him terribly. As if he were the greatest love of my life. And maybe he is. Maybe all of them are. Raphael, from last summer, became an ideal only after he'd returned home to Montreal. Javitz remembered that while Raphael was still here in Provincetown, I'd twice not wanted to take his calls. But once he was gone, he became the boy who got away, the boy who stole my heart, the boy I never was.

And now Eduardo. Who *are* these children? I can't sleep. His sweet breathing is driving me crazy. I slip out of bed and pad through the quiet three-room flat. It's a hot dry stretch of late June, a respite from weeks of dripping humidity. From the deck overlooking the bay, I smell cigarette smoke. Javitz is outside, smoking, watching the inky waves lick the eroding beach like a sick kitten. The moon is high, and the stars are out, scattered across a dark gray sky. The only sound is the foghorn from Long Point—the saddest sound I know: the call of the men who trudge on back to their guesthouses alone, rejected even by the desperate outside Spiritus at 2:00 A.M.

"Hey," I whisper, respectful of the night and Javitz's space.

He turns, exhaling smoke. "All done?" he smirks.

I smile. "He's asleep."

"A name?"

"Eduardo."

"I caught a glimpse as you came in. Beautiful."

I nod, sitting on a deck chair, propping my feet up on a small table. "And so *young*."

"How young?"

"Twenty-two."

Javitz sighs dramatically. "Are there such things as twenty-two year olds anymore?"

"One's sleeping in my bed right now. Go take a look." I close my eyes. "What did *you* do tonight?"

"Went to the dunes. Got fucked twice."

"Really?" My eyes are open now. "Is that why you're not sitting down?"

He laughs. "And neither of them was twenty-two," he tells me, hardening his lips. "When are you going to sleep with a *man*?"

"I *do*," I say, cattily. "His name is Lloyd."

"*Other* than your boyfriend," Javitz says, archly.

"I *should* probably try," I admit. "All these kids want is love and marriage."

"This one too? Already?"

I nod.

"They've got it easy," Javitz says, exhaling smoke. "All they're looking for are boyfriends."

"They all think they're so far advanced—'Oh, I've been out since I was fourteen,' or 'I brought my boyfriend to my junior prom.' But they don't know anything about being gay. You know, I hate this age I'm at: stuck in the middle. A foot in both camps. You on one side, the kid in my bed on the other. Sometimes it feels as if I'm on a merry-go-round and it keeps going faster and faster and everything around me is getting all blurry and I can't make out what side I'm on anymore. It's like everything is spinning out of control, like at the end of *Strangers on a Train.*"

"You were like him once."

"No, I wasn't." I've thought about this. "I knew all of you guys. He doesn't." I laugh. "Who does he have to teach him how to be gay?"

"You?" I can't tell if he's being sarcastic. "Here's a test," he says. "Go in and ask him to explain the difference between Blanche Hudson and Blanche Dubois."

I laugh. "But that's just it. I can't expect him to know. Those old movies were yours to share with me. They aren't mine."

He sighs. "I imagine there *will* come a time when gay men know Judy Garland exclusively from *The Wizard of Oz.* Who do the queens do up here now in their acts? Madonna? Joan Rivers? *Oprah?* What a loss." He takes a long, melodramatic drag on his cigarette.

"I thought you were trying to quit," I say.

"I've decided I want to die of lung cancer," he answers, deadpan, and then guffaws, that hoarse, throaty laugh that sounds like a fork caught in the garbage disposal, a laugh I don't think I'll ever be able to forget, not even when Javitz has been dead for thirty years.

I'm smiling. "Wouldn't *that* get them?" I say. "Javitz died of *what?* Lung cancer?"

"AIDS activist succumbs to cigarettes," Javitz laughs. Now wouldn't *that* be something?

"What should I do?" I ask. "The kid's asleep in my bed. I can't sleep next to someone unless it's Lloyd."

"You need to decide what kind of a summer it is you want," Javitz says, suddenly serious.

"Yes, yes," I say, annoyed at the lecture.

"Youth isn't the only instant in time in which we don't know what the fuck we're doing."

I know he means himself as well as me. This summer, next— the winter in between. What is it that we want from them? From each other? How much time do we have?

"It's so weird," I say to him. "Sometimes it feels as if I'm this survivor of a spaceship wreck on another planet. I manage to camouflage myself and fit in, but I know I'm just biding my time, because eventually they'll discover me—like Donald Sutherland did to Veronica Cartwright at the end of *Invasion of the Body Snatchers*."

"Dawling," Javitz says, and when he wants to make a point, as he does now, his Bronx accent becomes thicker, "the merry-go-round metaphor worked, but barely. Now your symbolism is showing. You're a writah. You can do bettah than that."

I sneer, "Can I?" I've been having a miserable time writing ever since I got here last week. I've produced nothing.

"Yes," he says, serious now, "you *can*."

"Aye, aye, sir," I say.

"And Lloyd will be here tomorrow," he advises, "perhaps early."

"You know, I want to go in, wake Eduardo, and ask him if he's ever seen *All About Eve*."

He arches an eyebrow. "And if he hasn't?"

"Kick him out," I smile.

"Why don't you try something easier? Like *The Wizard of Oz*?"

I stand up. "All right. I'll give him a break."

I leave Javitz to his cigarettes and lung cancer. It's almost 5:00 A.M. I'll be up in a few hours. Have breakfast with the kid. Send him on his way. Get down to writing. Wait for Lloyd. I know the routine. I know the tricks of the trade.

Yet when I open the door, Eduardo is gone.

I feel as if I've been punched in the gut. The sheets are still warm and the scent of his semen haunts the room. I look around. There is nothing in the room but a bed, a dresser, a pair of dumbbells, my boots on the floor, and the cold dusty radiator against the wall.

And I have the nerve to ask what happened to the boy?

Hah. As if I didn't know.

CRACK

• KEVIN MARTIN •

The Sixth Avenue Liquor Store still had that two-for-one deal on my brand, Joe Camel Wide Lights in the hard pack, so I got two, of course. As I walk out, he's right behind me, so I'm standing there on the street, on the corner, and I don't notice him till he says, "What are you gonna do with that extra pack?" I wheel around without looking, not even seeing him, before I say, "Smoke 'em, what would you do?" I see his face, nothing special, but skin so dark it nearly reflected the afternoon sun, white eyes with black-ringed irises, lids hanging over them and a little half smile showing mostly straight teeth, one gold cap and before I knew it I was off, already I could feel the tingles in my groin. My dick starting to get stiff made me shift my legs, and I went a little weak in the knees, stumbled just a bit toward him but caught myself right then, didn't want to give anything away, could be dangerous, but that *smile*. I was fumbling so much with the cellophane binding the two packs together that before he even could answer me back, I held both of them out to him and said, "If you can get 'em apart better 'n me, one of 'em's yours."

He took them from my hand, his long, thin fingers just grazing mine and sending goosebumps up my arm. He found the tab on the cellophane and pulled, separating the two packs, opened one and tapped two cigarettes out, put one between his lips and then, fingers on the unfiltered end of the other, steadily pushed it to my lips, through the space he forced, across my teeth and into my mouth. I had the matches so I lit one and brought it to his cigarette. He steadied my hand, his fist circling my wrist, then let it go, puffing out a ball of white smoke into the air between us. He says, "Say, friend, I'm fresh out till my check comes in next Monday. Can you spring for some beers?" I squinted, gave him the eye. I had eighty bucks, less the two and change for the cigarettes, and that had to get me through till next payday. But his eyes were on me, steady, and I was still feeling that pressure between my legs. Really, I had nothing going on and a six is a buck and a half or not much more for Bud or Old Milwaukee, and besides, my shorts aren't so baggy that he couldn't see that hard prong chafing the metal on my zipper, poking through my boxers. Man, he had me. "Yeah, I guess so," I said, and we went back into the liquor store, straight down the middle aisle. I was reaching for the case nearest me, but he slipped through, opened the one on the right, and picked up a six of Corona and some forty ozs. of malt. He was almost at the counter before he looked back over his shoulder. I hadn't even left the cases, stunned, but he hissed, "Come on, man," and I made my way up to the counter.

These two Korean guys, they both looked at us from behind the counter with their eyes narrow. They're never friendly to me anyway—I'm just some white face on Washington Avenue—but they just stopped everything when we came back in together. My beer hustler, whatever his name, all of a sudden he was in this breathless rush. "Pay the man—shit!" He put the beer on the counter in front of the bulletproof panel, took the cigarette out of his mouth and punched it in the air in my direction. "Come on, man, got things to do!" I looked at the beer and the men behind the counter. The older one stood behind the shorter, stockier young one, who said, "Must see I.D. from both of you. Both I.D. now please!" I handed mine over out of my billfold, careful to shield my cash out of sight. He reached into the front pocket of his jeans. I saw then, thin as he was, taut belly under that T-shirt, dotted boxers showing above the waist band of his baggy, slouched jeans, that he was definitely something special in the dick department. I couldn't take my eyes off it. That mound ran down farther than his hand reached into his pockets, pulling out bits of paper, gum wrappers, raggy pink Kleenex, some other stuff he pushed back in before it came out, and a old, dog-eared state I.D.

My face flushed and a fever rose up to my ears. I felt dizzy in the presence of a dick that, soft, seemed to go down to his mid-thigh. I couldn't make out the name on his I.D. before he passed it to the men behind the partition. They handed mine back to me right away but held onto his, poring over it, whispering between them looking at the photo, then at the man by my side. Christ, I thought, it's just beer, and I'm paying, what's the fucking problem? He looked back at them, silent, nothing on his face, hands gripped at his side, cigarette taut in his right fist, breathing through his teeth. "What your name is?" the younger one demanded. "It's on the paper, man," he said, eyebrows burring up and eyelids raised. I respected him for that. "We know —you tell us." "It's Glendon Thomas Cooper," he said, and, under his breath, "like you can read."

"And what you birthday?" You could see his nostrils flare, but his expression didn't change a bit. "August 3, 1969." It came out like steam. Their eyes bore into him for another minute, then they tossed the I.D. back into the change retriever. So maybe he was a familiar face, and maybe he wasn't a regular customer—who knew? The Asians behind the counter didn't let up. Anyway, I was paying, which I'm sure they knew because they looked in my direction when they said, "Eight dollars and sixty-six cents," which made me break the ten dollars I'd just gotten in change a minute ago. I slipped my last three twenties into my front pocket with my change, trying to look cool. The Koreans were staring at me, like they wanted to say something, who knew what, and who cared. They were too rude. Glendon, or Glen, or whatever, grabbed the beers and we headed out the door. He stamped his cigarette out just inside, cut a loud fart and stepped onto the sidewalk, laughing.

"Man, fuck them Ko-reens. They just wanted to hassle me 'cause it's my birthday." I hadn't thought, but it was just a couple of days after the date he gave. I started backing up off the curb. "Well, happy birthday. Glad I could help."

"Hey, man, you got a car?" I had my keys in my hand, so I figured it wouldn't work to tell him I was going to walk the mile to my house through this neighborhood. "Uh, yeah, but I'm pretty busy." "Come on, man, give me a lift. I just stay two blocks from here. My beer'll be warm if I walk in this heat." It was his birthday, and I felt kind of sorry he got such a hassle in the store. He didn't look like a bum, and maybe it was my imagination, but I think he was showing off the profile of his crotch. "OK, my car's right here."

I popped the door and hoped he didn't think my ten-year-old Z looked too nice. It was a sweltering day, and late afternoon when the low sun just burned the sky to a white crisp. I figured a few minutes in my car couldn't be a bad thing. He put the bag between his legs and extended his hand to me as I eased my way down into my bucket seat. "They call me Tommy, usually. You might know me though," he said. "You ever watch porn?" I did, but no, I didn't recognize him from any, but, man, how did he peg me so fast? I tried not to let on. I laughed. "But they give me different names in my flicks. Sometimes people know me by that. The ones I did for Jeff Stryker they called me Long Johnson, and I did a few for Black Forest—*they* called me T. J. Jackson." Yeah, those names were a little familiar. "The white dudes up in Nebraska who buy that shit wanna hear a nigger name for they money. Shit, money's good, too. Listen, just go up Sixth here to Pico and turn right."

That was about two blocks, so I started off. Up at Pico, he said, "Go on up here to Third and take a left." As soon as we made the turn he said, "Pull over here right quick. I got to go have a word with my cousin." Before I could say, "But . . ." he'd sprinted out of the car, leaving the beer inside and the door open. I thought for a second I'd peel off from the curb, door swinging, beers flying, big U-turn and back down the boulevard to my house. But I didn't. I saw him talking through the screen door of a big old house, then he came back down off the stoop to the car, bowlegs and that cracked smile of his under those heavy lids. "I'm right around the corner." I doubted it, and I was right. Around the corner and three more blocks, past Arlington to Gramercy and up toward Eleventh Street, was an old four-story brick building with barred windows all the way up and a grimy, windblown, faded-yellow FOR RENT/SE RENTA SINGLES & BACHELORS sign hanging limply off the roof. "This is it, man. Park it here." I pulled against the curb, idling the engine. "Come on, man, turn it off. You coming up, right?" "I don't think so, I got to get goin'." "Man, it's my birthday, man, you got me the party favors, least you can do is come up for a minute, just. Let me give you a beer. You ain't got nothin' to do at four-thirty on a Saturday." He was right, that's for sure. "Well, yeah, I got time for a beer." "All right, then. Sure as shit beats the heat."

His door opened up against a small sink, the only running water in the room. To the left of the entry was a small, dorm-sized single bed, unmade. Beyond that he had a little color portable TV droning away on a stack of boxes, and behind it, more cardboard boxes stacked floor to ceiling. The only walking space, between the closet and the bed, was covered with a small braided rug. There were no chairs. He stepped in and kicked off the rubber flip-flops he was wearing. "Make yourself comfortable, Blondie. I'll pop the beers." He put the malt liquor and four of the Coronas into the fridge, placing the other two on top of the TV. Lucy Ricardo was plotting with Ethel to play a trick on the boys. I sat on the edge of the bed. Tommy lifted his T-shirt over the top of his head, baring a thin but defined chest. I could make out the ridge of his backbone and the ribs on either side of his back. He opened the beers one by one with a bottle opener and handed me one. "Where are those cigarettes, man?" I didn't answer. I just stared at the two heavy steel rings pierced through each of his nipples. He laughed, touched the heel of his beer against his right nipple. "Jeff Stryker paid for these after we wrapped *Forcible Entry*. I did a few extra cum shots for some guys who couldn't make their nut and he paid for these at the Gauntlet, on top of the cash. Come on, Blondie, where're those cigarettes?"

I fished two out of my pack, gave him one and lit them, reaching up to him standing above me, eye to crotch level next to the bed with my match. I took a drag, then sucked on my beer. Tommy looked down at me. "You don't have to just look at them. You can touch 'em." He put his arms down to his side, beer in one, smoke in the other, and thrust his wiry chest out toward me. I placed my beer on the floor, reached out with my free hand and traced the outline of his left nipple and the steel ring. "Oh, man, come on, give it some juice." He grabbed my fingers and squeezed them together over his nipple. I looked into his face, his eyes closed, reading nothing, nothing at all. I put my cigarette into my mouth and extended my other hand to his right nipple, hooking both rings with my pinkies and giving a steady, firm yank. "Pull it, man. Like you're gonna tear those suckers off." Eyes closed, he swayed back, leaning away from me to heighten the tension. I pulled, pulled, till his nipples were straight out from his chest, and he began rubbing his crotch up and down with the angled base of the beer bottle. "Yeah." He put his cigarette into his mouth and curved his palm around the fabric covering his prick. He took half a step closer to the bed, moved his hands to my shoulders and pulled me forward. "On the floor."

I knelt in front of him, putting my cigarette into the cracked ashtray at the side of the bed, curling my fingers in his belt loops and doing a hoover on the soft mound in his jeans. "Hold on," he said, springing open the top button and unhitching his belt. His loose jeans slipped off easily, down below his knees and I slid his undershorts off after them. The skin at the base of his belly and top of his thighs was chalky black, and the hairs around his crotch were glistening. His dick itself was a long, long limp boat, longer than most I'd ever seen hard. I licked that thing up and down, then fluted it as far as I could down my throat. Still, a few inches hung out. Lucy was still on, a different episode. She was sunburned, walking stiffly down a runway in a tweed jacket and skirt. "Gentle with it, man. Use your tongue."

He pulled away, stepped out of his jeans. "Listen here, man. Loosen up my hole." He laid on his back at the edge of the mattress, leaning on his shoulders. He held his legs up and open wide, displaying his asshole. I figured, Why not? I was here already. And when he got off I could jack myself off then leave. I placed my tongue at the center of his sphincter. He grabbed his cheeks and pulled them apart. He whispered, "Come on, baby, gimme a little tossed salad." It was fresh, moist, and pretty clean tasting, especially given how steamy hot it had been during the day. I dug in, giving him tongue, tooth and spit, pressing along the sides of his outer ring of muscle to open it up, his fingers pushing in alongside my tongue, and into my mouth as well. "You like that, baby? Well, watch this." He took my chin in one hand and pushed me back. With the other, he guided that big dick of his over his balls and toward his ass. I sat back on my haunches, slack-jawed, as he pressed his thick but still soft dick straight down, pulling his balls aside as he worked his dick toward his own ass. I'd never seen this before, never; photos, video, nothing. The head and a good part of the shaft extended past the opening. I watched as he took his fingers and pressed the head inside his body. A bell rang on the TV and two cute guys and a girl took a run for the border. The head submerged completely. A photo of Michael Jackson and Lisa Marie Presley, eyes covered with a newspaper. He grimaced, like it was hurting, then breathed out hard and said, "Give me a hand, man." I slid forward on the floor and pushed some of his shaft up his hole, real gentle. "Oh, man." I was sure he was wincing, so I stopped until he said, "Get up there. Put your finger in." He grabbed my hand and drew it to him. I extended my index finger and pressed on his dick, opening a groove for my finger to slip in. "Push it," he said. "Push it on in." Finally, probably three inches was up him and the rest of his shaft and root lay taut along his groin. It didn't look half bad, really. I played with it, licking it, biting it. He liked that.

A little more of that, and then he said, "I got to smoke some blow. You want some too?" He rolled himself up on the bed and slowly pulled his dick out of his body. I answered quickly, "No man, thanks. I don't do that." "Okay." He pulled a slim glass tube out of a box under his bed. Lucy was back on, in California again, hiding under a bear rug in William Holden's house while Ricky and Bill plot to play a trick on the redhead. "You don't know what you're missing." "Whatever." Maybe if he got high on this crack, I could get him off and go home. He pulled out a tiny plastic bag and handed it to me, steadied the pipe at his lips with one hand and held his lighter in the other. "Load me up, man." I'd only seen this on TV. I thought—it's crack, and I'm going to help a junkie crackhead get high. This is serious. Even if it's his birthday. Weird . . . Well, it's his body, I thought. Maybe he read my mind, because he said to me, "Get the fuck over here and load me up. You don't have to smoke it." So I pulled two small rocks out of the few in the bag and placed them on the metal screen in the pipe. He fired it up. There was a kind of crackling sound coming off the rocks. They glowed blue with their own flame. Tommy drew smoke through the length of the pipe, stopped, blew out, then quickly pulled all of the smoke into his lungs. Just a faint gray mist left in the pipe.

He held it in for a few seconds, then opened his mouth, breathed in, and said, "Kiss me." I figured it's some drug ritual to kiss whoever's around after you smoke, so I put my hand on his dick, leaned over, and placed my lips on his. He opened my lips with his tongue, then breathed out, harsh and fast, into my throat. I swallowed before I could think, and he laughed, "That your first hit of C? Tell me if you feel anything." I was speechless. In fact, it tasted like nothing. Nothing. I sat there for a second, a little disoriented—it was years since I'd taken anything, coke, whatever, and I never thought I'd be sitting next to a porn actor who'd just fucked himself and was slipping me crack in a French kiss. I waited, fearing the worst—I'd pass out, start seeing things, get paranoid or frantic. But after a few minutes, still, nothing.

So, when he held the used pipe up to me and said, "There's just a trace left. Hardly a thing. Give it a try," I surprised myself by taking the pipe right up to my own lips and firing it up myself. The smoke was hot and acrid, and I pulled it away, hacking. "Give it less fire, man," Tommy said. "Be cool with it." I drew the last wisps out of the pipe slow and smooth. Tommy took the pipe back and slipped it back into the box, then faced me, holding his dick up between his legs. "You gonna get a good taste of this dick now, baby. Get out of those clothes." I missed Lucy on TV. Three Latin guys were running around a stage in front of some big Mayan backdrop. The longhaired one was cute, but the bald guy looked sexy. And the short one—he looked like the meanest fuck of all.

I pulled off my shirt and shorts, kicked off my shoes and pulled at my socks. "Man, you are one pale motherfucker," he laughed. "Get down on the bed and let me see that ass of yours, Blondie." That seemed like a great idea to me. I ate him out, now he can return the favor, for all I care. But he didn't eat me. I heard his lighter flick and that familiar crackling sound. He took a deep inhale, then placed his lips on my ass and blew in with gale force. I'm full up to my stomach. "Keep that in, boy."

I lay there dumb, wondering just who gave him the right to pump my ass up with crack . . . but I didn't say nothing. I'm fully inflated and I heard him stand up and take another long hit, then a second. He started playing with my ass, greasing it. He said, "You're gonna feel this now," but I didn't. He bore into me. I braced myself for his dick to hurt, but it didn't. I just felt it slide in slowly, then out and in again deeper. I was sure it wasn't hard from how I felt it bending before it went in.

There's a knock at the door and Tommy pulls out, fast. He says to me, "Get behind the door." I push my clothes along the floor and stand next to the sink, starting to freak out that we were being busted. He looks through the peephole, then undoes the locks and opens the door. "It's cool, man," he says to me. I wonder, Cool for who? I'm face to face with a broad-shouldered, shaved-head big black man with dark, thick eyebrows, staring hard at me, a naked white man standing next to the sink. Tommy says, "This is my cousin, Keith. An' this my pet, Blondie. Keith has some more party favors. Get a beer, man.

"Keith, you gotta see my little blond boy's ass, look just like a pussy. Serious." "A pussy? No shit?" Tommy says, "Get on your belly and open up your ass, baby." Pussy, he says. I get my knees up on the bed and pull my cheeks apart. Tommy was showing me off for his cousin now, showing me off, I guess, like I came equipped with a pussy for his pleasure. Well, I'll give him a show, I thought. I opened my cheeks, shoulders on the bed, and worked my ass muscle open and closed. Tommy slapped my ass a few times. I liked the attention. It didn't hurt or nothing. They both laughed, and somebody wriggled a finger up my hole. "Sure as shit looks like a pussy," Keith said. I heard Tommy whisper—can he think I don't hear? "This bitch do anything. He's gonna open up that pussy and take my fist."

Then Keith says, "You got the cash for this, man?" And Tommy says, "Hold on." He runs his fingers along my back and through my legs, leans over and whispers to me, "My cousin got some really fine party favors and we're almost out, baby. If you want to party some more, you got to ante up. You got twenty bucks?" I looked up at him without saying a word. What did he think I was—crazy? I had sixty-something bucks on me, but I sure as shit wasn't going to supply his habit all night long. "Yeah," I said, "I got twenty bucks and some change I need for gas money. I'll get you the twenty." I grabbed for my shorts before Tommy could get his hands on them, fishing in the front pocket and pulling out, luckily, just one bill. "This is it, man."

Keith handed Tommy a little bag and said, "Let me fire you up with my stash." He pulled out another bag and Tommy handed him the pipe. "No, give Blondie the first blow." "No," I said. "Thanks, I'll pass." "Oh, I forgot, you like me to blow it to you. Keith, give my boy a crack kiss." Keith and Tommy sat on either side of me and Keith fired up. He took a deep blow, then leaned over and blew smoke deep inside me. Then he took one for himself. Tommy did the same, kissing me deep on the lips with that white smoke, then taking one for himself. "*Now* you're feeling something," Tommy said, pinching my nipple and pulling one of his rings at the same time. "No I'm not, I'm not feeling nothing . . . but, uh, it does kinda feel like my ass is opening up by itself." It was true. I had this sensation that some ghost or something was placing gentle fingers on my ass, that pussy they were talking about, and spreading me open.

"Yeah, you're feeling it." I slid my ass off the edge of the bed and Tommy knelt next to me, putting three or four fingers inside. Or something. I don't know how many, really, maybe five, who the fuck knows. It felt good to be so open. I heard Tommy say something about "up to my knuckles."

Somewhere along there Keith left, I'm not sure when. But he wasn't there later, when Tommy pulled his fingers out and said, "This stuff is *good*. Let's fire up another bowl," and I said, "Okay." He turned his head and looked at me like he was shocked. "Yeah, let's fire it up," I said, something of a shock to myself but, I figured, I'm in this far, might as well ride it to the end. "You gonna take this?" "I'll do it," I said. "Well, we're just about outa rock. If you want some, you gonna have to give me some more money. I owe it to Keith." "Uh, I might have another twenty in my pocket, I think." Tommy fished it out and pulled out another bag. He popped a large rock and two small flakes onto the screen and handed it to me. I held it up above my lips, as I'd seen them do, and started the ritual again. Draw in, hold, blow out, then a mighty suck. I held it then Frenched off blows to Tommy. He drew his own too.

I started feeling comfortable, so I leaned back and spread my legs apart. Tommy smiled and leaned over, kissing me deeply, sliding his left hand under my left leg, lifting it up and spreading my cheeks with those long fingers. Elegant, you might say. Yeah, he could do whatever he wanted. Him I trusted.

He took his time and I lay back, him digging up inside me deeper, flexing his fingers, and I opened up for him, feeling a pulse passing between us—like he had an energy coming off his fingers and he was plugging it inside me. His tongue was down inside my throat and he was feeding a steady stream of spit into me. I was completely receiving, every way, and I brought my ass up as far into the air as I could to make it easier for him to deliver himself into me. He got up to where I gasped, then he stopped. "Baby needs another rock to open up that pussy for me." The pipe went right up in my mouth, already packed. He fired me up. I drew in and waited . . . waited . . . waited . . . still I felt nothing. Nothing to ride over me, nothing to crest atop me, nothing to drown me. It was nothing. It was all nothing. Hell, I was nothing.

Seconds of pressure against my ass passed. Seconds, minutes, whatever. Hours—who could tell? I let the feelings rise and subside and then . . . then it was like a solid pop. Almost like the giving and trembling of an earthquake, cracks surfacing from beneath the silent earth.

I could feel my hole stretch, shrink, then a massive fullness in my bowels. I heard Tommy say, slowly, like breathing out air, "Man, what the hell I got. You opened up for my whole fucking hand." I felt him screwing in circles. I heard him say, to himself, I guess, "Just make it past the curve."

Tommy was moving, bellying up inside me, touching a place so deep I could feel it. Finally, I could taste it. Taste his fingers walking up inside me into my heart, into my throat, pulling, grasping, wanting more of me, more. "Yes!" he said, "Open it up, baby." I didn't know what was happening, what I was feeling—or not. There were flashes of silver on the inside of my lids. I could feel all of his arm to his hand spreading me out like the horn of plenty and I was spilling out, spilling open, and there it was, the floodgates, the tides, a blood tide of static energy, not anger, fear, shame, joy or whatever, just a wracking, roiling tide that convulsed me, it consumed me and I just started wailing. Out loud, piercing, not sure if I was laughing or crying, what I was reaching for, but there was a veil of tears pooling in my eyes and crisscrossing my cheeks. I pulled away, away from the shore and ran the current of the tide surrounding me, swimming away.

Tommy was silent. I didn't know what I was saying, even if I was saying anything. Maybe I was speaking in tongues, maybe quoting the Bible or the Torah, the Koran or the mysteries of some other holy book I didn't even know. But the pressure was going down, less and less. Tommy started to withdraw, he pulled out slowly, deliberately, delicately even. I could feel everything. I was still crying, moaning. He stood up and crossed the rug to the sink, washing his arm and hand meticulously, like a priest preparing for Mass. I watched him. First just my head, then my whole body snapped up, risen to attention, eyes wide. He said, "Baby, didn't I give you what you wanted? Didn't I give you what you been looking for?" He looked small against the corner of the room. I said Yes I said, yes.

In a daze I grabbed my stuff, pushing my feet into shoes without socks, shorts without my boxers. The rest in my arms. Tommy made no move to stop me. But I could not move fast enough. "I gotta go, man, see you later." I was out fast, running down stairs, wondering, Would he come after me? Did I want him to?

It was pitch dark in my car. The clock read 3:24 A.M. Not long to dawn.

I watched the rear-view mirror as I pulled into my parking lot, making sure the automatic gate closed me off from the street. I headed in the back, straight to my bathroom, unlading my arms straight onto the tile floor, stepping out of my clothes and into the shower.

I let the water get hot on my skin, the air turn white with steam in the dim light. Only when the water started to scald I stepped back, letting the heat drench me, my face, my chest. I turned around, let the water run rivulets down my back and into my ass cheeks, spreading them wide and washing the sticky skin around and in my hole, deeply and thoroughly. It amazed me how easily I slipped my fingers inside myself, into the passage he named for me, named my pussy. I turned the water off and stood in the tub for a moment, the air chill on my skin in the weak light of dawn.

In my bedroom I went through my pockets as I folded my shorts. Less than a dollar in change. Maybe I dropped some bills. I leaned over against the bed and again felt the skin at the kernel of my ass—my pussy. I felt the skin carefully, exploring its touch. I stippled the edge of my hole with the tip of my finger. I spread the flesh apart to feel if it would smooth. I was on my knees and shoulders again, on my bed, pulling my cheeks apart, feeling the cool air of dawn up against my ass.

I wanted to see this pussy, this source of my feeling, this power, this point where Tommy entered, spread his energy, where my energy rose, grew, expanded. This woman's power—my power. Man—woman. This red hot center. This pussy, entering. This transformed heat, something, some bright thing, from nothing.

I placed my hand mirror on the floor next to my bed and leaned back over the mattress, legs straddling the mirror, my back propping my ass in the air above the reflection. I craned my neck and shifted my weight to get a good view of my opening ass. My tea-rose pussy. Serrated folds of deep pink centered by a dark red knot, fullest in the middle. I stared into my reflection, imagining how the loose flesh around my hole could look to someone just like a pussy. I gazed hard at the deep mystery, trying to peer into the pure center of its vision, the porous separating wall of hanging skin, the bruised, slightly swollen nodes, the fringe of straggly hair, imagining the void within.

The light was getting stronger, coming up over the eastern mountains and cracking through my drawn blinds. It was going on 5 A.M. Sunday morning. The Muslim muezzin in the mosque a block over was calling the morning prayers. Soon the Mexican church across the street would be ringing its bells. Maybe I could sleep. Probably eventually. Later would be easy. I had nothing planned.

GRAHAM GREENE
IS DEAD

• ACHIM NOWAK •

For ten days life unravels as I always thought it should. A Hollywood B-movie.

It's a story of forbidden love, in a country wrenched by war, and I play the soldier without a cause, swept up in a drama so much larger than my own. Hidden passions, hidden fears, they're turned inside out, right there for everyone to see. Life is sudden and raw. And for these ten days I know the line between terror and fun, between danger and death. It is very thin indeed.

It begins with a round of phone calls, early on a Friday night. A little after seven, the Atlantic is already shielded by a dark gray mist, no shimmer from the moon, the evening veiled by squatting clouds. The ferry from Trinidad is on time, for once. I watch it slip past my line of vision toward the harbor in Scarborough. I recline on my sofa, lit only by the light from the broken reading lamp and the overheads in the kitchen. Lift the last slice of pizza from the cardboard box on the floor, the pizza from the Teaside Inn that has everything on it, onions and peppers and pineapples and mushrooms and olives and thick chunks of tomato, and the phone rings. I turn onto my stomach and reach down to the floor behind the lamp, pick up the phone.

"Have you watched the TV?" It's Tony, his voice a quiet whisper and fresh with contained excitement.

"I don't have a TV," I tell him.

"Well, it just went off the air. Someone announced that Robbie is dead, and the rest of the government is being held hostage in the Red House. They were all there for a cabinet meeting, and the Muslims are running the country now."

"What?"

"I said that Robbie is dead, and the Muslims . . ."

"Yes, I heard you."

I've been in Tobago for only three weeks now, but even I know who Robbie is: A. N. R. Robinson, the prime minister of Trinidad and Tobago, or, as the locals like to call their nation, T&T. I hold on to my receiver in a moment of sustained silence, an unwitting moment of quiet for the dead Robbie perhaps. The Atlantic slams into the boulders below the terrace; it provides my steady, unrelenting wall of sound. I feel nothing if not a certain numbness. I certainly don't know what to say.

"I don't know when I'll see you again," Tony picks up on his end, in Trinidad. The melodrama is sweeping his voice, it quivers in a low, hushed tremble. This is a man I met four days earlier, on a side street in Port of Spain, just two blocks from the Red House where the government is now under siege. We chased each other through downtown Port of Spain; before we finally stopped and talked, at the edge of Woodford Square, we marched freely through the Red House, right past the uniformed guards. It was clear, even then, that this was a country for the taking.

"The phones may go down. Anything could happen, we just don't know. If you can't get through to me, please write. Please." Tony's voice is solemn as he gives me his work address first, then the one at home. I melt as I write them down. Even after only four days I know what his gesture means. He's willing to receive my letters at home, in the house of homophobic dragon mom. Tony's twenty-nine and his mother suspects; she asks a lot of questions. But Tony isn't out. So he's willing to lie away the mail from this boy from New York. I know Tony likes me. But this is a gesture of despair.

I hang up the phone and walk onto the terrace, away from the night chirps of the frogs by the road, into the roaring sound of the sea. The phone rings again.

"Have you heard?" It's Lillian, my Puerto Rican friend from Brooklyn who's staying over in Scarborough.

"Yes, I have. What do you think?"

"Well, nobody really knows what's going on. The Muslims have taken over T&T Television, but the radio's still broadcasting. Just listen to the radio. I don't think it's going to affect us here in Tobago at all."

Lillian sounds so utterly calm. I'm a little disappointed. I'm in Tobago, and I want to be affected. I want to throw myself into the heart of this unfolding drama. Hold a hostage in my own little Red House, dodge bullets on my living-room floor, watch blood trickle down my terrace, toss a dead body into the sea. Instead I hang up and walk to my radio to find a station with news of the events. The phone rings again.

"Have you heard what's going on?" A voice is yelling into the receiver on the other end. Nurse Pitt. She lives on the Old Road, around the corner from me.

"Yes, I have!" I yell back.

"It's terrible. It's absolutely terrible. Go listen to the radio."

"Well, I was just about to turn it on when you . . ."

"Robbie is dead. This is not good. Robbie was from Tobago. This is very bad for Tobago. Very bad. Do you have food?"

"Well, not much, you know, but I go to market every day."

"Buy food first thing tomorrow morning. And come by if you need anything. But go and buy food. Go."

"But Mrs. Pitt, why? This is going on over in Trinidad."

"I know my country. I know my country." And with that she sighs and hangs up. I find a Trinidad radio station on the dial. Sinead O'Connor is singing "Nothing Compares to U." Then an announcer cuts in. He sounds as anxious as Tony and as loud as Nurse Pitt. Word is, he says, that Robbie is dead. Nobody knows what's going on. Everyone is urged to stay calm. Everyone is urged to stay at home.

I lie down on my bed, burn two mosquito coils, keep the windows to the ocean wide open and listen to the roar of the sea, and for the first time tonight a wave of excitement sweeps my chest.

———

I wake up as I always do, with the lighting of the sky. Gray lifts off the Atlantic, the boulders, the palms, the mango trees, the fence. They separate. Blocks of gray dissolve into sticks of green and brown. The clouds this morning puff and droop. The water bounces lighter than usual, a silvery black. I pick up the remains of the coils, slip my feet into my flip-flops and smudge the ashes into the floor. Turn on the kitchen light, drop the base of the coils into the trash can. As I fling open the French doors, I notice, way in the distance, the sliver of light that breaks the sea from the sky. Then I remember.

I hurry into the living room and turn on the radio. A Beethoven sonata reaches its crashing end, then the announcer comes in. He sounds tired and his voice trails before his sentences are over. I check the clock on the dining-room table. It's five-thirty in the morning. "Downtown Port of Spain is burning in flames," he says. "I can see it from the window outside of my control booth. There has been looting going on all night. The hospital reports eight people dead. The Jamaat Al Muslimeen have taken control of the Red House and the Television Building. The airports are closed."

I step back onto the terrace. It's so silent here this morning, and none of this seems real at all. Eight people dead. I feel the sharp, sudden stab of those words. But just as quickly I feel it slip away. After all, I have the foreigner's edge. It's not my country that's going down the tube, it's someone else's. It's always someone else's. The airports are closed, that's the statement that sticks. I came to Tobago to escape my queer life in New York—the endless hospital visits, the memorials, the easy sex. I came here to escape, and all of a sudden I can't; I've been robbed of the one privilege I cherish above all others, the privilege to run away whenever I want. I don't like this, I don't like it one bit. But then the silence of the morning falls over my terrace again. I listen to the radio, and all I hear is another set of words.

When I return to the kitchen, I flick the hot-water switch. Turn the faucet, there's water for a change. So I run a full bath and settle into the tub. Watch the sky blossom to a milky white above the turquoise curtains that cover the lower half of the bathroom windows. My skin wrinkles and sags with the hot water, it kind of folds and collapses, but inside I start to feel taut, like a pinball right after the trigger has been pulled. Tony calls at seven, just as I climb out of the tub. He's never called this early before.

"Oh good, the phones still work." He sounds so relieved to hear my voice. I, too, am relieved. And very glad to talk to him.

"Have you heard about the looting? It's the Guyanese and the Dominicans that are doing it."

"How do you know that?"

"Trinis don't do that kind of thing."

"Tony, you can stop defending your country to me. Trinis committed the coup."

"That's different. They're Muslims."

"Trini Muslims."

There's another silence, when the bristling of the ocean bleeds with the static of the phone line. For a moment it seems Tony is gone, his voice swallowed by the sound of the sea. I miss him, I realize it that instant. I miss him a lot. And it catches me completely by surprise. Tony returns, seconds later, and his voice is again wrapped in the drama of the day.

"Be safe, baby," he whispers in a soft, sweet tremble, overflowing with his five-day-old love for me. "Be safe."

Oh, that moment when he speaks I feel so very, very close to him. He blazes across my terrace in a sudden flash, just as he did that first afternoon on Sackville Street. I see him as I saw him then, walking toward me in his immaculately pressed shirt, the shoulder-length hair that whips from his face, the chestnut sparkle of his skin, the three-day stubble that spells danger. My GQ Indian fantasy man. The second we hang up I yearn to hear his voice again, yearn to be utterly swept away by the thrill of this courtship. Instead I decide to get out of the house. I find it hard to be alone, for long, in my apartment on Seventh Street, in the East Village of Manhattan. It's harder in a house such as this; this building is larger, emptier. The solitude multiplies as I walk from room to room. The walls stare with a brutal candor. The windows rattle with the wind. Clatter, bang, ache, they don't ever stop.

I close the front door and walk down the Old Road. It's deserted, as always. But this morning I see it so clearly for what it is: A crumbling potholed road, a forgotten village bypassed by a new highway. A tiny island just north of the equator, miles away from home. When I reach the row of bushes that shield Nurse Pitt's house from the street, I shortcut onto her lawn. The top half of her kitchen door is pried open, a sign that Nurse Pitt is up. Her house is a disintegrating island Victorian. Everything, the windows, the doors, the roof, has survived the hurricanes by shifting off base. And everything looks like it has shrunk, like it's a size too small.

Nurse Pitt sits on a miniature stool right next to her kitchen cabinet, her head pressed into a red plastic boom box that rests on top of the counter, right by the shiny chrome napkin holder. A flowered house smock covers her stocky body, a navy kerchief covers the tight metal curlers that sit in her hair. I knock on the lower ledge of the door. Nurse Pitt quickly motions me in and gestures me silent, all at once. I pull up the other stool and sit close to her, rest one arm on the kitchen cabinet. Lillian took me to meet her the day I arrived in the village of Lambeau. Nurse Pitt held the keys to my house. Lillian introduced her as Mrs. Ferguson, but I soon realized that everyone else in Lambeau knows her as Nurse Pitt. She is just this side of seventy now. She hasn't worked in the island hospital in over ten years, but once a nurse always a nurse. Maybe that's the reason I like her so much. Nurse Pitt needs someone to take care of, and I've always searched for those who will take care of me.

"I just called you," she admonishes. "I was worried. I'm glad you've come."

Then she tilts her head closer to the radio and turns the dial again.

"Radio Grenada," she whispers to me. "They have Debbie Ransom. She's the only reporter who really tells it like it is. She's right in downtown Port of Spain. You must listen to Radio Grenada."

I settle into my moment with Nurse Pitt; sink into the unabashed melodrama of the day. We huddle together, our eyes, our ears very near, intent only on the radio; listen for words that will seal this island's fate. Her fate, my fate. I strain, but mostly I hear a lot of whistling and whooshing and voices screaming and vanishing. Then one voice settles for a few seconds. "That's Debbie," Nurse Pitt says excitedly. It, too, is swallowed fast.

Nurse Pitt tries to pull her voice back in, she barely touches the dial, but all she draws is more noise and then a screaming Venezuelan DJ.

"It's terrible," Nurse Pitt says, and I sense for the first time how truly upset she is, how deeply troubled by it all. "Debbie says the sky over Woodford Square was as bright as a fireworks display. She could see people running down the streets, carrying refrigerators and washers on their backs." She pauses and quietly shakes her head. "It's the Guyanese that are doing all this, you know."

I stifle a laugh. Nurse Pitt lifts herself from her stool, heaves for a moment and then leads me out into the garden. She walks with a quick step, a sure determination. Picks a clump of calaloo leaves from the grass, a cucumber, a lingering mango, yanks some balls of prickly soursop from a stem. This piece of land has been her family's for a good eighty years. There has been no coup on this property, there's order on this slope. I watch her, and for a moment I almost believe that this is where I was destined to come all along, that this is my land, too. Nurse Pitt retrieves a crumpled plastic bag from deep within her smock and thrusts it into my hands. "Here, put it all in here. And I want this bag back, you never give me back my bags." I marvel at the imperious toss of her forehead. I can tell how much she has enjoyed raiding the garden for me, especially today, when a nation is under siege.

"And you must go shopping," she insists. "You must."

Lillian's Toyota thunders down the Old Road. It's high noon, and I'm so glad she came by and picked me up, glad she rescued me from my house. I only wish she knew the Old Road better. Lillian hits all the potholes instead of circling them, our buttocks levitate and crash. And we laugh, a loose, falling overboard kind of laugh that's only possible among those who live in ignorant bliss. I love her face, love the way it breaks into that vast, easy smile, the way every muscle in her face bursts open. Lillian's the one who got me here in the first place. "I found you a house in Tobago," she said last spring when she called, a delirious excitement in her voice. It was that simple. She spots another pothole, and this time she aims right for it, goes straight for the hit. We roar again. We're both utterly caught up in the thrill of this ride, and we drive with a boastful swagger, a reckless arrogance, as if our laughter alone could will this coup away.

Nurse Pitt was right, of course. I know that the moment we swing onto the Noel Highway. Traffic is heavy. An army of cars stands in front of the first mini market in Bon Accord. Lillian throws me a quick glance, and then we, too, jump out and rush into the store. I take one look. A chill wraps my spine. Right in front of my eyes a store is coming undone. Half of the shelves are already empty, and people are yanking more and more items into shopping carts. The carts press into a tight, long line, trying to check out at the two overwhelmed cash registers. We can't find any empty shopping carts at all and simply start to pile items into our arms. The items I want, eggs, milk, lettuce, are long gone. So I grab what I can find, ketchup, sardines, mosquito coils, toilet paper. More people press into the store, and nobody seems to get out. The July heat hangs still amidst all the commotion, and the checkout girls move as slowly as they always do in every store on the island. Lillian and I stand in line, silent. By the time we pay we're drowning in sweat. We stash our groceries into the trunk of the car and flop into the seats. Lillian turns on the radio again.

"President Noor Hassanali has interrupted his vacation and returned to Port of Spain," the announcer says. "He will lead the negotiations with the Jamaat Al Muslimeen for the release of the hostages. The country will be under curfew from six o'clock tonight until noon on Sunday. Only authorized emergency personnel will be allowed on the streets during curfew times."

Lillian looks at me and says: "Shit."

We don't laugh as she hits the gas. It's two in the afternoon now, that leaves four hours in the day. We head to the end of the Bon Accord Road, all the way to the airport, and park the car at Store Bay, just behind the terminal. Music booms loud from the bar. The picnic tables throng with European tourists and Trinis from the neighboring hotels getting drunk. Lillian and I get some Caribs and settle into a little cove to the left of the main section of the beach. The sun has started its descent toward the horizon, just beyond Pigeon Point where the invisible Grenada lies. The water at Store Bay sits still as if in a lake; it shimmers in an emerald green, its cover sealed with streaks of silver light. We take our beers into the water and float. For a moment the breeze and the water seem to merge, and my head tilts farther back. With one hand I hold the beer bottle up high, with the other I cup the water beside me. My head turns toward Lillian. She also floats, head back into the water, beer pouring down her throat. Then she turns to me and smiles. It's a wise and weary smile, and I'm so happy to see her familiar face. Quietly my eyes fall shut. Light shimmers expectantly below my lids. Slowly, steadily I drift with the water closer to the beach. In the distance the loudspeakers from the picnic area drone. But then all I hear is the stillness. The stillness of the water. The stillness of the light. And, I realize with a burning twitch, the stillness of an airport where planes no longer fly.

Night falls early and fast in Lambeau. By six the light begins to harden and coalesce. By six-thirty the moon rises behind Nurse Pitt's house, and the tops of the palm trees in Little Rockly Bay merge to the sharp-toothed ridge of a comb. Tonight the Old Road is deserted. I don't know why that surprises me, it almost always is. I walk out of the house, up to the fence by the road. Look to my left and to my right. There is no one in sight. No people, no cars. Up the hill, no one in sight. Lambeau is observing the curfew.

"Hi, Baby."

I'm so glad when I pick up the phone and hear Tony's voice.

"Hi, Baby." My shoulders snuggle into the two-seat sofa, I want to call it a loveseat but that's not what it is, it's just a sofa that's too small. Tony's voice sounds hushed and soft. My legs curl in tight, my head tilts into the hollow circle of light from the reading lamp. Ready and yearning for another round of melodrama.

"There are more people in the streets." Tony whispers as he tells me the news. "At least twelve dead. It's just terrible . . ." And then his voice squeaks just a little as he asks the next question: "Do you think the Americans are going to invade?"

"I doubt it. This isn't Grenada, you know. I don't think most Americans even know this is going on. I've had no calls from the States."

"Well, you're my American, and you have already invaded me." Tony sounds so irresistibly coy as he utters these words. I adore this line of conversation. Especially since we're caught in a coup; Tony's in Trinidad, far, far away, and there's nothing either of us can do about any of this.

"I didn't invade you yet, sweetheart." I can be obnoxious when I like someone. Thank God Tony doesn't mind. And it's true. He came up to my room at the Queen's Park Hotel the second night we met, and it was definitely a preinvasion visit.

"I want you to, I really do." His voice seems to lower an octave, it slobbers and woos. In an instant Tony becomes my restless native, my begging courtesan, and I his shipwrecked captain, his elusive master, stranded on a distant shore. Thrown together and at once torn apart. "And in a way you already have."

I'm moved by the sincerity in his voice, it's so completely without fear. The coup seems to have killed his trepidation, it has set Tony free. I remember a moment that second night, minutes before we dropped his friend Liz in St. James and Tony came up to my room. We were parked in the empty parking lot of a soccer field. Liz sat behind the steering wheel, Tony to her right, I in back. We were an odd threesome that evening, trapped in Tony's little Toyota. During a moment of silence, as Liz lit another cigarette and I scanned the lights above the Savannah, Tony leaned back and reached for my right wrist. The touch of his hand sent shock waves up my arm. I don't think any man has ever touched me with such affection, such charge. I looked down at the slender, bony skin of his arm, the beautiful sweep of black hair that pointed to his wrist, and watched him slide a braided leather strap around my wrist; bend a copper hook into a matching eye. He performed this act with a delicacy that startled me. And he did it quietly, without saying a word. The moment he was done he turned away and stared at the darkening soccer field. This exchange took seconds only. It had been planned, clearly, a sweet and calculated act of seduction. Maybe that's what moved me so, the care and the planning. In the seconds of silence right after, Liz turned back to me and whispered, like the translator for an act that required no translation: "He really likes you, you know."

I knew it that evening, just five days ago. But there's a danger here tonight, a sharper, more daring seduction that was impossible then.

"Do you know the Silva method?" Tony asks me.

"No, what is it?"

"The Silva method is very popular here in Trinidad. It is where you learn to concentrate all your thoughts and all your energies on something that you really want, and you do it several times every day, you really put your thoughts to it, and then those things will start to happen."

"Do you practice the Silva method?"

"Well, I haven't been, but I think I will."

"And what will you wish for?"

Tony is silent. In that moment I feel so unspeakably close to him. The Silva method I can understand. I, too, believe in the power of the mind, it's my bridge across uncrossable waters. I wonder. If I could center all my thoughts on one thing, what would it be? Right now, this very second, I wish for this coup to go on and on, forever and ever.

"Call me tomorrow," Tony whispers. "If the phones work."

"If they work."

I open the windows in my bedroom and wedge the little hooks into their eyelets. Bring two mosquito coils from the kitchen and let them burn. Then I lie down on my bed and drape a sheet around my legs. The Atlantic beats against the boulders with a strong, steady bang. The light of the moon falls in blue shafts onto my bed. Twelve people are dead. Tony sounds close, so truly close. I'm very, very happy tonight.

Little changes for the next three days. I wake early with the lifting of the night, rise and turn on the radio first, before I switch on the kitchen lights or prop open the windows or do anything else. The news trickles, much like the faucet in my bathroom. The fires have stopped but the death toll is rising. Hassanali's people are negotiating with Abu Bakr, the leader of the Jamaat Al Muslimeen, for release of the hostages. Businesses are shut down. Banks are closed. Food stores stay open and run dry. And I? I stand on the terrace of my house and wait for the phone to ring. Wait for the curfew to end. Wait for Lillian to come by and take me to Store Bay. Wait. It's the hardest thing in the world to do for a willful soul like me.

Tony calls in the morning, I call at night. That seems to be the unspoken rule of our courtship. I hunger for him more and more with each passing day. We talk of nothing really. This is a courtship of the voice, of the ocean roaring behind us like a prerecorded soundtrack. But sometimes his voice disappears, so suddenly and quickly, right while we talk. It slips and drops. And then it vanishes completely.

"Tony, I can't hear you!" I yell into the phone. I know he's on the other end, he doesn't speak but I sense his breath, he's still there.

"My mother," he whispers finally.

"What," I ask. "She just walked into your room?"

"No, she came by the hallway."

"Well, why don't you shut your door?"

"I couldn't do that!"

"Why?"

"Well, I've never done that before. It would upset her."

"Tony, you're twenty-nine. You're allowed a room with a door that can be shut!"

But there is always the moment, right afterward, when the scenario becomes endearing again. When I snuggle into my sofa and the night wind rattles the bedroom windows and slams the French doors back into their frame, when the electricity goes out and my one candle flickers wildly on the floor. Every time Tony's voice returns it sounds closer. I love the way it topples with excitement, as if it talked to a lover for the very first time. I love the way it's mushy on the edges, so soft, like a mango from my mango trees waiting to be sucked to the pit. And it gets closer and closer. By Monday night I feel it quiver on the sofa right beside me. On Tuesday it crawls down the empty sheet of my bed and scales my neck, nuzzles my ear, so sweet and tender and close, and then I actually feel his breath tickle my lobe: "Hi baby."

That night I know I have to tell him. It's a bit cooler than it has been, a drop of only a few degrees, but a notable change in a place where heat is the one reliable force of nature. The sky is ravishingly clear, blue-black as the ocean. The stars shine like fireflies tonight, distant and sharp. When I call Tony he picks up right away. "Hi baby." His voice has melted so low it seems to seep through my pores, into my bones. I know no other way but to put it to him directly. "There's something I've been meaning to tell you, Tony."

"Yes, baby." His voice wraps itself around my telephone cord.

"You know about HIV, right?" I pause. I've opened this door before, I've walked through it countless other times, so why does it seem so difficult today? So impossible? In a quick swoop I feel the weight drain from the telephone cord. "Well, I'm HIV positive, and I thought you should know."

There's a gulp on the other side of the line, and all of a sudden it feels like he really is on the other side of the line and no longer right here in my room. I hear two loud, heavy breaths, as if someone is losing all air or having a stroke. Then there is a sharp clang and Tony's receiver hits a solid object. The telephone line bristles with static, we're still connected but Tony's gone, and this time, I know, it's not because of dragon mom. I hold onto my receiver and wait. A burst of terror clutches my chest. For a second it occurs to me that I may not ever hear his voice again. It hadn't occurred to me before, only now. The light of the moon frames the terrace in a subterranean glow. I feel myself sink below water, below the black surface of the Atlantic. I hold onto my receiver, hold it with a tighter and tighter grip, and the static of the phone connection invades my shoulders, my arms, the lining of my stomach. I hear the drone of the static, and then I, too, fall into utter silence. My eyes quiver with the light of the moon, and all sounds, the ocean, the phone, the night frogs are swallowed by a silent fear. I don't know how long this lasts. Curfews are measured in time, but this moment lasts longer than any single curfew period. When Tony returns to the phone it happens with another loud clang of the receiver. I hear two more thumping breaths, sighs that seem to draw air from the bottom of the sea, and then Tony's voice starts to wail.

It's a quiet, tender wail, the door to his room is open after all. He cries and cries, sweet, birdlike sobs. When his voice finally speaks he sounds like a very little boy, so innocent, so near.

"Are you dying, baby?"

"I'm not dying, Tony, I'm HIV-positive."

My answer feels like a letdown, I know. People are dying in Port of Spain every night, the moon this evening is so full and pure, so why shouldn't I play the dying lover for him? Let Tony be my island widow, let him nurse me into death, let him mourn and bury me, on a hilltop high above Little Rockly Bay, under another iridescent moon.

"Are there any more surprises?" Tony asks. It's a legitimate question.

"I don't think so."

"How's the weather over there?"

"Clear."

"Yeah, same as here."

"Good night baby."

"Good night."

This evening I can't bear to be inside the house. I listen to the ocean batter the rocks below the garden, it batters them hard. Like it's willing the rocks to surrender, like it wants to rush into the garden, to the house, to me. I do it suddenly and without thought; I have not done it before. Climb down my garden to the boulders below. Past the two mango trees the earth falls fast. I skitter, lunge for a tree trunk for support. Hold on, then skitter to the next. Rip the halter out of my right flip-flop while I jump down the precipice. Land on a fallen cocoa trunk. The first gusts of water splatter my body. I slide further down to the boulders, they're large and slippery and dark. My hands dig into the earth above the boulders, they dig for strength, but then I let go. I suddenly stand alone on a rock licked wet by the sea. My torso wobbles, my feet press into the sharp crevices of the stone, press down hard so I won't fall. I cannot see the house, just sixty, seventy feet above me. The Lambeau I know has vanished. For a moment it all feels so terribly, painfully clear. I have simply traveled too far. Water sprays the tree trunks, the boulders, my ankles, shoots up my chest. The sound of the ocean whips and howls, it burns my ears. My toes let go of their clamp on the rock, and I start to slide down into the sea. My legs are lashed cold by the ocean. My chest slams into the boulders and scratches, the scratches start to bleed. Tony, HIV, this coup. This very instant it all seems too much. If I let go, the Atlantic will swallow me up and spew me back out, and no one will know, no one will hear my call. The thought paralyzes me. But suddenly, as if out of nowhere, I feel a push from deep within, and I start to inch my body back toward land. My ribs scratch and burn, my head swirls, more skin tears as I slide up a boulder, and then, finally, my hands dig into their first chunk of sweet, solid earth.

It happens early the next morning, right after Tony's first call, before Lillian comes by to pick me up for the beach. I sit with a cup of oversoaked tea and a slice of toast that's buried in sugary guava jelly, there is no other food left in the house. My hands leaf through a library copy of Gerald Durrell's *My Family and Other Animals*. It's his account of growing up a British boy on the island of Corfu. It's either that or one of the Graham Greene novels I have in the house. I simply can't reread those again. I've checked every one of them out of the island library before. I like Durrell, his book is sweet but this is my third reading, and it just reminds me again that these are the nineties, not the thirties, I'm not a twelve-year-old boy, Tobago isn't Corfu, and Graham Greene is dead.

The phone rings, and Nurse Pitt's on the other end, her voice yelling with more than usual vigor: "The Muslimeen have surrendered. Hassanali has made a deal."

"Why would Hassanali make a deal with the Muslimeen?" I'm very skeptical.

"Well, listen to the radio!" Nurse Pitt is clearly annoyed with me. She grunts and hangs up at once. I turn on the radio, find one of the Trini stations. Nurse Pitt was right, as always. "At noon," the announcer says, "all the hostages will be released. Until further notice the curfews remain."

A rage erupts in me as I hear the news. The coup is over, and nothing has changed. Nothing. The curfew remains, for security reasons. I have no food in the house. I have no money. And all the banks are still closed. That afternoon Lillian and I drift out into the ocean again. The sun floats over Pigeon Point, lazy and fat, and I know I don't want to burn here on Store Bay for one more second. I want to suck it all up, the beauty of this beach, the view from my terrace, the majesty of the palm trees, the shimmer of the moon, the sky. I want to swallow it hard so I can chew it all up and spit it back out and never, ever have to look at it again.

"Isn't it wonderful that the whole situation is over now."

Tony sounds joyous as we speak that evening. I don't buy it for a second, he's putting on an act. It's a cautious jubilation. A slippery joy. It meets my cautious sadness, my seething venom. Part of me, I confess, longed for more, much more bloodshed. More fires, more killings, more death. Only thirty-two people killed. A minor coup.

"I miss you, baby. I want to come over and be with you," I say to Tony, my voice now melting into puddles on the floor. Doesn't he understand? This very second the urge is so terribly, terribly strong, it overwhelms. I want to get on a plane, fly to Trinidad, I want to walk through the ruins of downtown Port of Spain, make love to Tony among the smoldering flames. I want to burn in his arms.

"I miss you too, baby," Tony answers. Our vocabulary has been reduced to the same ten words which we recirculate again and again. And then he surprises me and assumes the voice of reason. "But there's only one flight a day now, and you know there are no seats, and if you came here I couldn't see you anyway, you would just be sitting in a hotel."

A few more words, and then I hang up the phone. Step out to the terrace, haul myself up to the stone ledge that frames the house, lie down. My body quivers. He infuriates me, he really does. Why does he have to be so damn rational, now that the coup is over? Especially since I'm becoming so utterly, uncontrollably obsessed: I have to get out of Tobago. I have to see him now.

Two days later the moment comes. Lillian and I are racing down the Noel Highway, guzzling the last two Caribs from our six-pack when we hear the news: The curfews will lift early on Saturday, at eight in the morning. Eight to six, that means ten hours, a whole day almost, to be out and about, to be free. I call Tony the second I get back to the house.

"I'm coming to Trinidad tomorrow."

He answers, the excited but cautious pragmatist: "How are you going to get here? There have been no flights. And where are you going to stay?"

He's right, of course. I can't stay with him. And I imagine all the hotels in Trinidad are filled to capacity with foreigners trying to get out. It will be impossible to get a seat on a BWIA flight to Piarco, people have waited all week to leave Tobago. And I have absolutely no money left. None.

"Look, Tony, just call one of your friends at BWIA and see if they can sneak me on the passenger list for a flight, OK? I'll see what I can do about the rest."

I'm on a mission now. I'm throwing all caution to the wind. These are desperate times, I must be reunited with my lover, and nothing will stand in my way. Nothing. I ransack all my belongings in the house, every piece of clothing, every suitcase, hoping to find some money stashed away somewhere, anywhere. It's my search for a tangible miracle, a sign that someone wants me on that flight. As often as I've done this in the past, something has always turned up. Today, from deep inside the pockets of one of my traveling bags, I retrieve a twenty-dollar bill. Twenty U.S. dollars. I remember it now, that's the bill I had saved for my reentry into the States. Airport money, that's what I call it. The flight from Crown Point to Piarco costs the equivalent of $13.00. So I can get there.

The rest is easy. Nurse Pitt changes the money for me. Tony calls early on Saturday and tells me my name is at the top of the reservation list for the midday flight out of Tobago. "Well, I'm glad you've slept with all the right people," I tease him. Tony's not in the mood for sex jokes, he retreats into a sulk. Though that lets me know I probably hit the nail on the head. And then, just before I head out to the airport, I call Lillian. It's a call I've looked forward to all morning.

"Look, Lillian, I'm flying to Piarco today so I won't be coming to the beach. I should be back in a few days, I think . . ."

I must admit, I gloat a little as I speak. I know I'm about to desert her, my friend, my last tenuous link to life back home. Lillian gasps for a second, it's a gasp of disbelief. She knows that no one in their right mind would think of going to Trinidad at a time like this. No one. Tobagonians avoid Trinidad the way Long Islanders avoid Manhattan. They certainly wouldn't go in a time of war. But then she clues into the romance of it all. I know her voice so well, and I believe she sounds just a little jealous when she finally responds. "Ah, you and Tony," she says with a wilting sigh. "It will be so nice."

I don't see him at first. I stand on the sidewalk outside the domestic waiting hall and fight off the taxi drivers that try to whisk me into their cars. Other passengers stream past me, into the arms of waiting relatives or lovers, into screams of joy and spontaneous cries. The entire sidewalk, in fact, seems to erupt in an orgy of embraces. For a moment I feel quite lost, looking for a man I know mostly from phone calls whispered during a coup. And I don't see him coming. He suddenly just stands next to me, like a genie that's sprung from the pavement. Tony looks slimmer, smaller than I remember, more like a scrawny, over-grown boy. A smile skips across his mouth. I watch it almost in disbelief, as if I'd never seen this smile before. And I stare at the beauty of his skin, the creamy smooth glow of his face. The vicarious toss of his black-blue hair as it sweeps from his fore-head, straddles his chin. The nervous waver of those beautiful lashes. The terror in his eyes as he tries to look at me.

We don't hug or touch. This is Trinidad, after all, and we're two queer boys. And not just any two queer boys. No. We're an Indian boy and a white boy. And the white boy is not a local white, he's a foreigner, that's clear enough for anyone to see.

No, I know this much about Tony by now. We don't touch in public.

He rushes me across the road to the parking lot. We run in silence, separated by the intensity of our phone calls, the close-ness of our voices in the night, a closeness that can't be repli-cated on a Saturday afternoon in the sunburned parking lot at Piarco. We're much too close, in fact, to feel anything.

Tony hunches into the steering wheel, throws me a nervous smile. I look straight ahead, watch the cars race toward us on the other side of the divider, glance back at Tony as we shoot into Port of Spain. The ride feels supremely unreal, as if I'm dreaming it, everything I see is framed by the blurs of speed. I want to say Tony and I are racing into that blur, but the truth is, it's he and I who are the blur, and the cars around us very solid and real. I glance at him again. The beauty of his face, the tender, sweeping lashes, the patrician nose, the long, long neck that seems to leap to the sky; they banish my doubts, for a second.

We swing through Independence Square, just blocks from the Red House where we met, thirty-two dead bodies ago. Today the Savannah outside of the Queen's Park Hotel is a green desert. I jump out of the car and turn to Tony who suddenly slumps behind the wheel.

"Well, aren't you going to come in?"

He squirms in the seat, looks at me with a sullen face. I get angry. I've forgotten all the little games we played before the coup.

"Look, they already know you're sleeping with me, so get over it. Your face is known at the Queen's Park Hotel."

And with that I march into the lobby, up to the nice little Indian lady who dozes behind the desk. The lobby is deserted. The screaming Venezuelan kids and their nannies who owned this lobby ten days ago are nowhere to be seen. A porter lies on the sofa, eyes shut. The Indian lady jolts awake as I press the table bell. Her eyes dart as if she feared the Muslimeen had just invaded the hotel.

"So you're the one who called from Tobago," she says with a glint of bemused discretion. As she takes my credit card, Tony wanders into the lobby and lingers, close enough so he can hear my conversation with the clerk, far enough to make it clear that he isn't really with me, that we're certainly not a couple. When she hands me the key, he follows to the elevator as if he also just happened to go up to his room. The elevator is empty. The hallway on the fourth floor is empty. My room is large and also very empty. Two double beds are covered in bordello red, just like the room in which I stayed a week ago. The air hangs still and dead. I open the windows at the far end of the room and look down to the pool. A gust of hot, humid air slaps my face.

The pool, too, is deserted. I turn around and watch Tony stand far away from me, by the bed closest to the door. He looks lost and very ill at ease. That's when it hits me. My God, Tony and I are the only guests at the Queen's Park Savannah Hotel. There are sixty-five rooms in this hotel, the former crown jewel of the Port of Spain hotels, and everyone has left. A blast of energy sweeps my chest. The thought of being alone with Tony in this colonial dinosaur titillates me. And all at once it makes me feel even more stuck with him.

Tony sits on the edge of the bed and studies one of the hotel brochures.

"Let's take a shower," I suggest and don't wait for an answer.

"Now?" Tony looks up from his reading and looks genuinely surprised.

"No, tomorrow morning." I don't like it when my sarcasm cuts through, but Tony is pushing his luck. I toss my clothes onto the bed and disappear into the bathroom. The water burns, it's instant and hot, and I lean back and let it pound my chest.

"Tony, are you coming?" I realize that he still hasn't appeared in the bathroom.

"I'll take a shower when you're done."

"That kind of defeats the purpose, doesn't it?" He irritates me and at the same time, I must confess, I enjoy this little game of his. He wants me so badly, and yet he puts up such a fight. A second later he appears in the doorway to the bathroom, looks at me with mournful eyes and whispers, "I have never showered with a man before." With any other man I might get annoyed at such a bold-faced statement. But I actually believe he's telling the truth, and with us the truth has become part of the game, anyway. I jump out of the shower and start to tear off his clothes. Water drips from my body onto the floor. "No," he protests, "no," as he half fights and half assists in the stripping of his shirt. This struggle is invigorating, it's our first touch since we met at the airport, I'm enjoying it and Tony is, too. I surprise him, lift him up, try to drag him into the shower. "No." He's still protesting as he stumbles out of his underwear, steps onto it, almost slips, kicks it away onto the slippery floor. Then our bodies pounce on each other, slam into the tile wall. I feel the full force of his rib cage as he drops into my chest. His body is so slender, so bony, and yet it folds so perfectly into mine. We clutch each other and slip, hold onto each other very tight, then our bodies slide again under the hard stream of water. Our lips lock, they press and plunge, so tight it feels like an attack. Tony's tongue lashes and whips. His breath is hot, it sears the back of my throat. When we reach for air, water shoots into our mouths. We gurgle and spit, lunge for more air, wrap our mouths again, squeeze the eyes shut. My tongue swoops down and wraps his nipples, twirls them until my teeth bite down hard. Tony squeals, and then he nuzzles his head into my neck, bites back. We're two missiles who've hit their target, we dig and scratch and wound. And then I simply can't wait any longer. I drop down to his groin, grip his thighs and take him, all of him. His penis quakes like the rest of his sweet body, it's a delicious fit. I draw him in, deeper and deeper. We're both racing for the place where borders collapse, where countries merge, and treaties are signed. Tony gasps and yelps. His groin assaults me, rougher and harder, and then he can't wait any more either and lets go and shoots straight into my mouth, so fully, so completely, straight down to my heart.

When I open my eyes again and shut off the water Tony looks at me. His little-boy chest still heaves, his eyes are full of yearning. The afternoon light penetrates the bathroom. The white tiles of the walls drip with dew, the floor is puddled, and I feel like I'm emerging from a dive, the light so blinding and bright, this world so much less real than the one where I just was. Tony steps out of the tub, pulls a towel from the rack and carefully gathers his clothes, disappears into the bedroom. When I step into the bedroom Tony is meticulously folding his clothes and laying them out, piece by piece, on the far bed. I flop onto the other bed and watch him. He continues to fold his shirt, his pants, in silence, with utmost concentration, then he quickly slides onto the bed next to me. We lie still but don't touch. I wonder if he thinks about the HIV; if he understands that it's a danger much more final than this coup.

"That was really nice," Tony whispers after a few seconds. I love the way he says it, so softly, the way he stretches the word "really." It sounds like he really, really means it, especially in that sweet cadence of his Trini lilt.

208 · ACHIM NOWAK

"Yes, it was," I say and bite his ear.

"No," Tony says firmly and pushes me off. It is, I'm beginning to learn, one of his favorite words.

"I want to go to the beach tomorrow," I tell him. "To Maracas." Maracas, it is said, is Trinidad's most beautiful beach, and I have never been.

"I don't know if my car will make it all the way to Maracas," Tony announces sheepishly. "It was with the mechanic two weeks ago, and it still isn't driving right."

"What do you mean it's not driving right? You picked me up at the airport and it drove fine. And the airport is as far away as Maracas!"

"But you don't understand," Tony says; it's another favorite phrase of his I'm rapidly getting used to. "The road to Maracas is steep and full of curves, it's not like taking the highway from the airport."

"You mean I came all the way over from Tobago, and we're not going to Maracas?"

I'm really pissed. Never mind the fact that I live on Tobago, home to the most beautiful beaches this end of the Antilles.

"Well," Tony offers a compromise, "we could drive by Sandra tomorrow. She lives in Maraval, that's on the way to Maracas, and we can leave my car there and go with her in her Jeep."

I'm boiling now. Sandra is his best friend whom I'm in no hurry to meet. He thinks she's a lesbian and she doesn't know he's queer, and they do everything together, and they never ever talk about "it." I don't understand why they can't just fucking talk about "it." Although, I have assured Tony, I'm certain everyone knows he's queer anyway. This charade aggravates me. I'm in no mood to participate in a scene with Sandra. I see Tony as he sits there on my bed, looking sincerely helpless. I can't believe it. For a week we've been so far away, at opposite ends of the phone, an ocean apart, and now he doesn't even want to go to the beach with me!

"Look, I came here to be with you, Tony, not with Sandra. I don't want a fucking chaperone around every time I see you."

"But Sandra goes to the beach on Sundays anyway."

"Fine, let her go to the beach. We'll run into her there. But

I want to go with you." I thought Tony would enjoy my outburst of possessiveness and see it as a token of my affection. Instead he looks even more worried. We settle into another silent interlude before he glances nervously at his watch, twice, and announces he has to leave. I know. At night Tony goes home to Mom. Especially during curfew time.

"So what about tomorrow?"

"I will pick you up at ten and we'll go to Maracas."

"Nine!"

He looks at me and wants to protest, I can tell, he wants to tell me that no one in their right mind goes to the beach on Sunday at nine in the morning, only someone like me who doesn't know anything about anything would think of such a thing. Instead he relents.

"OK, nine." And then he bolts out the door. A maid scurries past the corner by the elevators, she had been listening at our door, no doubt. I walk to the window and pull aside the curtains, survey the room. I feel so terribly lost in here without him. So I, too, run down to the lobby. Tony is gone. The door to the street is already locked. The entire staff has left the building to beat the curfew, and a new night clerk sits on the sofa. It's he and I, alone, shut in for the night. An episode of *The Cosby Show* flickers on the television screen.

We pull away promptly at nine. Tony wears a cheery smile and is just a little too perky. His khaki shorts, his white shirt, his sneakers, everything has a scrubbed, intensely clean look. Mom takes care of her boy, a bachelor like me never looks that clean anymore. We grab some breakfast at the Kentucky Fried Chicken on Maraval Road and then head into the mountains. "That's where Sandra's family lives," Tony announces as we pass a gathering of villas on a slope to our left. Sandra, like Tony, like most Trinis in their twenties and thirties, lives at home with her parents. I ignore his comment and focus on the climb. Our roles today are clear. Tony plays the tour guide—it accounts for his cheeriness, I'm convinced, and it keeps him in complete control of the day. I play the helpless tourist for him—willing to follow his lead, willing to be entertained, willing not to challenge him. As the road curves higher, the terrain to our left suddenly falls away. Several hundred feet below, the Caribbean glistens with a bright, charcoal sheen. It's a startling view, this sharp, quick drop. I imagine all the cars who've shot past the railing and vaulted their drivers to their deaths. I love the fact that Tony and I are riding so very close to the edge. After several more turns the road rapidly descends, and then, magically, Maracas Bay sprawls into view, like a flash from a primordial dream. Maracas is a long, flawless sweep of sand, wedged into a narrow break in the Northern mountain range. The water looks pristine, the palm trees that enclose the beach ferocious and dark. This is a true Trini beach, and part of the primordial dream, of course, is a place such as this that has not been claimed by tourists like me.

"This is where I always lie!" Tony announces as we plunk ourselves into a spot near the center of the beach. I'm surprised. I was convinced he'd settle in a section very far from here, so as not to be seen with me. Maybe I underestimate him. Maybe he wants to show me off, after all. The beach is still empty, it's just after ten in the morning. Tony, of course, was right—nobody goes to Maracas this early in the day.

We run into the ocean at once. I don't think I will ever be truly close to a man who doesn't enjoy water, who doesn't crave the slippery, wet danger of the sea. Tony does. He hurls his slender body into the waves, attacks them with a fiery determination. The waves are tipsy baby waves, but we throw our torsos right into them, and when we hit a crest, we flip over flat and catch a ride. We both, I see that so clearly today, are driven by the same dark forces of the sea. I slam my chest and glide, slam and glide until, very suddenly, I reach the point I've longed for all morning, the point when something in my back seems to snap, when I know that today I can swim free of everything, free of all the petty squabbles and fears, free of Tony, yes free of him, and as soon as I know that I, of course, want nothing more than to swim right back into his arms.

When I finally run out of the water I collapse into my towel. The beach around us has started to fill. Tony, I notice, is checking the scene like a hawk. Whenever he sees people he knows to be gay—and I realize quickly that everyone in the scene, everyone that is gay that is, knows everyone else in the scene, or at least knows that they're in the scene—he points them out to me. The beach starts to transform into groupings of gay boys and girls, right in front of my eyes. They stroll along the water, always in threes. Two men and a woman, two women and a man. It's a casual yet carefully orchestrated undercover game. They're all impeccably behaved, there are no flamboyant touches here, no public displays. At no point do I see two boys together without a chaperone. And suddenly I understand. That's why Tony fought so vehemently to have Sandra along. We're like a tricycle that's missing a wheel. We're so terribly naked in public, two boys alone. I feel a rush of very tender feelings towards Tony as I realize this. I want to tell him. I want him to know that I know. But then I think it might make him even more uncomfortable. And so another thing remains unsaid.

Sandra never shows. But I receive a sudden jolt, sometime early in the afternoon. Tony and I lie on our towels, curled into a hypnotic beach sleep. I lift my eyes, and for a second I think this can't be, this really must be a dream. There are soldiers on the beach. Not just one or two, no, it looks like an entire platoon. It looks, in fact, like the beach has been invaded. I roll up and press my hands into the sand and blink my eyes. I don't know where they've come from so quickly, it's almost like they've marched out of the sea. The soldiers are moving from the far ends of the beach toward its center, toward us, they're walking right along the water's edge. This scene is a cliché, right out of a bad Hollywood movie. They wear combat fatigues, their machine guns are pointed up and out, their fingers on the trigger. They walk with a squat, predatory bounce, their hips weighted low, the strut wide, their torsos held rigid as they step through the sand, past families and children and trios sprawled on beach blankets. They cross in silence. Some of the bathers are still in the water, oblivious to what's going on. But everyone else on the beach has sat up. Their silence matches that of the soldiers now, the bodies of the beachgoers sit still, as rigid as those of the troopers. It's a stillness I have heretofore only known at a beach when I've been alone. The soldiers look to be Trini soldiers, their crossing lasts maybe five minutes, no longer, then they vanish into the palm groves behind the beach. A hush lingers after they have left. I look at Tony as he sits next to me.

He looks so impossibly beautiful with his salt-licked wet hair, his three-day stubble that endows him with a toughness he doesn't have. And suddenly I'm gripped by a chilling fear; it grips me with a brutal punch. I want the future with Tony to live up to these last ten days, to the drama of this moment, and I know it can't. I see the inevitable so clearly: As restrictions disappear life will return to normal. Without restrictions Tony and I will collapse. This is a courtship based on separation and the fear of death. The battles now will no longer be outside of us, they will be our very own. They will be small and petty, I fear. They will be the dramas of everyday life. And those are the dramas I fear the most.

There's only one more thing I must do before I return to Tobago: I have to see the ruins. The next morning I leave the Queen's Park Hotel and wander down into the business district. The Red House and Woodford Square, where I first talked to Tony a little less than two weeks ago, are still shielded from the public. As I walk down Frederick Street, along the east side of the Square, stores are opening for business. I turn into Queen Street and walk over to the corner of Henry, where most of the fires were reported. Several three-story department stores have burned down. Their walls are smoke-stained and scarred, their roofs now cave toward the street, their front walls are gone. They look like skeletons of steel, stripped naked, with beams that jut out of joint. Other shops stand empty behind the broken glass of their display windows; many are boarded up. Henry Street is eerily deserted, there's no room for traffic to maneuver, and no other gawkers have shown up. I'm a little surprised that I can so readily walk about. After all the curfews and restrictions it seems that no one really cares. I stand for a moment in the middle of the street and breathe in the scene. So this is what's left. There's a certain beauty in this rubble, in these plundered windows. But it's a fast and fleeting pleasure. A wave of deep disappointment sweeps through me. And I think of Peggy Lee as she sings, "Is that all there is?"

I turn and walk down to Independence Square, jump into one of the many waiting taxis that can take me to the airport. The driver and I battle for the fare.

"It's sixty-five TT Dollars to Piarco," he states when I ask for the rate.

"I'll pay you thirty," I tell him.

"What?" He scowls at my offer and sounds genuinely outraged. "This is the official fare. It's on the official government fare listings. They're posted at the airport." He's right, of course. I also know that they're government-sanctioned highway robbery, these official tourist rates. No Trini pays that much for a cab ride. This is part of the day-to-day warfare between the foreigner and the local. I hate it. It gets me riled up this morning as it often has in the past. And it's not about the money, it's about the principle. It always is.

"Look, I won't pay the official rate, I live on Tobago."

This statement does the trick. In one fell swoop I have erased the realities of who he and I are. The statement lets him know that he was wrong, that he has jumped to conclusions. I'm not a foreigner after all, Trinidad and Tobago is where I belong. I want to cling to this little delusion, I want to believe it's true, but deep down I know only too well: He wasn't wrong. And Trinidad and Tobago isn't my country. It never will be.

THE WHITE BLACKBIRD

• JAMES PURDY •

Even before I reached my one hundredth birthday, I had made several wills, and yet just before I put down my signature

Delia Mattlock

my hand refused to form the letters. My attorney was in despair. I had outlived everyone and there was only one person to whom I could bequeath much, my young godson, and he was not yet twenty-one.

I am putting all this down more to explain the course of events to myself than to leave this as a document to posterity, for as I say, outside of my godson, Clyde Furness, even my lifelong servants have departed this life.

The reason I could not sign my name then is simply this: piece by piece my family jewels have been disappearing over the last few years, and today as I near my one hundred years all of these precious heirlooms one by one have vanished into thin air.

I blamed myself at first, for even as a young girl I used to misplace articles, to the great sorrow of my mother. My great grandmother's gold thimble is an example. You would lose your head if it wasn't tied on, Mother would joke rather sourly. I lost my graduation watch, I lost my diamond engagement ring, and, if I had not taken the vow never to remove it, my wedding ring to Will Mattlock would have also taken flight. I will never re-move it and will go to my grave wearing it.

But to return to the jewels. They go back in my family over two hundred years, and yes, piece by piece, as I say, they have been disappearing. Take my emerald necklace—its loss nearly finished me. But what of my diamond earrings, the lavaliere over a century old, my ruby earrings—oh, why mention them? For to mention them is like a stab in the heart.

I could tell no one for fear they would think I had lost my wits, and then they would blame the servants, who were I knew blameless, such perfect, even holy, caretakers of me and mine.

But there came the day when I felt I must at least hint to my godson that my jewels were all by now unaccounted for. I hes-itated weeks, months before telling him.

About Clyde now. His Uncle Enos told me many times that it was his heartbroken conviction that Clyde was somewhat re-tarded. "Spends all his time in the forest," Enos went on, "failed every grade in school, couldn't add up a column of figures or do his multiplication tables."

"Utter rot and nonsense," I told Enos. "Clyde is bright as a silver dollar. I have taught him all he needs to know, and I never had to teach him twice because he has a splendid memory. In fact, Enos, he is becoming my memory."

Then of course Enos had to die. Only sixty, went off like a puff of smoke while reading the weekly racing news.

So then there was only Clyde and me. We played cards, chess, and then one day he caught sight of my old Ouija board.

I went over to where he was looking at it. That was when I knew I would tell him—of the jewels vanishing, of course.

Who else was there? Yet Clyde is a boy, I thought, forgetting he was now twenty, for he looked only fourteen to my eyes.

"Put the Ouija board down for a while," I asked him. "I have something to tell you, Clyde."

He sat down and looked at me out of his handsome hazel eyes.

I think he already knew what I was to say.

But I got out the words.

"My heirloom jewels, Clyde, have been taken." My voice sounded far away and more like Uncle Enos's than mine.

"All, Delia?" Clyde whispered, staring still sideways at the Ouija board.

"All, all. One by one over the past three years they have been slipping away. I have almost wondered sometimes if there are spirits, Clyde."

He shook his head.

That was the beginning of even greater closeness between us.

I had given out, at last, my secret. He had accepted it; we were, I saw, like confederates, though we were innocent, of course, of wrongdoing ourselves. We shared secretly the wrongdoing of someone else.

Or was it *wrongdoing*, I wondered. Perhaps the disappearance of the jewels could be understood as the work of some blind power.

But what kind?

My grandfather had a great wine cellar. I had never cared for wine, but in the long winter evenings I finally suggested to Clyde we might try one of the cellar wines.

He did not seem very taken with the idea, for which I was glad, but he obeyed docilely, went down the interminable steps of the cellar and brought back a dusty bottle.

It was a red wine.

We neither of us relished it, though I had had it chilled in a bucket of ice, but you see it was the ceremony we both liked. We had to be doing something as we shared the secret.

There were cards, dominoes, Parcheesi and finally, alas, the Ouija board, with which we had no luck at all. It sat wordless and morose under our touch.

Often as we sat at cards, I would blurt out some thoughtless remark: once I said, "If we only knew what was before us!"

Either Clyde did not hear or he pretended I had not spoken.

There was only one subject between us. The missing jewels. And yet I always felt it was wrong to burden a young man with such a loss. But then I gradually saw that we were close, very close. I realized that he had something for me that could only be called love. Uncle Enos was gone, Clyde had never known either mother or father. I was his all, he was my all. The jewels in the end meant nothing to me. A topic for us—no more.

I had been the despair of my mother because, as she said, I cared little for real property, farmlands, mansions, not even dresses. Certainly not jewels.

"You will be a wealthy woman one day," Mother said, "and yet look at you, you care evidently for nothing this world has to offer."

My two husbands must have felt this also. Poring over their ledgers at night, they would often look up and say, "Delia, you don't care if the store keeps or not, do you?"

"You will be a wealthy woman in time, if only by reason of your jewels," my mother's words of long ago began to echo in my mind when I no longer had them.

My real wealth was in Clyde. At times when I would put my hand through his long chestnut hair a shiver would run through his entire body.

He suffered from a peculiar kind of headache followed by partial deafness, and he told me the only thing that helped the pain was when I would pull tightly on his curls.

"Pull away, Delia," he would encourage me.

How it quickened the pulse when he called me by my first name.

Yes, we came to share everything after I told him without warning that bitter cold afternoon.

"Clyde, listen patiently. I have only my wedding ring now to my name."

I loved the beautiful expression in his hazel eyes and in the large, almost fierce black pupils as he stared at me.

"Do you miss Uncle Enos?" I wondered later that day when we were together.

"No," he said in a sharp loud voice.

I was both glad and sad because of the remark. Why I felt both things I don't exactly know. I guess it was his honesty.

He was honest like a pane of the finest window glass. I loved his openness. Oh, how I trusted him. And that trust was never betrayed.

I saw at last there was someone I loved. And my love was as pure as his honesty was perfect.

My secret had given us a bond one to the other.

In those long winter evenings on the edge of the Canadian wildlands, there was little to do but doze, then come awake and talk, sip our wine so sparingly (I would not allow him to have more than half a glass an evening), and there was our talk. We talked about the same things over and over again, but we never wearied one another. We were always talking at length on every subject—except the main one. And I knew he was waiting to hear me on that very one.

"How long has it been now, Delia?" His voice sounded as if it were coming from a room away.

At first I was tempted to reply, "How long has it been from what?" Instead I answered, "Three years more or less."

"And you told no one in all this time?"

"I could not tell anyone because for a while I thought maybe I had mislaid them, but even as I offered this excuse, Clyde, I knew I could not be mistaken. I knew something, yes let that word be the right one, something was taking my jewels. Oh, why do I say 'my'? They never belonged to me, dear boy. I never affected jewels. I did not like the feel of them against my skin or clothes. Perhaps they reminded me of the dead."

"So that is all you know, then," he spoke after minutes of silence.

I had to laugh almost uproariously at his tone. "I am laughing, dear Clyde, because you spoke so like an old judge just then. Addressing me as a dubious witness! And dubious witness I am to myself! I accuse myself—of not knowing anything!"

"Could we go to the room where you kept them?" he wondered.

I hesitated.

"No?" he said in a forthright, almost ill-humored way.

"It's a long way up the stairs, and I have never liked that big room where I kept them. Then there are the keys. Many many keys to bother and fumble with."

"Then we won't go," he muttered.

"No, we will, Clyde. We will go."

Ah, I had forgotten indeed what a long way up to the big room it was. Even Clyde got a bit tired. Four or five or more flights.

"Well it's a real castle we live in, my dear," I encouraged him as we toiled upward.

"You must have a good heart and strong lungs," he said, and he smiled and brought his face very close to mine.

Then I pulled out my flashlight, or, as my grandfather would have called it, my torch.

"Now the next flight," I explained, "has poor illumination."

As we approached that terrible door, I brought out the heavy bunch of keys.

"Put this long key, Clyde, in the upper lock. Then this smaller key when you've unlocked the top one, place it in the lower one here."

He did it well, and we went through the door, where, of course, another bigger door awaited us.

"Now, Clyde, here is the second bunch of keys. Put the upper key to the large keyhole above, give the door a good shove and we can go in."

He fumbled a little and I believe I heard him swear for the first time. (Well, his Uncle Enos was a profane old cuss.)

We entered. There were fewer cobwebs now than when I had come in so many months before.

"See all those red velvet cases spread out over the oak table there?" I said. "In the cases were the jewels. Their jewels."

He looked around and I gave him my torch. But then I remembered there was an upper light and I turned it on.

He shut off the torch. He seemed in charge of it all, and much older than his twenty years then. I felt safe, comfortable, almost sleepy from my trust in him.

"Look there, will you!" he exclaimed.

I put on my long-distance glasses and looked where he pointed.

He bent down to touch something on the floor under the red velvet cases.

I took off my glasses and stared.

"What is it, Clyde?" I said.

"Don't you see?" he replied in a hushed way. "It's a white feather. A white bird's feather. Very pretty, isn't it?" He raised up the feather toward my trembling hand.

A strange calm descended on us both after Clyde found the white feather. At first I was afraid to touch it. Clyde coaxed me to take it in my hand, and only after repeated urgings on his part did I do so.

At that moment the calm descended on me as it had many years ago when, during one of my few serious illnesses, old sharp-eyed Doctor Noddy had insisted I take a tincture of opium.

Why, I wondered, did the glimpse of a white bird's feather confer upon both me and Clyde this unusual calm? As if we had found the jewels, or at least had come to understand by what means the jewels had been taken. I say "us" advisedly, for by now Clyde and I were as close as mother and son, even husband and wife. We were so close that sometimes at night I would shudder in my bed and words I was unaware from where they came filled my mouth.

Clyde, more than the jewels, then—let me repeat—was my all, but the jewels were important, I realized dimly, only because they were the bond holding us together.

That evening I allowed Clyde a little more than half a glass of red wine.

"The only pleasure, Clyde," I addressed him, "is in sipping. Gulping, swallowing, spoils all the real delicate pleasure."

I saw his mind was on the white feather.

He had put it on the same table the Ouija board rested on.

"We should see it in a safe place," Clyde said, gazing at the feather.

His statement filled me with puzzlement. I wanted to say, Why ever should we? But I was silent. I spilled some wine on my fresh white dress. He rose at once and went to the back kitchen and came forward with a little basin filled with water. He carefully and painstakingly wiped away the red stain.

"There," Clyde said, looking at where the stain had been.

When he had taken back the basin he sat very quietly for a while, his eyes half-closed, and then:

"I say we should put it in a safe place."

"Is there any such, Clyde, now that the jewels have been taken?"

"Just the same, I think we should keep the feather out where it is visible, don't you?"

"It is certainly a beautiful one," I remarked.

He nodded faintly and then raising his voice said, "It's a clue."

My calm all at once disappeared. I put the wineglass down for fear I might spill more.

"Had you never seen the feather before, Delia?" he inquired.

The way he said my name revealed to me that we were *confederates*, though I would never have used this word to his face. It might have pained him. But we were what the word really meant.

"I think it will lead us to find your jewels," he finished, and he drank, thank heavens, still so sparingly of the wine.

I dared not ask him what he meant.

"I think the place for the feather," I spoke rather loudly, "is in that large collection of cases over there where Cousin Berty kept her assortment of rare South American butterflies."

"I don't think so," Clyde said after a bit.

"Then where would you want it?" I said.

"On your music stand by your piano where it's in full view."

"Full view?" I spoke almost crossly.

"Yes, for it's the clue," he almost shouted. "The feather is our clue. Don't you see?"

He sounded almost angry, certainly jarring if not unkind.

I dared not raise my wineglass, for I would have surely at that moment spilled nearly all of it, and I could not have stood for his cleaning my white dress again that evening. It was too great a ceremony for ruffled nerves.

"There it shall be put, Clyde," I said at last, and he smiled.

Have I forgotten to tell how else we whiled away the very long evenings? Near the music stand where we had placed the feather stood the unused old grand piano, by some miracle still fairly in tune.

Clyde Furness had one of the most beautiful voices I have ever heard. In my youth I had attended the opera. In my day I heard all the great tenors, but it was Clyde's voice which moved me almost to a swoon. We played what is known as parlor songs, ancient, ageless songs. My hands surprised him when he saw how nimble and quick they still were on the keys. My hands surprised me, as a matter of fact. When he sang my fingers moved like a young woman's. When I played the piano alone they were stiff and hit many wrong keys.

But I saw then what he meant. As I played the parlor songs my eyes rested not only on him but on the feather. What he called—the clue.

I had suggested one or two times that now that Uncle Enos had departed, Clyde should move in with me. "There's lots of room here; you can choose what part of the house you like and make yourself at home, godson."

Whenever I'd mentioned his moving in up till then he had always pouted like a small boy. The day we found the feather I felt not only that something had changed in me, in the house, in the very air we breathed, but that something had changed in him.

As I went up to kiss him good night that evening I noticed that over his upper lip there was beginning to grow ever so softly traces of his beard.

"What is it?" I inquired when he hesitated at the door. He touched the place on his cheek where I had kissed him.

"Are you sure as sure can be you still want me to move my things here?" Clyde asked.

"I want you to, of course. You know that. Why should you walk two miles every day to Uncle Enos's and back when it's here the welcome mat is out?"

"You certainly have the room, don't you?" he joked. "How many rooms have you got?" he grinned.

"Oh, I've almost forgotten, Clyde."

"Forty?" he wondered.

I smiled. I kissed him again.

The feather had changed everything. I must have looked at it every time I went near the piano. I touched it occasionally. It seemed to move when I picked it up as if it had breath. It was both warm and cool and so soft except for its strong shaft. I once touched it to my lips and some tears formed in my eyes.

"To think that Clyde is going to be under my roof," I spoke aloud and put the feather back on the music stand.

Dr. Noddy paid his monthly visit shortly after Clyde had come to stay with me.

Dr. Noddy was an extremely tall man but, as if apologetic for his height, he stooped and was beginning to be terribly bent so that his head was never held high but always leaned over like he was everlastingly writing prescriptions.

This visit was remarkable for the fact that he acted unsurprised to see Clyde Furness in my company. One would have thought from the doctor's attitude that Clyde had always lived with me.

He began his cursory examination of me, pulse, listening to my lungs and heart, rolling back my eyelids, having me stick out my tongue.

"The tongue and the whites of the eyes tell everything," he once said.

Then he gave me another box of the little purple pills to be taken on rising and on getting into bed.

"And shan't we examine the young man then?" Dr. Noddy spoke as if to himself.

He had Clyde remove his shirt and undershirt much to the poor boy's embarrassment. I went into an adjoining closet and brought out one of my grandfather's imported dressing gowns and insisted Clyde put this on to avoid further humiliation.

Dr. Noddy examined Clyde's ears carefully, but his attention seemed to wander over to the music stand. After staring at it for some time and changing his eyeglasses, he then looked at Clyde's hair and scalp and finally took out a pocket comb of his own and combed the boy's hair meticulously.

"Delia, he has parted his hair wrong. Come over here and see for yourself."

I took my time coming to where the doctor was examining my godson, and my deliberateness annoyed him. But all the time nonetheless he kept looking over at the music stand.

"I want you to part his hair on his left side, not on his right. His hair is growing all wrong as a result. And another thing, look in his right ear. See all that wax?"

Dr. Noddy now went over to his little doctor's bag and drew out a small silver instrument of some kind.

"I will give you this for his ear. Clean out the wax daily, just as I am doing now." Clyde gave out a little cry, more of surprise than of pain, as the doctor cleaned his ear of the wax.

"Now then, we should be fine." But Dr. Noddy was no longer paying any attention to us. He was staring at the music stand and finally he went over to it. He straightened up as much as age and rheumatism would permit.

It was the feather, of course, he had been staring at so intently, so continuously!

He picked the feather up and came over to where I was studying the instrument he had recommended for Clyde's ear.

"Where did this come from?" he spoke in almost angry, certainly accusatory tones.

"Oh, that," I said and I stuttered for the first time since I was a girl.

"Where did it come from?" he now addressed Clyde in a tone of rage.

"Well, sir," Clyde began, but failed to continue.

"Clyde and I found it the other day when we went to the fourth story, Dr. Noddy."

"You climbed all the way up there, did you?" the old man mumbled, but all his attention was on the feather.

"May I keep this for the time being?" he said, turning brusquely to me.

"If you wish, Doctor, of course," I told him when I saw his usual bad temper was asserting itself.

"Unless, Delia, you have some use for it."

Before I could think I said, "Only as a clue, Dr. Noddy."

"What?" Dr. Noddy almost roared.

Taking advantage of his deafness, I soothed him by saying, "We thought it rather queer, didn't we, Clyde, that there was a feather in the room where I used to keep my grandmother's jewels."

Whether Dr. Noddy heard this last statement or not I do not know. He put the feather in his huge leather wallet and returned the wallet inside his outer coat with unusual and irritable vigor.

"I will be back then, in a month. Have Clyde here drink more well water during the day." Then, staring at me he added, "I take it he's good company for you, Delia Mattlock."

Before I could even say yes, he was gone, slamming the big front door behind him.

Dr. Noddy's visit had spoiled something. I do not know exactly how to describe it otherwise. A kind of gloom settled over everything.

Clyde kept holding his ear and touching his beautiful hair and his scalp.

"Does your ear pain you, Clyde?" I finally broke the silence.

"No," he said after a very long pause. "But the funny thing is I hear better now."

"We always called earwax beeswax when I was a girl," I said. Clyde snickered a little but only, I believe, to be polite.

"He took the feather, didn't he?" Clyde said, coming out of his reverie.

"And I wonder why, Clyde. Of course Dr. Noddy is, among other things, a kind of outdoor man. A naturalist, they call it. Studies animals and birds."

"Oh, that could explain it then, maybe."

"Not quite," I disagreed. "Did you see how he kept staring at the feather on the music stand?"

"I did. That's about all he did while he was here."

I nodded. "I never take his pills. Oh, I did at the beginning, but they did nothing for me that I could appreciate. Probably they are made of sugar. I've heard doctors often give some of their patients sugar pills."

"He certainly changed the part in my hair. Excuse me while I look in the mirror over there now, Delia."

Clyde went over to the fifteen-foot-high mirror brought from England so many years gone by. He made little cries of surprise or perhaps dismay as he looked at himself in the glass.

"I don't look like me," he said gruffly and closed his eyes.

"If you don't like the new part in your hair we can just comb it back the way it was."

"No, I think maybe I like the new way it's parted. Have to get used to it I suppose, that's all."

"Your hair would look fine with any kind of a part you choose. You have beautiful hair."

He mumbled a thank-you and blushed.

"I had a close girl chum at school, Irma Stairs. She had the most beautiful hair in the world. The color they call Titian. She let it grow until it fell clear to below her knees. When she would let it all down sometimes just to show me, I could not believe my eyes. It made me a little uneasy. I like your hair, though, Clyde, even better."

"What do you think he wants to keep the white feather for?" Clyde wondered.

We walked toward the piano just then as if from a signal.

I opened the book of parlor songs and we began our singing and playing hour.

He sang "Come Where My Love Lies Dreaming." It made the tears come. Then he sang a rollicking sailor's song.

But things were not right after the doctor's visit.

"It's time for our glass of wine," I said, rising from the piano. "We need it after old Dr. Noddy."

A great uneasiness, even sadness now came over both of us.

I have for many years had the bad habit of talking to myself or, what was considered worse, talking out my own thoughts aloud even in front of company.

Dr. Noddy's having walked off with the feather Clyde and I had found in the jewel room was the source of our discontent.

Thinking Clyde was dozing after sipping his wine, I found myself speaking aloud of my discomfiture and even alarm.

"He is making us feel like the accused," I said, and then I added more similar thoughts.

To my surprise I heard Clyde answering me, which was very unlike him.

I felt we were in some ancient Italian opera singing back to one another, echoing one another's thoughts.

"I didn't like the way he stared at us, holding the feather like it was proof of something," Clyde started up.

"Exactly, godson. The very words I was trying to express when I thought you were dozing."

"What does he aim to do with it?" Clyde raised his voice.

"And what does he mean to do with it regarding us?" I took

up his point. "He acts more like a policeman or detective than a doctor where the feather is concerned."

"You take the words right out of my mouth," he spoke loudly.

"Oh Clyde, Clyde whatever would I do without you?"

"You'd do all right, Delia. You know you would." He picked up the empty wineglass and to my considerable shock he spat into it. "It's me," he said, "who wouldn't know where to turn if I wasn't here with you. I would be the one who didn't know up from down."

"With all your talents, dear boy!" I cried, almost angry he had spoken so against himself. "Never!"

"Never what, Delia? You know how I failed in school and disappointed Uncle Enos."

"Failed him, failed school! Poppycock! Then it was their fault if you did. Uncle Enos adored you. You could do no wrong in his eyes. Oh, if only he were here to tell us about the feather. And about that wretched doctor. He would set us straight."

"Now, now," Clyde said, rising, and he came over to my chair and all at once he knelt down and looked up into my troubled face.

"Does old Dr. Noddy know your jewels have disappeared?"

"I think so."

"You think so?"

"I'm sure I told him when I was having an attack of the neuralgia that they had all vanished."

"And what did he say then?"

"It's not so much what he said, he never says much, it was the way he stared at me when I said, 'All my jewels are gone.' "

"Stared how?"

"As he stared at us today when he held the feather. Stared as if I had done something wrong. As if I had done away with my own jewels."

"Oh, he couldn't think that against you, Delia."

"He thinks against everybody. He feels anybody who needs him and his services has something to be held against them. If we are ailing, then we are to blame. That's what I gather from old Dr. Noddy."

"And now, Delia," he said, rising and standing behind my chair so that I could feel his honey-sweet breath against my hair.

"And now," he went on, "we have to wait like the accused in a court of law."

"Exactly, exactly. And, oh my stars, what on earth can he do with a feather, anyhow? Make *it* confess?"

We both laughed.

"I can't go to bed on all of this we're facing now," I told Clyde. "I am going to the kitchen and make us some coffee."

"Let me make it, Delia."

"No, no, I am the cook here and the coffee maker. You make it too weak. I must stay alert. And we must put Doc Noddy on trial here tonight before he can put us in the witness box and call us liars to our face."

With that I went into the kitchen and took down the jar of Arabian coffee, got out the old coffee grinder, and let Clyde (who had followed me without being asked), let *him* grind the beans.

"What a heavenly aroma," I said when our chore was finished. "And I made it with well water, of course, for as old Doc Noddy says you must drink well water religiously, dear lad."

We felt less threatened, less on trial at any rate, drinking the Arabian brew.

Then a great cloud of worry and fear descended upon me. I did all I could to conceal my feelings from my godson.

The source of my fear was, of course, who else but Dr. Noddy.

I recalled in the long heavy burden of memory that Dr. Noddy was nearly as old as I, at least he must have been far into his eighties at this time. But it was not his age which weighed upon me. It was the memory of Dr. Noddy having been accused a half century or more ago of practicing hypnotism on his patients. And also being suspected of giving his older patients a good deal of opium. But the opium did not concern me now, has indeed never worried me. He only gave it in any case to those of us who were so advanced in age we could no longer endure the pain or the weight of so many years, so much passed time.

No, what gave me pause was hypnotism, if indeed he ever had

practiced it. His taking away the feather had brought back this old charge. But my godson sensed my sorrow. He watched me with his beautiful if almost pitiless hazel eyes.

At last he took a seat on a little hand-carved stool beside me. He took my right hand in his and kissed it.

"You are very troubled, Delia," he said at last. He seemed to be looking at the gnarled, very blue veins on the hand he had just kissed.

"I am that," I said after a lengthy silence on my part.

"You don't need to say more, Delia. We understand one another."

"I know that, godson, but see here, I want to share with you all that is necessary for me to share. I want you to have everything you deserve."

"I don't deserve much."

"Never say that again. You don't know how precious you are, Clyde, and that is because you *are* perfection."

He turned a furious red and faced away from me.

"Let me think how I am to tell you, Clyde." I spoke so low he cupped his ear and then he again took my hand in his.

"I can see it's something you've got to share."

"Unwillingly, Clyde, so unwillingly. Perhaps, though, when I tell you, you won't think it's worth troubling about."

He nodded encouragement.

"Clyde, years ago before even your parents were born, before the days of Uncle Enos, Dr. Noddy was charged with having practiced hypnotism on his patients."

Clyde's mouth came open and then he closed it tight. I thought his lips had formed a cuss word.

We sat in silence for a lengthy while.

"That is why his taking away the feather has worried me."

"And worries me now," he almost gasped.

"My worry over the white feather finally recalled the charge he had hypnotized some of his patients."

"But what is the connection," he wondered, "between a bird's feather and hypnotism?"

"I don't know myself, Clyde. Only I feel the two have a connection we don't understand."

He smiled a strange smile.

"We must be calm and patient. Maybe nothing will happen at all and we will resume our old quiet evenings," I said.

He released my hand softly.

Looking into his face, yes, I saw what I had feared. My trouble had fallen upon him. And so that long evening drew to its close.

For a whole month we could do nothing but wait in suspense for Dr. Noddy's return. Now that I come to think of it, how happy I would have been if there had been no Dr. Noddy! Yes, I do think and believe that had he never appeared out of the fog and the snow and the bitter winds, Clyde and I would have been happy and without real sorrow forever. Dr. Noddy, having found the clue, the feather, began to dig and delve, uncover and discover, sift evidence, draw conclusions and then shatter all our peace and love along with our parlor song evenings and Clyde's solos on the Jew's harp. All was to be spoiled, shattered, brought to nothing.

But then, as someone was to tell me much later (perhaps it was one of the gypsy fortune-tellers who happen by in this part of the world), someone said to me, *"Had it not been Dr. Noddy, there would have been someone else to have brought sorrow and change into your lives."*

"Then call it destiny, why don't you?" I shouted to this forgotten person, gypsy or preacher or peddler or whoever it was who made the point. Oh well, then, just call it Dr. Noddy and be done with it.

"In our part of the world, nature sometimes is enabled to work out phenomena not observed by ordinary people," Dr. Noddy began on his next visit, sounding a little like a preacher.

Dr. Noddy had tasted the wine Clyde had brought him from the cellar even more sparingly if possible than was our own custom. (I had felt the physician needed wine to judge by his haggard and weary appearance.)

To my embarrassment he fished out a piece of cork, tiny but, as I saw, very distasteful to him.

"Fetch Doctor a clean glass," I suggested to Clyde.

Dr. Noddy meanwhile went on talking about nature's often

indulging in her own schemes and experiments, indifferent to man.

"She in the end can only baffle us. Our most indefatigable scholars and scientists finally admit defeat and throw up their hands to acknowledge Her inscrutable puissance."

I looked into my wineglass as if also searching for pieces of cork. Clyde had meanwhile brought Dr. Noddy a sparkling clean glass. He had opened a new bottle and poured out fresh wine.

"Dr. Noddy was saying, Clyde, whilst you were out of earshot, that Nature is an inscrutable goddess," I summarized the doctor's speech.

"Yes," Clyde answered and gave me a look inviting instruction. I could only manage a kind of sad sour smile.

"The feather," Dr. Noddy began again, pulling it out now from his huge wallet, "is one of her pranks."

Clyde and I exchanged quick glances.

"But we should let Clyde here expatiate on Dame Nature's hidden ways and purposes. Your godson was known, from the time he came to live with Uncle Enos, as a true son of the wilderness, a boon companion to wild creatures and the migratory fowl."

Clyde lowered his head down almost to the rim of his wineglass.

"Our young man therefore must have known that nearby there lived a perfect battalion of white crows, or perhaps they were white blackbirds!"

At that moment Clyde gave out a short stifled gasp which may have chilled Dr. Noddy into silence. To my uneasiness I saw Dr. Noddy rise and go over to my godson. He took both Clyde's hands and held them tightly and then slowly allowed the hands to fall to his sides. Dr. Noddy then touched Clyde's eyes with both his hands. When the doctor removed his hands, Clyde's eyes were closed.

"Please tell us now," Dr. Noddy moved even closer to Clyde, "if you know of the birds I am speaking of."

"I am not positive," Clyde said in a stern, even grand tone so unlike the way he usually spoke. He kept his eyes still closed.

"You must have known there were white crows or white

blackbirds, what some who delve into their histories call a sport of nature."

"I often thought," Clyde spoke musingly and in an almost small-boy voice now, "often would have sworn I saw white birds in the vicinity of the Bell Tower."

"The Bell Tower!" I could not help but gasp. The Bell Tower was one of the many deserted large buildings which I had long ago sold to Uncle Enos at a very low price.

"You see," Dr. Noddy turned to me. "We have our witness!"

"But what can it all mean?" I spoke with partial vexation. "It is so late, Dr. Noddy, in time I mean. Must we go round Robin Hood's barn before you tell us what you have found out?"

"This feather," Dr. Noddy now held it again and almost shook it in my face, "let Clyde expand upon it." The old man turned now to my godson. "Open your eyes, Clyde!" He extended the feather to Clyde. "Tell us what you think, now, my boy."

Clyde shrank back in alarm from the feather. "It could certainly be from a white crow if there is such a bird," my godson said.

"Or a white blackbird, Clyde?"

Clyde opened his eyes wide and stared at his questioner. "All I know, Delia," Clyde turned to me, "is, yes, I have seen white birds flying near the Bell Tower, and sometimes . . ."

"And sometimes," Dr. Noddy made as if to rise from his chair.

"Sometimes flying into the open or the broken windows of the Bell Tower."

"And did you ever see a white crow carrying anything in its beak when you saw it making its way to your Bell Tower?" Clyde's eyes closed again.

"I may have, sir, yes, I may have spied something there, but you see," and he again turned his eyes now opened to me, "you see I was so startled to glimpse a large white bird against the high green trees and the dark sky, for near the Bell Tower the sky always looks dark. I was startled and I was scared." Some quick small tears escaped from his right eye.

"And could those things the white bird carried, Clyde, could they have been jewels?"

At that very moment, the wineglass fell from Clyde's hand and he slipped from his chair and fell prone to the thick carpet below.

Dr. Noddy rushed to his side. I hurried also and bent over my prostrate godson.

"Oh, Dr. Noddy, for pity's sake, he is not dead, is he!"

Dr. Noddy turned a deprecatory gaze in my direction. "Help me carry him to that big sofa yonder," he said in reply.

Oh, I was more than opposed by then to Dr. Noddy, seeing my godson lying there as if in his coffin. I blamed it all on the old physician. "You frightened him, Doctor," I shouted.

I was surprised at my own angry words leveled against him. I would look now to my godson lying there as if passed over and then return my gaze to Noddy. I must have actually sworn, for when I came out of my fit of anger I heard the old man say, as if he was also in a dream, "I never would have thought I would hear you use such language. And against someone who has only your good at heart, Delia. Only your good!"

Taking me gently by the hand he ushered me into a seldom-used little sitting room. The word hypnotism seemed at that moment to be not a word but a being, perhaps *it* was a bird flying about the room.

"What I want to impart to you, Delia," the old physician began, "is simply this. I must now take action. I and I alone must pay a visit to the Bell Tower. For in its ruined masonry there lies the final explanation of the mystery."

The very mention of the Bell Tower had always filled me with a palsylike terror, so when Dr. Noddy announced that he must go there I could not find a word to say to him.

"Did you hear me, Delia?" he finally spoke in a querulous but soft tone.

"If you think you must, dear friend," I managed to reply. "If there is no other way."

"But now we must look in on Clyde," he said after a pause. At the same time he failed to make a motion to rise. A heavy long silence ensued on both our parts when unexpectedly my godson himself entered our private sitting room. We both stared without greeting him.

Clyde looked refreshed after his slumber. His face had resumed its high coloring, and he smiled at us as he took a seat next to Dr. Noddy.

"I have been telling Delia, Clyde, that I must make a special visit to the Bell Tower."

Clyde's face fell and a slight paleness again spread over his features.

"Unless you object, Clyde," the doctor added.

As I say, the very mention of the Bell Tower had always filled me with dread and loathing. But I had never told Clyde or Dr. Noddy the partial reason for my aversion. I did not tell them now what it was which troubled me. My great-uncle had committed suicide in the Tower over a hundred years ago, and then later my cousin Keith had fallen from the top of the edifice to his death.

These deaths had been all but forgotten in our village, and perhaps even I no longer remembered them until Dr. Noddy announced he was about to pay a visit there.

While I was lost in these musings I suddenly came to myself in time to see Noddy buttoning up his great coat preparatory to leaving.

"But you can't be paying your visit there now!" I cautioned him. "What with a bad storm coming on and with the freezing cold and snow what it is."

"This is one visit that should not be postponed, Delia! So stop once and for all your fussing."

He actually blew a kiss to me, and raised his hand to Clyde in farewell.

I watched him go from the big front window. The wind had changed and was blowing from a northeast direction. The sycamore trees were bending almost to the ground in a fashion such as I could not ever recall.

I came back to my seat.

"Are you warm enough, Delia?" Clyde asked with smiling concern.

"Clyde, listen," I began, gazing at him intently.

"Yes, Delia, speak your mind," he said gaily, almost as if we were again partaking of the jollity of our evenings.

"We must be prepared, Clyde, for whatever our good doctor will discover in the Bell Tower," I said in a lackluster manner.

Clyde gazed down at the carpet under his feet.

I felt then that if I were not who I was I would be afraid to be alone that night with Clyde Furness. But I had gone beyond fear.

"Shan't we have our evening wine, Delia?" he said, and as he spoke fresh disquietude began again.

"Please, dear boy, let's have our wine."

We drank if possible even more sparingly. I believe indeed we barely touched the wineglasses to our lips. Time passed in a churchlike silence as we sat waiting for the doctor's return. I more than Clyde could visualize the many steps the old man must climb before he reached the top floor of the Tower. And I wondered indeed if he would be able to summon the strength to make it. Perhaps the visit thither would be too much for his old bones.

It was the longest evening I can recall. And what made it even more painful was that as I studied my godson I realized he was no longer the Clyde Furness I had been so happy with. No, he had changed. I studied his face for a sign, but there was no sign—his face was closed to me. Then began a current of words which will remain with me to the end of my days:

"It's hard for me to believe, Clyde, our good doctor's theory that it is a bird which has taken my ancestors' jewels."

Clyde straightened up to gaze at me intently.

"Ah, but, Delia, do you understand how hard it has been for me over and again these many weeks to have to listen to your doubts and suspicions!"

"But doubts and suspicions, Clyde, have no claim upon you where I am concerned."

"No claim," he spoke, in a bitterness which took me totally by surprise. "Perhaps, Delia, not in your mind, but what about mine?"

"But Clyde, for God in heaven's sake you can't believe that I regard you as . . ." But I could not finish the sentence. Clyde finished it for me.

"That I am the white blackbird, Delia? For that is what you think in your inmost being."

Then I cried out, "Never, never has such a thought crossed my mind!"

"Perhaps not in your waking hours, Delia. But in your deepest being, in your troubled sleeping hours, Delia, I feel you think I am the white blackbird."

I could think of no response to make then to his dreadful avalanche of words launched against me. Nothing, I came to see, could dispel his thought that I considered him the thief, the white blackbird himself. My mouth was dry. My heart itself was stilled. My godson was lost to me, I all at once realized. He would never again be the young and faithful evening companion who had given my life its greatest happiness. As he returned my gaze I saw that he understood what I felt and he looked away not only in sadness but in grief. I knew then he would leave me.

Yet we had to sit on like sentinels, our worry growing as the minutes and the hours slipped by.

It was long past midnight and we sat on. We neither of us wanted more wine. But at last Clyde insisted he make some coffee, and I was too troubled and weak to offer to make it myself.

As we were sipping our second cup of the Arabian brew we heard footsteps, and then banging on the door with a heavy walking stick.

Clyde and I both cried out with relief when Dr. Noddy, covered with wet snow and carrying three parcels, stomped in, his white breath covering his face like a mask.

"Help me, my boy," Dr. Noddy scolded. He was handing Clyde three packages wrapped in cloth of old cramoisie velvet.

"And be careful, put them over there on that big oak table, why don't you, where they used to feed the threshers in summers gone by."

As Clyde was carrying the parcels to the oak table, I saw with surprise Dr. Noddy pick up Clyde's second cup of Arabian coffee and gulp it all down at one swallow. He wiped his mustache on a stray napkin near the cup!

"Help me off with my great coat, Delia, for I'm frozen to the bone and my hands are cakes of ice."

As soon as I had helped him off with his coat and Clyde had hung it on a hall tree, Dr. Noddy collapsed on one of the larger settees. He took off his spectacles and wiped them and muttered something inaudible.

Because he kept his eyes closed, I thought for a while the doctor had fallen into one of those slumbers I had observed in him before. My own eyes felt heavy as lead.

Then I heard him speaking in louder than usual volume:

"I have fetched back everything, Delia, that was missing or lost to you. And I have wrapped what I've found in scraps and shreds from the crimson hanging curtains of the Bell Tower."

His voice had an unaccustomed ring of jubilee to it.

"Bring out the first package, Clyde," he shouted the order, and as he spoke he waved both his arms like the conductor of a band.

Clyde carried the first bundle morosely and placed it on the coffee table before us.

"Now, Delia, let us begin!" Noddy snapped one of the cords with his bone pocket knife and began undoing the bundle of its coverings with a ferocious swiftness.

I felt weak as water as he exposed to view, one after the other, my diamond necklace, my emerald brooch, my ruby rings, my pearl necklace and, last of all, my sapphire earrings!

"Tell me they are yours, Delia," Noddy roared as only a deaf man can.

I nodded.

"And don't weep," he cautioned me. "We'll have no bawling here tonight after the trouble I've been to in the Tower!"

At a signal from the doctor, Clyde fetched to the table even more doggedly the second package, and this time my godson watched as the doctor undid the wrappings.

"Tell us what you see," Dr. Noddy scolded and glowered.

"My gold necklace," I answered, "and yes, my diamond choker, and those are my amethyst rings and that priceless lavaliere and—oh see—my long-forgotten gold bracelet."

I went on and on. But my eyes were swimming with the tears he had forbidden me to shed.

Then the third bundle was produced, unwrapped and displayed before us as if I were presiding at Judgment Day itself.

"They are all mine, Doctor," I testified, avoiding his direful stare. I touched the gems softly and looked away.

"What treasures," Clyde kept mumbling and shaking his head.

My eyes were all on Clyde rather than the treasures, for I took note again that it was not so much perhaps Dr. Noddy who had taken him away from me, it was the power of the treasures themselves which had separated my godson and me forever.

And so the jewels which I had never wanted in my possession from the beginning were returned again to be mine. Their theft or disappearance had plagued me, of course, over the years as a puzzle will tease and torment one, but now seeing them again in my possession all I could think of was the fact that their restoration was the cause of Clyde's no longer being mine, no longer loving me! I was unable to explain this belief even to myself but I knew it was the truth.

The next day Clyde, holding his few belongings in a kind of sailor's duffel bag, his eyes desperately looking away from my face, managed to get out the words: "Delia, my dear friend, now that the weather is beginning to clear, I do feel I must be returning to Uncle Enos's so I can look after his property as I promised him in his last hours."

Had he stabbed me with one of my servants' hunting knives his words could not have struck me deeper. I could barely hold out my hand to him.

"I have, you know too, a bounden duty to see that his property is kept as he wanted me to keep it," he could barely whisper. "But should you need me you have only to call, and I will respond."

I am sure a hundred things came to both our lips as we stood facing one another in our farewell. Instead, all we could do was gaze for a last time into each other's eyes.

With Clyde's return "in bounden duty" to his Uncle Enos's, there went our evenings of wine sipping and parlor songs and all the other things that had made for me complete happiness.

I was left then with only the stolen jewels, stolen, according to our Dr. Noddy, by a breed of white blackbird known as far back as remote antiquity as creatures irresistibly attracted to steal anything which was shining bright and dazzling.

Shortly after Clyde had departed for his uncle's, I had called some world-famous jewel merchants for a final appraisal of the treasures. The appraisers came on the heels of my godson's de-

parture. The men reminded me of London policemen or de-
tectives, impeccable gentlemen, formal and with a stultifying
politeness. As they appraised my jewels, however, even they
would pause from time to time and briefly stare at me with
something like incomprehension. They would break the silence
then to say in their dry clear voices:

"Is nothing missing, ma'am?"

"Nothing at all," I would reply to the same question put to
me again and again.

I had by then taken such a horror to the jewels and to their
beauty which everyone had always spoken of with bated breath
that even to draw near them brought on me a kind of fit of
shuddering.

After I had signed countless pages of documents, the appraisers hauled the whole collection off to a famous safety vault in
Montreal.

Then for the first time in years I felt a kind of relief that
would have been, if not happiness, a kind of benediction or
thanksgiving, had I not been so aware I had lost forever my
evenings with my godson.

WAITING ON EURYDICE

• J. E. ROBINSON •

In high school, dating was done by Martians. Everyone save I dated. There were those who went out; they had quickies in the back of Fords, or nightlongs in someone's room, aborted, occasionally gave birth, sometimes married, but I cowered in the dark and knew myself. A second's satisfaction, rested in guilt, and someone knocked on the door to ask what I was doing. Most of the time, it was my mother, come to see how I was before going off to some meeting with quaint old ladies in discreet dresses and wigs who would ask "your baby, Rose—now, he's still available, ain't he?" I told her I was thinking—I was, really, about Romeo for the thirty-fifth time of the day, wondering how in the world someone fourteen and in leotards could possibly get a twelve year old without either set of parents knowing about it.

I wish I had his luck. My parents knew my every move, my every thought even before I did and they had a bevy of friends to help in the surveillance. If I dared think about looking at a girl sideways through a rearview mirror, they would find out. My father was the best at that sort of thing, his rich black eyes peering through his pipe smoke giving me that sort of "who you trying to fool?—I know what you're thinking" look. This was especially frightening back in first and second grade because he would always leave court in time to pick me up just as I zipped up and came down from Chris Wilson chasing me after school.

I almost wetted every time I heard his Saab's engine because he saw, I know, and of course I didn't explain: a strawberry-haired ten year old trying to touch me and then chasing me up a pear tree is something I hardly think he would ever believe could possibly be done to me. Besides, I couldn't explain, what with the way his eyes warmed up when Chris came and spoke and said "See you tomorrow, Skip" and he would ask if Chris was sweet on me, as though she were my girl, and invariably it became an issue at dinner, sounding suspiciously like marriage, and, if my older brother Ted was home, he would egg it on, and was I scared. Then, as older, I took refuge in my father. I would lean against his body on the sofa in his den, luxuriating in that slick and queer smell of potpourri that comes from used pipe-tobacco grounds burnt by a cigar tip and staring blankly at the green, amber, and red equalizer lights dance to an orchestral, every now and then watching his omnipresent pipe puff clouds topped by rings of smoke that floated upward, fibers twisting and rotating, giving the smoke flight into disintegration, sometimes sucking his cigar until tar peed from the butt, I the pensive, moody, seeking child always, always hoping he had no idea what I was thinking, though his look made that hope vain. His hand would lift, the smoke would part, the fin de siècle of Brahms complete with hoop skirts waltzing would bid the lights dance, and I leaned against his body like so many children, finding sanctuary, my head bobbing at the will of his lungs, and I would try to imagine my father with my mother on the floor, waltzing, of course, as they had done at my sister Adele's wedding reception in the Park across the street, but I saw my mom up in her attic workroom transplanting philodendron cuttings and the Judge down in his chambers shrouded by stratus clouds of smoke and thick drifts of pulp, commanding his clerks to use their heads for something more than just passing kidney stones, and I was left to stare at bodices, careful to stare not too hard. When I did, the masks of the Dan frowned, told my parents, their look saying that was something I ought not do, and I awoke to the airy breath of my afghan descending upon me in the Captain Black–scented pitch of my room.

I suppose I was fourteen, maybe fifteen, before I saw girls as something other than Amazons and I was told they thought of me as something other than fresh meat. It was slowly turning eleven-thirty, and Drew Ford and I laid out on my bed, wrung out from a morning of playing tennis in the continental humidity of July. The room smelled of the quiet rancor of boys sweating, and Drew had it especially bad: before I could get him a towel, he had taken off his shirt and used it to wipe the sweat from his face, then hung it to dry down his front. His chest was a water-pale pinkish white, the umbra of his tits standing pink like the tip of a tiger-lily's tongue, his upper arms and thighs sunburn red from having used the wrong suntan lotion with the wrong sunscreen, and the light silky hairs of his forearms and lower legs were sweat brown, as dark as his bangs, and there was a large suspended oval pressing against the flap of his fly that I couldn't help noticing. My father's red Abyssinian Bert joined us temporarily, sniffed out bodies, and left, her sleek body floating like Torvil and Dean on Bosnian ice. After playing Queen, my stereo was still on and, not knowing so, we were serenaded by a Haydn string quartet that made us languish in the air conditioning even more. Like Drew, I had a Coors he had carried as a six-pack all the way from his house in Whitman Township—as we played, it stayed with his bicycle in a backpack, making it warm, and for that reason I nursed it. We were alone, my parents at work in their offices downtown and not expected home for lunch, though I listened for any sound saying they were coming, hearing nothing more than the Kidds' husky Henson chasing a swift hutch of rabbits Brian Kidd and the lawnmower had spooked out next door. We lay, we drank, he talked about burns, rashes, and pimples, and I listened. After adjusting himself and groaning that he hoped he wasn't coming down with jock itch, he said he heard there was a girl in one of his classes that sort of liked me.

"Who?"

"Kathy Lawrence. She's blonde 'n' big—you know—" He cupped his breasts with his hands. "A real nice body. Not a bad face, either." He found my yearbook and showed me her; from her picture, she looked as he said. When school started in September, he showed me her in person on our way back to the boys' locker room after an activity in the girls' gym; in flesh, she was everything the picture promised, only more so. He wanted

to call her attention to us, but I shook him off, letting her concentrate upon chemical formulae rather than see us in our shorts
and those irritating jock straps. Instead, she came to me in the
dark and stayed with me a couple nights; I looked for her at
school and saw her occasionally in the parking lot with the other
Whitmaners and watched her talk and smile easily. I heard
Whitmaners snicker. For a semester, I chose things in the girls'
gym just so I could walk by the chemistry room and see her up
close and, for a semester, Drew went as well and offered to
introduce us and, for a semester, I refused, and then the semester
ended and Driver's Ed came in and moved a fourth of us soph-
omores to a PE hour in which for me there was no Kathy
Lawrence en route to the girls' gym. Drew thought it a shame.

The start of our junior year meant meeting Kathy Lawrence,
and Drew Ford finally getting his wish. All summer, he tried to
get me to think enough about her to see her face to face, and
he took me out to Whitman Township after tennis to show me
where she lived, and he even got her phone number—more than
once, he called her wherever we were, handed me the phone,
and I always hung up when someone answered. Then, he asked
"Don't you wanna meet her?" Our junior year, he was elated a
chance of scheduling had dropped us into the same Dr. Levin
American Lit class. He came rushing out just before I walked
in and, grabbing me, exclaimed "she's here!—she's here!" I
looked—in a room half full with hes, the only she was Dr. Levin,
hardly something for Drew to get spastic about.

"Who? Dr. Levin?"

"No, no! Kathy Lawrence!"

By then, that name had a way of making me sick and it was
doing it again. I couldn't help but stare when she entered, and
she stared in kind—"love," I think it was. She was soft in her
selection of yellows and whites and the scoops of her chest made
me oblivious to almost everything else—away and at a distance,
she seemed not quite real, then near she was, and I turned pre-
occupied with her; to all, I was daydreaming. That sick-to-the-
stomach feeling of gas just being gas and heading nowhere came
over me and it became worse as I glanced periodically at the
slowly nonmoving time pieces of the class reaching for the hour
of lunch . . . tension made us grin, and she had good teeth.

When lunch came and Dr. Levin's class was over, I started my way to her to introduce myself, but she beat me to it.

"Skip Macalester—"

"Kathy Lawrence—"

"Hi."

"Hi."

Casually, we walked to the next hour—I had lunch, she Trigonometry with Gerald Banks, whose niece he thought would go well with me. I was gone before Mr. Banks could see me. That was all we saw of one another that day, and it was over a year in the making. Drew called that night to see how we fared without him. "We did well," I said, and he was happy. Come that Saturday, he said, we were to go to her house.

Saturday morning, I was up earlier than usual. Of course, my parents were surprised. They were having breakfast on the terrace in the backyard. The Judge sat back from the table, knees casually crossed, hands leafing through the *Courier* before contemplating the obituaries, two *jodh*-shaped streaks juxtaposed on the face of his black onyx ring shining in the sun, glasses sitting flipped-up on his bald head, fresh cigar smoke dissipating close to the gray left in his hair. Mom was just as intense, removed from the table with some briefs she was mending for the firm, pausing time and time again to pick death from some maidenhair that belonged in the solarium, and, at times, I think she thought about something Macalester, Wharton, Stone, and Parker was doing, since the firm's doings involved her. They looked up as I came through the French doors, their readings and other considerations giving way to me, and it was part of that parental intuitive to look me over. Unlike other September Saturdays, I was really dressed. I had khakis like theirs and a red rugby shirt striped oatmeal and blue (both of which our maid pressed for me). I wore no socks; neither Mom nor the Judge liked that. I wore cologne.

I ate a piece of bacon before sitting on the edge of a planter of mixed roses. I read part of the paper and listened to Mom and the Judge go back and forth over a case being granted cert by the Supreme Court last term. Then, they looked at me. Why, they seemed to ask, why, on an early September Saturday morning, why was I up, dressed like that, scented like that, eating like that. Were Drew and I going to play tennis as usual, or could it be I would be off to see a girl?

Drew was my salvation. When he came, the Judge's cigar was down to a stub and he flung it past the roses and waved the smoke away. He always did that for guests. Drew was used to it. As he came around from the front, he was grinning (he always grinned around Mom and the Judge, even though I told him to stop it). They smiled back, and offered him breakfast. When Drew sat down across from me, he looked like he was about to laugh. He was in no place to laugh: he had been cleaned, neatened, and oiled. He smelled better than usual, and had even brushed his hair. He wore his usual shirt and shorts, but he also wore loafers. As usual, he wore no socks. He winked. I looked at the table. Mom fixed him a plate, then disappeared. (I think the phone rang.) After she was gone, I watched the Judge watch Drew eat. Then, Drew looked at me.

"What's wrong," Drew asked.

"Nothing," I said. I cleared my throat, and drank a glass of orange juice real slow. I cleared my throat again. "We're going out to see a girl."

"Oh," the Judge said. "Who?"

Casablanca fans and high, arched windows with miniblinds, as they are at the firm's offices in the St. Croix building downtown, sun and shade-lit, smoked Republican in oyster-white paint and walnut parquet flooring—that was the Judge's world. Would Kathy fit? . . . she lived in a tri-level, on a cul-de-sac, in a subdivision, in the middle of nowhere in Whitman Township . . . the Judge kept three-by-five dossiers locked in the cherry buchershrank in his den—there was nothing there under "Lawrence." Sooner or later, he would ask someone what they knew about her family, but I knew they wouldn't know. I knew she wouldn't fit.

I said nothing. The Judge creased his napkin and set it in his plate. Then, he examined his glasses, cleaned them, and placed them on his knee. Mom finally came out. She began watering the flowers, which could have waited for the yardman, if you ask me. While she did so, she loitered around the terrace. Drew was quietly, blissfully eating. Then he smiled again. Something was feeling my leg.

"Anything the matter," the Judge asked.

"No," I said. I pretended to drop part of the paper, and, when I picked it up, I looked under the table. Bert was under the table.

"So," Mom asked finally, "what's on the agenda today?"

"Nothing," I said.

"They're going to see a girl," the Judge said.

"Oh," she said. I shrank. "Who?" she asked.

I shook my head. "You don't know her. Just a girl."

It was just eleven when Drew and I left. The clocktower at Main Street Presbyterian Church began tolling from the other side of Milton High School and Antioch Baptist Church to the northwest of us on White Street answered. There were also lawn mowers. On any other Saturday morning, my parents and our neighbors the Howells would be out and, being the same age, they would be reminiscing. I used to hear them talk about their high-school years, the time before "prep" became "yup," the years before the world crashed into hell and proved too improbable to fix, and, since September is nearly a month before the start of the Second Season, normally they tied it all in with baseball, the bits and pieces of the Cardinals that won the World Series their senior year of high school, and, as always, they remembered the names: Lonnie Smith, Tom Herr, Keith Hernandez, George Hendrick, Darrell Porter, David Green and Gene Tenace and Dane Iorg, Willie McGee, Ken Oberkfell, Ozzie Smith, Andujar and Forsch and Kaat and Sutter. After all these years, the Judge still couldn't forgive Whitey Herzog for trading Ted Simmons. The Judge would shift his weight, cross his legs, and wax with Mr. Howell over half-drunk bottles of Beck's that cancer is still cancer, the Space Program is still talking about sending a man to Mars within the decade, shopping is still done at the grocery store, chicken still lay eggs and food is still solid, "The Day After" is the closest anyone has come to nuclear war, a ride from Vienna to Moscow is still hampered by border guards, guns, and barbed wire, and walking in the Geneva woods is still the best way for the benignly bellicose Superpowers to come to their senses and try acting like everyone else, no behemoth had been born in Bethlehem and hundreds of thousands—like hundreds of thousands a millenium before—left Armageddon on January 2, 2001 after seeing nothing more than a change of four seasons, their alma mater Milton High School still has yet to win a Homecoming game, the Earth still revolves around the sun, birth is hard, as is life, and death before ninety is still surer than taxes—the greatest technological changes they witnessed were the death of Ma Bell and the introduction of a counterfeit Coke that tasted like Pepsi, hardly events heralding a Brave New World. They all were just around sixty, and, for the Judge and Mr. Howell in particular, the lack of change meant little. The Judge's finger goes around the bottle mouth once, then back, and, should they be talking that morning, he would move the conversation back to baseball, since that was Cleveland's year, and, like everyone else, he was rooting for the Indians, because of Satchel Paige. Then, the Judge and Mr. Howell would laugh and the Beck's would be gone.

We left at eleven, while the bells tolled. Sonia Kidd came out with Henson as Drew pulled his car from under a poplar across the street into our drive, backed up, and turned around. Drew asked if I wanted to speak to her. I said no.

Drew had to see my cousin Marshall Langston, who lived a block away. Marshall had something from Physics Drew needed. We found him on the Langston patio. Like me, he wore a rugby, but his was a wrinkled and oversized one worn in his own, disheveled, who-cares way. Marshall was reading, but not in his contemplative manner that made him the visual personification of those Byronic adagios he plays on his cello, nor in that very own whimsical style showing that dash of Mr. Mistoffolees within his streak of Old Deuteronomy, but irritated, increasingly so, or at least a bit annoyed. He was drinking lemonade and listening to *The Flying Dutchman* on the radio. His younger brother Pik was doing the grass; every now and then, Marshall would watch Pik cut, blowing a whistle and snapping *"PETER"* each time Pik missed a spot, which annoyed Pik to no end (it was Pik's fault: he worshipped Marshall like no younger brother should). Drew and I seemed almost unnoticed as we sat next to Marshall at the patio table. "What'cha reading," I asked.

Drew notwithstanding, Marshall showed us. It was a Dartmouth recruiting bulletin, green, slick-glossed, plenty colored in every photograph. "It's Mrs. Stuart's idea," he said quickly, referring to the white-haired resident liberal of the high-school counseling department. "She says they're looking for 'qualified minorities.'"

"And, what did you say to that," Drew asked.

"To *that*? I asked her how big an effort are they putting into looking for qualified Whites—you know *her*: she didn't go for that." His Lockean New Negro got up and mumbled "qualified minorities" and rolled his eyes, tossing the bulletin onto the patio table. "What a hypocrite."

"She probably meant nothing by it," Drew said quickly. "Maybe, maybe it was that she just didn't know."

"Maybe," Marshall said, "but she should've. Really, it didn't surprise me all that much. She likes Norman Mailer, after all— who knows?—after reading Allen Ginsberg, she probably even comes through here at dawn thinking she'll find an 'angry fix.'" He paused and drank lemonade. Marshall always drinks lemonade when he gets hot. "You're here for that stuff," he asked Drew, and Drew nodded.

We went inside. Inside was quiet, except for a radio in the kitchen. Everyone was out doing something somewhere, and Marshall's bit was refilling the lawn mower because their parents thought Pik was still too young to do that for himself. Before going upstairs, Marshall made a fresh pitcher of lemonade.

"So," Marshall asked. "You two going to see that Lawrence girl?"

"What 'Lawrence girl,'" I asked.

"'What *Law*rence girl,' *please*!" Marshall rolled his eyes. "The whole school knows about her, cousin dear. Next time, before trying to deny it, take a bottle of castor oil, go to the bathroom and see what comes out, because, cousin dear, you're a terrible liar."

With that, Marshall ran upstairs to his room. Drew and I stayed downstairs in the living room. Marshall's father Ken came in a little later.

"Looks like you boys aren't tempted to battle Marshall's room today," Ken said, flashing a broad smile.

"No, sir," Drew said, very crisply, like he couldn't forget Ken was an assistant principal at the high school.

Ken excused himself to the kitchen and drank lemonade. The Langstons have this thing about lemonade. Marshall came down while Ken was in there. When I say "came down," I mean "slid down," on the banister. He tumbled into the living room and landed with a thump so hard it shook the grandfather's clock in the hall. Marshall stood. He smiled. He had changed from the rugby into a candy-striped Oxford shirt and a Howard University sweatshirt ("prep," they used to call it—so utterly "prep"). Ken came from the kitchen with his hands on his hips.

"And *what* is supposed to be the meaning of *this*?" Ken demanded.

Marshall looked at his clothes. "I spent all morning looking at Dartmouth green," he said simply. "This afternoon, I wanna be seen in Howard blue."

Ken started laughing and Marshall took Drew and me outside. To his credit, Pik had a third of the yard cut, and he was dumping the bag of clippings into a compost pile.

"I made some lemonade," Marshall announced. "And Dad's here. So, if you wanna drink some, better hurry, else Dad'll get it." Pik nodded. Then, suddenly, Marshall picked up a football that lay on the ground, whistled, and signaled for Pik to go out for a pass, and, with an ease belying his size, Marshall threw the ball, sending it on a high, tight, spiraling arc through the air that would have eventually met Pik in a reception, but a wind hijacked it, rendering its spiral and flight eccentric. Pik, however, picked up the ball. He faded back parallel to its track and, as its flight quickly corroded, he dove, caught the ball, and landed in a thicket of peonies near the middle of the yard.

"If only Milton could have him," Marshall said. "*Yo!* If only Milton could have you!"

"*Naw*—they'd still lose." Pik wiped his hands on his shorts and stretched his hands along the laces. He gripped the ball, and threw it back. The ball bounced past us.

"What's he trying to do," Marshall mumbled, "trying to be funny? *Yo!*—you trying to be funny?"

Pik didn't answer. He only smiled and went in for lemonade.

We left. Marshall had to run back in to get his Physics notebook because he had left it in his bedroom. After that, Drew chose the quick way to Whitman Township. That meant going through the heart of Jefferson Heights. Everything on my side blended into flowers, shrubs, and trees. Then came the tiger lilies in the yard of Mr. Howell's funeral home; I could hear Grandma Macalester talk about the way Aunt Hilda said Uncle Bug planted them when Grandpa Macalester's Grandpa Wright owned the place. The church was before the last turn. Old ladies meant for Sundays in stewardess white and deaconess gray had work clothes on, and the ivy up the red-bricked sides waved at me (or so I thought). The church looked as it did at Adele's wedding. Whenever I see the church, I think about Adele's wedding, and the Judge in his swallowtailed heather-gray morning coat, and Adele in a long, flowing white dress, and Mom crying, and I am always chilled by the realization that, of the millions of billions of people to have graced this planet, everyone—my mom and the Judge included—had come about via something as Oedipal as sex.

I told Drew I was thirsty. "I want ice cream," I said. Drew joked that was from watching the Langstons drink all that lemonade. I thought Drew would take me to his house (I knew he had ice cream, and his house was not that far), but he made a couple quick turns and we ended up on the state highway. In a few minutes, we were at Steak 'n Shake.

We had malts. It was still early. Inside, the place still smelled of soap water. Beside us, there was a pair of waitresses whose hair had been teased into Medusan tentacles. One of them kept making eyes at Drew; Drew kept twirling on the counter stool. He turned quiet when seven or eight of our classmates came in. My cousin Brad was among them. Like the Langstons, he was a cousin through Grandma Macalester, although he scarcely looked the part. Of a mother of Polish extraction having a dash of the British that shows up in him as it shows up in no one else, skin pale and unsuntannable, hair muskrat brown, nose sleek, eyes gray, with lips that—if one looks hard enough and close enough—only hinted some far-off ghost of negritude, Brad was vaguely European, and a looker. Drew watched as well. Like the others, Brad gave a meek muted wave, veered off quickly, and sat at a table near a window.

Brad's young brother Alan sat near him. Alan (he preferred that to his more ethnic first name Aaron) was of a type Brad was least comfortable around most, and, though a bit more colored, his was the off-white look of polite compromise between his parents. His nose was a parental compromise, neither Negroid, thanks to his mother, nor Jewish, thanks to his father, but a simple, nondescript one going comfortably with his skin, surrounded by freckles by the splattered, as though someone in Art had taken a mix of purple and yellow and flicked it at him when the teacher wasn't looking. The boy sweats easily, like that day, and in the sweat and its humidity, his sandy curlyish hair took the consistency of a Libyan's, and he had wayfarers that must have been too sweaty to wear. Alan would prove a looker, too. He also gave us a wave.

I returned to my vanilla malt, and Drew wiped his mouth with the back of his hand. Everything was quiet for a while until something happened at Brad's table and Alan almost walked out. I was able to get him to sit with us. I ordered a root-beer float for him. When the float came, Alan watched the grooves in the glass. He was pathetic. He said nothing. He drooped so badly he seemed to collapse between his thighs. He had his straw in his mouth, but he sucked like the suck was forced upon him. He shuddered—or did he shiver?—the air was running cold in there—he fidgeted and his shorts rode up past the tanline on his thighs. He looked almost too pathetic. I tried rubbing his back.

"Hey, what's *with* you," he demanded, pushing my hand away. "You *know* I don't go for *that* kinda *stuff*!"

"What happened," Drew asked.

"Nothing," I said quickly. Then I turned to Alan. "The Judge did that when you were a baby. You used to like it then."

"Yeah, but—that's fine. That's fine for him to've do it back then. But, *that* was when I *was* a baby. I'm not a baby anymore, you know."

Drew mumbled an apology for me. Alan shrugged. Afterward, Alan was very quiet. He finished his float, licked his mouth, pushed the glass away, and waited for us to finish. For a while, he looked my way.

"So," Alan finally said, "you guys going anyplace?—or're you guys 'just out'?"

"Both," I said.

"Skip's going out to see a girl," Drew said. "Judge Macalester just sent me along to make sure he behaves. You?"

"Him?" I asked. "He's just out to get some sun."

"Actually, Brad had to take me out to get something for my bike—just some grease, that's all. Then we ran into *those* guys." Whatever happened at Brad's table was still sore for Alan; he preferred pecking through glass to talking about it. A burst of laughter roared from Brad's table and Kay Reece said "you dick—you *dick*" and pulled ice cubes from his shorts. Alan continued tapping. "I got the grease."

Drew offered to drive Alan home. The Morgans—Brad and Allen's family—lived in a part of Whitman Township that was not exactly on our way, in a subdivision of trees, marigolds, large yards, and custom-built houses with cobblestone driveways shooting into courts in the back, in a house owned by the hotel their father Dennis managed. Alan sat back and became lucidly gregarious listening to Drew's music. He rested his head on Drew's gym bag on the seat and began to ramble: so, who was this girl?—was she cute?—did she have any sisters?—Brad was "in love," did we know her? . . . he sighed—was the door unlocked?—Brad's the one with the key, no telling when he'd be home—their little brother Ian had been worrying about his boa, it looked "green," whatever that meant, he might have taken it to the vet—could he get in through the back?—perhaps he might have to climb through a window. Then, suddenly, Alan sat up and looked outside thoughtfully with his mouth wide open.

"Skip," he said quietly.

"Yeah?"

"You like me?"

Smiling, smiling just before laughing, I looked at him. "What?"

"Do you like me?"

"You're a cousin"—third cousin, once removed, yes, but third cousins still count.

"Yeah, I know—but, do you *like* me?"

"How the—what kinda question is that to ask a *cousin*?"

"It's a question for you to answe'—could you JUST answer the *goddamn quest*ion, will you?"

I shrugged. "You're a cousin"—Alan fell back onto the seat

in frustration—"as hokey as it sounds, being family still means something—"

"Being family means nothing, as far as that's concerned. Do you like me?—yes or no, that's all, nothing complicated. Just yes or no."

I shrugged again. "Yeah. Why?"

Alan didn't answer. Instead, he leaned forward and asked Drew the same question the same way for the same answer, then plopped back down in the seat. For a stretch, Alan just breathed, staring at the warp-stained vinyl car top—perhaps he was thinking, perhaps just thinking about thinking for the sake of thinking, then a pause, something in the air, thoughts change, the Rolling Stones blaring through Drew's speakers, Alan rages his knuckles with the drums on the back of my seat, then the song ends, Alan stops, silence again.

"I was just wondering," he said suddenly, " 'cause, I never know just how you guys think of me, or whether you guys like me or not—you know, sometimes, you guys just treat me like I'm a pain in the ass, or something like that, like it's just a nuisance 'n' something of a bore to be around, or something like that—"

His voice trailed off, his body faded, his eyes turned blank. I thought he was asleep, but that was until the music changed. Then, almost immediately, his knuckles began raging again. All became quiet again when the grade changed and we headed down the lane to his house. Alan sat up and looked, not just at each house and at every yard, but at the whole thing, as though all of it (or almost all of it) were new to him. At one point, the sun creased along his chin and turned it as identifiably like my family as Marshall's, or mine, and those freckles notwithstanding, he looked a little more like us; then, when the sun crinkled and moved away, that look was gone.

The Morgans' was the last, or second to the last, house. No one was home, and Alan had no key. He ran to the side of the house and climbed the trellis to a bedroom window and we waited in the driveway. For a while, Drew seemed tense, and said nothing.

"You gotta be more careful," Drew finally said. "Promise me

just one thing, will ya: that before you *do* or *say* anything, that you just stop a minute 'n' *think*, especially around one of them."

"What's that supposed to mean?"

"Whaddaya mean, 'what's *that* supposed to mean,'" he exploded. "Goddamnit!—you mean I gotta spell it all out for you? You know those guys that were in there! You know where's their heads! You know how they talk! You mean to tell me you got absolutely no clue how that stuff'll all sound when it gets back to you on Monday? You mean to tell me you just simply don't understand things like that? And, what do you think I'm supposed to say when they ask me what's your problem?"

I shrugged. "I don't know, just call me a faggot," I joked.

"You're a faggot," he yelled. "Now are you happy?"

Things dim here. All I remember is how hurt Drew looked through all that . . . I think he muttered "why can't you just understand" as he drove off. After that, he was quiet until after we were on the Post Road across Whitman Township. I remember he made some crack about a kid we passed that struggled on his bicycle, then he became quiet again when we saw that kid was a middle-aged woman. I don't think he said another word until after we got to Kathy's house. But, then again, going through her subdivision, I was not paying attention to Drew. I was thinking about her, getting nervous, and for once I wished I had socks. The car stopped, and Drew mustered something of a quivering smile. He was tense again.

"Well, we're here. Ready?"

"As ready as I'll ever be," I said.

"Nervous?"

"Me?—of course not."

"Then, we're in trouble." Then he did something he had never done before. Slowly, almost painfully, he traced the length of my nose, then caught himself. Afterward, he held onto the steering wheel so tight his knuckles turned completely white, and he stared into the speedometer. He was biting his lip. "Skip—sorry. Your lips're dry, they might even be chapped."

"I'll be sure not to kiss her, then."

"No," he said, almost looking at me, but not quite. "No, go ahead. Kiss, if you want. Just be careful when you do."

We left the car (*I* left the car—Drew was a little slow leaving).
Amazingly, I felt calm about going to Kathy's door, but, when
I got there and was stared at by her peephole, that feeling of gas
just being gas and heading nowhere which I had come to know
so well came again.

"Arthur Melvin Macalester," I heard myself say quietly, "you
should leave now, now that you have the chance."

In truth, I had no such chance. Drew was right behind me.
Although his eyes were red, he smiled and rang the doorbell,
then he turned around and snorted. It took a while for someone
to open the door. It was a thin, angular boy with straw-colored
hair, who took a single, long, skeptical look at us, then let us in.

"You guys're here for her," he asked, taking off his shoes and
socks just behind the door. " 'Cause, she's not here right now,
but that's O.K., 'cause she'll be back real soon, or that's when
she's *supposed* to be—you know how *girls* are, you never know
whether they'll come when they say they're comin' —so, you
guys can wait in here for her, if you guys want."

It smelled in there. From the looks of the place, someone
forgot to hire a maid. The boy, Kathy's brother Wallace, led us
through the house to the family room downstairs. It took up the
entire basement, complete with a wall of glass overlooking their
deck and a small in-ground swimming pool. Part of the family
room was sunken, and a hearth sat in the middle of it. On the
other side of the hearth, two boys in towels and damp swimming
trunks lay on a chaise lounge while a guy, slightly older than us,
drew on a sketch pad with charcoal. One boy watched me intensely, his hands always moving, always twitching, drumming
fugues and tarantellas in a sharp *rattatatat*, a beat, then our eyes
met, brushed, blushed, batted down, and did it again, again, a
little longer this time, a little softer, a little less frightened, the
hands stopped, his face flushed, shrugged for knowing how to
shrug, puckered as if to speak, fell silent against my almost raised
palm, quivered up nervously at its corners into something of a
smile and stayed there a tense second before easing into something more natural, and I smiled back.

"You weren't born for this," Drew whispered into my ear.
"So, just *try* to behave—*please*."

The guy doing the drawing had sharp blue eyes and jet black hair. His skin was naturally pale. He wiped his hands on his jeans periodically. He flipped his head back to get the hair out of his eyes, smiled, and showed us what he was drawing. Did they know he was doing their feet? Nothing is a greater aphrodisiac for me than bare feet.

I couldn't stay. I left as quickly as I could. Drew was not far behind. Although we must have stayed in front of Kathy's house for just a few minutes, it seemed so much longer. I couldn't get out of my mind the boy who was watching me. I think he was twelve, about the same age as Alan and Wallace, and he had hazel eyes and a look that reminds me of Rosy in O'Faolain's "How to Write a Short Story." I still ask myself, while all that went on, was I doing IT to him, or was he doing IT to me.

"Sorry," I finally said in Drew's car. "Maybe, we can try again some other time."

"Yeah. Maybe. But don't worry about it."

That was Drew's way of saying forget it. I tried the best I could, but Drew was driving me home, and soon, there was the Park, and its esplanade, and its rose garden. In a year, I was to be in the Jefferson Heights Cotillion, and how was I uncomfortable about girls.

Drew pulled into our driveway. Mom's Volvo was gone, but the Judge's Saab was still there. Drew turned off the engine. For a short while, we just looked at one another. It was, I think, almost one.

"I don't think we'd be able to find a court for a couple of hours, if you wanna play tennis today," Drew said, scratching his nose. "So, whaddaya say 'bout just going to a movie later, maybe get some pizza afterward?"

"O.K."

"Say, you find the movie and call me, O.K.?—around five?"

"O.K."

"Say." He paused. "You all right?"

"Yeah."

"You sure?"

I said I was. In a way, I found it hard to convince even myself.

I watched him drive away. I don't remember much, except for the Judge calling me into his den, and the way he pulled a short strand of brown hair from my shirt, and the way it spiraled to the floor. Then, I went to lie in my room, soothed by Schubert and soughed in dreams.

BLACK AND BLUE—
A TALE OF MIXED COLORS

• SANDIP ROY •

"Today morning," said my mother, "I met Mrs. Basu in the fish market. And she said 'Mrs. Mitra you are sending your Sanjay to America. I think you should get him married first. Just the other day my sister-in-law's brother wrote from Texas that he is getting married to some American girl. And such a fine boy too—never stood second in his life. First class first in physics. And his mother now cries all day.'"

My mother gave a nervous half laugh and looked at me. That was my signal to reassure her that I would protect the family honor against evil, gum-chewing, cigarette-smoking, home-wrecking, disrespectful American women. I imagined them waiting at JFK airport in New York—hordes of buxom blondes in tight shorts and skimpy tops ready to snap up naive, god-fearing, rice-eating Indian boys as they stepped off the plane.

Unable to extract any reassurance, my mother plunged on. "Why, look at your uncle Shobhan's son. He went to America just like you and then came back after four years and married that nice Radha. What a sweet girl and a doctor too."

"But you always said Radha was fat and dark," chimed in my sister.

My mother glared at her. "And you'll be ten times darker if you don't put on that cucumber-milk paste like I tell you to. All day long—just run around in the sun with no protection. Mark my words, you will turn as black as charcoal and then we'll see what prince will marry you."

Undaunted by her dismal future my sister continued, "Well, if he married an American girl at least you would have nice, fair grandchildren. All white with red cheeks and blue eyes. I've always wanted blue eyes."

"But they'd be no-good Anglo-Indians," said my mother fiercely, "neither here nor there. Where would they fit? And anyway these American girls don't make good wives. Look at Sushil—breaks his mother's heart and marries some American. And she just leaves him after five years. Two little children, too."

"She was not American," said my sister, "she was Romanian."

"All same!" said my mother grimly. "These white women have no sense of family."

"But who said that if Sanjay married an American she'd have to be white?" interjected my father looking up from the newspaper. "She could be black too."

"Negro!" My mother's mouth fell open in total horror. Almost beseechingly she looked at me. "Then I will have a heart attack," she said weakly and closed her eyes. I know she was seeing little grandchildren with flat noses, shiny black skin and thousands and thousands of tiny braids. "Like snakes, like millions of little snakes crawling all over their heads," she said with a shudder. Snapping her eyes open she glared at my father. "And you, just sit with your nose in the paper all evening. And then put all these nonsense ideas in my son's head!"

I had no intentions of following in the footsteps of Mrs. Basu's sister-in-law's brother. I was going to go to America and look up Tom Cruise. My friend Amit said his cousin had brought a magazine from America which said that Tom Cruise was actually a homosexual. And did I know that all the universities there had a GLU.

"Glue?" I asked bewildered.

"Not glue, stupid. G-L-U—Gay and Lesbian Union."

I wondered if my little midwestern university had a GLU too. I read the prospectus from cover to cover. But it said nothing about GLUs.

The airport was a whirl of lights and noise. "United an-

nounces departure of Flight . . ." "Will passenger John Hodg-
man on American Airlines Flight . . ." I emerged dazed and
blinking out of the dark, safe shadow of my mother's love and
made my way to the end of the winding queue at the immigra-
tion counters. The official who looked at my papers was a big
white man with a ginger mustache. He sized me up over his
glasses and said something. The words just seemed to get lost
in his bristling mustache. I must have looked clueless because
he straightened up and said slowly "Can I have your passport
please?"

I handed it over.

"All you Indians and Chinese come here to study. And not
one goes back." He shook his head and stamped the form.
Handing it back to me, he said in a bored voice, "Next." I was
in America.

On the flight from New York to Deanville, I was sitting next
to an overweight man with a red face. He sold cars, and he
advised me to buy only American cars. "The parts are cheap.
But you touch a Honda or a Nissan and you are looking at one
hundred dollars at least." Converting quickly to rupees, I looked
suitably impressed. He said he knew many Indians and ha ha
not all of them were Patels!

Across the aisle was this real cute tall blond man in shorts.
The seat beside him was empty, and I wanted so bad to sit there.
I wanted to look at his long legs—the golden hairs glinting. But
I did not know what excuse to make. The stewardesses started
serving salted almonds and drinks. I started to read the in-flight
magazine with great interest but could not shut out my
neighbor.

"My doctor," he announced with great pride, "is an Indian. I
call him Sam but he has another Indian name. Did you know
that almost all Chinese take an English name when they come
to America?"

I wondered if like the Chinese I would take a new name
too—a kind of second birth. Unlike the Chinese we learn to
speak English early. When I arrived at Deanville, there was a
huge scandal because this white student had told a Chinese student to go back to China and learn some English first. The
white student was a husky farm boy who had never even known

Chinese food before he came to Deanville. Then suddenly he found himself floundering in a jabber of Mandarin, Korean, Vietnamese, Thai. . . . I wanted to hold those callused farmboy hands and look into his blue eyes fringed with golden lashes. And I wanted to say, "We are not all like that. I spoke English from the age of four."

Little towns in India have a dusty, unkempt look—yapping dogs, open gutters and swerving cyclists. But Deanville was a picture-postcard town—little white houses along streets lined with trees. It was fall and the trees were all ablaze with orange and gold. I loved to hear the leaves go crunch as I walked over them. It was a friendly, cute town but it was not San Francisco. I had heard about places in San Francisco where young boys oiled their smooth buff tanned bodies and stripped naked while you ran your hands over their wondrous hard curves. I had heard that in San Francisco you could go to baths and have sex amidst the steam and showers.

The first time I went to the locker room at the gym in Deansville, I was scandalized. All these men just roaming around naked, their white towels slung over their shoulders! In India it is common to see men holding hands on the street. But people there tend to be very shy about their bodies. I remember hopping around on one foot as I struggled to wiggle out of my swimming trunks and into my underpants without untying the towel around my waist. I do not remember having ever seen my father naked. And now here I was surrounded by swinging penises and untanned butts. I kept my glasses on till the last minute as I took mental snapshots of each man—the swell of his buttock, the heft of his circumcized penis, the sudden flaring of pubic hair. In the shower I kept my eyes firmly on the wall uncertain how my own member would react to the sight of these ripe athletic bodies vigorously soaping themselves. A black guy stepped up to the shower next to mine.

"How you doing?" He nodded.

I had never really seen a black man before I came to America. Certainly not a naked one! Out of the corner of my eyes I took a peek at his sex. Even in repose it seemed heavy—almost menacing. I wondered how much larger it got when erect. I did not find him erotic. He was almost a little scary—so big and dark.

The powerful jet from the shower struck his body and then trickled tamely down through rivulets of white foam. He was a magnificent man but just not my type. I would have bristled if someone had called me a racist. After all when I was fourteen, I had, in a voice quivering with emotion, recited Martin Luther King's "I Had a Dream" at the school elocution contest. But physically black men did nothing for me. "It's just physical," I reassured myself. "They are just not my type. It's not about race."

Black men in Deansville drove huge ramshackle gas-guzzling American cars blaring the most god-awful rap music. I didn't like the music, I didn't like the aggressive bristle of their flat-tops and I didn't like to look in their eyes. There was a guarded watchfulness in them, and I felt if I peeled the guard away like a contact lens I would fall into a bottomless pit. In Deansville the rail tracks neatly split the town into two halves. "On the east side of the tracks," the president of the Indian Students Union had informed me, "the rents are cheaper. But that's also where most of the *kallus* (blackies) live. So it's not too safe." I, Sanjay, fierce opponent of apartheid and admirer of Martin Luther King, meekly let the racist slur pass as I made my home on the west side of town.

Deansville was no San Francisco, but it did have a GLU on campus. However it took me almost two months to summon up courage to go to a meeting. The notice had said "GLU meets in the Juniper Room at 7:30 P.M." At 7:25 I wandered into the student center looking for the Juniper Room. An Indian boy I knew went by. I was sure he was going to ask me "Why are you going towards the Juniper Room?" But he just walked on by. I walked down the long carpeted corridors of the student center, past the snack machines. Right next to the Juniper Room was the Pine Room where the Film Society was meeting. I tried to look as if I was deeply interested in the workings of the Film Society and then ducked into the Juniper Room. There were about eight or ten people hanging around making small talk. They looked up as I went in and returned to their chit-chat. I stood on the outskirts of their conversations with a nervous half smile. I spotted some sodas on a table and picked up one just to give myself something to do.

"That will be fifty cents, please," said a chubby man with a silver bracelet.

"Oh," I said, rummaging in my pocket.

Shit, in my nervous rush I'd left my wallet behind.

"I guess I must have left my wallet behind," I said lamely, putting my drink down.

"It's O.K., Vince, I'll pay for it," said a voice behind me.

I turned around and fell headlong into eyes which were as blue as the Indian sky in October after the last rains had gone. When I was young, I had the stupid notion that eyes and hair were somehow bound together. Blond people had blue eyes, redheads had green eyes, and brunettes had black or brown eyes. And here stood this black man with tight curly black hair looking at me out of the bluest eyes I'd ever seen.

"Hi," he said extending a hand, "you must be new around here. I am Glen."

"Hi, thanks. Sanjay," I mumbled, shaking his hand.

"San-jay," he said slowly, "so where are you from, San-jay?"

Glen was from California. He was studying law. He looked like he should have been studying dancing. Or gymnastics. He'd gone to Europe for the summer and wanted to live there. Most of all he wanted to get out of Deansville.

I hoped he was stuck in Deansville as long as I was.

"So have you been to A Different Beat?" he said. "Oh, but you must; hell, it's the only gay bar in town."

How could I admit to this suave, poised young man of the world that I had never even been to a gay bar? My hesitation must have been evident on my face, for he said, "Why don't you give me your number? If I go there on Friday night I'll give you a call."

Was this, oh my god, was this a date? Could this be a pickup line? Dare I breathe?

I scribbled my number on a grocery receipt and handed it to him.

He stuffed it in his pocket, smiled and said, "Nice meeting you, Sanjay. But I have to run. I told Sean I'd meet him at nine."

"Sean?"

"My boyfriend. He's Irish. You'll meet him Friday night."

I walked home utterly bewildered. Was he coming on to me or was I reading too much into a purely friendly gesture? Anyway I wasn't supposed to be attracted to black men. But then why did I want to drown an Irishman named Sean?

On Friday when I came home from school my roommate Satish was busy making dinner.

"Oh, Sanjay," he said, "someone called Glen or Len called you."

"Oh, O.K.," I said. Then I added casually, "Do you need the bathroom? I'm going to take a shower."

"Again?" he said startled. "Didn't you take one today morning?"

I ignored him and said, "If Glen calls, tell him I'll call him back."

"Who is this Glen?" he asked suspiciously. "Is he Indian?"

"Just a guy I met recently," I said stepping into the shower.

"Where?" he persisted.

I turned on the shower and pretended I had not heard him. It was like having my mother as my roommate. Was this what I left home-cooked food for?

I was shaving when the phone rang. I jumped for it with my face full of lather. It was Glen.

"So you up to going out tonight?"

"Sure, let's go," I said trying to sound cool and not swallow any foam.

"Gimme your address so I can come and pick you up."

I gave it to him.

"Apartment number?"

"Five hundred and," I said. Then I suddenly glanced at Satish, industriously chopping onions and said, "Never mind, I'll be downstairs at 8:30."

"I'll be going out," I told Satish, rather needlessly, since he'd been listening to every word I'd said.

"Will you have dinner at home?" he asked tossing the onions into the hot oil.

"No," I said returning to my shaving.

"You should have told me earlier," he said crossly, "I made too much rice."

At 8:29, freshly shaved and cologned, I was on the corner waiting for Glen. Two Indian boys I knew saw me and stopped to chat.

"So where you off to?" said one.

"Out," I said shortly.

"Hot date, huh?" leered the other. "Man, did you bathe in aftershave or what?"

"What's she like, man? Where have you been hiding her?"

"Very funny," I said hoping my monosyllables would drive them away before Glen came. I could just see them running up to my apartment.

"*Arre* Satish, know what, we saw Sanjay going somewhere with this *kallu*!" And then Satish would say accusingly, "How did you become friends with this *kallu*?"

And what would I say? "But he had blue eyes!"

Unable to pry out any juicy tidbits the boys got bored and wandered off before Glen drove up.

"Where's your boyfriend?" I asked, getting into the car.

"Oh, he has a terrible toothache and went to sleep."

"Oh" I said, trying to sound concerned. I knew someone who had died of an infected tooth.

"So," I said, trying to sound casual, "do you and Sean live together?"

"Oh no. We've only been dating a couple of months." Abruptly changing the subject he said, "It's too early to go dancing. Let's go get something to eat."

We went to a pizza place. It was Friday night and the place was bustling with students. I just prayed that all the Indians I knew were at home eating rice. I was sure that Glen and I were sticking out as a very unlikely pair. I wished he wasn't wearing such a big hoop in his ear. I tried to remember if it was the left ear or the right ear that was the gay ear. "So tell me," he said in full earshot of the shrieking students at the next table, "how do you pick up guys in India?"

I was so relieved when it was time to go.

———

I don't know quite what I expected from my first gay bar, but A Different Beat was quite a modest place. It was dimly lit, and the blaring music bounced off the walls producing a strange vibration. People jostled on the cramped dance floor. Women with short hair balanced their beers on the edge of the pool table as they took aim. The noise and cigarette smoke swirled around me in ever-tightening circles, and in sudden panic I clutched Glen's elbow. He was cutting though the crowds with flamboyant ease, and I trotted along behind him. Men with outrageous bouffants hitched their falsies up and looked us up and down. Guys in flannel shirts and blue jeans hung around the pool table drinking beer. Glen seemed to know everyone there. They all shrieked and pecked him on the lips. No one used names. Everyone was either "darling" or "bitch." I was introduced over the blare of music.

"This is Sanjay. He just came from India this semester."

"San-J?"

"What was that again?"

"Sanjee?"

"Sorry, I didn't get that."

Now I know why people rename themselves John and Steve in America.

"So," said this blond guy with streaky blond hair, "do they have bars like this in India?"

I was saved from answering when Glen materialized at my side and said "Let's dance."

We elbowed our way onto the dance floor and tried to carve out a little space. I had never really danced before and was anxious about stepping on his feet. But I needn't have worried. It was so crowded I just needed to sway my hips a bit and the crowd did the rest. Glen danced beautifully, tossing his head and shaking his hips. He slid his slim hips close to mine and put his hands on my hips and grinned and said, "Relax, Sanjay. Just let it go." I had never been turned on by pictures of black singers or black athletes. But this man was just making my heart pound as he swiveled around on the dance floor. Perhaps it was those flashing blue eyes. Perhaps it was the gin fizz I had drunk. Perhaps it was the fact that I hadn't had sex since I came to America.

All I knew was that when he sashayed up to me and rotated his crotch dangerously close to mine I was ready to explode.

Every little gesture seemed pregnant with double meanings. Every comment was spiced with a dash of flirtation. Glen was not quite twenty-one and I bought him a drink. I watched him sip his margarita. A few grains of the salt that crusted the glass clung to his lips, and if I had had one more gin fizz in me I'd have reached over and licked them off. He was sweating after all that dancing and his silk shirt clung to him like wet kisses. I put my hand on his and he did not move his away. He just smiled and said, "Are you having a good time?"

On the way back he said, "Would you like to see my apartment? But I should warn you it's an absolute mess."

Was this the equivalent of asking me up for coffee? Especially since neither he nor I drank coffee.

He had a little studio apartment with movie posters on the wall. Black sheets tangled on an unmade bed. Fashion magazines full of beautiful men with high cheekbones. His hair dryer was still plugged in, the bottle of hair gel on the side of the sink. He checked his answering machine. Someone called Richard wanted to meet for breakfast.

Ann was wondering if she could get a ride with him.

No messages from Sean of the aching tooth.

"Would you like some tea?" he said, rummaging in his kitchen cabinet.

"That would be lovely," I replied. Any excuse to stay a little longer.

"Peppermint, chamomile or orange blossom?"

What I wanted was some good strong Indian tea boiled with lots of milk and sugar to clear the cigarette smoke and boom-boom rhythms swirling in my head.

"Chamomile," I said.

I heard him humming as he filled the kettle with water.

I idly leafed through the men's clothing magazines, rummaging for something to say. Something sexy, funny, a come-on with room to withdraw if it misfired.

"Oh," said Glen. "Have you ever seen any gay porn magazines? I have some in that drawer beside the bed."

The last thing I needed was more stimulation. But I'd never

seen a gay porn magazine before. I pulled one out from the midst of a tangle of underwear and socks. Glen had some skimpy black underwear. I wondered what he was wearing tonight.

I flipped through the pages of buff tanned men with bleached blond hair. Most of the men had blue eyes but none had Glen's bitter-chocolate skin to set them off. Glen had taken off his sweaty shirt and was rubbing himself dry. His chest was a shade lighter than his face and arms and the hair in his armpits was crisp and dark. I tried not to stare but it was all I could do to keep myself from running my fingers over his skin. Pulling on a T-shirt he set the cup of tea down in front of me and flicked on the TV. I wondered if he was going to look at the magazine with me. But he just flicked through the channels and yawned and stretched.

"Are you tired?" he said "I'm getting kind of sleepy. Why don't you just crash here tonight? I'll drop you home tomorrow on my way to the gym."

For a moment I saw Satish's face. What if my mother called tonight? What if my aunt called early in the morning? What if?

"Oh, that'll be fine," I said, trying to sound cool and collected. Like I did this all the time.

"I think I even have an extra toothbrush somewhere," he said.

My God, had he planned it all?

I put down the magazine and sat down on the bed beside him. He'd turned down the TV real low. I took a deep breath. It was now or never. I stretched and took off my glasses. In all the seduction sequences in movies the woman takes off her glasses. Then she loosens the tight knot of her hair so that it cascades down like a waterfall. My hair was too short so I just took off my glasses. Glen went into soft focus and I hoped my eyes looked bigger and softer. He laughed and said, "Stop looking at me in that way."

"What way?"

"You know, kind of dopey and gooey."

"Why?" I said putting my hand on his shoulder.

"You know I have a boyfriend," he said but he did not move away.

"*You* don't have to do anything," I lied as I traced my finger down his chest and over his nipple. He didn't answer but took my hands and played with my fingers. Oh my God, it was going to happen. My first man in America. As our lips met I just hoped I wasn't going to faint. We just played with each other's bodies that night. We explored and caressed and stroked each other with our hands, our tongues. Just before he came he shuddered deeply and whispered, "Oh God! I'm going to come. I can't hold back anymore." It was almost a confession. When I came all over his belly I looked deep in his eyes. My first American man. And he had blue eyes!

When it was all over he kissed me gently and reached under the bed for a handful of tissues.

"Here, wipe yourself off."

I lay there my head on his arms watching blurred images flickering on the TV. At that moment I trusted him deeply and implicitly. I was not worrying about grades, calls from Mother, suspicious looks from Satish.

"Talk to me," I said.

"About what?"

"Anything. Tell me about the first time you had sex."

He told me. Then he turned to me and asked, "Now can I ask you something?"

"Sure."

"Why did you want to sleep with me?"

I wondered how to start. I wanted to tell him that I had never found black men attractive. But he was different. Special. Or I guess I just hadn't learned to look at them. Until I met him. And fell headfirst into his blue eyes. I wanted to ask him who in his family had blue eyes. Was he perhaps mixed?

"Turn off the lamp," I said.

But before I could say anything more, he said, "Hang on, I need to go to the bathroom."

He went into the bathroom and turned on the light. I lay in bed admiring the fluidity with which the muscles in his long back and pert butt played together. I watched him brush his teeth. He wiped his face on the towel and turned back to the mirror. Very carefully he reached into his eyes and plucked out the lens. One left lens, one right lens. Even from the bed I knew they were both blue. I watched him put each one carefully in its little round case. He squeezed a few drops of soaking solution in each container.

When he turned off the light in the bathroom I turned off the lamp as well.

In bed he put his arm around me and said, "Well, what attracted you to me in the first place?"

I turned my face away because I could not meet his eyes. But I needn't have worried. In the dark I could not see their color at all.

I pulled my shame over me like a blanket and buried my face in his neck.

HOUSE OF DIFFERENCE

• WAYNE SCOTT •

Our sons will not grow into women.
Audre Lorde, *Sister Outsider*

"Speculum."

He had learned a new word. He loved the way the sound started running in the back of his throat and, breaking from his lips, leapt into the air. SPEC-u-lum. He was waiting in the living room for a shipment of toys and clothes from his father's house. Except for the GI Joe he had carried to the police station, he had nothing else. To entertain him, his mother had shown him a box full of gadgets.

"Speculums," she announced. She was a gynecological nurse. "Doctors use it to examine the insides of a woman, to make sure she's normal."

He examined the gadget in his hand. He did not ask the question in his mind: what insides? The speculum did not look like anything helpful.

That summer, the summer he was returned to Chicago, he crept on the edges of his mother's strange world. He heard forbidden words. He tasted the vegetables—wildly colored, oddly shaped—that she gathered from produce stands. Every summer she searched farmers' markets for odd-looking vegetables—yellow rutabagas, dirty chanterelles, misshapen red peppers—returning to the apartment, her arms stuffed. He manfully tried the concoctions she made: brown rice mixed with sautéed tomatoes and chickpeas, soup made of crushed asparagus and peas (*velouté*, she called it), and escarole leaves mixed with walnut oil and bitter cranberries.

Speculums looked like the heads of dinosaurs cackling, a fossilized record of the merriment of prehistoric beasts. Cold metal speculums, jaws adjusted by moving joints; small blue speculums with plastic gums; and clear speculums, cracked white in places. Some of them were broken into pieces. One was lined with sparkling zirconian diamonds, tied with a red satin ribbon. He held it up for his mother.

"That's a joke," she explained, "from a friend."

"Speculum!" he blurted. The mean jaw in his hand crashed down on the head of GI Joe and swallowed him. "No, no, no I'm being eaten alive by the SPECulum," he screamed in a high voice.

His mother frowned. "You're acting like a child," she said. With slight pressure—it reminded him that they had grown apart over the years—she took the gadget from his hand. In the background the other gadgets rustled, murmuring, "speculum speculum speculum," as if they, too, were intent on destruction. "Why can't you act more mature?" she asked. "Don't you want to be grown up?"

It was the summer of in-betweens, a season of worry and uncertainty. Everywhere Adrian went he knew that he was in between. He strolled on a sidewalk that was neither the busy street nor the shady courtyard. When he walked, his steps, guided by some unknown rhythm, seemed to fall onto the cracks, no matter how much he thought about avoiding them. Some part of him was determined to be unpredictable and different. He was in between elementary school and junior high school. Not even elementary school, but in what they called in some suburbs "middle school," a place for wedging sixth graders. When he thought about all the in-betweens, he was unsure whether in between was one word or two. *Inbetween.* In between his mother's city apartment, two flights up, and his father's sprawling house in Evanston; in between buoyant spring and the fading, brown fall, in the hot press of summer monotony; in between childhood and being a teenager; in between bodies, differences that multiplied daily.

He leaned against the yellow brick of the apartment building and listened to his mother argue. Since his arrival, she had been debating with her friend Peg Flanagan. It had something to do with him. Passersby, walking and jogging and biking along Broadway, glanced at the second-story window where his mother was shouting and Adrian, who did not know whether to be embarrassed or proud, smiled shyly back at them. Her high-pitched words spilled from the living-room window.

"I told you, Peg, he's only eleven! I swear it!"

He knew that he was, in fact, twelve years old and that his mother, though well intentioned, was lying to her friend on the telephone. He leaned against the bricks, his white body almost disappearing in the glare from the summer sun. His mother called the bricks "cream city bricks." They were imported from Milwaukee, Wisconsin, sometime around the 1920s, when the apartment building was built. The yellow building stood in contrast to the buildings on either side. Their ordinary bricks, once crisp, maroon rectangles, were chipping and purpling with age and weather. His mother's building stuck out like an exaggeration.

Adrian reached his hand into the right pocket of his pants. He had found, through practice, that by slipping his hand into his pocket and sliding the cotton pouch to the side, he could touch his penis without anyone noticing. He looked like any other boy on the street, but he was clutching his scrotum with three fingers. "Acting like a child," he murmured to himself. He was thinking about the bodies before him on Broadway: the black bodies of three girls, their skin flickering with shades of bronze and red and gold, jumping rope in the recess of sidewalk at the brim of the courtyard; the bodies of ladies, old and wrinkled, hobbling by with bags of groceries; and the bodies of men, grown up and lean, striding confidently down the street.

He had found that, if he squinted, focusing on the tan patch on the back of a man's jeans, he could detect his waist size and the length of the leg. He scanned the crowd that trickled by, wondering about the most perfect measurements. Too stocky at waist 36, length 31? Too bony at waist 29, length 35? He rated each one against an evolving standard. He was thinking, then, about his own body, barely adolescent, and how pale he must look, almost invisible, against the evenly laid, cream city bricks that were perfect and clean and bright in the summer air, except for one ugly scar: a spray-painted, black-blue signature, its letters bigger than his head.

It said, in bold capitals, LESBIAN RAGE.

"Peg, we're going in circles," his mother continued speaking. Her friend owned a coffeehouse for women and children only. His mother had taken him there, when he was younger, to hear music, but the coffeehouse had a rule about boys over eleven years old. "I'll tell you the conditions. No birth certificate. No proof. You take my word for it."

Vandals had sprayed the building long before Adrian came to live in the apartment overlooking Broadway. It was strange that no one seemed bothered by the words. He had seen sandblasters removing gang graffiti from the red brick walls of tenements in Uptown, just a few blocks north on Broadway, but they never came to the building labeled LESBIAN RAGE. It was as if the words belonged there, black and fuzzy against even lines of brick. The label agreed with the residents of the courtyard building, opening like a U onto the street, and it agreed with the pedestrians who witnessed the silent cry, as they bustled up and down the street with shopping bags. Neighbors called it the "LESBIAN RAGE building," with the same indifference that they called the main street "Broadway" or the cross street "Cornelia," as if the meaning of the pulled-together letters had sunk below awareness. "The cleaner's is two doors down from the LESBIAN RAGE building," they would say, or "You'll pass the LESBIAN RAGE building on your way to the best hotdog stand in Lakeview."

What, he wondered, would another newcomer—someone whose parent was not a lesbian—expect of this building? Would he imagine women with snakelike hair and beady eyes, lurking in the courtyard shadows? Would he expect hissing curses, screams about injustice, or large feet stomping in frustration? Or would he see Adrian's mother, Miri, with her cheekbones rising like the crests of an apple-red heart, the wave of her honey-colored hair, staring at the yellow stains on the bathroom floor, the toilet seat propped up—so *unnaturally*—exposing the cool, wet porcelain? Would he hear that firmness that crept into her voice? "Adrian, Mommy is unhappy with you." Would he call that pink trace of irritation LESBIAN RAGE?

"Male role models!" his mother shrieked. "Male role models! No, Peg, he can't stay with his father."

Down the center of Broadway, in the distance, the black skyscrapers loomed, like devils, wreathed by the low mists pushing in from Lake Michigan. Red lights blinked at the tips of their horns. Adrian imagined his father hiding downtown. He was crouching, perhaps, in the underground tunnels that lined the Chicago River (a dark, wet place, Adrian imagined, the curve of its walls streaked with algae and green river slime). He was scavenging the food-encrusted litter that slipped through the grates on Wabash Avenue. Though no one really knew where his father had gone, Adrian suspected he was nearby. His father was sending him messages through the blinking spires of the tallest buildings, the Sears Tower and the Hancock Building: cryptic, red monosyllables that called out to him in his new home.

"I . . . miss . . . you. . . ."

"I . . . love . . . you. . . ."

"Please . . . don't . . . tell. . . ."

Those words had been told to him, as his father packed a suitcase that last night in their house in Evanston. His father, whom his mother detested now more than ever; his father, whose crimes covered the front page of the city section of the newspapers that she tried to hide from him; his father, who had broad shoulders (but never broad enough) and a jaw set at a masculine angle (but never square enough); his father, whose stomach was wrapped with a pillow of flesh that he lamented but that Adrian loved to lay his head upon; his father, whom Adrian sometimes missed and sometimes wished had never existed; his father, who had fled in disgrace. He had been gone for three weeks.

"I don't know if he's hit puberty," his mother whined from the window. "Not to look at him. That's irrelevant. Some boys hit puberty at ten!"

In front of him, the girls were laughing and jumping rope. They swirled their double ropes like cake beaters, whipping and snapping against the sidewalk. He watched one girl, standing outside the blades of jump rope, her head bowing into its rhythm. Quickly, she dodged between its strokes and, encircled within the prism of the beater, she bounced from one foot to the other. Swishing the rope around her body, her two friends cheered: "Oooooooh, girrrrrrrl! Yeah, girl! Yeah, girl! Oooooooh, you hot girl!" He wondered how he could explain what he was doing, leaning against the LESBIAN RAGE building, holding his penis, enviously watching them, thinking about the bodies of pedestrians and squinting at the labels on the backsides of men's pants, but he could not explain it to anyone, because the word to say it, like speculum, was still so foreign, so frightening. He was waiting for a "transsexual."

Two weeks ago, lolling against the bricks of LESBIAN RAGE, Adrian had spotted an eye-catching creature: tall, so slim she made him gasp in wonder, her stick-like legs curving softly at the knee and pencil-thin heels that curled into the high arches of her feet. Suspended upon those magical shoes, her body bent over subtly, revealing only the slightest bondage to gravity and fashion. An explosion of hair, alive with stripes of blond and red and brown, fell below her shoulders. She wore a shimmery fabric of washed coral that slipped off her bony shoulder. She walked with a self-possession that, for someone who looked so extreme, invited his gaze, as if she were defining the norm on this stretch of tiny boutiques and coffee shops with green marble-topped cafe tables and chairs made of black wire, looped like opaque signatures.

In spite of the pretty garb, she had a notch at her throat and a jaw like the jaws that his father had wanted: square and heavy. At first, Adrian did not know if it was an elegant woman or a man in lady's clothes. As the creature stepped along, a floral bag draped from her shoulder, looking like it weighed as much as she did, Adrian was drawn by this confusion. He had missed something—some sure sign to her sex. He did not know what the sign was or where on her body it would appear, but he knew that, if, for just a moment, he could get close enough to study her, as he had studied the patches on the backsides of men, he would find it: the secret to her identity, the missing clue that would tell him to which group she belonged.

That first day he had followed her, marveling at her buttocks.

Her hips swayed too much for the paltry flesh; the clingy pants were splashed with grimacing petunias and laughing roses. They created the illusion that her hips were larger, fuller, more voluptuous than they were. She stopped at the corner of Broadway and Cornelia. Adrian turned, pretending to read the sign on the Chinese Laundromat. He could see her there, standing alone, in the reflection on the glass. Maybe, he thought, she was hoping to be noticed by a pedestrian or a driver behind the wheel. The red stop sign enveloped her head and the cars slowed, halted and moved on, unperturbed by her presence.

For a moment he forgot where he was and he watched her image projected on the window. Her image glittered against a background of hanging white shirts, wrapped in plastic, and a pile of multicolored laundry, unsorted on the Laundromat counter. She met his stare. Adrian's head cocked awkwardly, his hands smudged the glass, and his jaw dropped. "Hi there!" she said, winking. Her voice was low and raspy, as if she smoked too many cigarettes. He turned and gaped at her as she flung the pouch over her shoulder and, laughing, crossed the street with a flourish.

He had heard his mother calling. "Adrian!"

It was nearing dinner time. The corner of Cornelia and Broadway was a mutable place. During the daylight, it was crisscrossed by shoppers and cafe-hoppers and citizens going from store to store, picking up exotic groceries and speciality foods, but as dusk approached and the street grew darker, it changed. Lanky women in high skirts moved in and out of the light of the hotdog palace at the corner; cars paused at the intersection and the women leaned into them, unconcerned, their legs bent slightly in a soulless curtsy. His mother, who worried about him, had seen him talking to the creature.

When he arrived upstairs, his mother was peeling and slicing a white vegetable (*jicama*, she called it) that he had never before seen or tasted. "That was a transsexual," she explained to him, cutting the *jicama* into cubes and tossing them into a salad bowl. Natasha Staller was their neighbor, a friend of Miri's. She lived in one of the elegant townhouses on Cornelia, between Broadway and the lake. "She's an actress," his mother said. "She plays a cicuit of gay clubs and comedy theaters. I've seen her perform twice. She's quite funny, I think." His mother paused, then added, "for a drag queen, I mean." As she talked, his mother poured a mixture of orange juice and grated peel over the cubes of *jicama*.

Over the last three months, Natasha—whose friends nick-named her "Nasty"—had had her picture splashed on the side of the theater that faced the busy intersection of Diversey and Halsted. It made her a minor celebrity. In the picture—which seemed, Miri explained, to celebrate her recent transformation into a woman—Natasha stood, shocked and delighted, as a heat-ing grate blew her billowing white dress high into the air, re-vealing a smooth stretch of newly reconstructed crotch.

"She *used* to be a man?" he asked.

"She had an expensive operation," she explained. "Not many people knew she was a boy. She's been in drag since she was a teenager and dressing full-time for the last eight years. We were used to her."

It was the first of many confusing messages that his mother would give him that summer. "You don't really want anything to do with a transsexual," she told him that night.

"I thought she was a drag queen."

"Same difference."

"But I thought she was your friend, Mom."

"She's trouble." His mother sealed the container that held the *jicama* and placed it in the refrigerator.

"Why?"

"Never mind," she said, looking ashamed. "Forget I said any-thing."

His mother's costume, he suddenly noticed, seemed so simple: a white T-shirt, with spots of peanut butter on the chest, a badge to her imperfect parenthood, and faded denim pants with no belt. His mother, wearing garb that was fashionable for a mid-western lesbian surviving in the big city, was relentlessly and passionately plain-looking.

That summer, the summer of in-betweens, the season of worry and uncertainty, he had decided to try to forget his father.

Once, long ago, his father had read him *Peter Pan*. After bed-time, the mother, whose name was Mrs. Darling, would come to her children's bedside and tidy up their minds, sorting thoughts they had collected during the day. She would pick and choose, organizing what remained in their minds like laundry in an underwear drawer. Adrian wished for that power to separate himself from events, to pluck out familiar names—street signs, lunchtime games, old friends, and Daddy—and to discard them like clothes he had outgrown.

Charlie, Matthew, Normie. His father usually preferred for Adrian to play with certain kinds of children. "Lost boys," his father called them. Soft-spoken boys who were poor or lonely; children from the kind of home they called "broken"; boys whose families had been splintered by calamity. Charlie was pale and he stuttered when he spoke; he was smaller than any other boy in the sixth grade. Matthew's father spanked him every time he made a mistake; he was fearful and talked to no one. Normie lived with his great-aunt; he was always wondering where his mother had gone.

All of Adrian's friends loved his father. He was not like the other parents. He disdained rules and nighttime quiet and fixed bedtimes. He had constructed a treehouse with a firepole exit in the backyard. He hung a tire swing from a thick oak branch. It swung in wide, dangerous circles. When Adrian was a little boy, he had not known the words to describe his father's peculiar way when the lost boys visited: deciding with keen interest which friend came on which weekend; pressing down on Adrian and these friends with kindness; creating so many daredevil circumstances in the backyard—rope ladders, swings, and parallel bars fashioned from sawhorses. Adrian knew that his father was popular, more so than he was, and he realized that the cost of his appeal was this pressure. As he grew older, he referred to it as "the problem," without thinking about what happened when the lost boys were with Daddy. His father once said it was jealousy. The lost boys never said they were bothered.

That last spring, however, his father had changed. An urgency seemed to hang in the air. It began one night when Adrian was taking a bath, filling the tub as high as he dared. His knees popped out of the water. Lying there, creating meek waves that carried broken, fluttering images of his torso, he studied the bathroom door. Ever since he had started washing himself as a little boy, his father insisted for safety's sake that he keep the door ajar.

When his father came to brush his teeth, he glanced down. "Oh, I knew this, I suspected," he said, dropping the toothbrush. Although he had intruded on Adrian's bath time in the past, on this occasion he looked surprised. He left quickly. Adrian felt his face grow red. The heat of that one exposed moment lingered for a long time. He could not shake it. He could feel the nameless problem with all of his senses, but the words to say what it was were beyond him.

His father began to seem less careful in his choice of friends, and less secretive. He started noticing other boys who played on the playground, the boys Adrian avoided: handsome Kurt, a soccer player who was taller than the others; thirteen-year-old Max, the oldest of the boys, who was stocky and bullied other children; Marcus, the most intelligent student in the sixth grade, who was always taking his friends aside and telling dirty jokes. These were confident, happy children; they were not like the lost boys.

One morning his father called, "Why don't you ask Marcus to spend the night?" He had just turned off the shower and stepped onto the slippery tile. Outside the half-open door, waiting in his green flannel pajamas, Adrian glimpsed flashes of terrycloth and his father's white limbs amidst the steam. "He seems like a nice guy."

"Marcus?" Adrian asked. He touched the soft, dry edge of the towel draped around his neck. "He's twice as big as me!"

"He seems like a fine young man," his father assured him. "Why don't you ask him to spend the weekend. We'll build a tent in the backyard."

"I want to ask Normie," Adrian said. Quiet Normie had been abandoned by his mother.

"It'll be good for you to socialize with some different kids for a change."

"But Normie—"

"Normie just visited two weekends ago," his father answered. He opened the door to let out a cloud of steam. Adrian looked away, trying to seem casual, but he noticed his father's body

peripherally: the roll around his middle, the patches of conceal-
ing, dark hair, the penis interrupting his body like a comma.

"They're my friends," he countered. "I want to ask Normie."

"Ask Marcus."

Adrian pouted for a moment, but he did not argue. Marcus
came home for the weekend with him, just like the other boys.
They played in the treehouse and stayed up late at night. His
father made caramel apples and let them jump in their underwear on the king-sized bed. Soon Adrian felt proud that Marcus
wanted to be his friend, even though it was his father, not him,
that Marcus really liked.

But that weekend something happened. In school on Monday,
Marcus avoided Adrian. He picked him last in kick ball. He
slapped his hand hard when he was crossing the monkey bars.
He bullied him on the swings. Once he called him "faggot." In
class, Adrian noticed, Marcus no longer waved his hand, sure of
the answer. He gazed out the window, looking like he was going
to cry. Adrian knew it was his fault for having brought Marcus
home.

At breakfast on Friday, Adrian and his father sat in the
window-lined pocket of the kitchen. The light that poured in
had lost its hint of winter blue and, because there were neither
shades nor curtains, it glared brilliantly all around them. Adrian
and his father were accustomed to squinting and suffering. He
ducked his head behind the cereal box, puzzling over the word
"riboflavin," while his father sipped from a cup of coffee, reading the newspaper.

"I'd like to have Marcus come for the weekend again," his
father said, turning the page. Merciless and hot, the yellow
blades of sunshine cut into the breakfast nook. "How would you
feel about asking him, Aid?"

Adrian was afraid that if he said anything, he would no longer
have the father all the boys admired. The special world he shared
with his father, who was good to him and yet lonely, was breaking down. Only he recognized this fact. He stared into his cereal
bowl, pretending not to hear.

"What's the matter, kiddo?" his father asked, setting down
the newspaper. "I thought you enjoyed having Marcus visit."

He had a crumbling feeling inside his body. His father was staring hard at him. In the bright light the expression on his face was fading into silhouette.

"Daddy," he started. He and his father had never discussed the problem. "I think Marcus is going to tell."

His father let his newspaper fall onto the floor. "Oh, I didn't realize," he said absently. "I didn't. . . ."

Adrian glared at the low puddle of milk in his bowl. They had abandoned the lost boys, who were quiet and grateful, for someone who was handsome and cocky. He clenched his teeth and wondered, for the first time, why his father had become so clumsy. He wished he would disappear.

"I shouldn't have done it," his father said finally, his deep voice wavering. "I should have stopped." He paused, sweating, and his eyes became moist. "It's just that I was afraid I might hurt you instead."

That night in his mother's apartment, after a frustrated search for his transsexual, it was oppressively hot. Adrian laid awake in bed, listening to sounds on the street: the honking and cursing of traffic on Broadway; the occasional bands of men, drunken and happy, singing lyrics from musicals; the jukebox playing distantly from the bar around the corner. Gloria Gaynor was shouting, "I will survive." He walked over to the window and curled against the cool plaster wall, his chin resting on the ledge. He stared at the street below him: the purple shadows seething in the alley; the crumpled papers that, caught in a windstorm, blew in circles; the garbage flattened in the crease by the curb. In the distance he could see the Hancock Building, the red light at the tip of its horn, blinking at him.

"I . . . love . . . you."

The first thing he heard was the clicking of her high-heeled pumps on the concrete. Natasha Staller folded her arms across her chest, wrapping herself in a black coat that descended below her knees. An ivory evening gown, glittering with sequins, peeked out from her collar. Her voice, deeper and more threatening, muttered, "I told you to leave me alone!"

Two men were following her down Broadway. She wanted to

cross the street, but they blocked her path. One of them pulled at her colorful tresses. "Come on, baby! I just want to see if it's real!"

"Is any of it real?" the other man taunted.

She stood pressed up against the wall. They surrounded her. "Didn't you used to be a gay guy?" the first man asked. His face was inches from hers.

"We used to see you in the bars, right?"

"You were a slut. You slept with anybody who'd have you."

"Yeah, I remember you."

"I'm a woman," she answered, looking away from them. Her teeth were clenched. "I have never been a gay man."

"Oh right—"

"What exactly are you, you liar?" the second man asked. "A transvestite?"

"A transsexual?"

Adrian's ears sizzled at the words.

She looked the man in the face. Her eyes narrowed. In a deeper voice, she answered, "Yeah, a transsexual, guys. I just had my penis lopped off last night—"

They hooted with laughter. Adrian bit his lip hard and tasted a little blood. His heart thumped. He thought they were drunk.

She looked furious. "I'm a woman, damn it."

"Oh, yeah?" the first man said, laughing. "How deep is your vagina?"

She glared at him. "How big is your dick, you classless moron?"

They laughed harder.

"Get out of my face!"

"Don't overreact, sweetheart."

"Yeah, we're not hurting you—"

"We're just curious," the first man added. "How deep *is* your vagina?" He put his arm around Natasha's shoulder.

"Fucking idiots!" Natasha slapped the first man with her fist. The second man grabbed her neck. She screamed. Adrian gripped the window ledge. He was not sure, but it looked like she bit his arm. She ran up to the LESBIAN RAGE building. Adrian heard an ugly buzz in the living room.

"Come on, come on," she was saying.

The men followed her down the street, but slowly, unsteadily. "Aw, damn—" the first man whined. "She's getting away."

Adrian could hear her—the broken sounds coming from her body—in the courtyard. He heard her open the door of their building. Her sobbing rebounded, trapped noises, in the stairwell outside his mother's apartment. He heard knocking on the door.

"Miri!"

"What on earth!"

Adrian slipped over to the bedroom door and parted it. Hidden in the darkness, he stood, watching his mother talk to her. He clutched the door and felt light-headed, like he might fall.

"What happened to you?" Miri asked, taking her arm and helping her to the couch. Natasha had blood on her neck and white collar.

"I'm sorry," Natasha said, shaking. "I shouldn't have come here. I didn't know where to go."

"It's O.K.," his mother answered. "Let me get something to clean up that scratch." She disappeared into the bathroom. Natasha stopped crying when his mother left. She looked shaken, her eyes streaked wet and red.

"Here," his mother said. She touched the scratch with a washcloth. "This might hurt a little. It'll clean out that scratch. What happened?"

"There were two of them," she announced. She started crying again. "They followed me home from work, to that alley across the street. They pushed me down in the garbage and cursed at me. They said they wanted to rape me."

Adrian ducked his head farther behind the parted door, into the darkened room. He could not believe what he was hearing.

"Oh my God," his mother said.

"I didn't know what to do," she continued, wiping her eyes with the tissue Miri handed her. "They were going to gang rape me. One was holding back my arms, while the other pulled down his pants. They beat me." She buried her head in her arms. The room seemed to vibrate with her tragedy. Adrian felt the shattered feeling in his body, as if he were the person talking to his mother.

"I don't see any other marks," his mother said, looking confused. She was a nurse, not easily fooled. "Just this scratch on your neck. You say they pushed you down."

"But they were, they were beating me!" She looked at Miri as if she were cornered.

"I'm sorry," his mother said. "I didn't understand. I don't understand. How did you get away?"

There was a long pause, as if the silence were absorbing her tears. Adrian had never witnessed such misery.

"They saw it," she confessed finally. "When they pulled up my dress, they saw. They didn't want me anymore." She was crying hard. "They could have killed me, but they let me go. I'm so ashamed, I'm so frightened and ashamed."

"What did they see, Natasha?" she asked. His mother's voice seemed more confused than ever. The story did not make any sense. "Two months ago you said you finished your surgery."

"I didn't have enough money—"

"But you told us—"

"I didn't have enough money!" she shouted. She hiccoughed. "If I had had the surgery already, they would have destroyed me tonight. Destroyed me! Don't you understand? They wanted to rape me."

Adrian felt a thin well of blood on his lip. It tasted rusty. He closed the door softly. "Oh, damn," he mumbled, trying to control the sounds escaping from his body. It was the type of crying that wanted to be loud, but he was frightened to have anyone, even his mother, hear him. He was crying because Natasha was a liar. He was crying because her story made him remember his father. He was crying because she was still a man. He had wanted her to be something else: neither a man nor a woman.

He heard his mother at the door. "Adrian?"

"Go away!"

"What's the matter?" she asked. "Did you see it?"

"Nothing," he said, whimpering, pulling his pillow over his head. "Nothing, nothing, nothing."

Peg was stocky and tough-minded, dressed in a black suit jacket with squared shoulders. "How ya doin', kid?" she asked him. He shrugged and eyed her warily. He did not like her.

Whenever she visited the apartment, Adrian retreated outside, no matter how humid the weather. His mother would ask him to leave anyway. She had been arguing with Peg all summer.

The three black girls were playing jump rope again in the recess of the courtyard. He stared through the eye-shaped snapping of the double dutchers' ropes.

From the window, he heard his mother talking to Peg. "You keep your discussion about puberty and age limits and patriarchy to your dyke's group," she said. He wondered why they were still friends. "If I hear one word in front of him, I'll raise a stink."

He was growing dizzy at the way the whirling cords wrinkled and broke apart images on the other side of the street, when he glimpsed her, the flamboyant Natasha Staller, looking cool and perfect in a feathery, white lace coat dress and a creamy broad-brimmed hat that flapped in the breeze. She turned the corner at Cornelia, walking toward the tunnel under Lake Shore Drive, the tunnel that led to Lake Michigan.

Without thinking, he crossed the intersection and trailed after her. A driver honked at him for running across the street. She entered a gate in front of a brownstone. It had a narrow staircase ascending, it seemed, to an unapproachable door. She turned, at the top of her stairs, and looked down at him.

"Oops," he said.

She stared at him.

Finally, he asked a question. "Is this where you live?" The building was elegant. The black rods that held up the banister were shaped like a garden of iron daisies; the carved oak door contained a stained-glass window with triangles of alternating burgundy and forest green.

"Who are you?" she asked meanly.

"My mother knows you," he declared. "Her name is Miriam Birkin."

Like an elegant dragon-woman, Natasha Staller looked only ruffled. Her lip angled and she forced a steaming strand of cigarette smoke into the air. Annoyance, like a bright scarf, seemed a part of who she was. "Your mother is an amazing woman," she said. "She's a saint."

"She told me you're a drag queen."

Natasha wrinkled her nose. "That's what she said? A drag queen?" She held the wand of her colored cigarette slightly, her fingers swishing in S shapes, sending curls into the air like the beginnings of some blue-white lace. "I am not—" There was a stylish pause. "—a drag queen."

"You aren't?"

"What I am," she said, "is misunderstood."

She had a way of inserting pauses into her sentences, dismantling them, with spaces uncluttered by sound.

"I don't understand," he said.

"Little boy," she said, curling her tongue deliciously around her L's. It sounded more like *LEEtle buoy*. "A drag queen is a man who dresses as a woman, but makes no attempt to disguise the fact that he is a man." She spewed her ghostly breath into the atmosphere. "A female impersonator masquerades as a woman and conceals every sign of her male body. I have been called all of these things, and I am none of them."

She had an accent, but he did not know what country she was from.

"I saw what happened to you the other night," he said. He wanted to confront her, to name the lies she told, but the pounding of his heart trapped the words in his body. "I saw those men bothering you from my window."

She threw out her hand, as if she were casting away litter, and she took rapid puffs on her cigarette. "That kind of thing happens to me a lot," she said. Her eyes grew soft.

"I don't like being teased either," he said to her.

She looked at Adrian briefly, but turned away. "You know, I used to think I belonged to gay men like them," she said sadly. "Every night on the stage I would look into a crowd of them. They were cheering me, thrilled to be near me. In my mind I was like Bette Midler or Barbra Streisand or any of those campy hags who got their start in gay clubs. But, at some point, I stopped saying I was doing drag. I finally told them, 'No, sweethearts, this is who I really am. I have finally transformed into myself and I feel glorious.'

"No one wanted to hear that. No one clapped or cheered when I said it. It was as if I had betrayed them. Perhaps I had. I made them think it was a costume—it *was* an extreme outfit, an outrageous posture I took—when it was my real self. I was a woman. But they thought I was one of them."

She did not look at him. It was as if he were anonymous, surrounded by an audience of accusers. He felt a forbidden sense of privilege, to be near her, listening to a story of her life.

"Last night I wanted to tell those men something, but I was too afraid."

He hesitated. He wanted to forgive her her deceptions and to hear the stories of her life, because they were beginning to seem beautiful. He wanted to tell her that he knew she was both a liar and a man. "What was it?" he finally whispered.

"I wanted to say to them: 'I have always dressed as a female as long as I can remember and I have always felt myself to be a woman. I am, simply, a different kind of woman.' "

He felt that the exotic creature was beyond him—she was so adult, so glamorous and special. He was mesmerized. Invisible waves, starting in a hot spot in the center of his body, rolled outward, leaving his fingertips and toes trembling with an expansion of flesh. His throat grew dry. His crotch tingled. "My mother," he added clumsily, "is a woman, too."

She relaxed her pose and smiled. She seemed to look at him again. "Well, now," she said, pressing her lips into a tight, rosebud smile. "You and I will have a lot to talk about, then, won't we? It's time for me to leave. I have a show tonight. You're a sweet little boy, and very safe." *LEEtle buoy.* The luxurious syllables floated in the air, expectant, like blown kisses that never land. She looked over her shoulder, at Broadway, and she spoke to no one in particular.

"Fags, you know, aren't the only ones who get bashed in this neighborhood."

"Good-bye," he said. It was a parched sound in the back of his throat. After she disappeared into the brownstone, he felt the noises and sights of the ordinary world seep into his awareness again: the honking of buses and the steady *whoosh* of traffic, the click of jump rope on the cement and the arguing of the double dutchers. When he returned to the LESBIAN RAGE building, he heard his mother talking to Peg, but in subdued tones. He guessed that she had negotiated a place on the floor of the women's coffeehouse for him, a place where, sitting at the feet of his mother and her lover, who would be holding hands in the safest place they knew, he would masquerade as an eleven year old, his legs clenched at the knees, hiding the subtle hairs that were growing, inevitably, frighteningly, between his legs. How much longer, he wondered, would his mother be able to lie about who he was? What would happen to him when she could no longer shield him with untruths? Twelve, thirteen, fourteen . . . Adrian leaned against the LESBIAN RAGE building and, staring at the black spires shooting through the mists of downtown, like a far-off bad dream, he shielded his eyes, unable to see, although it was not bright outside.

9.2

• DAVID VERNON •

As we drive down the Number 15 freeway I tell Louis about the dream I had last night where I was hosting *The Tonight Show* and my guests were Joseph Stalin, Charo, Jacqueline Suzanne and the June Taylor Dancers. The audience was filled with families, eagerly waiting for the show to begin. Then, I called my mother to remind her to watch. She told me she'd try but there was a hurricane heading in the direction of Burbank. As I hung up the phone a powerful wind burst into the studio and blew away the audience, the band, and finally the guests. Even the June Taylor Dancers, every last one of them.

Louis nods as I relay this to him. He is wearing a pair of khaki shorts and blue tank top, his dark wavy hair tossing in the wind. The only part about the dream I'm making up is the part about my mother. In the dream it was actually Louis himself who broke the bad news about the storm, but I don't want to start another argument.

He keeps his eyes on the road and considers my dream. Dreams are important to his family and a dream without a meaning, however clumsy, would be like an unsolved algebra equation to a mathematician. (Once I told his sister Marie that I dreamt our cat, Tammy, was wearing braces, to which Marie responded in utter seriousness, "You *worry* about her.")

Louis clears his throat to let me know he has solved the mystery.

"You feel like you are always on the verge of a great success but your mother holds you back, creates havoc in your life."

I smile at him and wonder what kind of great success I might be on the verge of—Head Substitute Teacher, the Mr. Chips of substitute teachers, perhaps. Louis looks off, proud to have solved the puzzle as we drive through a stretch of road that looks just like the last thirty miles of road we've passed.

We approach a sign announcing only forty more miles to Victorville.

"Forty miles," Louis echoes.

This bad habit endeared him to me early in our relationship but now sends me searching the glove compartment for a knuckle wrench.

"Pretty out here, isn't it?" he tells me in the form of a question.

I look out at the desert and the scattered rows of Joshuas looking like Charlie Brown Christmas trees and frankly, I worry. Louis' family lives out here in this desert that looks like one of those Australian end-of-the-world movies where all the survivors of the nuclear holocaust run around with dirty hair and scabby knees. If we're not careful we could end up living here too.

The truth is, although I love his family (mine I would trade for baseball cards but I really *love* his family), I'm growing weary of these frenzied trips to Victorville. I keep hoping they will help save our relationship, but every Monday morning after we return I find myself physically exhausted from the drive and Louis seems even more distant.

Louis comes from a large third-generation Mexican family. He is the youngest of five children. In 1985 most of his family moved from Glendale to Victorville because of the lower property rates and also because it seemed to be a safer place to raise their children.

Louis has a seventy-eight-year-old grandmother, Melena, whose dreams are filled with warning. Kenny, Louis' nine-year-old nephew, explains that Grandma Melena's dreams are like the six o'clock news. "Tomorrow's six o'clock news," he adds. In her time Grandma Melena has dreamt of the Sylmar Earthquake, the assassination attempt on Gerald Ford, and the explosion of the *Challenger*. Unfortunately, she has also dreamt of a bomb that would blow up the Liberty Bell, a tidal wave separating San Francisco from the rest of California, and for five years straight, the death of Bob Hope.

"I swear it's gonna happen this year," I remember her promising to the table last Thanksgiving. "Bob's gonna drop."

Every few months for the past year Melena had been predicting earthquakes that never came to pass. From what I could tell, *The Weekly World News* has a better track record than this lady.

Two nights ago we received a call from Louis' sister, Sophie.

"Grandma Melena dreamt of an earthquake last night. A 9.2. She sees a lot of destruction in Los Angeles. You guys better come over!"

"What do you think?" Louis asked once he got off the phone. We had been laying in bed together, reading separately.

"I don't know," I whined, "she hasn't been right about anything for a long time. There was an earthquake she predicted in January. And she swore she was right about the one she predicted in April. I feel kind of silly driving out there again."

A few minutes later Louis' mother called asking us if we were going to drive up for the earthquake this weekend.

"Mom, you know she's never right," Louis told her.

"But mijo, the receptionist at the doctor's office heard on *Entertainment Tonight* one of Shirley MacLaine's spirits predicted a big earthquake in Los Angeles this month."

Just as we were dozing off Louis' brother, Franklin, called and asked us if we had heard about Grandma Melena's dream, adding that he had a friend who worked for the Victorville Fire Department. They were on special alert due to an alarming drop in the water table under the San Andreas Fault.

Grandma Melena, Shirley MacLaine *and* the Victorville Fire Department—not the three most reliable sources. Still, wouldn't it be tempting fate to not spend the weekend in Victorville with the Delgado clan who have enough provisions holed away to open their own Price Club.

I admit I felt foolish as I removed our paintings from the walls and Velcroed the crystal wineglasses in the cabinets. I was never brought up to be superstitious. No stock was put in fortune cookies, coffee grinds or bad dreams. When I was ten I was haunted by a story I had ripped out of the newspaper and brought into my class for Show and Tell. It was about a ten-year-old boy, Milo Dunk from Norfolk, Virginia, who was kidnapped and tortured by his parents' canasta partners, a couple they had known for years. For weeks no friend of my parents' escaped my scrutiny. Were they really who they claimed to be? Or were they members of some underground children-haters society, waiting patiently for the perfect moment to cart me away? My mother, finally noticing I had stopped eating, set me straight. She knelt down and in the most patient voice she could muster said, "Dale, listen to Mommy. Nothing is going to happen to you. Just think about it. Nothing ever happens to *anyone* in our family. Nothing monstrously good. Nothing monstrously bad. It's a family curse and you're just going to have to accept it."

And I've lived with that belief ever since.

"Ten miles," Louis calls out as we pass a sign. He scratches at his goatee, a new addition to his face. The goatee has only grown in partially, but I'm certain it's something he's doing just to annoy his conservative family. But I don't see why if they didn't mention anything about his pierced ear and assorted unusual haircuts he's shown up with in the past, why they'd mention this new spot of growth on his chin.

"Who's going to be there?"

"Almost everyone, except maybe for Renayaldo and Clydie. They're going to Vegas."

I nod, trying to remember exactly who Renayaldo is. I'm not good at remembering names. It doesn't help being a substitute teacher and seeing all those different fleshy faces every day. I swear if Louis and I break up I'll never date anyone who has more relatives than members of the U.S. Senate.

Louis and I both grew up in Southern California and were raised knowing that the "Big One" would probably occur in our lifetime. When I was in fifth grade there was a film shown in the auditorium called *Listen to the Sounds of Warning*. The reddish, grainy sixteen-millimeter film showed a brother and sister, Rick and Sandy, during an earthquake drill at school. Sandy listened attentively as her teacher advised the class on what to do. Rick, a wiseacre with a blond buzz cut, horsed around during the demonstration, ignoring the safety procedures. In the next scene an earthquake strikes during class and Sandy knows just what to do while Rick runs panicked into the hallways. The last shot of the movie showed one of Rick's tiny hands sticking out from under a pile of cement. The narrator closed the film saying, "If Rick had just listened to the sounds of warning, he would have survived."

Louis has told me that in grade school he was taught that an earthquake was like an overweight man in loose pants with a thick, expansive belt. When there was tension he would move his belt up a notch and his belly would rumble. When the pressure on this overweight man became too terrible he would pull the belt in and unbuckle. This is the image that stayed with Louis: when the "Big One" occurred, the earth would be unbuckling beneath him.

A car in front of us backfires loudly and we both gasp. I realize I am clutching the steering wheel white-knuckled, like the safety bar on a roller coaster.

If it's going to happen, I find myself praying, let it happen here. A spot halfway between our home and his family's, away from our jobs and ambitions and away from the person I suspect Louis is having an affair with. The city would be wiped out and we'd have to start all over. Certainly, if Noah and his wife were having marital problems before the flood, they'd just have to get over them. I could get used to the desert, roasting cactus, hunting for dinner, making love under a quilt of stars. Maybe without the anxieties of our day-to-day lives we could recapture something primal, something necessary about our relationship.

I listen to the faint music of the desert, expecting the worst as we drive on.

In Victorville we arrive at the home of Louis' sister, Carmen. It's a buffer. After weeks of just the two of us in our one-bedroom apartment it's a way to dip our toes into the familial pool before diving into his parents' house, the nucleus.

Carmen was the last holdout in the Delgado clan (barring

Louis) to make the move to Victorville. She survives by shopping vigorously through the mail from department stores out of her reach: Macy's, Neiman Marcus, Saks. Her house resembles a photograph from one of her catalogues. Even though I've grown accustomed to her overaccessorized design, I still expect to see an arrow pointing in the direction of a halogen lamp or glass coffee table with the letter "D" or "E" in bold floating above us.

Seconds after we ring the bell, Carmen's seven-year-old daughter, Carrie, swings open the door and screams, "Uncle Dale! Mom, Uncle Dale's here with Louis!"

Louis tosses me a dirty look. He doesn't encourage any of his relatives to refer to me as part of the family.

"We're packing for the earthquake," Carrie tells me, her voice tremoring with excitement.

I give her a smile to let her know I share in her sense of adventure.

"Carrie, I told you, we're going to Grandma and Grandpa's to keep them company just in case of an earthquake, but there isn't going to be one," Carmen says as she approaches us wearing an oriental robe I remember seeing circled in one of her Victoria's Secret catalogues a few months ago.

"Hi boys."

She gives both of us a hug.

At thirty-three Carmen is only two years older than I am, but the stress of raising Carrie and five-year-old Ricardo has made its mark on her. Her mess of wavy black hair hangs like a cloud above her head.

"I don't know about you two but I'm so tired that if that 9.2 does show up tonight I'd probably just sleep right through it."

"Let me show you what I'm packing," Carrie says as she pulls me into her room.

"I'm bringing my blanket in case we get to sleep outside and my new Step Aerobics Barbie so we have something to play with," Carrie tells me as she empties her suitcase. "And I'm taking my nurse kit. In case I have to fix someone up."

From the den I hear Louis and Carmen talking. I split my attention, hoping to overhear their conversation to see if Louis is telling her how we haven't been getting along, how I've been suspicious of this new friend of his he's been seeing an awful lot of lately.

Louis and I had what our friends refer to as a "cute meet." Louis is a librarian at the downtown branch of the Public Library, although he was working at the West Hollywood branch when we met. I came in requesting a copy of *The Fountainhead* to be put on hold. After two weeks I could care less about *The Fountainhead*, it was just an excuse to come into the library and stare into Louis' gorgeous black eyes and ogle his chest as he would report the book still hadn't been returned. Finally, on the fifth week, Louis asked me out and showed up at the door with a copy of the book. It was perfect, except for the fact when I finally read *The Fountainhead*, I didn't care for it much.

When we met, Louis was estranged from his family. He said they didn't fully accept his homosexuality. He had come out to his family the previous year, and although they were supportive, they would blanch whenever he would discuss the more intimate details of his sex life with them. Louis took this as an insult, even though none of his family, even the married couples, ever say anything about sex. I encouraged Louis to give his family another chance. Even though it's never mentioned, I think Louis' family credits me with bringing him back to them. I was amazed at how well his family has grown to accept us; of course, Louis won't be satisfied until he can discuss sodomy over chorizo and eggs at their breakfast table. Louis says families are not sexy. Louis says I have an unhealthy fixation on the archetypal concept of families. Louis says I am paranoid and jealous; that I am someone to worry about. Indeed, three years into our relationship, when I picture him at work I imagine him smiling at young guys in tight jeans, bearing them bouquets of Fitzgerald, Hemingway and Plath.

When Carrie and I return to the den, Louis and Carmen stop talking, both throwing me a nervous look.

The heat is unbearable, easily up near a hundred degrees, as Louis and I drive up to his parents' house. It is a spacious territory resembling a ranch, a mini Ponderosa but without the horses or lively theme music. Antlers hang above the archway over the wood plaque whose burnt-out letters read: *Delgado*. Two of Louis' nieces jump rope in front of the house and they wave as we pull into the driveway.

Impending disasters follow the same etiquette as holidays at the Delgado household. There are four zones. The men who have married into the family and Louis' father sit in the living room in front of a towering big-screen TV, always watching a boxing match or a ball game. The women populate the expansive kitchen either cooking or keeping up to date with the Delgado family saga. The backyard is where Louis' brothers and all nephews over sixteen hang out, shooting baskets, drinking Dos Eqis beer, and telling penis and vagina jokes. The den, the front yard and the upstairs guest room is usually littered with nieces and nephews playing with their latest booty from the Victorville Toys-R-Us.

Louis and I walk through the rooms and exchange greetings and hugs. The house is abuzz with activity. I haven't seen this much excitement at the Delgados' since last Thanksgiving when they spent two hours trying to negotiate the Secret Santa.

My first holiday here was confusing. I didn't know which group I belonged to. Technically, I was a male who had married into the family which would mean I would be relegated to watching the husbands watch sports. But I love to cook, and didn't most of them think of me as Louis' wife anyway? Hadn't I earned a coffee mug with my name on it? I also enjoy playing with the younger nieces and nephews, learning all the games I had missed out on as a child: the trick to winning a game of Old Maid, the ethics of jumping rope. And since the boys in the backyard practiced serious denial about mine and Louis' relationship, wasn't I really just another dude entitled to shoot hoops or at least watch Louis' godlike nineteen-year-old nephew Leo work up a sweat.

My position in the Delgado family seems difficult to define. I feel at home here. Truly I had almost totally abandoned the idea of family before I became part of theirs. After my first visit I asked Louis "So, how did I do?" Sporting a look of disdain, he told me, "Did you have to enjoy yourself so much?" Louis is not as close to his family as I am.

Louis' mother breaks free from the kitchen crowd and embraces me and then her son. She is a short, energetic, upbeat woman with a swirl of gray hair. Always well-dressed, today she is wearing one of her church dresses and as I get closer to her I notice she smells of Oil of Olay.

"How was the drive?"

"Endless," Louis groans. "Where's Grandma?"

"Napping. She wants to be rested for all the company and for the earthquake."

"When is it supposed to happen?" I ask.

"I don't know. Gee, I hope it happens this weekend though," she says, betraying her excitement. "That is, if it has to happen at all."

"Where do we put our bags?" Louis asks.

"You two get the guest room upstairs," she says leading us up the staircase. "Did you ever see such commotion?"

I gaze over at Louis. I'm floored by her act of kindness. The upstairs guest room is a highly coveted spot, everyone else will have to sleep on the floor or on the couch. And the room contains only one bed.

"Ma! We'll sleep in the living room," Louis demands.

"I've made the arrangements," she says sternly.

"It's O.K., let someone else sleep up here. I'll crash on one of the couches and Dale can sleep on the floor."

"You'd make poor Dale sleep on the floor?" she asks, incredulously.

"Yes, he can sleep on the floor. And his name is Dale. Everyone in this family seems to think his first name is 'poor,'" he says, his voice raised as high as I've ever heard him raise it to a family member.

"Well, too bad. Dale *is* family and I'm not letting him sleep on the floor."

"I give up."

"It's settled," she tells us dismissively, "I've got to go and check on dinner."

As she retreats downstairs, I wonder if she is giving us the guest room because even she has recognized our relationship is in perilous waters.

"What was that all about?" I ask.

"You are *not* family," he growls. "You're my queer boyfriend. They're trying to change what we are and make it into something they can understand. We're not like them. We're not a married couple. Maybe I like sleeping on the couch and sneaking into your sleeping bag and fucking you while everyone else is sleeping. You think the best you can get is to be accepted by my heterosexual family. I think it's more important not to lose sight of who we are."

Clearly I don't know how to respond to this outburst. He throws his suitcase on the floor. "This is my worst nightmare," he says under his breath as he heads downstairs.

After I unpack and write "Fuck You Louis" a hundred and fifty times on a sheet of paper, I join the party downstairs where Franklin is trying to assemble everyone, except for Grandma Melena who is still resting, for an earthquake drill. Franklin is a high-school basketball coach, and strangely enough the shortest of the Delgado children. He talks to us as if we were his team and there were only twenty seconds left in the game.

"O.K., now listen up 'cause this is serious business. The safest places to be in this house when the earthquake hits are the doorways and under the table." Franklin points out all the doorways with the precision of an airline steward then warns the family to steer clear of the windows. "I want to try this once."

The room breaks out in a rash of excitement.

"I want everyone to go to a different part of the house and when I yell 'Earthquake' I want you to run and take safe cover. So now just go and pretend to do what you'd normally be doing."

Rena, the seventeen-year-old daughter of Louis' sister Marie, announces she has to go fix her makeup. Rena studies art, dresses provocatively and talks down to most of the family. Louis doesn't care for Rena, he finds her arrogant. Personally, I'm thrilled by her.

The rest of the family disperses. I settle in front of the television and Louis strikes up a conversation with Carmen, in the kitchen. I watch whatever boxing match is on the big screen and try to pretend I have no idea disaster is about to strike. I clear my mind and find myself surprised at how easy it is to shift focus. Then I remember all the years as a child when I ignored the inevitability of my parents' divorce. I used to watch TV and pretend I didn't notice the arguing and the violence going on in the next room. Some natural disasters you see coming and yet you just keep turning the volume on the TV set higher and higher.

From a back room we hear Franklin yell, "Earthquake, earthquake." The children race from down the stairs, screaming in mock terror. People are running, pushing and giggling as they try to get under the large dinner table. For a moment I am disoriented. For a moment my mind translates this as real. I don't see Louis and I'm aware of how desperately I love him and how frightened I've been about what is happening to us. To *our* family. I scan the room and still can't find him. It may sound very Tammy Wynette, but if there's a disaster I want to be right next to him.

"Come on everyone," Franklin yells out impatiently, "you're acting like you're on your way to church. Shelves are shaking! Windows are cracking!"

"Dale, I'm here," Louis calls out. He's already under the table. I squeeze in right next to him.

"I was a jerk. I'm sorry," he says as he touches my hand.

"Where's Dale? I want to be next to Dale," Carrie says. She scrambles from under the table, races to the other, climbs underneath again and wedges herself between me and Louis.

I peer out from under the table and see Rena has taken shelter under the frame of the front door. She has her arms extended across the doorway, her chest in her black halter top pushed out. Her makeup is excessive and she is wearing her black leather boots with one leg hitched up against the doorway. I imagine her framed by the doorway with tumbling telephone poles and flying debris and realize she is the poster girl for the apocalypse.

Finally it is quiet until a sound of something moving upstairs becomes audible. It is soft footsteps followed by a *clump* sound. Nobody says a word. We hear step, *clump*. Step. *Clump*. Step. *Clump*. Grandma Melena appears at the top of the stairs with her cane, wearing a black, multiveiled dress that at one time must have looked gorgeous on her but unfortunately now seems two sizes too big. She walks down the steps gradually with the use of her cane. Footstep. *Clump.* Footstep. *Clump.* Once at the bottom she peers under the dining-room table.

"What the hell is all this?"

"We're practicing for the earthquake, Ma," Louis' mother calls out.

"Practice? We're talking 9.2 here. Total destruction. You can't practice for that," Melena says as she leaves the room, disgusted with the whole bunch of us.

Soon more guests arrive. Word of Grandma Melena's dream has spread. A tiny woman with flaming red hair is introduced to me as Aunt Antonia from northern California.

"Salinas," she says as she shakes my hand.

The party is under way. The house is vibrating with the sound of people laughing. Children chasing each other in the hallways and up the stairs. From inside the kitchen you can hear knives chopping against cutting blocks, the oven being opened and closed and pots bowling over. This is the sweet music of dinner being prepared.

In the dining room Rena sits in a corner with her sketchpad and focuses her attention on the people around the table.

"What are you drawing?" her mother asks as she walks in from the kitchen, wiping her hands on her apron.

"Just drawing," Rena responds, moving the pad away from her mother's view.

"Can I see what my talented girl is drawing?"

"It's personal," Rena says without looking up.

"It better not be making fun of God or the family, that's all I can say," her mother warns as she walks away.

I take a trip up the stairs to look for Louis, and I'm filled with a sense of family. I was always the one who scoffed at all the Hallmark commercials, laughed at all the "baby in the blender" jokes. I was the one who wished awful things on the Bradys, Partridges, Waltons, the close-knit families of the world. I thought as a gay man I could never have a family or be a part of one. But as I pass by a hallway lined with glossy family photographs, I imagine one up on these walls of Louis, our cat Tammy and me. Recently when I walk this hallway, I feel like the Grinch at the end of that Dr. Seuss holiday special, the one I used to watch by myself every Christmas, when his minuscule heart finally grows.

I can even imagine a K-Mart eight-by-ten in this hallway of Louis, Tammy, me, and a child of our own. Someday.

I hear Louis' voice inside his parents' bedroom. I open the door and find him sitting on the bed, his back to the door, talking on the phone. Startled, he looks at me and covers the mouthpiece.

"I'll be off in a few minutes."

Wanting to get a snippet of his conversation I loiter in the bedroom, pretending to notice the small print under a plaque titled, "World's Best Grandmother."

"Something you need?" Louis asks impatiently.

I nod my head no and leave the room.

Downstairs two of Louis' nieces, Jewel, who is six, and Claudia, who is nine, tug me into a room where Carrie, draped in one of her grandmother's caftans, has the lights dimmed and is playing fortune-teller.

"What is that you're wearing, Carrie?" I ask.

"My name is Madame FooFoo," she answers, her voice deep and high at the same time.

"Is it two Foos as a first name or is Foo your first name and your last name?"

Jewel and Claudia giggle.

"Dale," Carrie says sternly, "stop playing around."

From one of her flowing sleeves she produces a Magic 8-Ball. "Ask Madame FooFoo a question."

"OK, Foo," I say, "when's the exchange rate going to even out?"

"Gots to be yes or no," Jewel calls out.

"You have to ask a yes or no question," Carrie asserts, losing her patience. "Like, does Dale have a girlfriend?"

She shakes the Magic 8-Ball, turns it over and squints to read the response.

"It says, My answer is no." She shakes the 8-Ball again, full of verve, the way one shakes a bottle of juice before opening. "How about," she continues, "is there any girl who likes Dale?"

Jewel and Claudia nod in agreement.

"It says, Don't count on it."

Carmen knocks on the door and steps in.

"Wash up for dinner." She eyes Carrie's get-up. "And hang up Grandma's dress."

After they dart out of the room I pick up the thumb-smudged Magic 8-Ball and decide I have a few questions of my own.

"Is there going to be a major earthquake soon?"

Don't Count on It.

"Should I trust a fortune-telling device manufactured by Hasbro?"

Ask Again Later.

"Is my relationship in trouble?"

Outlook Not So Good.

"Is Louis having an affair with this new friend of his, this Geoffrey?"

Better Not Tell You Now.

In the dining room Louis and I are seated at the main table with the other married couples. Years ago, Louis brought over a guy he was dating and his family seated them both at the children's table.

"If we're going to die tomorrow, we might as well eat well tonight," Louis' father says as he passes a plate of steaming, homemade corn tortillas. Louis' father is a short man in his early sixties who has been retired for several years. He spends most of his free time in his garden, and since his retirement his skin has turned leathery and dark brown. I have no idea whether he knows Louis and I are lovers. He treats me like one of the family, and at any dinner table he makes certain my plate is full.

The table is alive with food. Besides the Swedish Table Smorgasbord in Culver City, which my father would take us to on *special* occasions (like announcing his divorce from my mom), I can't remember ever seeing so much food on one table. I smell the strong fragrances of cilantro and fresh chiles from the Delgado garden. Carmen made spicy chile rellenos topped with a thin red salsa. There are empanadas filled with ham and cheese. Someone brought cheese and chicken enchilladas. There are bowls of rice and black beans. One of Louis' other sisters cooked up a tangy meatball soup.

During dessert most of us eat buenellos while a few people attend, with some trepidation, to a lime Jell-O Carmen had made in the shape of a chile pepper. All eyes are on Grandma Melena, who has been strangely quiet all evening. Finally Carmen's husband Al breaks the ice by asking, "So a 9.2, huh?"

"You can bet your bottom dollar," she promises.

"There's never been one that big before, Grandma," Leo says.

"Well there's gonna be."

Melena straightens herself up in her chair.

"How do you know it's going to happen this month, Grandma?" Sophie asks.

"I saw a newspaper in the dream. It was this month."

"Did you see the exact day?" Al asks.

"With my eyesight?"

If there was a spotlight in the house it would be on her right now.

"It happened like this," she tells us softly, forcing all of us to move in closer. "I was walking to Vons and the sky was orange like cream of tomato soup. I could hardly walk there was so much rubble in the streets. Broken glass everywhere. The buildings looked twisted. I passed the dry cleaners, and there was a sign swinging in the window saying, 'Closed Until Further Notice.' "

She pauses for dramatic effect as I wonder how many times she has rehearsed this presentation today.

"Then I see a newspaper in the machine and the headline is enormous. It says '9.2 Arrives.' I go over to get the paper but then I realize I don't have enough change. Isn't that the way it always happens?"

The room nods in agreement.

After buenellos and coffee I join Leo, his cousin Victor and two twenty-year-old friends in the back. I don't know if I've ever seen a sky with this many stars. It's chilly yet the guys are wearing tank tops. Leo plays with the basketball, and it bounces on the cement, creating an echoing thud I imagine traveling across the desert.

"What do you think about this earthquake stuff?" I ask the group.

"I believe it," Victor says. "A friend of mine heard something about water levels."

"No disrespect to your grandma, man, but there's never been no quake that big. That'd be one big motherfucking mess," one of the friends says.

"Maybe she's dyslexic," Leo says as he bounces the ball and shoots. "Maybe there's going to be a 2.9."

Leo smiles at his own joke and looks over at me to see if I'm laughing. I'm not but I smile to let him know I *want* to think it's funny. As he continues playing ball, I stand frozen and try to find the correct word for what I was experiencing as he looked at me. It takes a minute before I recognize that the correct word is swoon. There is no end to Louis' irritation over my attraction to Leo.

"When you look at him," Louis once told me, "it's the look of a man who drives a Chevy gazing at a BMW."

"Maybe it's like, you know, when the telephone wires get crossed and you can listen in to other people's conversations," Leo says as he passes the ball to Victor. "Maybe her dreams are like that. Maybe somewhere in another country or another planet there's gonna be an earthquake or some disaster. Like one of those cable dishes, maybe her dreams are vibrations from some other world or civilization."

"Pendejo!" Victor laughs as he throws an empty beer can at Leo.

I don't know if it's because I'm drunk off the richness of the evening or if it's because I imagine Leo explaining his theory to me out in the desert under this canvas of stars, but I swear I think it's about the most beautiful theory I've ever heard. I'm damn near teary until Victor lets out a loud belch, and the guys start talking in Spanish.

In truth, I've formulated my own theory about Grandma Melena's dreams that is not far off from Leo's. Once when we received a call saying Melena had dreamt of a 3.5 earthquake, Louis and I argued that night over whose turn it was to clean out the refrigerator. Another time when she predicted a flood, we argued all evening. The last time we came to Victorville, Grandma Melena had predicted a 7.5, which never came to pass and Louis and I fought the whole ride home over a joke he had made at my expense in front of his family. That argument snowballed, and I ended up moving out of our apartment for three days. There is no doubt in my mind Louis would call it egotistical, but I've been suspecting that Grandma Melena has tuned into *our* channel by mistake. In her dreams she is measuring the seismic waves of our relationship. But now she sees a 9.2, total destruction. Leaving the backyard and entering back into the house, I find myself almost desperate for an honest-to-god earthquake. 7.5. 8.8. 9.2. It can be of the buildings-falling and the continents-drifting variety. I don't care. I'll walk through rubble, stand in line for rations, help rebuild the city. I'm ready for the end of the world, just not the end of my relationship.

In the guest room Louis and I sleep at separate ends of the king-size bed.

"Would you believe, no one even mentioned my goatee?" Louis says. "I think I'm just going to shave the damn thing off."

I look at Louis laying near me. His body is a map I know intimately.

"Can I put my head on your chest?" I finally ask.

"Are you crazy? Somebody could walk in."

"Nobody's going to walk in," I say.

"This is my family's house. People don't knock before they barge in."

"Oh, please. You know as well as I do there's an invisible sign on this door the size of a billboard saying 'Queers At Work—Sodomy Occurring—Stay Out.' We could stay in this room for a month, and no one would even check us, they're too afraid of what they might see or hear."

"Not the younger kids," Louis offers, "not Ricardo or Carrie or Jewel."

I don't say anything because he has a point. I imagine they view us in the same manner I used to think of Uncle Bill and Mr. French in *Family Affair*; just two confirmed, fussy bachelors who enjoy each other's company.

"I think that since your parents let us stay in this room, it's as if they're giving you permission to fool around with a guy, and suddenly, now that it's allowed, it's just not as attractive."

"Will you stop with this crap," he begs. "Pretty soon you'll be talking about my internalized homophobia, and I'm going to go sleep on the roof. I swear to God, Dale, I'll sleep on the roof."

Louis stays on his side of the bed but leans in to give me a frugal kiss.

"Good night. I love you."

As he settles in, preparing for sleep, I ask, "Louis, who were you talking to on the phone?"

"When?"

"In your parents' room."

"Estelle."

"I don't think I know her."

"From work. The one with the British accent whose son is bipolar. She took my shift today, and I wanted to thank her."

"You couldn't wait till we got home?"

"Fuck. I can't even call someone. I can't have that much space without you getting panicky."

"I'm sorry."

"Who did you think I was calling?"

"I thought maybe you were calling Geoffrey," I say, feeling a bit guilty.

"Figures."

"So you weren't?" I ask, trying to get a direct denial.

"Fuck," Louis says again, then pauses. "I told you, I was calling Estelle. Can we sleep now, is it O.K. with you Dale, do you mind all that much?"

I try to sleep but I find myself thinking of that movie from the seventies, *Earthquake*, where Los Angeles is leveled by The "Big One." Louis and I rented it a few months ago for a kick. In it, Charlton Heston is in a loveless marriage to the shrewish Ava Gardner while having an affair with an aspiring actress played by Genevieve Bujold. In the end, Ava is sucked down into a sewage pipe, wearing a devastating Edith Head gown, as Charlton and Genevieve look on. He has to make a quick decision between old love and new. As the John Williams score climaxes, Charlton waves good-bye to Genevieve and jumps in, to his certain death, after Ava.

Maybe Louis isn't having an affair with Geoffrey. But why

then haven't things been adding up? Why has Louis been so distant and irritable lately? Everyone knows that his sullenness is one of Louis' most exciting qualities, but this moves beyond sullen. And wouldn't it be just like him to fall for a Jeffrey who spells his name with a G. A blond Geoffrey, Louis has admitted. Perhaps I am being too neurotic I think as I turn to go to sleep. But I can't shake the feeling that if Louis, Geoffrey and I were together in an earthquake-ravaged downtown Los Angeles and I fell into a sewer, it would be a long, dark fall, and I'd be doing it alone.

I awake Sunday morning with a view of the stucco ceiling jerking side to side. I feel the motion of the bed shaking unevenly. The effect is more nauseating than frightening. I sit up and catch Jewel and Carrie holding tight to different ends of the bed. As soon as they see I'm on to them they let go of the bed and dart out of the room, giggling. The other side of the bed is empty.

I leave the bedroom wearing a plaid flannel bathrobe I found in the closet. The first person I encounter is Louis' mother who kisses me good morning.

"Hungry?"

I nod.

"Me too. I always get hungry after a good night's sleep," she says smiling. "Just ravenous. Tell Louis to get out of the shower because we're serving breakfast."

I enter the bathroom across from the guest room and make some space at the crowded sink for my toothbrush and toothpaste. The room is filled with steam and Louis is taking one of his legendary all-day showers.

"Save some for me," I call out.

"Who's there?" It's a voice I can't make out.

"It's Dale. I'm sorry. I just came in to brush my teeth and I thought you were Louis."

"It's Leo. Don't worry about it. Go ahead and brush."

I start brushing my teeth slowly, thoroughly, and glance over at the steamy, clear glass door where, his muscular frame arched forward, he's washing his hair. He pushes his head over the shower, his hair wet and almost comically matted, and asks me to pass him his razor that is sitting on the sink. I pick up his razor and see his lean body pressed up against the glass window, his cock squeezed up against it. I hand him his razor and he thanks me. As I brush my teeth while sneaking further peeks at Leo, I acknowledge to myself I'm not the lecherous type. I don't linger in the showers at the gym, my eyes never trespass territories at public urinals, but with Leo giving me permission to practice dental hygiene in the same room while he showers, I want to find a comfortable armchair, a pair of opera glasses and a tub of popcorn. After I finish flossing my teeth for the second time, I remind Leo breakfast is ready, and slip out of the bathroom.

"If it was going to happen, it would have happened this morning," Al explains to the group at the breakfast table. "For whatever reason most earthquakes happen in the morning. It's a fact."

"It's still morning," Grandma Melena calls out, annoyed, from the kitchen.

"My teacher at school says it has to do with the pull of the tide," Ricardo says, sitting next to Ellen and across from his mother. Breakfast seems to be going in shifts, and this one, I gather from the amount of dishes already in the sink, must be one of the middle shifts. Ellen passes around a plate of blueberry pancakes.

"There's also cereal," she says to me, pointing to the boxes the size of television sets.

"Did you go to an army-surplus store and ask for bomb-shelter size to get these?" I ask.

"We like to be prepared," Ellen replies.

Marie comes in from the kitchen with Grandma Melena, carrying another plate of pancakes.

"I dreamt of a baby last night," Marie tells the table. "It had thick lashes and it was just crying and crying."

"Whose baby was it, Aunt Marie?" Ricardo asks.

"I couldn't tell. It was on a big bed, just laying there by itself."

"What do you think the dream means?" I inquire.

"It means somebody is going to have one," Grandma Melena says, rolling her eyes at me. "What a stupid question."

Carmen is looking through catalogues over a cup of coffee. I think to myself she must have been up for a while now because she's already worked through the better catalogues. As I eat she is making large circles in the Harriet Carter catalogue. Louis comes in and joins us at the table.

"Where's Dad?" he asks as he pours himself a bowl of Life cereal.

"He went to get some Ben-Gay," his mother tells him. "He said the sounds of all the people sleeping in the house kept him awake."

Louis gives me a broad look, telling me he's in a better mood today. He stares over at Carmen and her Harriet Carter catalogue.

"Find anything good?"

"A few interesting items."

She shows us a few things she has circled in red felt: a reusable coffee filter that comes with a three-year warranty, a baby's bib reading, SPIT HAPPENS, and a one-inch gold cross with the entire Lord's Prayer inscribed in the center.

"For Christmas," Carmen tells the table.

Rena saunters into the dining room wearing sunglasses, a black halter top and tight short pants. She sits at the table and pulls out her drawing pad.

"Do you want any coffee mieja?" her mother asks.

"Black."

"Aren't you going to have any breakfast?" Ellen asks her.

"I took a diet pill." Rena opens up her sketchpad to a particular page and starts drawing.

"Are you still taking that art class?" Carmen inquires.

"No," Rena says without looking up. "My work was too experimental for them."

"I told you, don't do that while people eat," Marie shrieks. "People ought to be able to enjoy a meal without having to worry about posing."

"I'm just drawing the table."

"Take it to another room."

Rena lets out a deep breath, letting everyone at the table know how exasperated she is with them. After she leaves the room Grandma Melena screams at Marie, "That girl of yours, she's got the manners of a stripper. Wearing sunglasses at the table!"

"It's a different scene today, Grandma," Marie explains, "they need to feel out their individuality."

Melena waves her hand dismissively at Marie. "Individuality! They think they're so special. Girls' problems are the same from my day. It's how they wear their makeup that gets worse and worse."

When the table clears Marie takes me outside and asks me if I'll drive Rena to the store.

"Maybe you could talk to her, try to find out what's going on. This is one of those times I think she needs a man to confide in." She must notice the blank expression on my face because she adds, "You know, *guy* questions."

I agree to take her to the store but don't have the heart to tell Marie that it appears to me any questions Rena had about men had been answered some time ago.

Inside I pass the kitchen table, carrying my coffee cup to where Grandma Melena is sitting alone reading the newspaper. I nod my head politely. No need for conversation since she never talks directly to me, which is why I'm surprised to hear her say something in Spanish as I walk by.

"Pardon," I say.

She points a finger at me to join her.

"Let me read your cup."

I take the final sip of coffee and hand her the cup. Melena turns it upside down for a moment then picks up the cup and stares deeply at the grounds. She is wearing a long-flowing black-flowered dress that covers her chair completely. Her face has thick wrinkles that arch together as she concentrates on my coffee cup. She wears a flower-scented perfume that collides with the perspiration she is gathering from this long, heavy dress. It is a smell that comes across as dying flowers. Melena looks closer at the cup then puts it back down on the table.

"What is it?" I ask her.

"Who believes in those things, anyway," she says, turning away from me, letting me know that my presence is no longer welcome at the table.

I go upstairs to get my wallet and find Louis sitting on the bed in the guest room. I tell him about my conversation with Marie and my experience with Melena. When I kiss him good-bye he asks me to sit on the bed with him for a minute.

"I'm feeling guilty about last night. Not the argument, but the fact I lied to you about who I was talking to on the phone."

I put my hand on the bed's headboard.

"I *was* talking to Geoffrey. But really Dale, you don't have anything to worry about. He's just a friend. I didn't want to tell you I was talking to him because I didn't want to fight again. It has to be okay for me to have friends in this relationship and not have you flip out."

I kiss Louis. I find his honesty attractive. He surprises me by returning my kiss, pressing his tongue inside my mouth. He unbuttons my jeans and pulls them down to the floor.

"What about your family?"

"We'll just have to take that chance."

Louis maneuvers me so my face is up against the door and in a minute he is inside me. He thrusts and I try not to make too much sound up against the door. His rhythm is perfect.

"Is there anyone else?" I whisper.

"No," Louis moans, his voice full of passion.

"Do you do this to Geoffrey?"

"No."

"No?"

"Only you, Dale, I fuck only you."

Louis pinches my nipple, pulls out and comes. After I come, we fall to the floor and barricade the door in a sweaty heap.

Rena brings a backpack and her sketchpad, and I drive her to a beauty-supply store, located next door to the Happy Hocker Pawnshop. At the beauty-supply store she buys a bag full of cheap cosmetics for six dollars.

"If there's going to be a disaster, this shit might be hard to find for a while."

She then instructs me to get on the freeway and drive for a few miles. She wants to take me someplace.

Although Rena and I haven't spent much time together in the past, I think we share a mutual admiration. We've always been honest with each other, and in a way we're both radical new offshoots of a relatively conservative family.

After a few barren miles we thankfully get off the freeway and drive to an abandoned stretch of desert.

"This is it," Rena announces.

We get out of the car. There is nothing but desert as far as I can see.

"Where are we?"

"I don't know the name of it, but it's one of my favorite places."

"Are there scorpions here?"

"How should I know?" she answers, losing her patience. "Just follow me."

She grabs her backpack and leads me to a point where there is a deep crack in the earth.

"What is it?" I demand.

"VFL. Visible fault line. The San Andreas." She looks at me with a poker face. She wants me to be impressed and I am. She lays a beach towel over a section of the fault line and pulls out a bottle of Coppertone.

"I brought a towel for you, do you want it?"

I shake my head no then crouch in what we used to call in Boy Scouts "Indian Style."

Rena starts polishing her arms with the waxy yellow liquid.

"Are you and Uncle Louis getting a divorce?" she asks.

"Queers don't get divorces," I tell her.

"What do they get?"

"New boyfriends."

"Oh, I see."

Rena sits up, wipes a drop of sweat off her forehead and looks over at me. "So what's the deal with my mom?"

"What?"

"You know, why she wanted you to take me out."

"How did you know?"

"I'm psychic," she says, annoyed. "I saw her talking to you."

"Well, off the record, she says you're acting strangely. She thinks it's boy problems."

"It's her and those fucking dreams! It's a pain in the ass, everyone in the family dreaming shit all the time. Why can't they just take a Valium and get a good night's sleep!"

This is something I've noticed about Rena, she has a temper like out of a Greek tragedy. As she spurts out the remaining dab of suntan lotion and tosses the bottle into the air, I realize the wind is still and the sounds of the distant highway hushed, as if in awe of her anger.

"This pisses me off big time. I can't do anything without worrying she'll know." Rena leans in closer. "Can you be trusted if I tell you something?"

At this point I'd be willing to promise just about anything to find out what this is all about.

"There's this guy . . ." She rummages through her backpack and pulls out a photo and hands it to me. "His name is Waffle."

"Waffle? As in, 'I'm at the House of Pancakes, should I order French toast or . . . ?' "

"Don't make fun," she warns me.

"No, I'm not," I apologize, realizing this is serious business. I look at the photo glossed with a thumbprint of suntan lotion. Waffle is a stocky fellow, wearing a black L.A. Raiders cap, a baggy raincoat, a small hoop earring and a thin mustache. In the picture Rena stands next to him with arms around his waist.

"We met in school last year but we never got together 'cause he got in some trouble and he had to go live with his brother in Arizona. But during that time we've been writing to each other." Reading my mind she adds, "I had him send the letters to my friend Raquel's house. Read what he wrote on the back."

I turn the photograph over and read Waffle's inscription.

HERE IS ANOTHER MEMORY OF ME. DAMN BABY LOOK AT YOUR CURVES. BABY YOU GET IT. I'M TIRED OF DREAMING ABOUT YOU. I CAN'T WAIT TO GET YOUR GOOD LOOKS IN MY ARMS AND LET NATURE TAKE ITS COURSE. SIGNED YOUR #1 MAN (GUESS WHO).

I return the picture to her.

"He's gonna be in town next weekend for his sister's wedding.

I'm gonna tell my mom I'm staying over Raquel's and we're going to spend the night together."

"What if your mom figures it out?"

"I'm going to see him regardless," she tells me, putting her photograph back into her bag. "There's nothing you or my mom can do to stop me."

I consider breaking into a chorus of "A Boy Like That," but then I imagine being left alone in the middle of the desert standing on the VFL waiting two years for a yellow cab to happen by. I tell Rena I find the situation very romantic. I also tell her she should proceed with caution, and she can trust me to keep my mouth shut. Rena sits up and stretches. She starts brushing out her hair before we leave.

"It's like I was telling Raquel, we have this science class together and last week there was this lesson on meteors and scientists know when one is going to hit Earth. They can see them through their telescopes from far off just building speed and building speed and becoming more and more intense, but they can't do anything to stop them from landing. When they do land, it's BOOM!" Rena thrusts her hand into the ground and tosses a handful of gravel in the air. "In class I whispered to Raquel—it's like me and Waffle. Inevitable. Like these stupid earthquakes, even if you did know when it was supposed to happen, what good is it?"

Back inside the car I notice her sketchpad and ask her what she's been drawing this weekend. Rena skims through the pad and stops at a particular drawing. It is a scene of the Last Supper but the table is clearly the table in her grandparents' living room. In the sketch the ceiling is caving in and the disciples are under the table, their hands waving out in terror. Jesus crouches in the center of them, his hands folded together covering his neck.

"I call it 9.2. Do you like it?" Her voice is timid for once.

I nod in approval. "I'm just glad it doesn't mock religion or your family though," I say as we drive off.

We return to the Casa Delgado where a group of people, including Louis, are finishing up a late lunch made up of leftovers before they head home. Somehow the magic of the much-discussed earthquake has dissolved. I can feel the difference as I take a seat in the living room.

"Where's your grandmother?" I ask Louis.

"They made her go lie down. She started getting excited, going overboard, you know, talking about the end of the world, scaring some of the kids."

I pick at a chile relleno without making a commitment to eat the whole thing while Louis' father tells the table about a story in the newspaper about two twin sisters from Oakland who were driving separate cars from opposite ends of the city and were killed when they had a head-on collision together in the center of town.

After a while Louis and I pack our bags and say our good-byes. Ellen gives us a bag of leftovers to take home with us.

"I don't even want to think about what you two eat when there's no one to cook for you."

We each get a generous hug, the same exact hug, it appears to me. Marie brings us a gallon of water to take with us "just in case" and walks us to the car.

"How was your talk with Rena?"

I think about science class, meteors and people trying to predict earthquakes and I just tell her, "Fine."

We drive back to the 15 South which will lead us to the 10 West, then to the 101 North, which will bring us home, then to bed, a place filled with unsolved equations.

Louis and I compare notes about our weekend. He tells me about a talk he had with his father, and I tell him about my trip with Rena, although I don't disclose any information about Waffle. When the conversation is depleted I look out the window at the thick black night, the stars overhead, and my mind wanders to Rena and her date. Then I think about the baby in Marie's dream, and I wonder if maybe this baby might somehow be in our future. Or perhaps it's one of those dream/metaphor things, representing something like a fresh start. I try to picture this baby, but having very little experience with them I get the proportions all wrong. The baby in my mind has a tiny sliver of a body but a huge head and eyes that are round and needy.

I rest my hand on Louis' thigh and he removes it immediately.

"I need to concentrate," he says. "The roads are so dark."

"Do you want me to drive?"

"No, I'm doing okay."

"Well I think it was a pretty exciting weekend. I thought your mother looked good."

"Yeah, she did."

"Carmen's put on weight."

"She's been on Slim-Fast. She put on ten pounds."

"Your parents' house was immaculate," I tell Louis. "It's hard to believe with all those people. What, does your mother get up and vacuum in the middle of the night?"

"She's always been that way," Louis says, but his mind seems somewhere else.

"Louis, do you ever see us like your parents, with our own house somewhere, lots of people visiting?"

Louis doesn't answer me, instead he turns on the radio.

"Louis?"

"What?"

"I'm talking to you."

"What?" His voice is verging on anger.

"Did I say something wrong?"

"You've been pushing me all weekend, Dale. I just feel like I'm going to explode. I can't keep it to myself anymore." He starts sobbing first quietly then almost hysterically. I can barely make out what he is saying.

"You just have to know, Dale, that I . . . Geoffrey and I, we didn't plan . . . didn't want any of this to happen this way. Especially telling you. Especially that."

I look away from him. We're passing a stretch of desert that is isolated and dark. There is a ballet of headlights of cars driving in the opposite direction. I look back over at Louis crying jagged tears and wonder if it is only me feeling the road quivering furiously, the earth unbuckling beneath the two of us.

CARTOGRAPHY

• KARL WOELZ •

Trees sway gold and green and rust leaves in the brisk wind that whistles around the corner of the squat gray house with the carefully trimmed shrubs and forest-green shutters beside windows cleaned to sparkling. The seasonal wreath on the front door encircles a gleaming brass knocker and nameplate upon which, dead center, the deeply engraved *Hargrove* beckons like the heart of a target.

Bryan traces circles on the top of the kitchen table with the hard white end of his ballpoint pen, his mind settled on nothing in particular. The neat stack of bills on the table before him. The patch of sunlight in which a squirrel sits in the backyard, head tilted to one side as if listening to the quiet hum of the refrigerator. The occasional clunk of the ice-maker. *Mr. and Mrs. Richard VanHoffstatt request the honor of your presence* peeks out from beneath a sky-blue envelope from the orthodontist, a bill yet unpaid. The invitation, its elegant, looping script printed on heavy cardstock, has been addressed to Trevor and Philip Hargrove and Bryan Lefflin, the third name by itself on a line of its own, separate from the others.

Bryan looks at the small, cream-colored envelope which rests on top of his bills, addressed to a young woman he barely knows whose name will soon change, and examines the stamp unlike those he has just used—*Love 29¢*—in the upper right-hand corner of this delicate square of cream-colored paper. He can see the girl, leaning over the dark-brown counter of the post office, her hand, soon to be ringed, gracefully tucking a swath of hair behind her ear as she pores over a laminated sheet of brightly colored stamps while her mother pulls a crisp, twenty-dollar bill from the back of her thick, black leather checkbook.

Weddings, Bryan thinks. Smiling glassy-eyed women. Self-satisfied men, husbands or boyfriends or lovers, their arms resting on the backs of oiled wooden pews, casually marking off territory. Pastors or priests or reverends, talking always of the sanctity of Union. *Does Philip own an appropriate pair of shoes?* Bryan taps his pen on top of the checkbook. *Which card can hold a pair of shoes?*

It's unlikely that Philip will allow himself to be seen in a pair of loafers, although one never knows. Bryan remembers shopping with his mother. *Is it too tight? Do you have enough room? Are you sure you like that color? What about this one?* He tries to avoid saying things like this when out with Philip, but he hears the words coming out of his mouth all the same, as if the words have a will all their own. He's one of the few men he knows who hates to shop. His friends, and Trevor too, can spend hours rummaging through antique shops, men's furnishings or housewares departments, record stores. "Are you *sure* you're a fag?" they ask, as he hangs back, bored silent, listening to them compare and argue and haggle. "Can we see your membership card, please?"

He hasn't even thought about a gift. Shoes and a wedding present. *Might as well get both out of the way at the same time. Maybe Philip will have some ideas; he's closer to the girl's age anyway.*

Bryan hears the Mustang pull into the driveway and looks at his watch: 4:20.

"I'm home," Philip calls as he opens the front door.

"Kitchen," Bryan answers, hearing the heavy click of the lock as the door swings shut.

"You know, I leave in the morning," Philip says as he comes into the kitchen, a rush of cool air in his path, "and you're sitting at the table. I come home and you're still sitting here." He puts his books down on the island countertop and opens the refrigerator.

"I'm turning into Ann-Margret in *Carnal Knowledge*," Bryan says.

"Yeah, but she stayed in *bed*."

"I'm working up to that."

Philip takes a glass out of a cabinet next to the refrigerator and pours himself a glass of Coke. "You want some more coffee?"

"Sure."

Philip returns Bryan's coffee mug to its place beside the stack of bills, pulls out a chair, and sits down at the table. "So how was your day? You didn't go in to the shop?"

"No. I left Melisse in charge. It's pretty slow this week."

"Man of leisure."

"And how was your day?"

"The usual. A high-pressure trough of boredom with scattered showers of enlightenment in the low-lying areas."

"When was the fall of Constantinople?"

"You're a funny man. World History was last year, anyway. Do we have anything sweet to eat?"

"I think there's a couple brownies left in the bread-saver, unless your father finished them off."

Philip gets up from the table again. Bryan listens to him rummaging through the pantry, hears the lid of the Tupperware bread-saver being popped off and placed on the counter.

"Hey, he actually left me more than a crumb. For once."

"Your mother dropped some stuff off for you," Bryan says over his shoulder.

"Oh yeah? What'd she leave?"

"Brochures, mostly."

"Europe stuff?"

Philip returns to the table, half a brownie in his mouth, the rest wrapped in a napkin in his hand. Bryan slides a thick gray envelope across the surface of the table, the logo of a nearby travel agency stamped along its left edge, but Philip only glances at it and pushes it aside.

"Aren't you going to open it?" Bryan asks.

"Later," Philip says. He looks at the stack of bills next to Bryan's hand. "Is that Heather's wedding thing there?"

"Yep."

"I don't really have to go, do I?"

"Uh, *yes.*"

"Oh come on, Bryan. You're not really going to make me go to that pud-fest are you?"

"Don't look at me. It's not *my* decision." Philip grimaces. "And don't use the term 'pud-fest,' please."

"But why do *I* have to go? Heather Van is the lamest piece of crap around," Philip says, popping a chunk of brownie into his mouth. "Just because her mom and my mom were in the same prehistoric sorority, I have to have my whole Saturday night ruined? Can't you talk to Dad about it?"

"It's one Saturday night in the grand scheme of the universe. Six weeks away, at that."

"You're a big help."

"You could bring a date."

"Yeah, right."

"I'll sneak you a beer or two."

Philip rolls his eyes. "*That* is pretty lame bribery, Bryan. Can't you *please* convince Dad that I don't need to go?"

"Hey," Bryan offers, "you can get a new pair of shoes out of it."

Philip looks at Bryan, the image of his father, an eyebrow raised and his head cocked to one side. "You are *joking.*"

"Do your toes have enough room?" Bryan asks.

Philip glares at him. "I feel like I'm on my way to a sock-hop."

"But are they comfortable?"

Like a temperamental fashion model, Philip walks away from Bryan and the salesclerk, the heels of the loafers clicking sharply on the parquet floor that surrounds the carpeted island of the men's shoe department. He turns and walks back toward the two men, his head lowered either in embarrassment or examination of the denim bunched around his ankles.

"I hate them."

"They'll look better when you're wearing the right pants," Bryan offers.

"They hurt across the top of my foot."

Bryan looks at the salesclerk, a thin blond not much older than Philip, who wears too much gold. Several rings, a tie clip, a delicate bracelet. His perfectly clipped fingernails look as if they've been painted with a layer of clear polish.

"How about a wing tip?" Bryan asks the young man.

"Do you really think so?" he replies, giving Bryan a look not unlike that of a mother trying to explain why a cookie before dinner is not a good idea.

Philip sits down heavily in the chair beside Bryan and immediately removes the offending shoes. The salesclerk gently places them back in their box, folding a sheet of tissue paper over the shoes like a baby blanket, tucking it around them, carefully placing the lid back on the box.

I'm too young for this, thinks Bryan. *This is Trevor's job*. As an adolescent, he had always resented being dragged from store to store like a life-sized doll, living proof of his mother's control over the universe. He realizes now that those excursions had been as humiliating for her as they had been for him.

"So," the salesclerk says, looking at Bryan. "Wing tips?"

Philip looks at Bryan. Bryan looks at the salesclerk. The salesclerk looks at Philip's white-socked feet.

"Just bring us a pair of your plainest black shoes," Bryan says. "Lace-ups." The salesclerk disappears into the stockroom, a rush of lemony cologne in his wake.

"We are buying this pair of shoes," Bryan says, "even if, in the ten seconds they're on your feet, they turn your toes into bleeding stubs."

"Whatever you say."

"I should have made your father do this."

"He hates shopping with me."

"No small wonder."

"Here we are," the salesclerk says as he reseats himself on the ottoman in front of them. He holds up an ugly shoe free of all ornament. "Plain black lace-ups."

"We'll take them," Bryan says, offering his credit card to the young man. "Could you put the sneakers in a bag? He'll wear these out of the store."

———

"You know what I was thinking?" Philip says, looking out the passenger window of the Cherokee on the way home.

"About the Europe thing?"

"No, Bryan." Philip shakes his head. "I wasn't thinking about *that*."

"It's just that your mother—"

"I *know* what my mother thinks."

Bryan wants to look at Philip but doesn't, the boy's silence a reprimand to which the older man cannot respond.

"I was thinking," Philip says slowly, "that you and Dad could have some kind of ceremony. They do things like that now."

"I don't think so." Bryan keeps his eyes on the road ahead, squinting slightly at the headlights of cars in the other lane. "Can you see your father in front of an altar?"

Philip fiddles with his shoulder restraint. "You don't have to do it in a church or anything. You could do it in the backyard. Casual."

"It's not exactly our style, Philip."

"But people do that kind of thing after ten years, don't they?"

"Some people."

"We could invite some of your friends. Melisse. Art and Charles. The Murphs. Maybe a couple of my friends."

"Right."

"The cooler ones."

"Uh-huh . . ." Bryan says.

"Mom."

Bryan can't help but let out a laugh. "Your mother?"

"Just because her new husband's kind of a dweebus doesn't mean *she's* so bad. She's cool. She likes you, Bryan."

"*Now* she does."

"What are you always saying about water under bridges?"

"Thank you for throwing that back in my face. A natural ability you've obviously inherited from your father. Should we play 'Three Times a Lady' as I walk down the aisle?"

"*Har.* I'm sure we could find an appropriate k.d. lang song or something."

"Your father and I aren't *lesbians*, Philip."

"I don't know," he says, shrugging his shoulders and looking at the large hands resting in his lap, trying to make light of it all. "I just thought it might be something to do."

Bryan looks over at this handsome teenage boy, his responsibility by default, now staring out the window at the quiet, tree-lined neighborhood in which he has lived for the past ten years of his life. He sees the boy's face, mostly shadow, reflected by the dashboard light in the glass of the passenger window; a face he has washed and held and kissed and taught to shave. A face as familiar as his own. A face he will miss when Philip leaves for college in a few months.

"I'll talk to your father," Bryan says, knowing as he says it that he has already let the moment slip through his fingers.

"Forget it," Philip says, still looking out at the passing houses and their soft, golden squares of light from kitchen and living- and dining-room windows. "It was just an idea."

Bryan and Trevor lie in bed, each in his own pool of soft white light cast by a lamp on the nightstand by his head. Bryan flips through the pages of a large, glossy magazine. Trevor reads, glasses low on the bridge of his nose, from a thick, hardcover book.

"I wish you wouldn't open those cologne ads," Trevor says without looking up.

"I didn't," Bryan replies, glancing over at his partner. "Imagine how strong it would be if I had."

Trevor turns a page loudly.

"Will June be at the VanHoffstatt wedding?" Bryan asks.

"I suppose."

"You realize that Philip doesn't want to go."

"Because of June?"

"Because he's seventeen. Did you want to go to weddings at his age?"

"It wasn't a question of what I wanted to do at his age."

Don't pull that Father Knows Best *shit with me.* Bryan flips through several pages of his magazine at once. "I bought him a pair of shoes for the wedding today."

"I'm sure that was a pleasant experience."

"I can always use them for work."

"How much?"

"Eighty-something."

"Cheaper than sneakers."

Silence falls again. Bryan closes the magazine and puts it on the nightstand. He rolls over on his side, facing Trevor.

"You know what he said to me in the car on the way home tonight?"

"No," Trevor says, eyes trained on the page of his book. "What?"

"He thinks we should have some kind of commitment ceremony."

"You and I?" Trevor looks up from his book.

"A renewal-of-vows thing."

"What did you say?"

"I said I didn't think it was our style."

"Where did he get an idea like that?"

"God only knows. I thought it was kind of sweet. Misguided, of course, but sweet."

Trevor closes his book, removes his glasses, and places both carefully on the night table. He switches off the light, leaving the two men in the glow from Bryan's lone lamp. He takes Bryan's hand and holds it in his own.

"What's with the sudden romanticism, do you think?"

"I don't know," Bryan says. "Maybe he's tired of us living in sin. Maybe he wants to make an honest woman of me."

"That's my job, I think," Trevor replies, still holding Bryan's hand as he slides into a position from which he can face his lover. He kisses Bryan's forehead.

"He even mentioned some of his friends coming."

"God, what kind of postmodern *Brady Bunch* episode is this thing supposed to *be*?"

"Do you think Robert Reed ever sucked off Greg? That was the oldest one's name, wasn't it?"

"You're disgusting," Trevor says, pinching at Bryan's nipple.

Bryan reaches across the bed, turns off the light, and slides back into Trevor's arms. "Maybe we should do it."

"No," Trevor stage-whispers into Bryan's ear, wrapping his arms and legs around him, pulling him tight against his body.

"No? We could wear white linen and play a tasteful k.d. lang ballad or something."

Trevor slaps the flat of his palm against Bryan's rump. "For Christ's sake, honey, we're not *lesbians*."

Philip was eight years old when Bryan first met Trevor, a little boy whose new front teeth were too big for his face. He was a quiet child, watchful of the adults around him. His parents had divorced two years earlier, and he had spent those many months shuttling back and forth between the homes of his estranged parents—four days here, three days there; two tastefully quiet neighborhoods separated by a twenty-minute drive past Methodist churches, awninged dry cleaners, refurbished one-screen movie theaters with espresso bars in the lobby, and charming boutiques with heavy wooden doors in rich shades of cranberry and slate and forest green.

There are times, even now, when Bryan can still see that little boy. He stands in the open doorway of Philip's bathroom, watching him shave with a deliberateness—his brow creased in concentration—that reminds him of the boy with the tip of his tongue peeking out from between thin lips as he shades, so intent on keeping within the lines, the pages of his *Goofy and Friends* coloring book. Philip stands in front of the sink, a thick turquoise towel wrapped around his waist, unaware, Bryan thinks, of his beauty, of the handsome grace of skin and bone and muscle that defines his manhood.

"You know we're leaving in twenty-five minutes . . ." Bryan says.

"Yes," Philips answers, not taking his eyes off the mirror.

"And you still have to get dressed."

"Yes."

"And you know what your father's like about being on time."

"Bryan, you're not helping me move any faster by trying to chat right now."

"Sorry," Bryan says, turning away and walking over to the

bed, where Philip's clothes are laid out, as if waiting to come to life. "Just trying to avoid catastrophe."

Philip grunts.

The box of shoes, bought weeks ago, sits unopened at the bottom of the bed. Bryan removes the lid and unfolds the tissue paper. He takes the shoes out of the box and places them next to a stack of school books on Philip's desk. He runs the fingers of his right hand across the dull, black leather. These aren't Philip at all, Bryan thinks, struck, as he sometimes is, by the idea that there is someone—a son, no less—whose existence is so intimately connected to his own and yet, at the same time, so completely independent of it.

But I'm not his father, Bryan thinks, barely registering the feel of leather beneath his fingertips. There is no doubt that Philip loves him, that Philip accepts as part of "family" this man who cooks breakfast and demands chores be done and checks homework and sleeps in his father's bed. But where in his heart is the place for such a man? *What claim do I have to all this?* Perhaps there is no place, Bryan thinks, even though he knows better, even though he knows the flash of panic in his gut is unfounded.

"What are you doing?"

Startled by Philip's voice, Bryan's hand jumps, knocking the shoe beneath his fingers off the desk. Behind him, he can hear the gentle rustle of cotton pulled over skin, the crisp snap of elastic as Philip puts on underwear. "I was just thinking," he says to the floor as he bends over to retrieve the shoe.

"Well, try not to wreck the whole desk while you're thinking so hard," Philip says as he sits on the edge of the bed and pulls on his socks.

"No, I won't," he says, placing the fallen shoe back on the desk, his voice quiet.

"Bryan, please don't get all glassy-eyed on me, okay? I thought weddings didn't make you go all goopy?"

"They don't. It was just a momentary out-of-body experience."

"What do you think of this tie?" Philip holds up a bright red tie with suns on it; suns that look like the kind you find on old maps. Maps with faded-ink drawings of sea dragons. Archaic,

Bryan thinks, enjoying the word's hard vowel and the sharp click of the final "c." He sees bearded men hunched over tables lit by candles, coloring the boundaries of human experience.

"Mom got it for me," Philip says, laying the tie on the bed and picking up his navy blue pants. "For the wedding."

"Nice. Hurry up and get dressed. Dry your hair. I don't want to give your father an excuse for giving us any grief."

"Yes, O Perennial Peace-Maker."

"Smart-ass."

"Can I borrow some cologne?"

"Yeah, but I want it back," Bryan says as he begins to walk out of the bedroom.

"Smart-ass," Philip answers, throwing the tie at Bryan's back. "May I *have* some cologne?"

"What kind?" Bryan asks, stopping to lean against the frame of the bedroom door.

"I don't care. Whatever will make me smell irresistible." Philip grins.

Bryan tosses the tie back to his half-dressed son. "Dry your hair."

"Well," Trevor says, taking a sip from his wineglass, "the Van H's certainly know how to put on a good spread."

Bryan nods, fingering the stem of his own glass, which stands before him on the round table, presently empty, at which they're seated. "Are you surprised?"

"No. Grateful I'm never going to be father-of-the-bride, though."

Bryan lets out a barely audible "hmmm."

"Did you talk to June?" Trevor asks.

"Yes. And new husband."

"What did you think?"

"Philip's right: he is kind of a dweeb. Pleasant." Trevor nods in agreement. "But still a dweeb."

"Did she talk to you about the trip to Europe?"

"Of course she did," Bryan says, a little too quickly. "Why do you ask such a ridiculous question?"

"Why do you say it like that?"

"I thought the whole idea was that he was going with the Peterson boy."

"June is hardly going to pay for a friend to go *with* him."

"I'm not *suggesting* that—"

"What's the matter with you?"

"Forget it."

"Why are you upset about this? Philip shouldn't go abroad just because Jason Peterson got an internship with the *Tribune*?"

"You think it's a good idea to send Philip off to Europe by himself?"

"Don't you?" Trevor sounds surprised. "He's capable of handling a EurRail pass and youth hostels."

"I guess." Bryan sounds unconvinced.

The small band at the front of the long, tastefully decorated banquet room is playing a slow, romantic song. Bryan looks at the couples dancing; delicate heads resting on broad shoulders.

"I think it would be a good experience for him. Help him grow up."

"You take it for granted," Bryan mutters under his breath.

"What?"

"Nothing."

"Trevor!" a deep voice booms from several feet away. A tall, ruddy-faced man, one of Trevor's lawyer friends, approaches the table.

"Jack," Trevor says as he stands up to shake the man's hand. "What have you been up to?"

"Too damn much." He laughs, smiling widely and pumping Trevor's hand. "Hello Bryan. How are you?"

"Fine thanks, Jack," Bryan says, nodding and remaining seated.

"Mind if I steal this man away for a few minutes?" he asks.

"Be my guest," Bryan answers, hearing Jack say something about "that frigging Landers job" as he and Trevor head off in the direction of the bar at the back of the room.

Looking past the table's floral centerpiece, a carefully orchestrated explosion of green and white and peach, Bryan sees the bride on the other side of the dance floor, talking to a group of middle-aged women whose faces beam as if they'd just witnessed the Annunciation. The groom, an athletically handsome blond, stands jacketless at her side, holding a tall glass of beer from which he occasionally takes small sips. Pacing himself, Bryan thinks. He can see the groom's biceps straining against the sleeves of his crisp white shirt. *Solid.*

Philip in Europe, Bryan thinks. He sees Philip, a large duffel bag slung over one shoulder, standing in some dusty Spanish street with a half-folded train schedule in one hand, an obvious *turista*. Target. A gaggle of street urchins brandishing homemade weapons chase him down an alley á la Sebastian Venable.

Listen to me, Bryan thinks. *Molly Melodrama.* He takes a drink from his wineglass, clears his head of this vision, thinks briefly of the groom standing naked beneath a waterfall, an advertisement for some Hawaiian honeymoon paradise. *Philip is not an adventurous child.*

He can see the reflection of Philip's face in the windows of third-class train compartments as he hurtles across plains and over mountains, maybe meeting other American students along the way. Or not. Standing in front of paintings at the Louvre, by himself, without companions, thinking of the houses he calls home, eating at McDonald's because it's easier, doing what he must out of some sense of duty, some sense of keeping those who care for him happy.

"Are you having another out-of-body experience?" Philip asks, appearing out of nowhere, sitting in his father's vacated seat. "You are such a liar about weddings, Bryan. You have been funky all night."

"Have I?"

"Pensive is the word," Philip says, smiling. His eyes are bright. "Lighten up. Think of Heather naked, that should make you laugh."

"She's really quite pretty," Bryan says. "I don't know why you're always ragging on her."

"We go way back." Philip holds the rim of the table with one hand as he balances his chair on its rear legs. "To before you, even. I've known Heather since the *womb*, practically."

Bryan looks at Philip. "Do you remember when you first met me?"

Philip looks hard into the eyes of the man beside him. He brings the front legs of his chair back to the floor. "What's the matter, Bryan?"

"Nothing's the matter," Bryan says, conscious suddenly of the heaviness of his shoulders, the weight of his hands against his thighs. "Really. Nothing." Philip raises an eyebrow. "I'm just being *pensive*."

Underneath the table, Philip reaches out and touches Bryan's hand, his warm fingers wrapping themselves around those of the man beside him. "I wish you were having a good time," he says.

"I am."

"You have *never* been a good liar." Philip squeezes Bryan's hand. "I'm the one who's not supposed to be enjoying this, remember?"

Bryan smiles, masking, he hopes, the sudden dizzying sense of standing at the edge of the known world, staring out at territory yet undrawn.

"Hey, Hargrove," a voice behind them calls.

Philip looks over his shoulder, nods at his friend. "Coming." He turns back to Bryan. "Call of the wild."

"Go," Bryan says.

Philip squeezes Bryan's hand again and then the fingers are gone. "I'll be back," he says, scooting his chair away from the table and standing up to go. "You can't leave without me. I've got Dad's keys."

The house is quiet. Bryan listens to the steady sound of Trevor's breathing as his eyes adjust to the darkness. He had been dreaming, about what he cannot remember, when his eyes suddenly opened, as they sometimes do when a noise pierces deep sleep. He lies still, listening.

After a few minutes, he slides carefully out of the bed so as not to wake Trevor. The bedroom is blue-gray in the hazy streetlight that shines through the front window. He picks up a rumpled denim shirt from across the back of the valet and puts it on over his T-shirt and underwear. He walks down the hall to the kitchen, stopping at Philip's closed bedroom door. He puts his ear against the wood. He can hear nothing.

Slowly, like a thief caressing the lock of a huge steel safe, he turns the knob and walks silently into Philip's room. Here, too, the light is blue-gray, making everything look cold and unreal. He tiptoes to the bed and the long lump concealed beneath its covers. Philip faces the wall, the back of his head all that is visible in the room's weak light. Bryan leans over the blanket-covered form. Philip's breath is lighter than his father's, barely audible. Bryan stands there for some time, listening, until he realizes that his bare legs are growing cold, that his lower back is getting tight.

Bryan sits on the living-room couch, a blanket wrapped around his lower body. He sits in darkness, sipping from a glass of red wine, a trick he has learned to help beat his frequent bouts with sleeplessness.

And will you join with me, the reverend had said, his arms opened wide to include the entire congregation, *in support of the holy bond that Heather and Michael are making here before us today?* And the voices had called out, as one, *We do*. Bryan had felt the muscles of his throat move; had heard, as if from far away, the sound of his own voice saying the words. But what he saw, Heather and Michael and the reverend suddenly vanished, were his parents, who had no doubt envisioned a day in which *their* only son would stand before banks of flowers and rows of friends in their Sunday finery, all looking upon this spectacle as one. He saw his parents, now grown old, sitting in the morning sun on their patio, each drinking from a cup of coffee, the paper spread out between them, silently reading, the sound of waves pushing softly against the nearby beach a constant, quiet reminder of how little we can call our own.

They send Philip checks at Christmas and on his birthday, the cards written in his mother's elegant hand, signed with their Christian names: *Love, Marjorie and Clark.*

———

He hears his name. He feels a hand, insistent, on his shoulder. Again: "Bryan?"

He opens his eyes, sees Philip's face above him. "What?" His voice is hoarse with sleep.

"I made coffee."

"Wh' time is it?" Bryan says, pulling himself into a sitting position on the couch.

"Eight-thirty." Philip sits down beside him on the couch and holds out a coffee mug. "Want this?"

"Sure," Bryan answers, taking the coffee. "What are you doing up so early?"

"I don't know. Woke up and figured I might as well get out of bed."

"Have the Pod People taken over?" Bryan takes a careful sip from his mug. "You're not the real Philip Hargrove," he says in mock terror. "What have you done with him?"

Philip smiles. "Just drink your coffee, Mr. sleeping-on-the-couch-for-some-mysterious-reason . . . Dad kick you out of bed?"

"No. I couldn't sleep. Came out here—"

"Got sauced up." Philip nods at the wineglass sitting on the table next to the couch.

"Had *half* a glass of wine to relax me, thank you very much, and fell asleep."

"A likely story."

Bryan swats at him with one hand. "Why get up so early if you're only going to harass me, you ungrateful child?"

"You're drinking coffee made with my own two hands and *I'm* the ungrateful one?"

Bryan sets his mug on the table beside the half-filled wineglass. "Come here," he says, holding out one arm, waiting for Philip to slide in next to him. Philip rolls his eyes, sliding slowly under Bryan's arm, and leans back against the older man's chest.

"Aren't I a bit old for bedtime stories?"

"You're never too old to be hugged. Haven't you heard my mother say that a hundred times?"

"This is the last time I make you coffee if this is what I have to endure as a result of it."

"What am I going to do when you're gone?" Bryan asks, wrapping his arms around Philip's body.

"Make your own coffee, mow your own grass, run your own errands."

Bryan squeezes his arms together. Philip laughs, lets out a "hey!"

"You're so mistreated," Bryan says.

"There's a whole semester yet."

"What am I going to do, huh?"

"Miss me."

"That's right," Bryan says, lightly kissing the top of Philip's head. He waits a beat. "For about twenty minutes."

"You are such a *fart*," Philip says, wriggling out from under Bryan's arms. He scoots back to the other end of the couch, pointing his index finger: "*Fart*."

Bryan laughs, picks up his coffee mug and drinks. "So where are you going to go on this European adventure your mother wants to send you on?"

"Who says I'm going?"

"Don't you want to?"

"Maybe I could just take the money instead."

"Whatever you want to do." Bryan takes another sip of coffee. "I'm sure your mother would understand."

"What would you do?"

Bryan looks at Philip over the top of his coffee mug. "What would *I* do?" he says.

"Uh, that *was* the question, I think."

Bryan looks at his son, at the bright eyes and delicate planes of his face. He looks into the eyes he knows so well, the eyes now searching his own for an answer. There is so much, he thinks, so much unknown until felt.

"I'd go," he says.

"You would?"

"Yes," he says, the map of his heart unfolding. "Start in Florence." He can see the world stretched out before him, its faded colors marking off the boundaries of what we know as ours. "Work your way north from there. Vienna. Prague. Berlin. Do you want to do Scandinavia?"

"I don't know. Should I?"

"Why not? There's so much," Bryan says, the past's territories taking shape with each word, rivers and plains and forests pulsing into color all around him. "So much, Philip. Like nothing you've ever seen."

ANDREW AND I

• NORMAN WONG •

1. Playing House

Andrew and his boyfriend, Reed, finally broke up. Reed moved in with his new boyfriend, Jason, who also happened to have been a former fuck-buddy of Andrew's. A year ago, one evening, Andrew had brought Jason home from a bar for a ménage à trois with Reed.

Meanwhile, Andrew and I have also been seeing each other for the past several months. Andrew and Reed had an open relationship. Although I wanted to say to Andrew, "That's what you get when everyone's seeing someone else," I didn't; because Andrew was in mourning, and besides, for the first time, I was allowed into his apartment. In the living room, dark maple bookcases lined a wall, giving the apartment an intellectual feel. The bedroom was simply and elegantly furnished with a matching antique mahogany bureau, nightstand and bed frame, all passed down from Andrew's grandparents. Perfect white sheets. Lace curtains. Fourteen-foot ceilings and original prewar molding and wood floors. The model Americana apartment.

Andrew didn't like sleeping alone, so he told me that I could sleep over. Gradually I moved in my belongings, backpack by backpack, abandoning my dorm room.

It was 1982, I was a college freshman, and this was the first time I was living with somebody other than my own family. I liked waking up in his arms, sharing with him that first cup of coffee in the morning, bearing witness to his bathroom habits, making love night and day.

While living with Andrew, I discovered myself having inherited some of my own mother's odd, meticulous household habits. Like her, I would survey the kitchen, making sure that the stove was off, the refrigerator door shut, the faucets secured, the window looking out onto the fire escape closed tight. Upon leaving the apartment, after locking the front door, I always gave it a hard push, testing the lock's endurance.

Soon it became obvious that Reed had been the clean one. With him gone, dirty dishes accumulated in the kitchen sink for me to wash. Andrew discarded his clothes on the bedroom floor, underwear and damp towels on the bathroom floor.

"Why are you always washing my clothes?" Andrew complained.

"Because when they're on the floor, I assume they're dirty."

"Well, they're not. I just left them there. And did you put this shirt in the dryer?" Andrew held up a shrunken polo shirt. "Are you washing the whites and darks separately?"

"No."

"Why not?"

"Because my mother just washed everything together," I explained.

"Well, that's fine if you grew up wearing polyester."

Once, after starting a front-loading washer of whites, I noticed, through the glass door, a foreign red sock, left over from the previous wash. The washer's door was locked shut. I nervously sat, waiting for the cycle to end; at which point, I immediately took out the red sock, and rewashed the load, this second time with extra bleach.

Sometimes the toilet sat unflushed, yellowing. I even began spotting dried urine stains on the seat. And then one day, I discovered that the bathmat was soaked with piss. Had Andrew been peeing on the floor? And then it dawned on me. Long ago back in Hawaii, I'd discovered that Dad sometimes, while sitting on the toilet, absentmindedly urinated between the seat and rim: pee sliding down the side of the porcelain bowl onto the mat on the floor. As a kid, I would clean up after Dad, washing out the mat in the tub. Once Mom asked me why it was wet, hanging on the side of the tub to dry. Protecting Dad, I told her that I'd just taken a shower.

I also worried that the TV stayed on for too long. Back at my family's home in Honolulu, the TV was always on. As a child in the middle of the night, even though I couldn't hear it, I would often climb down my bunk and go to the living room to check if it was left on after a marathon night of viewing.

When Andrew went to the bathroom (to pee on the mat) I turned off the TV.

"Why do you always turn off the TV as soon as I walk out the room?"

"I thought you were finished watching," I said, innocently.

Andrew turned it back on. Then I grew fearful that turning it off and on in such quick succession would further sabotage its mechanism. An explosion was imminent.

Once coming home from class, I discovered that Andrew had left the iron on. That evening I reprimanded him, "You have to be more careful. You're going to start a fire."

"It's my apartment. I can do what I want," Andrew answered back.

After a month of living together, Andrew still maintained that we were only friends. It was too soon for him to be in another relationship. Going from one to another boyfriend, without an interim of reflection.

Although sometimes it did only feel like I was "playing house," it was still the closest thing to a happy home life I'd yet experienced.

2. Chinese Cooking

It was wintertime, and I began to feel homesick for Hawaii. I was always slipping on the slick walkways, foolishly grabbing onto whoever I was with or near, usually pulling them down with me. I especially hated when slush got into my boots, soaking my socks. If it got too messy out there, I would sometimes skip class.

One blizzard morning, while parked cars sat buried in snow

on the street, I asked Andrew to cut my hair. In preparation I washed my hair in the kitchen sink, as Andrew searched for the clippers. "My father used to cut my hair," I shouted from beneath the running water.

"Mine, too," Andrew said, returning with the clippers and its attachments. "But he always did a bad job."

"Will you do a bad job?"

"No. I'm really good at this."

I asked Andrew what he wanted for his birthday. His birthday was the following week.

"Nothing," he answered. "I don't like birthdays."

I sat on the kitchen stool. We didn't bother with a bib, since we were both only wearing our briefs in the always toasty apartment. Coffee burned in its maker. The buzzing clippers grazed my head.

"I love Chinese hair," Andrew said. "Thick, full and dark. Wei has beautiful hair."

Wei was Andrew's first lover. I listened attentively.

"It's because of Wei that I came to love everything Chinese. We were childhood friends, sweethearts. Each other's best friend. We were both nerdy and unpopular. The other kids teased us constantly—Ancient Chinese fortune, 'If there's an Andy, there's a Wei.' Ha, Ha."

"Where's he now?"

"He's in medical school in San Francisco with his law-student wife. They're the perfect beautiful Asian couple. Wei taught me how to cook Chinese."

"But you use a cookbook." I pointed to the kitchen counter.

"Wei gave me that cookbook. There's nothing wrong with acquiring new recipes. There's more to Chinese food than the bland Cantonese food you grew up eating. Wei is Mandarin. Spicy and tangy."

I wondered if I would be Andrew's second Chinese lover. Had Reed only been a white distraction? "What do you want for your birthday, if you had to have something? At least tell me what kind of cake you like."

"A pumpkin pie."

"Why a pumpkin pie?"

"Because that's what my mother served me after my father hit me." Andrew told me the story about his father hitting him so hard once that blood came to his mouth. His father then hit him again for staining the rug. Meanwhile, his mother was baking a pumpkin pie in the kitchen. Sweet and cinnamony. His father ordered him to clean up the blood. In the kitchen, his mother gave him a damp sponge. Afterward, she served him a slice of pie. The warm pumpkin soothed the cut in his mouth.

My hair tumbled off my body onto the linoleum. "My father used to hit me, too," I said. "But he never drew blood. He usually just ignored me. Actually, I think my mother hit me more."

"That explains why you're gay."

"But once when I was twelve or so, I grabbed the ruler out of her hand."

"And then you hit her?"

"No. She slapped me once with her hand, hard, backed away, and then screamed to Dad, 'Look at your son grabbing the ruler out of my hand. Soon he'll be beating his own parents. American school has taught him to rebel.' After that, she never hit me again. That's when I started to grow tall, taller than both of them."

"Rebellious ABC—American-Born Chinese—son living on the mainland, defying the wishes of his traditional Chinese parents. When I have kids, I'll never hit them," Andrew said.

Where are you going to get them from? Are you going to have them alone? With a woman? With me?

After the haircut, I took a shower, while Andrew went back to bed. (After showering, I always swatted the shower curtain, knocking off the excess water, as Mom would've.)

I rejoined Andrew in bed. As he slept, I lay awake hungry, wondering how our parents hitting had affected us and made us who we were. There must've been a connection between Andrew's abuse by his father and Andrew's obsession with Asian men. Because Asian men were smaller, daintier than white men, we could not hurt Andrew. And the reason I liked white men was because I wished that my neglectful father had been more attentive, dominated me.

After a while, I got up and went to the kitchen. In the refrigerator I found four slightly dried hotdogs, limp carrots and celery sticks, an assortment of Oriental sauces, and milk.

I returned to the bedroom to see if Andrew was awake. Maybe we could brave the cold and go out and get something to eat.

"Why are you waking me?" Andrew asked, with his eyes closed.

"Are you crying?"

"I was dreaming that my boyfriend left me. But then while I was dreaming, I realized, it'd really happened. Reed's gone. Wei's gone."

"I'm here for you. Are you hungry?"

Andrew sat up in bed. "We're not lovers. We're just friends. I thought I've made this clear to you. I can't be in another relationship right now. I'm not ready."

I stood silent. I told myself to pack my bags and leave, immediately. But it was too cold outside. I was too hungry to leave. Where would I go? Back to tropical Hawaii to work with Mom at the family restaurant? There would be plenty to eat there. "Are you hungry?" I asked Andrew again. "Do you want to go out and get something to eat? There's nothing to eat in the house."

"There has to be something to eat. I just went shopping a couple of days ago."

"There are four hotdogs, some carrots, celery sticks—"

"Sichuan hotdogs! Wei and I used to make that all the time when we were broke as undergraduates."

In the kitchen, both naked now, I cooked the rice while Andrew chopped up the hotdogs, celery and carrots.

"Is there any cooking oil?" Andrew asked.

"I saw some butter in the refrigerator," I said.

"You can't use butter for Chinese cooking. It won't heat up properly. What kind of Chinese cook are you?"

Andrew found a bottle of Wesson oil in the cabinet. He measured out spices and sauces with a tablespoon, referring to the stained pages of the cookbook. Dad would cook by sight, never having to measure anything out.

While cooking, Andrew attempted to correct my mispronunciation of words containing double *o*'s and *l*'s. "Say *school*."

"*Sch—ul*," I said.

"No. Long double *o*'s. Sch—oo—l."

"School."

"Say *noodles*."

"*Nu—dos.*"

"Noo—dles."

"Noodles."

"Good."

Soon the hotdog, celery and carrot pieces, a wokful of oranges, reds and greens, sizzled in a spicy, oily garlic sauce. The rice was also ready.

"Your hair," Andrew said, reaching over to stroke me, "is sticking in a thousand directions. Typical Chinese hair."

I closed my eyes and wrapped myself around Andrew. I liked cooking with Andrew. We were a family. I kissed him on his neck, his chest, and then bit his nipple. Andrew's skin was soft, warm, moist. Tiptoeing, I rubbed my erection against the side of his ass. He turned around to face the counter, all the while reaching for the Wesson oil.

I observed the food getting cold. Dad would've insisted that we eat immediately while the spices were still alive. Dad would yell at Mom to sit down. She could never sit still for more than a couple bites before having to get up to do something else—wash out a pot, get dressed for work, apply her makeup. I myself would sit sleepy at the family's kitchen table, prematurely awakened from my after-school nap. We ate early to accommodate Mom's work schedule. With my fork, I would push around the bland white rice, not hungry. Dad became upset when no one ate his cooking.

After sex, Andrew reheated the Sichuan hotdogs, and I scooped out the rice. We ate at the kitchen table.

"I'm starved," I said, picking up the plate of food and, with my chopsticks, shoveling some in my mouth.

"Why are you eating like that?"

"I always eat Chinese food like this at home."

"You Chinese are so uncouth. I've lost my appetite." He put down his chopsticks and pushed forward his plate. He got up and walked out the room.

I picked out the hotdog pieces from Andrew's plate.

3. The Other Man

Andrew's apartment was located in the unfashionable part of Hyde Park, on the edge of the university community.

Suspicious characters hung out on the front stoop. I couldn't figure out exactly who our neighbors were; people came and went. When I was home alone I would doublelock the door. This was the south side of Chicago.

From an apartment above, sometimes I heard shouting and a child crying. Once I stuck my head out the kitchen window and deduced that the noise was coming from the window directly above me. The yelling and crying sounded urgent, and then I thought I heard hitting, beating. What did the child do wrong? Rip his father's newspaper? Break his mother's lipstick? Whack, whack.

I wondered if I should call the police. But what would they do? Come over next week? Should I, instead, go upstairs and knock on their door and tell them to stop? "I'm going to report you," I could threaten. But wouldn't that only anger the parent more? Did he have a gun? Then suddenly the child stopped crying.

Complete silence.

I felt relieved when the shouting and whimpering resumed. I decided that I had to somehow distract the parent, bring him out of his violent state for a moment, so that he could have a chance to see the harm he was inflicting on the child.

In the refrigerator I found half a carton of eggs and carried them over to the window. Sitting on the sill, one hand holding onto the window, in the other hand an egg, I leaned out. I lobbed the egg upward. It went straight up and down, falling to its death three stories below. Five eggs to go. Aim better. I could see my breath and noticed dirt lining the windowsill. I would wipe it clean afterward. I took another egg and tossed it up. This one splattered on the intended window.

Enthralled by my success, I forgot to pull back in before the yolk and white dribbled on my head like birdshit. The crying and yelling continued. I reached for another egg, and with the same technique and precision, hit the window again. This time,

I pulled back in immediately. Suddenly the yelling stopped. The window above screeched open. Mission accomplished? The broken eggs were a warning from the kitchen god.

I returned the remaining eggs to the refrigerator.

But still it didn't feel all right. I still felt that same lonely feeling I would feel after being hit by Dad. Back then, I would lie in my bunk, plotting my escape. Presently I'd successfully run away from home; I would never live in Hawaii again. But why had these sad feelings followed me to the mainland?

One night, sleeping beside Andrew, I dreamed that Mom and I were speeding up a shopping mall's parking complex, ramp after ramp, going higher. Mom was driving. Suddenly, in front of us, the ramp ended, and we drove into the sky. I turned to Mom and told her that I'd had a good life. I woke up, just as I felt we were beginning to fall.

The following evening I arrived home to an empty apartment. There was no note; no message on the answering machine. Andrew and I had plans to make dinner together. A couple hours passed. I snacked on leftovers. Afterward I curled up on the sofa with a mug of herbal tea doctored with a shot of whiskey, and read *Persuasion*.

The front door opening woke me. Andrew stood there with another man. The man was white, handsome, a little shorter than Andrew, and had a bushy moustache and sideburns.

When I stood up from the sofa, the paperback novel thumped to the wood floor.

"Damon, Mike."

"Mike, Damon."

"Hi," Mike said and then asked Andrew, "Where's the bathroom?"

"Over there." Andrew pointed.

Andrew looked blankly at me for a moment longer before following Mike down the hall. I heard them both going into the bedroom and the door shutting behind them. I sat down on the sofa and lit a cigarette. Should I knock on the bedroom door and ask to speak with Andrew—alone? But what could I say? *We were not boyfriends.* And what about Mike? Would he think of me as a jealous drama queen?

I tiptoed down the hall to the bedroom and pressed my ear lightly against the door, the cigarette burning in my hand. I could hear the old lumpy bed making noises, accompanied by whispers and moans. Did Andrew and I sound like that? It was happening on the other side without me. Should I barge on in? Was Andrew expecting me to join them? I started to shake.

Back in the living room, I put out the cigarette, packed my backpack, and carried my mug to the kitchen. There, the mug slipped from my hand, breaking on the linoleum. Next I took a glass from the dish rack and dropped it. And then another and another. I sat down at the kitchen table and stared at the shards of glass twinkling. It was time to go.

When I got up from the table, the chair tipped over. Clunk. I pushed over another. I couldn't reach the third chair, pinned behind the table against the wall. I wondered if Andrew or Mike would step on the glass with their naked feet. In the pantry, I found the broom and swept the glass into a pile, into a corner. I leaned the broom up against it, and even decided to leave the kitchen light on, so they could see the sharp glass. I left the two chairs lying on the floor. In the living room, I put on my coat, and as I opened the front door, turned back to see light aching from the crack under the bedroom door. I braced myself for the cold.

Over the phone, the following morning, Andrew asked, "Did you have to break the glasses? I didn't have that many after Reed left."

"Was that how you chased Reed away?"

"No. I didn't do it to hurt you."

"Why did you do it?"

"I don't know why. I'm losing my mind. Come back so we can at least talk. I need you here."

"Where's your friend?"

"He's gone."

"Will you see him again?"

"I don't know. I've told you we're not lovers. I'm not ready for another boyfriend right now."

"I'll come back tonight to get my stuff."

"I didn't do it to hurt you."

That evening, when I arrived at Andrew's, I found him lying curled up on the bathroom floor.

"What's the matter? Are you all right?"

He was crying. "I can't take it anymore," he mumbled.

"Did you take something?" I didn't see any blood. "Did you take any pills?"

"No."

"Get up."

"I can't take it anymore."

I sat on the floor beside Andrew. I reached for the toilet paper, unspooled several sheets, and wiped Andrew's face. "It's all right. I'm here."

I managed to get him up off the floor, into the bedroom, and on the bed. Andrew held me tightly. I kissed him on the lips. Inhaling his perspiration odor, I climbed on top of him.

Andrew continued to cry. After a while, my erection subsided. I got out of bed, went over to the closet, got out my duffel bag, and began filling it, pulling shirts off hangers.

"What are you doing?" he asked, sitting up. From the ashtray on the nightstand, he picked out a relightable cigarette butt. "I don't want you to go. You can't leave me, too." He relit the cigarette.

"You should have thought about that before picking up someone last night." I walked over to the chest of drawers and picked out my T-shirts and pairs of underwear.

"I won't let you go," Andrew said. He reached over and grabbed my arm.

I pulled away. I wanted to hit him. Instead I began to cry. "I'm going. Are you going to be all right?"

"No."

"I'm sorry." I left the bedroom.

Andrew leapt off the bed, dropping his cigarette, and grabbed me by the shoulder. I pulled away and continued toward the front door. Andrew came up and pushed me against the wall.

"I never said I was your lover. Did I ever lie to you? You can't go."

"Let me go," I muttered. I dropped the bag to the floor. Andrew's face, wet and red, was up against mine. I could smell his stale cigarette breath.

"I never said I was your lover." His saliva hit my face.

"Let me go." I thought about grabbing away Mom's ruler. "Please, let go."

4. Chopsticks

In the morning Andrew tossed violently under the sheets. I was careful not to wake him. He has enough trouble sleeping as is. I wrapped myself tighter in my robe, feeling cold above the blanket. I wondered if in his dreams he knew that I was sleeping beside him. Not Reed. Not Wei. He pushed the blanket aside to reveal his naked chest. Long ago, in the afternoons, when he came home from work, Dad would lie shirtless in the chaise longue out back on the lanai. His skin never tanned, but rather barbecued pink-red. I reached over and dared to touch Andrew's chest, the symmetrical hairs surrounding each flat nipple. Under the sheet his penis was hard. I'd never seen Dad's penis. Just a dark patch in the crack of his underwear. Andrew began to play with his erection. I played with myself, looking on. He got up on his knees, panting and moaning, his eyes still closed, his hand grasping his dick. I remained noiseless beside him. I wanted to come at the same time as he did.

"You're too Chinese," Mom says to Dad.
Since Dad didn't get Mom anything for Christmas, Mom asks Dad for some money.
Dad gives Mom twenty dollars. She looks at him, shocked, and says, jeu choy um haum, that's not even enough to salt the vegetables.
Dad shrugs and says that's all he can spare. He says he's thinking about the future.
I pretend to play with my new plastic football. The price sticker was still on the box. $5.98. The leather football that I wanted was too expensive. Lily plays with her new Barbie. I want to play Barbie with

her but don't want to get Mom and Dad any more upset than they already are.

The day after Christmas, Mom, Lily and I go to Ala Moana Shopping Center. I spend too much time looking at the half-priced Christmas cards and get myself lost from them. I go to the women's department and look under the racks of dresses. Sometimes Lily hid under there. The smell of new clothes makes me sneeze.

I can't find them and start to cry. Then in the distance I see Mom standing in front of a mirror, holding a dress to her body. Lily stands nearby, holding another dress. I run to them.

"Mom," Lily says, "Damon's crying. What a sissy."

In between trading dresses with Lily, Mom hands me a tissue from her purse. "Why are you crying? I'm the one who can't afford either one of these. Dil (fuck)."

Downstairs in the candy department, while Mom is in the bathroom, an old Japanese saleslady comes up to Lily and me. The saleslady points at Lily, her other hand holding an open pack of candy. "I saw you poke this open," she says.

"I did not," Lily answers.

"I saw you," the lady repeats.

I remember that I'm still mad at Lily and say, "I saw you, too."

Mom returns, and the lady tells Mom about Lily opening the pack of candy. "And her brother saw her do it," she adds to the end of her story.

Mom looks at Lily and me. I don't say anything. Lily and I are frightened.

The lady makes Mom pay for the candy.

Outside the store, we sit on a bench under a palm tree, decorated with red garlands and silver balls. Lily says again, "I didn't do it."

"So why did you say that she did it?" Mom asks me.

I don't know what to say.

Mom hands Lily the candy.

Lily passes out the hard candy. They are in the shapes of tropical fruits, pineapples, mangos, bananas, oranges and guavas. They taste like the fruits they're supposed to be. Mom spits hers out, clinking it on the concrete walkway. "It tastes gross."

"What are we having for lunch?" I ask.

"Nothing," Mom answers. "This is your lunch."

I bite down on my hard candy, chew it soft, take another and swallow it whole.

For Andrew's birthday dinner, I bought a frozen pumpkin pie for dessert. I also decided to make stir-fry chicken with broccoli and rice. *I* learned how to cook by watching Dad. I placed the clean and dried chicken slices in a bowl, and added a splattering of soy sauce, a dash of sesame-seed oil, a larger drop of Wesson oil, sprinklings of salt, pepper and sugar, healthy pinches of minced ginger and garlic, and some chopped scallions. With my hand, I mushed everything together, then set it in the refrigerator. I started the rice in its cooker.

I steamed the broccoli, promptly taking the lid off the pot after three minutes.

The rice cooker clicked off. In a mini wok I heated some cooking oil and fried the raw brown-stained chicken slices, adding some sliced onion and crushed garlic. When the chicken appeared juicy-cooked, I added the drained broccoli spears, a squirt of soy sauce, a drop of sesame-seed oil, a sprinkling of pepper, salt and sugar, and a dollop of oyster sauce.

Before serving dinner, I put the frozen pie in the oven.

During dinner, Andrew attempted to correct my handling of chopsticks. Instead of holding them the proper way, I held them crisscross, in the shape of a pair of scissors.

"Hold them in the shape of a V," Andrew ordered, "not an X. Where did you learn to hold them like that?" He took hold of my hand and repositioned my fingers on the wooden sticks. But as soon as he let go, my hand reverted to its original position. The chopsticks again crossed each other as I reached for a piece of chicken.

"I guess if you learned it wrong in the first place," Andrew said, "there's no use trying to teach you to do it right. Why did your father let you do it that way?"

"I don't see what's wrong," I answered, annoyed. "I can still eat with them." I brought the bowl of rice to my mouth and shoveled in the warm white flakes.

"Like a barbarian."

5. Mice

When mice began to appear in the apartment, I promptly went out and bought poisonous green pellets and sticky traps. "How can there be mice when I keep the apartment so clean?" After a couple of days, the living room began to smell rotten. But when I returned to the spots where I'd set the traps, I didn't find any mice. The apartment continued to smell.

One day, while picking up a stack of Andrew's dissertation papers from the floor, I discovered a decaying, worm-eaten dead mouse. I screamed. It'd eaten the poison and then hid under the papers to die. With a piece of newspaper, I picked it up and tossed it out the window into the alleyway below, the apartment building's Dumpster.

One evening, stoned, sorting through dirty laundry (I liked to clean when I was stoned), I found some colorful scraps of fabric in the bedroom closet. I asked Andrew about them. He was watching TV; he liked watching TV stoned.

"Reed was going to make something with them. Pillows, curtains. They're from Paris," Andrew answered, relighting the joint. "He bought them when we were there last summer."

He passed the joint to me, and I took a hit before returning to the bedroom. I shut the door.

"What are you doing?" Andrew asked.

"You'll see."

From the bottom drawer, I found the fishnet stockings and the stash of makeup which Andrew'd saved from the previous Halloween. I undressed, pulled on the stockings, wrapped the loose fabrics around myself, a skirt, a blouse, a shawl. I applied red lipstick and blue eyeshadow. I found a towel and wrapped it around my head, reminding me of Mom after she'd washed her hair in the kitchen sink. (She didn't like washing her hair in the shower, because soap would get in her eyes.)

From behind the bedroom door, I called to Andrew, "Turn off the TV and the lights."

"What are you doing?"

"Just do as I say."

"They're off."

"Close your eyes."

"They're closed."

Coming into the living room, I walked over to the stereo and turned on the radio to a pop station. A new singer, Madonna, was singing, "I'm burning up, 'cause I'm on fire . . ."

I sang along, as I danced across the room in a combination of hula and disco moves.

"Can I open my eyes now?"

"Yes," I sang.

Andrew began to laugh. "You make an ugly woman." He laughed heartily. "You're no Suzy Wong." I moved across the room, stripteasing, unraveling the silky fabrics, dropping them on Andrew, bringing my foot up on Andrew's knee, seductively pulling down the stocking, one at a time.

Naked I fell upon Andrew. I got down on my knees, and pulled off his jeans. I sucked off Andrew, allowing his dick to come to the back of my throat, pulling away only when I thought I would begin to vomit. I told myself to relax and breathe through my nose, as I tried again.

With Andrew lying on the living-room floor, I mounted him. Closing my eyes, breathing deeply, I again told myself to relax. Andrew moaned. I felt in control of his pleasure. I was making him feel good.

After sex, I lit a cigarette, went to the bathroom and sat on the toilet. Scurrying noises sounded from the kitchen.

"Andrew," I called.

"What?"

"I think there's a mouse stuck in one of those sticky traps."

"Good."

"Please get rid of it."

"Leave it alone."

The mouse began to cry.

"Is it going to make that noise all night?" I asked. I dropped the lit cigarette between my legs into the toilet water, wiped myself, and flushed.

Walking to the bedroom, I said, "Andrew, can you please get rid of it? I got rid of the last one."

"Leave it alone," Andrew said again.

"What if it escapes?"

"It won't."

"Please."

"All right, all right," Andrew said, getting out of bed.

I followed him to the kitchen. Looking under the sink we found the mouse stuck in a glue trap.

"It looks so cute," I said.

Andrew picked up the trap and moved to the window.

"You can't throw it out like that," I said.

"Why not?"

"Because it'll starve to death."

"So?"

"Kill it first. Put it out of its misery."

"With what? I want to go to sleep," Andrew said, placing the trap down in the center of the kitchen floor. The fluorescent light above showing off the mouse's fine fingers.

"Just a second." I found a black and red can of roach spray under the sink. I sprayed the mouse wet.

"What are you doing?" Andrew asked.

"Killing it."

The mouse did not die. Instead it began to pull itself off the trap, the wet spray loosening the glue's hold.

"Look what you did," Andrew said, annoyed. "Get the broom."

Quickly, I slammed the broom down on the mouse and trap. When I raised it, the trap was stuck to the broom; the mouse came through the straw bristles. If it could only pull itself through, it would be free.

I screamed and dropped the broom on the floor. "It's going to escape," I shouted.

Suddenly Andrew went at it with a hammer. He pounded the broom. The mouse's skull cracked open. Blood seeped through the straw.

"Now we have to throw the broom away, too," Andrew said, angry, picking it up and sticking it out the window.

Afterward, he went to the living room to hunt for the roach, while I returned to the bathroom, where I washed my hands and sat back down on the toilet. I felt something else had to come out. I tried to remember what I'd had for dinner. Then I remembered that Andrew'd just fucked me.

"You want any more of this?" he called, referring to the roach. "I'm going to finish it."

"Go ahead," I shouted.

I wiped myself abrasively. I glanced down. The tissue was streaked brown and red.

THE MOST OBVIOUS PLACE

• RICHARD C. ZIMLER •

Just after we arrived at St. Gregory's, my mother said that I should see my older brother in his coffin so that I'd know for sure that he was dead. She sat me down in a pew and explained that for years after her own brother's death her mind had played tricks on her. "The times I saw Alan on the street, at the beach, in Central Park, on the subway . . . It was terrible. Then, when I'd rush up to him, I'd see it was only a man who looked like him." In disgust, she added, "Sometimes not even that. All that misery, all those ghosts, because I never saw my brother dead."

"But I don't want to see Harold dead," I said. "People are different. You needed to, I don't."

"You have to!" she said threateningly. "I'm telling you, you have to."

"No! It's enough I'm here for the funeral."

She scoffed. "The funeral's nothing. It's just the beginning!"

"I'm not looking at him. End of discussion!"

But the casket was open and his nose was pointing up like a bird's beak. I said to myself that whatever was in there wasn't going to look like him. But it did. Except for his texture; his face looked like wax dusted with fine powder.

The funeral was held on April 17, 1985. Since that date, I've never mistaken anyone on the street for Harold. No ghosts have appeared either.

Instead of being content about it, as my mom thought I'd be, I've always been disappointed.

She was right, however, about the funeral being just the beginning. Whenever I'd visit her, I'd sit for hours in the bedroom that I'd shared with my brother as a kid. Sometimes, I'd lie back and stare at the ceiling and wonder what had gone wrong. How does someone only thirty years old get a fatal disease and end up in a cemetery in upstate New York?

On these trips home, I'd spend most of my time visiting my brother's old hangouts. I'd always look around, half expecting to see him.

"Believe me, it's for the best that you don't," my mom assured me once, about two years after the funeral. "So stop torturing yourself waiting."

"Sometimes I can't remember what he looked like," I replied. When she looked at me skeptically, I said, "I can't. Not really. He's disappeared."

"You have photographs," she replied.

I let the silence accumulate between us because we both knew that I was talking about an internal image that had somehow dissipated.

She took my hands. "It's scary coming face to face with a dead person," she said.

"I accept that, but just a glimpse would be nice."

Another seven years passed. Just this past week, I finished my second novel. It's not really about Harold, but if you read between the lines . . .

Last night, I got up to go to the bathroom at three in the morning. I flipped on the light. And there he was staring back at me from the mirror above the sink. "Harold," I said, as if it was the most natural thing in the world to greet him.

Then I grew frightened; I remembered that he was dead. Yet there he was: his thin face, his dark, knowing eyes, his curly hair.

We stared at each other for a long time; after all my searching, he'd been hiding in the most obvious place all along.

ABOUT THE AUTHORS

David Bergman has edited *Men on Men* since 1992. He is the author or editor of a dozen books of poetry, criticism, and fiction, including *Cracking the Code*, which won the George Elliston Poetry Prize, and *Gaiety Transfigured: Self-Representation in Gay American Literature*, which was selected as an Outstanding Book of the Year by *Choice* Magazine and the Gustavus Myers Center for Human Rights. His most recent books include *Care and Treatment of Pain* (poetry) and *The Violet Quill Reader: The Emergence of Gay Writing After Stonewall*. He lives in Baltimore and teaches at Towson State University.

Bruce Benderson is the author of two works of fiction about Time Square: the novel *User* and the story collection *Pretending to Say No*. He is cowriter of the film *My Father Is Coming*, the translator of such French novelists as Sollers and Guyotat, and the author of numerous stories, articles, and reviews that have appeared in many magazines and collections here and in Europe.

David Ebershoff was born in Los Angeles and raised in Pasadena. He is a graduate of Polytechnic School, Brown University, and the University of Chicago Graduate School of Business, and has studied Japanese history at Keio University in Tokyo. His fiction, poetry, and reviews have appeared in *Alligator Juniper*, *Bay Windows*, *Chicago Literary Review*, *Chicago Review*, *Christopher*

Street, Puerto del Sol, and elsewhere. He lives in New York and works at Random House.

Born in Savannah, Georgia, **Jason K. Friedman** now lives in Seattle and teaches fiction writing at the University of Washington. His short stories have appeared in *The South Carolina Review*, *Asylum*, Baltimore *City Paper*, and in the anthologies *His: Brilliant New Fiction by Gay Writers* and *A Natural Beauty*. He is the author of the children's nonfiction book *Haunted Houses* and the children's novel *Phantom Trucker*. His adult novel, *The Creek Is Gone*, won a 1992 Associated Writing Programs Award. His essay on Southern gothic writing appears in the volume *Goth: Ethnographies of a Postpunk Subculture*.

A former fellow at the MacDowell Colony and the Helen Wurlitzer Foundation, **Philip Gambone** has been listed in *Best American Short Stories*. His collection of stories, *The Language We Use Up Here*, was nominated for a Lambda Literary Award. He has also contributed numerous essays and reviews to journals including *Bay Windows*, *The Harvard Gay and Lesbian Review*, *Lambda Book Report*, *Frontiers*, and *The New York Times Book Review*. His essays have appeared in *Hometowns*, *A Member of the Family*, *Sister and Brother*, and *Wrestling with the Angel*. In the summer of 1993, he taped a series of twelve hour-long interviews with gay and lesbian fiction writers, entitled "The Word Is Out" for WOMR radio in Provincetown. Gambone teaches at the Park School in Brookline, Massachusetts, and in the creative writing program at Harvard Extension School. He has just completed his first novel, *Pushing Off*, from which "*Gioia e Dolor*" is taken.

Philip Gefter is a subject and coauthor of *Lovers: The Story of Two Men*, published in 1979. He has just completed a novel, *Roman's Holiday*, about a gay man who explores romantic love with a woman.

Paul Gervais was born in Maine. His first novel, *Extraordinary People*, was a finalist for the 1991 PEN/Faulkner Award for Fiction. "Love in the Eyes of God" is excerpted from a new novel of the same name. He lives in Lucca, Italy.

Thomas Glave, a graduate of Bowdoin College, has received fellowships from the NEA/Travel Grants Fund for Artists, the New York Foundation for the Arts, and the Bronx Council on the Arts. His work has appeared in *Callaloo, Children of the Night: The Best Short Stories by Black Writers 1967–Present, Ancestral House: The Black Short Story in the Americas and Europe, The Kenyon Review*, and other publications. He is currently a Writing Fellow at the Fine Arts Work Center in Provincetown, Massachusetts.

Jim Grimsley is a playwright and novelist who lives and works in Atlanta, Georgia. His first novel, *Winter Birds*, was published in the United States in 1994 and won the 1995 Sue Kaufman Prize for First Fiction, given by the American Academy of Arts and Letters, and the Prix Charles Brisset, given by the French Academy of Physicians. The novel also received a special citation from the Ernest Hemingway Foundation as one of three finalists for the PEN/Hemingway Award. Grimsley's second novel, *Dream Boy*, appeared in 1995. He is the author of ten full-length and four one-act plays, including *Mr. Universe, The Lizard of Tarsus, White People*, and *The Existentialists*. He has been playwright-in-residence at 7Stages Theatre since 1986. For *Mr. Universe*, he was awarded in 1988 the George Oppenheimer Award for the Best New American Playwright, and in 1993 he won the first-ever Bryan Prize in Drama, presented by the Fellowship of Southern Writers for distinguished achievement in playwrighting. He is a member of PEN American Center, the Southeast Playwrights Projects, and Alternate ROOTS. He is currently at work on his third novel, *My Drowning*.

Paul Lisicky grew up in Cherry Hill, New Jersey, and was educated at the Iowa Writers' Workshop and Rutgers University. He has published stories in *Mississippi Review, Carolina Quarterly, Provincetown Arts, Black Warrior Review, Kansas Quarterly*, and in the anthology *Flash Fiction*. His awards include a National Endowment for the Arts Fellowship, a James Michener Award, the Henfield/*Transatlantic Review* Award, residencies from Yaddo and the MacDowell Colony, and two fellowships from the Fine Arts Work Center in Provincetown, where he lives, completing a novel from which "Lawnboy" is an excerpt.

William J. Mann is a journalist and fiction writer whose biography of the openly gay silent film star William Haines, *Wisecracker*, will be published in 1997. His work has appeared in numerous magazines and newspapers, including *The Advocate*, *The Boston Phoenix*, and *Frontiers*, as well as in such anthologies as *Sister and Brother*, *Looking for Mr. Preston*, *Queer View Mirror*, and *Happily Ever After: Erotic Fairy Tales for Men*. He is currently completing a novel from which "Tricks of the Trade" is an excerpt. He lives in Boston.

Kevin Martin is a Los Angeles–based writer and performance artist. His work has appeared in *Blood Whispers, Vol. 2: L.A. Writers on AIDS*, *OUT/LOOK*, and *Diabolical Clits*. Since 1991, he has presented seven performance pieces in Los Angeles, primarily at Highways Performance Space, including "Lives of the Saints," "How I Was Infected," "Queer Hearts," and "Crack," from which the story included in this volume was drawn. For the past five years he has been a member of the writers' group Live to Write/Write to Live. He is a recipient of a City of Los Angeles grant for HIV/AIDS educational dramatic writing.

Achim Nowak is a native of Germany who now lives in Manhattan. "Graham Greene Is Dead" is an excerpt from a forthcoming memoir of the same title. Other excerpts from this book have won a PEN Syndicated Fiction Award, been broadcast on NPR's "The Sound of Writing," and published in *The James White Review*. His performance work, created with Wendy Woodson and other collaborators, has been presented across the United States and Europe. Among his awards is a fellowship from the NEA and a grant from the Ludwig Vogelstein Foundation.

James Purdy is one of the most distinguished figures in American writing, having published novels, short stories, plays, and poetry throughout a long career. His first book, *Color of Darkness*, was published abroad in 1956, at which time he was hailed by Dame Edith Sitwell as "one of the greatest living writers of fiction in our language." His novels include *Malcolm*, *The Nephew*, and the seminal *Eustace Chisholm and the Works*. His most recent novels are *Garments the Living Wear* and *Out with the Stars*. Born in Ohio, he has lived for many years in Brooklyn, New York.

J. E. Robinson was educated at Howard University (B.A., Classical Civilization), at the University of Missouri-Columbia (M.A., Ancient History), and at the University of Chicago where he studied Ancient and Byzantine History. He is the creator, producer, and host of *Eavesdropping*, a half-hour arts and lifestyle radio conversation. His poems and short stories have appeared in *Galley Sail Review*, *Janus*, *New Directions*, *Unknowns*, and *The Wittenberg Review*. "Waiting on Eurydice" took twelve years to complete. He warns the reader: "Don't blink, you might miss something." Robinson makes his home in southern Illinois, near St. Louis.

Sandip Roy was born in Calcutta, India. "Black and Blue" is his first published work of fiction. He lives in San Francisco and edits *Trikone*, the world's oldest surviving magazine for South Asian lesbians and gays. He is a regular contributor to *India Currents Magazine*. His work has been included in such anthologies as *Looking Queer*, *My First Time*, and *Queer View Mirror*.

Wayne Scott received degrees from the University of Chicago and an M.F.A. in creative writing from American University in 1995. He has written theater and book reviews for *The Windy City Times*, *The Washington Blade*, *Outlines*, and *Metroline*. A psychiatric social worker specializing in posttraumatic stress and dissociative identity disorder ("multiple personality"), he has published clinical articles and chapters in *The Family Therapy Networker*, *Common Boundary*, *Differential Diagnosis and Treatment on Social Work*, *Clinical Social Work Journal*, and *Journal of*

Family Psychotherapy. "House of Difference" is from a novel-in-progress. He lives in Washington, D.C., with his partner Elizabeth Theilman.

David Vernon was born in New York and grew up in Los Angeles. He studied Film and Creative Writing at New York University. He works in the film industry. His short fiction has appeared in *His, Blood Whispers: L.A. Writers on AIDS, Volumes I and II, Indivisible,* and *Frontiers.* His story "Inside" appeared in *Men on Men 4.* He is working on a novel and a collection of stories and currently lives in New York.

Karl Woelz was born and raised in Great Britain, was educated at Columbia (B.A.) and the University of Texas (M.A.), and is completing his Ph.D. at the University of Kansas. Currently he lives in Lawrence, Kansas, where he teaches English at the University of Kansas.

Norman Wong was born and reared in Honolulu. He received his B.A. from the University of Chicago and his M.A. from the Johns Hopkins University Writing Seminars. His stories have appeared in numerous magazines and anthologies, including *The Kenyon Review, The Threepenny Review, Men's Style,* and *Men on Men 4. Cultural Revolution,* a collection of linked stories, was published in 1994. He is at work on his first novel, *ABC,* from which "Andrew and I" is excerpted.

Richard Zimler lives in Porto, Portugal, with his lover, Alex. His first novel, *The Last Kabbalist of Lisbon,* will be published this year in a Portuguese translation. His second novel, *Unholy Ghosts,* is also being published this year in London and in English. The winner of a National Endowment for the Arts Fellowship, his short fiction has appeared in *London Magazine, Panurge, Yellow Silk, The James White Review,* and other British and American magazines. His translations from the Portuguese have appeared in *The Literary Review* and *European Anthology.* "The Most Obvious Place" was prompted by the death of one of his older brothers in 1989.

PRAISE FOR THE
MEN ON MEN COLLECTIONS OF GAY FICTION

MEN ON MEN 1

"Some of the best gay fiction, past, present, and future."
—Martin Duberman

MEN ON MEN 2

"This collection includes some of the hottest (in other words, coolest) stories I've read anywhere."
—Brad Gooch, author of *The Golden Age of Promiscuity*

MEN ON MEN 3

"Even better than its predecessors: It's a rich mosaic of cultural diversity and a delight to read. A groundbreaking collection, it should be delved into by anyone interested in good fiction."
—*Lambda Book Report*

MEN ON MEN 4

"A series that consistently gives unapologetic, unashamed voice to the contemporary male writer. . . . The work in *Men on Men 4* is rich and complex. . . . True to its mandate, *Men on Men 4* heartfully and boldly tells us some stories that need to be told."
—*The Advocate*

MEN ON MEN 5

"David Bergman, the new editor of the *Men on Men* series, has kept George Stambolian's high literary standards but managed to broaden the social scope. This exciting book is the pot of gold at the end of the rainbow coalition."
—Edmund White

David Bergman has edited *Men on Men* since 1992. He is the author or editor of a dozen books of poetry, criticism, and fiction, including *Gaiety Transfigured: Self-Representation in Gay American Literature, Camp Grounds: Style and Homosexuality,* and *The Violet Quill Reader.* He lives in Baltimore and is a professor of English at Towson State University.